TREACHEROUS GAMES

"The destiny of the Olympics
was *never* more at risk"

Adrian

Best wishes

David Brodie

DAVID BRODIE

Published by David Brodie Books

This is a work of fiction. Names, characters, places and incidents
either are the product of the author's imagination or are used
fictitiously. Any resemblance to actual persons, living or dead,
events or locales (except known venues e.g. 10 Downing St) is
entirely coincidental.

First printed by Atlas Print Group March 2012

ISBN: 978-0-9571879-0-0

www.treacherousgames.info

www.davidbrodie.org

My thanks go to Tom, John, Adam, Jon, Luke, Jo, Helen and Megan
for their contribution and encouragement.

Cover design by Jon Willcocks Associates Ltd
Typeset by Georgina Pensri
Font: Minion Pro 10.5/14pt

FOR MEGAN, JO AND TOM

'Let us run the race that is before us and never give up.'
Hebrews 12.1

Contents

Chapter 1

"The games of the 30th Olympiad, 2012, are awarded to the city of ....London."

A huge roar crescendoed from the British bid team as they reacted to Juan Antonio Samaranch's announcement of the name 'London'. Faces changed from tension to exuberance. Clenched fists punched the air. Hugs and kisses were exchanged. The celebrations would go on long into the night.

* * * * * * * *

At exactly the same time in the UK, four men made final plans to travel to London to deliver maximum devastation to the public transport system and citizens of Britain's capital city. They knew the moment had come when they would be martyred for their faith in the prophet Mohammed. They had one final task. Each made an international phone call to unseen, unknown names who were committed to continue the struggle.

"It will be London. Allah be praised."

Within 12 hours London would see its worst atrocity since The Blitz of the Second World War, with 56 dead and more than 700 injured. But this would be nothing compared with the acts of terrorism planned for the 30th Olympiad. The year 2012. It will be London. Allah be praised.

CHAPTER 2

August 19th, 2008
Olympic Stadium, Beijing, China

The pistol cracked. The crouching athletes, with centres of gravity momentarily suspended over the start line, are instantly transformed into the most efficient running machines in the human race. The relative hush of the Olympic Stadium erupted into a roar of expectation, support and delight.

For this was no ordinary race. This was the 1500 metre final; the metric mile; the blue riband event of the Olympic Games. Since 1896, when Pierre de Coubertin had inaugurated the modern Olympics, no race has captured the public imagination like the 1500 metres. It was special. Successive generations have marvelled at the outstanding performances of Roger Bannister, Herb Elliott, Peter Snell and Sebastian Coe – all household names to the millions attracted to the pursuit of excellence.

TV producers punched buttons to get close up shots of the runners, for the billion TV screens worldwide and for the giant plasma screens around the track. Twelve athletes with one goal, one mission, one outstanding performance, one lifetime ambition, one final extreme effort… Olympic gold.

But this one was different, unparalleled, unique. Never before had athletes of such quality competed together. This wasn't a contest between two great athletes of the likes of Bannister and Landy. This wasn't an Olympic final with major nations absent by virtue of diplomatic embargo. This wasn't the golden era of English middle distance running when two or three outstanding athletes contested gold from within their exalted ranks.

Oh no, this was very special. This was the first time that twelve athletes had all been within two seconds of the world record in the semi-finals only two days previously. This was the first time that no single runner was quoted, even marginally, as race favourite. This race was as open as the English Grand National. Every runner peaked to perfection and within one and a half seconds of each other. The superlative contest, a lifetime of fame and wealth, the Olympic gold medal – the ultimate prize!

This was no tactical event with the contenders jockeying for position until the last 300 metres. Now, exercise physiology and sports psychology dictate the single strategy. The first lap at a pace which would have won the 400 metres in Barcelona, followed by three successive laps at equivalent speed. The theory is without question; the practice more tenuous. The 1500 metre Olympic final - a race of attrition. Twelve athletes all tuned by coaches, scientists, clinicians and therapists to match the available fuel in the muscles to the demands of two and a half minutes of exceptional running. And then as the fuel supply rapidly and inexorably runs out over the final 60 seconds, the one who suffers the least will stand on the podium to the sounds of his country's national anthem.

Twelve athletes starting with optimism based on the knowledge of a thousand gruelling training sessions, but the realism of knowing that each of his rivals has done exactly the same. Twelve athletes touched by their maker as gifted, as men above men, as fighters to the last breath, true gladiators of the modern era, yet beneath it all vulnerable, human and capable of losing the ultimate prize.

Forget the Olympic ideal, the friendly games, comradeship, the true essence of sport; these men are striving for one single moment in time – to subjugate their illustrious peers – to be written forever in the history books as the most dominant human on planet earth. This is their moment of destiny.

"And they're off." A hundred commentators bend forward at the waist pressing their lip mic's closer and sealing their voices from the roar of the crowd and from the background hum of the static in the media centre. Geoff Delaney of NBC scans the statistical information as it overlays his monitor. He confidently announces the fastest acceleration for an Olympic final since the Unisys computer started real-time speed analysis.

"Only twenty seconds into the race and Josh Silverman, the British 800 metre champion hits a pace unheard of for this distance. Phenomenal acceleration from a standing start."

The twelve athletes, the strain showing on their faces, jostling for position as they break from their lanes, still struggling to maintain rhythm amid the flailing arms of the tightly bunched group.

"The Italian Benito, showing his characteristic staccato cadence is on the Britain's right shoulder adding one stride to every fifteen as the bend unfolds."

"As they hit the three lap marker the positions stay the same, Silverman, Benito, the big Cuban Carrera, the Kenyan trio of Kipruto, Chortop and Ngeny, followed by Ho from Winhan province in central China and eighth but only separated by four metres an established front runner Gabet, the Moroccan."

At 400 metres, four billion viewers saw a split time displayed on the top left of their television screens, just three tenths of a second over the world record for the single lap.

Silverman looked calm, focused, 135 pounds of sinewy muscle. Slight, almost fragile, but with an economy of leg lift which seemed to defy human mechanics. He glided over the track so that there was no perceptible rise and fall of his upper body and in so doing, conserved every unit of energy.

The Italian kept his arms high and wide, a great asset in a bunched finish and cursed by those bent on overtaking. He'd been known to push, pull, tangle and strike. Disqualified twice from European Games for overuse of the arms, his upbringing in the slums of Naples never quite deserting him. In recent months the discipline introduced by his new German coach, Kurt Adam, a graduate of Leipzig Academy, had brought him to the forefront of world athletics. Perfectly placed and matching Silverman stride for stride, the contrasting styles mattered little in this company dedicated to the gods of elitism.

At 800 metres the split time once more flashed on the giant video screens and an incredulous world took time to register what they were seeing. An 800 metre time of one minute 42 seconds; a new Olympic record by three hundreds of a second yet within a 1500 metre final. Eight men within eight metres, having totally destroyed the field and dropped the American trio of Erchard, Fradley and Delves with the highly fancied New Zealander, Pinder, also totally out of contention.

Never in the history of championship running had this speed been achieved and yet relentlessly the race continued into the next lap with pursuing runners only metres adrift of the two at the front.

There was no time for the press corps to respond to this incredible feat. The big, powerful Cuban used the momentary distraction caused by the crowd reaction to the Olympic record to drive past the Italian and establish himself on Silverman's right shoulder. The Italian faltered momentarily, lost his rhythm, stretched to check the Cuban but the sheer physical presence of this six foot three inches powerhouse left him in an uncomfortable slipstream of solid muscular motion. Silverman, still staring at a point in space thirty metres ahead, had no need to shift his attention. He knew from the distinct foot pattern of the Cuban that it was the Pan-American champion beside him. The breathing pattern of Carrera, in perfect unison with every fourth step, was deeper, slower, more distinct than the British athlete. Silverman could hear each breath; it started in the deep recesses of his consciousness; he knew his own breathing was more variable, not laboured, not yet demanding his full attention, just different. The bell for the final lap sounded just twice before eight runners had passed the marker. Never before had a lead group of eight been so tightly packed. It was a miracle that such a bunched group had survived without serious contact, without incident, without any exhibition of irritation or aggression.

Gabet, the Moroccan, the only North African capable of the new approach to training, knew that he had to be in front at this point. He, more than anyone, knew that the pace made a mockery of the sprint finish. No athlete could run an Olympic record time for 800 metres, maintain that pace for another 400 metres and have a kick at the end. Any change in position over the last 300 metres may give the impression of acceleration, but the truth is that every athlete was simply tiring at different rates. But Gabet knew the futility of moving to the front quickly. At this pace it would immediately call on his final energy reserves, produce excess lactate and the pain would begin as surely as the sun rises daily over his native Moroccan mountains. Those mountains, renowned for their sand dunes on the lower slopes, provide the perfect conditions for endurance training. The relentless, twice daily session which starts with 45 minutes of non-stop dune running gave Gabet a cardiovascular system of unparalleled efficiency. Those dunes, each one charted and graded for sand depth, so the 45 minutes would alternate between fast running over a light covering of sand above the base rock and then to a slightly slower tempo through sand up to 20 centimetres in depth. With every stride the sand would cling, grasp, restrain his feet, defeating the efforts of his leg muscles to defy gravity. And then the sand grass, where his coach insisted that every step cleared the foot high grass, before plunging back into the loose sand.

Gerba Rashid, who once trained with Gabet in the Atlas

Mountains, but now running for Bahrain, was still seriously in contention. He was looking totally in control at the back of the leading group of eight. His vast experience now meant more than anything and his judgement of pace was known to be his greatest strength.

The sound of the bell, the final lap, the roar from 90,000 spectators, lifted the athletes for the 60 seconds of oxygen starvation. The prelude to exhilaration or despair; the zone of the psychologically strong; the moment of silent prayer; this was the time for survivors to survive.

In the final straight, the bunched athletes slowly evolved into a single line stretched across the track. Josh Silverman's muscles were screaming with pain; every breath was like a dying man fighting for life. The line was his with ten strides to go. The agony before the ecstasy, but the ecstasy never came.

There is nothing worse than coming fourth in the Olympic final. No medal, no ceremony, nothing in the record books, nothing to show the grandchildren. Nothing. Deep down Josh felt the pain, the anguish, the stark realisation that he was not going home in triumph. Josh Silverman had failed.

CHAPTER 3

August 19th, 2008
Beijing Dog Track, China

Josh Silverman was a freak. His grandfather had survived Auschwitz-Birkenau. His father had toughed it out from being the son of an East End tailor to become a respected cardiologist and his mother, the indomitable Sarah Sachs, was the first woman to conquer Everest and walk to both poles. He had the right genes and the right mental stamina to be the best. And he was. Josh Silverman was Britain's fastest and most exciting middle distance runner since the heady days of Steve Ovett and Sebastian Coe back in the 1980s. Josh Silverman was unusual in one other way. He was British and a practicing Jew. For some strange reason the Jewish nation had a limited history of producing world class track athletes in Britain. There were exceptions of course. The most famous being Harold Abrahams, but this was back in the 1920s. Josh was justly proud of his Jewish roots, but all this was secondary to the quiet pride in his natural, and in his view God-given, running ability.

Josh's pedigree and undoubted ability made his failure so much more acute. He was certain to follow the natural sequence of events for such a loss. The pattern of disbelief, anger, blame and in time acceptance could take weeks but right now he had to face an unbelieving and disappointed press.

The media were predictably intrusive, wanting answers when few could be given. Josh Silverman felt like saying "I was simply not bloody good enough," but kept his composure long enough to escape with a degree of dignity.

After a long and painful interview with the BBC, probing into tactical naivety, training schedules and mental state, Josh now felt the combination of physical and psychological strain utterly exhausting. He left the media centre in a state of bewilderment, lacking any focus or meaning to his very existence. This was more than a major disappointment, it was true personal devastation. Josh was a broken man and would need a level of support normally reserved for the military after times of horrendous conflict. His only immediate support was his sports agent, a certain Nigel Gressley.

Nigel Gressley's grandfather, Herbert Nigel Gresley, designed steam engines. He designed them so well that he was knighted. For some unexplained reason, Nigel Gressley's father added an extra 's' to the family name, most likely to avoid comparison with his illustrious father. Nigel was sent at the age of thirteen to be a boarder at a minor public school, Shipton College, on the River Thames. He was a disappointment as a sportsman, his highest achievement being to row at bow in the school's second eight. Although young Nigel showed little aptitude at playing sport, he compensated more than enough by his encyclopaedic knowledge of sporting events. If the school ever held a sporting quiz, Nigel was the first to be selected. Now as Josh Silverman's agent, Nigel Gressley was, without doubt, a man driven by financial reward. Nigel was in many ways the antithesis of Josh. Whereas Josh focussed on nothing other than being the fastest man in the world, Nigel was constantly exploring options, brokering deals, networking with anyone who could be useful to him and constantly hovering on the fringes of the murky world of bribery and corruption within sport. Josh Silverman was not his only client, but was undoubtedly his best performer. Nigel measured performance, not in terms of world records, but in terms of his personal financial reward. And he was good at his job. He came up regularly and consistently with the best sponsorship deals in the sport. Silverman's sponsorship with

Asics had been brokered over many months, but was reckoned to be the best in the business. Only the superstars of basketball, football and formula one, none of whom were on Gressley's books, had a better deal. Leading up to the Olympic Games in Beijing, Silverman was the brand that Asics promoted worldwide. He was literally their golden boy and the rumblings back at the UK head office in Warrington were already being felt. Who wants to promote an Olympic champion prospect who can only come fourth? Gressley felt the chill wind of change as sharply. But in the style of an old street fighter, he was not going to let this catastrophic result deflect him from a life of permanent financial security.

In addition to the differences between Gressley and Josh's motivation for success, their looks and dress could not be more different. Josh had the lean and rugged look of a dedicated athlete. His bone structure was well defined, with the film star appearance you might associate with the adventurer genre of 'Indiana Jones'. Gressley, on the other hand, had the look of a man who had let himself go physically many years before. He had that flabby appearance resulting from too many high calorie working lunches. Although his clothes were expensive, they never quite seemed to belong, in most part because of the portly frame that they failed to conceal.

Gressley, with an intuitive feel for Josh's psychological state, knew that distraction was essential. He fell into step with Josh as he struggled to find his way back to the athletes' village.

"We are going to the dogs," said Gressley, hoping that the trite pun might lift the mood.

"What?" replied Josh, still absorbed in his dark and destructive thoughts.

"I'm taking you dog racing," repeated Nigel. "In spite of this country's political leaning, they have opened a greyhound racing track just off the northern perimeter road in the Fanwin district of town."

"But I was led to believe that gambling was illegal in China," Josh muttered, slowly beginning to show an interest in something outside of his own mental state.

"It still is, except in highly controlled places, and the Beijing dog track is one of them."

Josh reluctantly appreciated his agent's efforts at giving him a focus, if only for a few hours, and soon the ill-matched pair were making their way to China's latest gambling attraction. Within thirty minutes the two of them were slamming the doors of the taxi outside a stadium of much smaller proportions. The Beijing dog track was home on Tuesdays and Thursdays to the city's canine elite. On Wednesdays and Fridays the track became a frenzy of fumes and flying cinders for motorbike racing and at weekends the infield was turned over to community basketball. Josh had never seen a live dog race before and had paid scant attention to the sport in the past. Tonight was different. It was to absorb their interest, energies, efforts, luck and enthusiasm for the eight national league races over the next two hours. Josh admitted to having little understanding of the minutiae of form, ground conditions, breeding or even the way to place a bet. The sounds, signals and rituals of the punters, the officials and the stewards were at first a total mystery. The track with its lights no more than two metres from the ground threw an eerie incandescence over the proceedings. The constant movement both sides of the track, coupled with the regular build up to the start of each race, gave an artificial excitement to the evening. It seemed like a rolling wave of activity as people passed from the track to the on-track betting stalls, from the bars to the stands and from the food stalls to the parade enclosure. The diversion was slowly working its magic on Josh and for a short time at least, he was able to put his failure to the back of his mind.

For the Chinese, the dogs were largely irrelevant. They were here to indulge in their favourite passion, but officialdom still held sway and the only way to gamble was through the state-owned tote. Nonetheless the enthusiasm was infectious and the two westerners were soon absorbed in the melee of the occasion.

It was hard for Josh and Nigel not to stand out in such a place, with Josh and Nigel's height, features and dress being out of place amongst the predominantly drab Chinese workers who thronged around the betting booths. Josh still sported his Asics tracksuit, specially produced for the Olympic Games, with the Asics emblem entwined in the Olympic rings. Nigel, as ever, in a rather brash Armani suit and open neck shirt, which looked considerably better on the mannequin in Bond Street than it did on Nigel's somewhat ample frame.

Josh, who had a natural love for dogs, was intrigued by the ritual that followed each race. Three dogs randomly taken from those in the race were immediately taken to a quiet area of the track where a white-coated official seemed to force a drink down each dog's throat, promptly resulting in the dog being sick. Josh, clearly shocked, grabbed Nigel by the arm to show him this disgusting practice.

"Oh they're just vomiting them," said Nigel casually, "it's common practice at all greyhound meetings."

"But what's it for?" asked Josh in alarm, "the dogs shouldn't have to suffer this humiliation."

"Simple," Nigel replied, "they vomit the dogs to make sure that they haven't been given a meal before the race. This could slow them down and change the betting odds for future races."

"So what slows them down?" enquired Josh, starting to show some interest for the first time all evening.

"Fish meal mainly, grass clippings, a variety of drugs." Nigel seemed incredibly well informed.

"So surely the vet cannot tell all this just by looking at the poor dog's vomit?"

"True, but the real test is that he has anything in his stomach at all. Dogs race semi-starved, so anything there would be suspicious."

"And I guess the lab would then take over to confirm the vet's suspicions?"

"Exactly. It doesn't happen often, but it's comforting to see that these sharp practices are under some sort of control in China as well as other countries."

"So all we need to do," said Josh more brightly, "is to wait four years and find ways to slow down all the other finalists and I get gold."

Nigel warmed to the joke, but as it was said something sinister clicked in his brain. He knew even then that this innocent comment could be the difference between failure and success. This could be the key to a large share in Josh's ultimate riches. Nigel had every reason to pursue this throwaway line with a vigour way beyond conventional morals. This was the moment when Josh's trusted agent changed from being calculating and selfish to becoming immoral and illegal. His outward demeanour would stay the same, but his thinking, plans and relationships would now shift to the dark side. The mission was success; the method would now be treachery.

"Leave it to me," Nigel responded, masking his deeper thoughts, "I shall personally feed a fish meal to all the other finalists in London. It'll be a breeze."

Josh was ready to go. The issue over the treatment of the dogs was starting to get him down. As the adrenaline which had been keeping him pumped up all day was now exhausted, he now felt genuinely hungry. Nigel, expecting this, had already planned a quiet Thai restaurant, well away from the athletes' village.

CHAPTER 4

November 23rd, 2009
Sayers Lecture Theatre, Loughborough University, UK

Professor Henry Coombe had for a short time been head of the world-renowned sports science department at Loughborough University. His elevation to this position was seen by many as remarkable. He had no track record of research, something that even in the 1970s was seen as essential. But he was incredibly astute and soon became a pro-provost of the University, normally a three year appointment. He was then offered a permanent position as pro-provost for alumni activities, giving him numerous opportunities for travel. These included countries which had led sports science in the period before democracy was introduced in Eastern Europe. This provided Professor Coombe with an insight into the questionable methods of performance enhancement.

Although Professor Coombe rarely gave lectures these days, his annual presentation on 'Cheating in Sports' was always well attended. Unusually the general public was invited to attend. Nigel Gressley made it his business to be there at least every other year, just in case there were any updates in the murky world of illegal sports enhancement.

"And in conclusion," intoned Professor Coombe, summing up the previous forty minutes of charts, images and statements citing drug abuse, blood doping, and a series of semi-legal practices endemic in the former Soviet countries, "we now face the constant battle between the chemist and the drug control officers. It is my opinion that with the rewards of sporting success as they are, cheating is on the ascendancy. Until the international authorities can establish a fool-proof test, most likely based not on urine testing, but on blood testing, then we will continue in sport to always be one step behind the determined cheat. It is my pleasure to announce that following a three million pound Sports Council grant, this University will host the new Institute of Performance Enhancement Analysis and we will be at the forefront of beating the sports cheats at their own game. Thank you for your attention and I invite questions from the floor."

"Professor Coombe," enquired an eager third year student, "can you tell us what will happen to the existing drug testing laboratories based at King's College in London and Northwick Park Hospital?"

"Final agreement has yet to be reached, but I am confident that the existing labs will transfer both human and physical resources to Loughborough and will result in their closure elsewhere within six months."

Gressley cautiously raised his hand, uncertain as to whether or not his question should be in open forum, "Professor Coombe, you have given us a fascinating insight into how sportsmen and women improve performance, but what strategies would an athlete use if he wished to underperform?"

"I cannot imagine such a situation occurring," Coombe replied after a lengthy pause to consider the options, "mainly because an athlete would simply not try as hard as he could in this unlikely scenario. I suppose one could envisage in the times of professional athletics such as the Powderhall sprints of the nineteenth century, when large bets were being placed, then some gains could be made by apparent underperformance. But as I have just said it would be considerably easier for the athlete simply to fake an exhausting performance and alter the subsequent betting. There is little doubt that in some sports like boxing, fights are thrown for a variety of reasons, but once again it is unlikely that the approaches I have described in my lecture would be the method of choice."

Professor Coombe was clearly getting out of his comfort zone, so he resorted to the well used strategy of buying time for a more considered response and invited Gressley to continue the discussion after the lecture had finished. A few more students and one member of staff enquired more specifically about drug composition and side effects and as the clock in the courtyard outside chimed for one o'clock, the lecture was drawn swiftly to a close. As nearly two hundred students noisily left the room, Gressley made his way to the front and stood patiently waiting for Professor Coombe to collect his laptop from the podium. As he waited, Gressley, with his perceptive mind and training in psychology, watched Coombe carefully. He rapidly deduced that Professor Coombe enjoyed his food. This was hardly a difficult assumption as he was clearly overweight and had the ruddy complexion of a man who enjoyed wine to excess. As Coombe turned, he showed no sign of recognition, but when Gressley introduced himself he forced a smile and said "Of course, you asked the question about slowing athletes up – a strange idea."

"You're probably very busy," said Gressley, "but if you could spare an hour over lunch, I would welcome the opportunity to pick your brains further."

"I cannot imagine I have anything to add," said Coombe, "but I do have until two thirty before I need to be back at my desk and I would welcome a short break."

The two men were gently but deliberately moving towards their individual agendas. Gressley saw Coombe as bringing him the knowledge he needed to plan his long term strategy for a gold medal. Coombe, on the other hand, had the short term interests of sampling some wine at one of the restaurants in town. He would also be exploring funding opportunities from someone who clearly had excellent connections in elite sport.

Gressley was, as usual, a step ahead and had already

prepared the ground for a lunchtime meeting. "Why don't we go into town and let me treat you to lunch?" he said, "I believe Sciroccos comes highly recommended, but would be happy for you to choose."

Coombe hid his satisfaction at such an excellent choice as Sciroccos, knowing it had a wine list comparable with that of any London restaurant. He demurred, but in doing so tried to give an impression of disinterest. Gressley was not taken in by this superficial performance and privately congratulated himself on his achievement so far. His mind was actively assessing how far he could push for critical information during the meal, or whether the topic should be kept on ice.

Gressley drove Coombe to Sciroccos, promising that he would return the professor by two twenty, in good time for his meeting. Sciroccos was an Italian restaurant with genuine pedigree. Its first generation owners had come over shortly after the Second World War and had built up a solid and authentic Italian cuisine which had, thankfully, been maintained by the family over time. The decor was simple, almost understated, but gave one the sense of an Italian bistro while maintaining the classic look of a quality venue. The starched white tablecloths with matching napkins set the standard and made it a place for an occasion as opposed to a casual meal.

They sat in a quiet alcove, well away from the entrance, in spite of the usual attempts by the maitre d' to place them in a table by the front window. Coombe had entertained many high profile visitors to the University here before and was well versed with the wine menu. "You choose," said Gressley, perhaps a little too hastily. "Although I enjoy good wine, when it comes to selection, I'm afraid I haven't much of a clue."

"I'm told that the Il Lago Riserva is especially good," said Coombe, shutting the wine menu to indicate that no further discussion was necessary. They deliberated over the a la carte options, both choosing a shellfish starter, with Gressley opting for rigatoni campagnola and Coombe settling for a simpler lasagne magro.

"As you know," said Gressley, "I am the agent for a number of elite sports stars. As such, I am becoming increasingly aware that these young men and women are at risk from others who may wish to influence their performance in some way. This is quite different from the more usual activity of enhanced performance, clearly your speciality, but one which concerns me in my professional capacity."

"I am listening," said Coombe, in spite of being engaged in the rather difficult operation of splitting open a langoustine without spreading it too far over the table and himself.

"The thing is," continued Gressley, having now decided to plunge in somewhat more recklessly, "the current enemy, for want of a better word, seems to be elicit betting organisations, mainly throughout Asia."

"This is hardly new," stated Coombe, with a look implying a modest level of boredom. "These guys have been involved in rigging the outcomes of horse races for sure, not to mention football matches, especially in the Italian league. The occasional rugby game has involved dodgy replacements to improve the odds of winning and we're all aware of the cricket match rigging involving the South African team. So what's new?"

"What's new, Professor Coombe, is that there is intelligence within certain sectors of the sporting world that some seriously unethical and illegal practices are being used to deliberately slow competitors down. Think back to the British Lions tour to New Zealand in 2005 when several of our key players went down with a non specific bug. It was assumed to be dodgy food, but the team doctor analysed swabs later. There is still a real possibility that an outside agent could have introduced a known pathogen."

"But surely this would have been made public if there was a shred of evidence to support such a thing," responded Coombe, becoming animated for the first time. "You're not telling me that the tabloid press wouldn't have nailed this one. They just love a conspiracy theory."

"My informants are pretty reliable," countered Gressley. "Remember I am the agent to three of the rugby players who were in that squad. It was kept under wraps mainly for political reasons. The New Zealand government wanted things to be seen to be above board as they were applying for the 2011 Rugby World Cup. To imply or even prove there had been a deliberate attempt at sabotaging any of our players would have been political dynamite."

"OK," Coombe accepted, "you have indicated one possible method of slowing athletes down, but timing would be critical. You cannot predict with accuracy the timescale of a viral or bacterial infection. The human body doesn't just work like that."

"But that's exactly why I am talking to you, Professor. You can help me with the details. I could then warn my athletes of such possible interference. Preparation is all in this game."

Professor Henry Coombe placed his elbows on the crisp, white linen tablecloth and put his outstretched fingers together to form an arch in front of him.

"And do you have other theories to propose slowing down athletes, presumably to favour others?" he enquired.

"I've no evidence at all of anything untoward with my athletes," replied Gressley. "All the evidence of match fixing comes down to individual players underperforming. In the racing fraternity it is illicit use of a variety of substances to slow the horses or the jockeys controlling them. And where jockeys are not involved, as in greyhound races, then special food is often given to slow them down and change the odds. That's why vets vomit the dogs immediately after races."

"Not my field," Coombe replied, "but interesting none the less. I am still intrigued as to why you are talking to me, when a lot of this stuff is probably on the net."

Gressley sensed that he had to go further as the bait of a good meal and wine was wearing thin. "Look at it this way, Professor Coombe. I am currently the agent for two international swimmers, two track athletes and this phenomenal young pentathlete Meghan Moir. You know these athletes well because they all came to this University and they feature strongly in your publicity as future Olympians. You're well aware of Josh Silverman because he is current world champion and missed out on a medal in Beijing by 0.2 of a second. These guys deserve the best shot and it is my job to give them every chance of doing so. We - that is the athletes, their coaches, me and even you - owe it to them to protect them from any adverse influences from whatever source. We can control certain things which could make a difference such as when they stay in the Olympic village. But we cannot put a surveillance team on them for 24 hours a day. I am looking for you to help me predict possible illicit attempts to ruin their chances of success at the Olympic Games in two and a half years time."

Professor Coombe, with his elbows still on the table, but his fingers now interlocked, looked straight at Gressley. The appeal meant little to him, but he was ready for a response which would make it worth his time.

"The way we do things in academia," said Coombe, deliberately keeping it one step removed from any personal involvement, "is to set this up as a research project and fund a researcher to do the work involved." Unusually Coombe hesitated as he mentally ran through the options. He had done this often enough to know that you start with the big hit and then work the costing down until the research sponsor bites. Coombe's hesitation reflected his concern for the shadier side of this work. A postdoc student would be far more difficult to influence. It struck him that it could even need someone working undercover. What better than a student aspiring for both athletic and academic honours. His mind was made up and he made his pitch.

"The University could set up a research project involving a PhD student over three years. With my personal supervision, he would explore all methods of influencing sporting outcomes with special emphasis on track athletics. In view of the sensitive nature of the work, his findings would be kept to me and you, right up to the time of the Olympic Games. They would only ever be made public with the expressed written agreement of both of us."

Gressley didn't hesitate as he knew that it was essential to have someone with the specialist knowledge that Coombe and his student could provide. He knew Coombe was astute, but if he had worked out that this knowledge could be used by him to ruin the chances of other athletes, then he was not showing it.

"And the cost of this research?" enquired Gressley, trying to appear casual, yet knowing full well that any investment would be coming from him.

"With tutorial fees of £3,000 per year, a bursary for the student of £12,000 per year, necessary bench fees of £9,000 per year and essential office and travel costs of say £3,000, you are talking in the region of £27,000 per year," replied Coombe.

Gressley took a deep breath, genuinely shocked at the amount involved. He was momentarily knocked off balance, a state he experienced rarely. Coombe noted a slight change in Gressley's skin tone as he assessed the financial implications. "Is there no alternative?" he explored, "perhaps some way that the bench fees or student costs could be reduced?"

Coombe was used to this response. He had heard it from drug reps, from pharmaceutical company agents and from private individuals all wanting knowledge on the cheap. His reply was well rehearsed. "The only alternative is to employ a research fellow. This will, with on-costs, be in the range of £36,000 per year before you even consider bench fees. Bench fees are a University requirement," continued Coombe, "but in the case of this student, or should I say potential student, who is likely to be travelling for part of his time, this could be reduced to a minimum of £7,000."

Gressley took little time to do the maths. An investment of about £75,000 over three years, would give him the best chance of a gold medallist. With sponsorship and appearance money, Silverman's potential earnings were in excess of £2 million and Gressley's 15% was worth at least £300,000. Gressley also recognised that with the Games still thirty months away he could pull the project once he had the knowledge he so sorely needed. He suddenly woke up to the fact that time was of the essence.

"How soon could your student start?" said Gressley, wanting to get back on track. Coombe was once again ready and framed his response with care.

"I have two students looking for higher degree work at present. A female swimmer who is on the verge of the British team and probably the more capable of the two. The other is a young lad from Moss Side in Manchester. Comes from a hard background and took time to settle at Loughborough. But he is streetwise and could be a good choice for something like this." Gressley, in spite of his public school background, warmed to this. "And his sporting credentials? Will he be accepted into the world of athletics as he makes his enquiries?"

"Not as good as the girl," replied Coombe, "but mainly because as a swimmer she is younger and could easily make the Olympic swim team with her dramatic progress at present. The lad is a fighter, quite literally. He boxes for the University and has just made the British student team. He is no slouch in the boxing world and if my experience is anything to go by, I would expect him to turn professional within five years."

Gressley, in spite of his career as a sports agent, had never ventured into the world of boxing. His view was this was best left to the promoters and those with inside experience of the sport.

"Sounds ideal," said Gressley, "when can we get down to business?"

"My only concern," said Coombe, immediately getting Gressley's attention, "is that the nature of this project may need cash to be drawn down quickly as the enquiries proceed. I am worried that our University finance department could be too slow to react in such circumstances."

"And your solution?" demanded Gressley, showing for the first time a note of concern in his voice.

"Oh, this isn't really a problem," said Coombe, "the student's bursary and fees are kept in the University main accounts, but all bench fees and overhead costs will be kept in a separate account I will set up for such purposes. Then I can access them quickly."

Gressley wondered how many of these 'separate accounts' Professor Coombe had accumulated over the years, but felt it wise not to enquire.

"So if we have a deal, I will introduce you to this student as soon as I get him on board. I can give you bank details at the same time. The first tranche of grant will be £25,000, payable immediately after our meeting and others will follow at yearly intervals." Gressley's colour had returned, now accepting that knowledge doesn't come cheaply. He gave a wry half-smile as he nodded his agreement. This was all that was required. No handshake. No contracts to sign. Just a tacit agreement between two men with different, but equally questionable motives.

"You'd better get me back to the day job," said Coombe, rising to his feet. "Thank you for a most pleasant lunch and here's to a successful outcome." Gressley noted that the card that was now handed to him had the words 'Sports Consultant' against Professor Coombe's name. His home address and details were in place of the more usual University information. Coombe picked up the momentary hesitation as Gressley studied the card and was quick to add "Might be best if we communicate through this route, at least for the time being. If our lad does start to unearth some worrying facts, then University involvement could make it all very tricky."

"Sure," said Gressley, slightly perplexed, but well used to difficult negotiations, "not a problem." Gressley settled the bill, while Coombe took a call on his mobile phone.

"Looks like you had better get me back pretty sharpish," said Coombe as the two left the restaurant. The Vice-Chancellor's secretary is after me and it sounds as if the old boy is in no mood to wait."

The drive back through town was uneventful. The shops and offices on the Ashby Road were showing the effects of decline following the building of the ring road in the 1990s. Rain spattering on the windscreen just added to the perpetual gloom of an East Midland November day. Gressley tried to lift the prevailing mood by asking about the prospects of Loughborough's students in the 2012 Games. But Professor Coombe was now back in academic mode, concerned why his Vice-Chancellor had called an urgent meeting. He was wondering if he could rely on his deputy-chair to handle the alumni relations meeting scheduled for that afternoon. Within minutes they were back at the main University gates and in spite of Gressley's offer, Professor Coombe insisted on walking from there to his office in the Senate building. They shook hands and as the pro-provost for alumni activities strode away, Nigel Gressley was left to contemplate the wisdom of investing in such an uncertain enterprise. Nigel was desperate to have his man on the podium of the Olympic Games, whatever it took and however it was to be achieved. Handled well, he had the confidence that it could be done. He knew it was going to be far more than preventing his man from suffering from any adverse events in his own training and performing. The truth was he'd need to find ways to influence the performance of the other key athletes. Nigel Gressley had the self-belief, determination and sheer arrogance to believe in his ultimate success. One thing he was sure of, it was going to get messy.

Chapter 5

December 8th, 2009
Ford Library, Loughborough University, UK

Two weeks later, Henry Coombe called Nigel Gressley at home just after eleven o'clock in the evening. Gressley was used to late night calls. It was par for the course in his job. Although he didn't recognise the number he very soon woke up to fact that the caller meant business. "Henry Coombe here. Just wanted to confirm our meeting." Gressley was sure that no meeting had been arranged, so took the word 'confirm' to mean that Coombe was planning a meeting and he was expected to be there.

"Next Wednesday at 10:00 am sharp. I have Senate in the afternoon, so I can only stay an hour, but that should be plenty to get young Stringer started. I have arranged a room in the Ford Library on the third floor. It is an internal room, glass all round like a squash court on TV, but fully soundproofed. Should be ideal. Any problem?"

Nigel Gressley was staring at his electronic diary and working out how he could shift a meeting at Molineux where he was negotiating photographic rights for half the Wolves team. If he got away from Loughborough by noon, he reckoned it would only be a ninety minute journey to Wolverhampton. A delay of just over an hour for a group of footballers who had nothing better to do with their time most afternoons shouldn't be a problem.

"Sure," he replied, "I've a meeting later that day in Wolverhampton, but should make it."

"Good, I'll get my PA to send you the details. See you

Wednesday." The phone clicked and Nigel was left staring at his handset. So things really were hotting up.

He was not a man to leave a job unfinished and immediately emailed his contact at Molineux to re-arrange his Wednesday meeting for two thirty. That done and now wide awake, he poured himself a single malt. Sitting down in the ancient leather armchair which was his respite from the fractious world of sports management, his mind ran freely over how he could ensure Josh Silverman became Olympic champion in two years time. Despite a second whisky, Gressley found his brain was now in overdrive. His golden rule was never to write when sitting in this armchair haven. It was supposed to be his one place of true relaxation. Reading was acceptable, preferably his favourite genre of autobiographies, but never to bring work 'home' to this well loved and well worn piece of furniture. He recalled the maxim that 'rules are for the obedience of fools and the guidance of the wise' and taking a single sheet of lined paper from a drawer in his nearby desk, he started to make brief notes.

Gressley's style was not to make notes in the conventional style of a student with headings, sub-headings and bullet points. At school he had constantly struggled with this approach, only later in life coming to the thankful recognition that he was in fact dyslexic. This explained a number of his scholarly issues, especially his examination performance. Although it was now far too late to change much, one thing he had found was the benefit of mind-mapping – a loose arrangement of thoughts in boxes, linked together by arrows and lines. He soon realised the folly of choosing lined paper because this was becoming inhibiting. Uncertain whether it was the whisky or the late hour, he chose not to walk the short distance to his printer and retrieve plain paper – far more suited to the task in hand. Over two hours the paper became a complex interplay of thoughts, some realistic, some crazy and a few simply evil. His central box initially had the three words 'SLOW THEM DOWN', but concern about the security of his thoughts made him rub out the word 'THEM'. This small change altered the script from a document which was planning the demise of others to become an assessment of the potential impact of others upon his own athletes. He had openly shared his apparent concerns about how the betting world could influence the outcome of a foot race. His personal plan to be the perpetrator – the one who would effectively be slowing the others down by means yet to be decided – would clearly never be shared with anyone, not at least until it became absolutely necessary. This small change seemed to settle Nigel. Drowning his third single malt, he carefully placed his mind map in a spring-back file innocuously labelled 'Future Plans'. This file he carefully locked in small desk drawer and placed the key with equal care in the small change pocket of his wallet. This done, and for the first time since his phone call now feeling in need of serious sleep, he went upstairs. For Nigel Gressley, there would be no welcoming arms of his wife at this hour, and he crept with all the care his heavy frame could muster into the guest bedroom. This for him was not an uncommon activity. His late and unpredictable hours did not suit Christine his wife, who was resigned to the fact that living with Nigel was predominantly a daytime activity. Not for her the regular routine of going to bed with a man, a good book and the pleasures of pillow talk and beyond. Sex in the Gressley household was pre-booked, fitting in to Nigel's schedule rather like his many business appointments. Christine Gressley was not especially happy with such arrangements. She preferred, like many women, an element of spontaneity. Yet, at least on the surface, she seemed to accept that for now this was the inevitable consequence of a lifestyle way beyond her original dreams. As a struggling psychology student, she had fallen for the undoubted charms of Nigel Gressley. She had supported him through the lean years, long before the sports agency business became the basis of her current comfortable existence. Nigel, avoiding a late night shower which would have undoubtedly disturbed his wife, slid between the crisp cotton sheets of the guest bed. The combined effects of the whisky and fatigue delivered him safely into the arms of Morpheus, a state which remained unchanged until long after breakfast had been served in the Gressley household.

Nigel Gressley's drive up the M1 to Loughborough the following Wednesday was tedious but uneventful. He was a great believer in mood music and wanted something to brighten up what was a miserable day even by the expectations of December in the East Midlands. He set his CD player to shuttle between Queen and Abba and the surround sound gave him the intense experience of being in a private concert hall. Such was his focus on the prospects of the meeting ahead that he almost missed the exit to Loughborough. Swinging sharp left as the slip road forked, the noise of the studs and gravel, combined with the violent movement of the car, quickly raised his stress level to a point that would cause his doctor real concern. Nigel Gressley was a man who needed to be in total control. He could sense the damp traces of noxious sweat on both his forehead and armpits. A mild ache in his groin, which he more commonly associated with looking down over steep cliffs or being suspended in an exposed chairlift, made him aware of his vulnerability. "Christ," he said to no one but himself, "get a grip. You don't want to go into a meeting stinking of stale sweat." Normally he kept a spare shirt in his car because even light exercise caused him to perspire to an uncomfortable level. Today, an unexpected call as he was about to leave had upset his routine and he now regretted the consequences. Nigel went through his routine of breathing in deeply to the count of two and exhaling sharply. By the time he reached the main gates of the University he was back in control with only the discomfort of his armpits still an issue. Professor Coombe's PA had done her job well with Gressley's name quickly checked by the porter on the security gate. He parked in the visitors' car park, consulted his precinct map and set off to the main library at a steady pace. After tightening his tie at the neck and adjusting his gold tie pin, he was well satisfied that, at least in outward appearance, he was ready. Gressley arrived at the impressive glass-fronted building, financed by a combination of wealthy alumni and the Ford motor company, and took the lift to the third floor. He spent little time finding the room which, as Coombe had said, resembled an elongated squash court. Coombe and Stringer had yet to arrive, so Gressley wandered over to a nearby vending machine, choosing an expresso with an extra shot. Cursing quietly as the extra hit caused him to spill the coffee over his right hand, he was wiping it down when Professor Coombe emerged from the lift. Simultaneously Jim Stringer pushed the door from the stairwell a little too firmly and dodged expertly as it swung back with vengeance.

Gressley stuffed a handkerchief quickly in his pocket and held out his now dry hand to Coombe who took it, yet noticeably avoiding eye contact. "Good to see you," said Coombe, somewhat gruffly, "journey OK?"

"Apart from nearly missing the Loughborough turning off the M1, it was fine," replied Gressley, and turning to the young man standing awkwardly to one side, "and I guess you must be our champion boxer?"

"James Stringer," came the response, "but only my mum calls me James, so please call me Jim." Jim Stringer shook hands with Nigel Gressley who, in spite of knowing him to be a boxer, was surprised at the force of his grip.

"Time is money," said Coombe leading the way into the room reserved for the next hour, "let's get down to business."

The room was sparsely furnished and clearly used for occasional meetings. It had ample power points and computer connections and had a digital projector fixed permanently below the ceiling to project onto a blank white wall.

Jim Stringer was dressed in chinos, an open-necked shirt, a Loughborough University sweat top and surprisingly in view of the December chill, no sign of an overcoat. He was slight, muscular and had his head shaved in the fashionable style which, combined with his hard features, made him look as though he had just been released from either the armed forces or prison. Coombe took his watch off his wrist and placed it deliberately in front of him on the table. He turned it round facing the other two, and then re-adjusted it to face himself. Gressley took this small act to signal that not only was time limited, but that Coombe had a finite amount of interest in this project. He was prepared to be little more than a bystander in the activity ahead, a situation which appealed to Gressley and was not appreciated by Jim Stringer.

"I've asked Jim to prepare a list of options. We are working on the brief that there is very real concern, though no hard evidence, that people unnamed may resort to illegal or illicit methods of preventing athletes achieving their potential," intoned Professor Coombe. "Jim, over to you."

Jim Stringer, somewhat in awe of the two men sitting with him, sat upright and took three single sheets of typescript from a black computer bag resting on his knees. "As you are aware, I've had little time to prepare so I thought it best to try to set out some broad headings. This is based on an initial web search of the topic, although it is clear that little will have made its way into the conventional literature. If you are happy to use this as a start, then my next plan is to trawl the grey literature – newspaper cuttings, private reports etc." By now Coombe and Gressley were studying the list with interest. Coombe was the first to speak.

"I see your headings appear to reflect your course work modules here. Do you genuinely think this is the best approach?"

Stringer was not at his most comfortable defending himself verbally, his preference having always been by physical means.

He drew a deep, but silent breath, knowing that this meeting was for him an unofficial interview.

"It is not the only option, Professor Coombe, but a reasonable starting point for discussion. As things evolve and I get hold of real examples, I may find that the headings change. For the moment though, this list gives me a basis to plan." Nigel Gressley had remained silent, but already felt some admiration for the way Jim would not easily be dissuaded. He saw elements in Jim's character which reflected his own and he was keen to get to know him better as well as use his skills as a researcher.

"So talk us through it," interjected Coombe, "a quick resume of your thoughts to date."

"My first heading," said Jim, "mechanics, reflects the potential for slowing athletes down by tampering with any aspects of the way they move. In track events the common denominator is the feet and many athletes have all sorts of prosthetics built into their shoes. Change the prosthetics and an athlete will underperform. Of course it would need some time to take effect. Hardly a quick fix solution."

"Any other mechanical methods?" enquired Coombe, somewhat testily.

"Not for now," Jim replied, "but I'm confident that there will be other examples when I've given it more thought."

"And the next on your list," said Coombe, "that of pharmacology?"

"Much more ground for speculation there," replied Jim. "The basis of most drug cheating in sport is pharmacological, but the clear difference, as you're both well aware, is the intent is to improve performance. Turning it around so that pharmacology is used to slow athletes down would be as difficult to hide as drug taking, but is nonetheless feasible."

"What do you mean by hide?" interjected Gressley, who up until now had remained silent. Gressley had a strange mannerism of pushing down on both arms of his chair and raising his backside very slightly up and forward as he started to speak. He settled back into his chair immediately, but Jim Stringer, who was trained to observe unexpected movements, noted this and added it to his neural database. Jim noticed that Gressley only did this when he was about to speak and wondered if it was a response to stress.

"Perhaps that's the wrong word," said Jim, "what I really mean is that anyone using pharmacological methods to slow athletes down would have to find a way of administering the drug. That in itself would not be easy. Dosage would have to be optimal and timing critical."

There was a momentary pause, which Jim took to mean he was to continue.

"My third heading," Jim continued, "is that of nutrition. As you are both aware, elite athletes are incredibly controlled about their diets, none more so than in my sport of boxing. Of course we have to maintain a maximum weight, but this doesn't apply much beyond contact sports and lightweight rowing. Nevertheless virtually all athletes at Olympic level have nutritionists monitoring their food intake. As they get nearer to competition the fluid levels are particularly crucial. Athletes will have specialist drinks made up for their individual needs. I suppose that anyone really determined to wreck an athlete's chance of success could tamper with their drinks. At this stage I have no idea how or what, but with more research I could come up with some options."

"This is brilliant," added Gressley, perhaps a little too enthusiastically, "I'll find a method of preventing any tampering with my athletes' drinks. It's the least I can do."

"And your physiology heading?" Coombe said, picking up his watch and looking at it rather pointedly. "How is a physiological knowledge going to help people bent on attacking an athlete?"

"I'm not sure yet, Professor, but as so many elite athletes are on training schedules based on physiological results, the results themselves could theoretically be doctored to alter training with a detrimental outcome."

"Interesting speculation," said Coombe, "and I for one cannot see just how betting cartels in Asia could influence the activities of British physiological labs."

"Nor do I quite frankly," said Jim, "but I guess that's the basis of my PhD – to turn speculation into fact."

Nigel Gressley indicated that he was about to speak by his strange movement and leaning forward said: "The next one intrigues me, Jim, injury. Are you suggesting that another party would deliberately injure one of my athletes?"

"It happens a fair amount in football, Mr Gressley. Teams can gain a lot by taking out a key player."

"Perhaps so, but it's surely a different thing with an athlete when competition is theoretically non contact?"

"Of course, Mr Gressley, but injury would not have to be restricted to the track. You must remember the case of Nancy Kerrigan back in 1994 when she was attacked by a guy with an iron bar, severely damaging her knee. There was a lot of evidence to suggest that the attack was an associate of her arch rival Tonya Harding who went on to win the figure skating championship that year in Detroit. And don't forget this was only eight months after Monica Seles was stabbed by a spectator with a kitchen knife while playing tennis in Germany. I accept these cases are thankfully rare, but I have to consider all options."

Gressley pondered the impact of such actions and started to get physically uncomfortable. He had bought into the notion of finding ways to put his man on top, but physical assault was, even for him, a step too far. All the more reason, he thought, to get Jim Stringer developing the methods which were impossible to detect.

Nigel Gressley was suddenly aware that his thoughts were causing him to lose contact with the flow of the meeting. He regained his focus quickly, hoping that this momentary lapse had not been picked up by the others. Pressing his hands on the arms of his chair, Gressley addressed Jim again. "Tell us about this intriguing heading – sociological."

"To be frank, Mr Gressley, this term is a bit of a catch all. My thoughts were concerned with the way people within society may act in a way which could influence a result. A home fixture in football is always reckoned to be worth a goal, but only when the crowd is a hundred percent behind their team. In my sport, where the venue is more intimate, it has always made a difference to me if the crowd is on my side. Not so much once the fight has started, but the buildup has a huge effect. Remember the Lions tour to New Zealand when the team hotel had local crowds partying outside most of the night. The players, quite rightly, believed it was a deliberate attempt to keep them awake before a big game."

"I accept the premise, Jim, but don't see this type of thing being a likely option for anyone trying to damage the chances of one of my elite athletes."

"I tend to agree, Mr Gressley, but, as I understand it, you and Professor Coombe are asking me to consider all options. What you could call anti-social behaviour has to be included, if only to eliminate it."

Professor Coombe looked at his watch for the second time in the meeting, clearly aiming to bring things to a close. "And your final heading sounds interesting, Jim - psychology. What exactly had you in mind here?"

"Well," responded Jim Stringer, now warming to the final theme. "This one has more potential than any of the others in my view. Less than a second could separate a gold from a bronze medal in an event like the Olympic 1500 metres and there has to be a massive psychological element. You see it in a sport like basketball when the player who has just scored a basket is consistently the first one back in defence. The score seems to give him new legs. Imagine if one athlete had received bad news just before the event. It could have a major impact on performance."

"You're not seriously suggesting that anyone from outside the athletic fraternity could spin bad news that would not be checked for its validity?" said Coombe, furrowing his brows in disbelief.

"I am sir," replied Jim, "especially with modern technology of texts and emails. All sorts of vicious rumours could circulate at a critical time before an event. These could have a massive impact on a susceptible athlete. These guys may be hardened to competition through training, but they are only human."

"Yes, but the impact would be uncertain," countered Coombe.

"That I accept, but any element of concern could easily take the athlete's focus away from the task in hand. If that was an Olympic final, it could be devastating."

Coombe nodded and started to pull his papers together, pushing them into a leather attaché case with the University logo embossed on the front.

"I need to go," he stated, with the authority assumed by his position. "I congratulate you Stringer on an excellent summary of your thoughts to date. As you get into this more, I fear that some issues will get both complex and sensitive. Because of this I am insisting that you keep all your findings between the three of us. Is that understood?"

"It is," replied Stringer, "but there are two issues I need to raise before you go." Professor Coombe, who by now had stood up and was moving towards the door, paused, turned and faced his student. Coombe was not used to having his plans interrupted, but before he could speak, Jim Stringer also stood up as if he were about to give a presentation. "I need a second supervisor, Professor Coombe, and what will I say when my friends ask about my work?"

Professor Coombe relaxed his grip on the door handle

and addressed Jim directly. "I have been thinking about these issues with care. The first is easy to resolve. I plan to appoint Mr Gressley as your second supervisor. It's perfectly legitimate. Mr Gressley is someone who can provide you with essential contacts within sport which would be impossible otherwise. He is not a member of the University, but it is not uncommon for someone, with let us say business connections, to play such a role. Presumably Gressley you would be happy to act in this capacity?"

Professor Coombe hardly gave time for Gressley to respond, taking his silence to mean assent. "And the other issue is slightly more tricky, but once again I have considered the options. From the point of view of the University authorities and indeed your friends, Stringer, I suggest a parallel thesis. Your title will follow my recent lecture and will be concerned with methods of enhancing performance in sport. We can change the title right up to three months before submission, so this presents no problem. Your task Stringer will be to play a little game with your friends and get them to think that you are working closely with me to update my annual lecture. As this will be a desk bound thesis it should be relatively easy to convince your friends of its legitimacy. For the time being you will be doing an intensive literature review which will logically stray into the areas you have outlined during this meeting. Any questions?"

Coombe's rhetoric temporarily stunned Nigel and Jim. They both saw the sense in his approach and shook their heads in unison.

"Good. Then I look forward to our next meeting."

The professor pulled open the door, stepped into the corridor stacked high with books and headed briskly towards the lift. Nigel Gressley, who was still seated, looked up at Jim Stringer who appeared rooted to the spot and raised an eyebrow as an expression of questioning uncertainty.

"What do you make of him?" asked Jim, quickly recovering

his composure after the rapid conclusion to the meeting.

"I'm not sure," Gressley replied, "he's difficult to make out, but he does have a reputation as a smart operator. On balance I think you should be grateful he is prepared to take you on."

"Oh I recognise that. It's just that I am not sure how closely he will get involved. He didn't seem to contribute much to the discussion. It's as though it will be all down to me with very little input from our learned professor."

"Actually I shouldn't let that worry you," continued Gressley, "you could argue that it's a sign of confidence in you. Sure he's a busy man with numerous issues to resolve on a day to day basis. But he wants you to succeed, I'm pretty sure of that."

"I hope you're right because I cannot afford to fail either. I missed the cut for financial support from Sport England and if I'm to make the Olympic team in two years time, I need the bursary that Professor Coombe put on the table."

"I suppose it's none of my business," said Gressley, "but what has he offered?"

"Nine grand," came the reply, "it's three grand below the current rate for a PhD bursary, but Professor Coombe said I won't be required to do any teaching or lab prep like the other research students do. The money will be tight, but at least it gives me extra time for training."

Nigel Gressley noted the discrepancy between the figure Coombe had quoted for the bursary and the amount being paid to Jim. Such issues could wait and he quickly returned his attention back to Jim.

"I cannot make any promises as this stage, Jim. It's still early days. But if things go well I will try to make up the difference from my own budget."

Jim made no reply, so Gressley continued. "I thought your summary of the options was excellent, Jim, and very much in keeping with my own thoughts. My brain doesn't work quite like yours, I'm more of a pictorial man, but you're welcome to share my thinking." Gressley took out the single sheet of paper he had created the night before and put it in front of Jim. "You can see that unlike you, I have made no attempt to subdivide the options in any way. But the examples I give are very similar to those you suggested in the meeting with Professor Coombe. I confess I never contemplated physical assault as a way to slow an athlete down, but accept the possibility, however unlikely. I also never anticipated what you have called the sociological group, largely I guess because it is difficult to see how anyone could organise such activities. But you are right on both counts, anticipation is key. My athletes need to be prepared for anything, especially in the last few days before a major competition."

"You can now see, Mr Gressley, why so many of the big names won't use the athletes' village at the Olympics. Why run the risk of infection, psychological intimidation or the distraction of the opposite sex? Even the effect of a different bed from normal could make a difference. So why risk any of this when you can be immune from it all in a quiet hotel out of town? Peak performance is far more than getting the training right."

"OK," said Gressley, "I can see that we're on the same wavelength. Your task now is progressively to put flesh on the bones of all these ideas, possibly others. It is only through the details that you provide that my athletes are fully protected and have the best chance of success. I look forward to hearing from you as soon as you have more information. Here are my contact details. Good luck."

Gressley opened his leather computer case, took out a business card and having passed it to Jim, shook him by the hand. This time he was prepared for the young man's exceptional grip, but for the second time in an hour was surprised at the force of it. The two left the room together and separated at the lift door. Jim turned away to the main body of the library, while Gressley waited a full, impatient minute for the lift to arrive.

The meeting had, for each participant, achieved their individual objectives. Professor Coombe saw another opportunity to place a significant amount of money into his personal account. Jim Stringer had been accepted to undertake a PhD programme, securing for himself a modest income for the next three years. Nigel Gressley now had someone working directly for him. Jim would essentially provide the knowledge needed to plot the downfall of any athlete who was in opposition to those in his own agency. Gressley knew that knowledge was the first stage in a complicated process. It would take influence, skill and considerable risk to put such knowledge into practice. Gressley knew the financial benefits would be huge when he got Josh Silverman on the Olympic podium. He was not a man to pass up this opportunity, whatever the cost. He had just over two years to get it right. There was no second chance and Gressley would be ready. On the drive to Wolverhampton, Gressley knew there was little he could do until Jim Stringer came up with details. He needed to refocus on the afternoon's meeting, but his thoughts kept returning to the range of ways to ruin an athlete's chance of success. How, and to whom, was still of academic interest, but soon this would all be for real. Worryingly, Nigel Gressley started to relish the prospect. Gressley's reverie was interrupted by the one thing that concerned him more than the complexities of his job. The dull pain in his chest had returned again. This time he couldn't put it down to his love of Indian food. He resolved for the umpteenth time to see a doctor, but somehow this personal information was something he was far more reluctant to access.

CHAPTER 6

Jim Stringer rarely enjoyed meeting Nigel Gressley. Jim felt strangely uncomfortable with him. It was as if there was an unknown agenda which Jim failed to fathom. Jim was well aware who paid the piper and without Gressley's sponsorship of the project, there simply would not be a project. Gressley always insisted in meeting at a neutral location, well away from the University and seemingly well away from Gressley's home, although to be fair, Jim was never exactly sure where Gressley lived. Adding to the mystery, they never met at the same place. Gressley was apparently always going to or coming from another meeting and the new location was a matter of convenience. On this occasion, Gressley had chosen the very public place of the Costa Coffee outlet at Watford Gap service station on the M1, just a few miles north of Northampton. This service station still had the dreary appearance of one of the first service stations on British motorways, but the Costa house style had at least done something to lift the pervading gloom of the place.

Gressley welcomed Jim with a hug which Jim found somewhat repellent. Hugging was a not a thing men from Manchester did and it was especially distasteful if the person hugging you had a tendency to sweat.

"Jim, how are you? You're looking in great shape. How's the boxing? I heard that you're gunning for the Olympic team."

Jim found Nigel's incessant small talk of little interest and somewhat tiring, particularly after driving over sixty miles to meet him.

"Anyway, let's get down to business. Bring me up to date with your research, Jim."

"Where would you like me to start, Nigel, with the medication or the equipment aspects?"

"Talk me through the medication issues first please Jim, these sound the most promising."

"Well as you're fully aware, use of any of the IOC banned drugs would inevitably result in any medal being void and the prospect of a life ban. If any of your athletes were given a banned drug, even up to six months before major competition with some of the drugs, then unless there was a programme of masking it would show up at drug testing."

"Hang on there, Jim, you're losing me. What's this about masking?"

"Masking is something the pharmaceutical guys have developed to hide the effects of illegal drugs. It depends entirely on the drug but an example would be using frusemide, a potent diuretic, to mask anabolic steroids by flushing them out more rapidly. The thing is, Nigel, the drug testing regime is now so advanced, particularly as it can use out of competition testing, that it takes a lot for the illicit chemists to keep ahead of the experts testing for drug cheats. To put it another way, the people involved in developing new performance enhancing drugs are only a matter of months ahead of the people preventing it. It's real cat and mouse."

"So who's winning the battle at the moment, the cheats or the enforcers?"

"Difficult to say because there are so many products on the market and new ones are constantly being developed. Also there is the complication of some of the drugs simply raising the level of a naturally occurring chemical in the body. It becomes a real debate as to what is the correct level for an individual and what is excessive."

"So from your research and experience, what is the extent of illegal drug use right now?"

"Sports vary dramatically. You've heard all about whole teams being either withdrawn or banned from events like the Tour de France. In athletics, in countries where out of competition testing occurs systematically, then no one with any sense would use any of the drugs when there are well-established testing protocols. Countries like China and Cuba could be rife with drug abuse, but even they would have to steer well clear of international competition while they are using them. They would either have very good masking agents to avoid detection or simply come off them well before competition."

"So what sort of time scale are we talking about to come off drugs before a major meeting where testing is guaranteed?"

"Once again, Nigel, it depends on the drug, some of the poetin family of drugs which can have a profound effect on endurance can still be detected three weeks after its last use. The benefits, of course, diminish by the day, so the trick is to continue to use the drug up to the last possible time that still allows washout to occur before the event. In the old days, countries in Eastern Europe, who were really big into this, would have precise timetables for each athlete. Of course since the shake up in the Soviet bloc, everything has become far more open and these countries are little different from those in the West. As I said before, the main threat is from countries that compete rarely on the international stage, and can keep their training programmes secret."

"So going back to my athletes, Jim, what is the main threat to them?"

"Number one is their own stupidity, when they use a banned drug unknowingly. Crazy really, because at the elite level they're part of, each athlete should be monitoring every morsel that passes their lips."

"All British athletes of Olympic standard are assigned

a nutritionist and a doctor and all are given a list of banned substances. More importantly, they all receive a list of products that might contain the banned substances," said Nigel, trying to impress with his knowledge of the topic.

"Exactly," Jim cut in, "but time and again, athletes blame some apparently innocuous over-the-counter medication when they are found to have a banned substance in their bodies. Some are really common products you can buy from supermarkets such as Sudafed or Day Nurse, which contain stimulants. But the athletes should know this. Look at the case of Linford Christie who failed a drugs test when he had drunk ginseng tea. In this instance, I guess his excuse was that the contents of the tea were not listed, but it very nearly cost him a ban."

"So Jim, what you're saying is that every one of my athletes will have to remain incredibly vigilant over anything they eat or drink including any supplements and treatments for any form of minor illness."

"Right, especially supplements. Most athletes believe in supplements such as glucosamine, but you can never be sure what potentially banned substances could be mixed in with them. In my sport, because we have doctors crawling around us to look out for brain injury and weight loss, we also have very comprehensive nutritional advice. The trouble is with the big shot athletes who get all the publicity, they can often become prima donnas and lose touch with the medical team set up to support them."

"OK Jim, this brings us back to the real problem for me, how do I prevent any external agency – you know what I mean, anyone wanting to get to any of my athletes, from doing so."

"There cannot be a failsafe system. Let's face it anyone determined enough could spike the drink of one of your athletes, contaminate the food by bribing a chef, or switch a crucial drink, even just prior to an event."

"Give me an example," said Gressley, trying hard to show a

level of interest which beguiled his true intent.

Jim took time to reply. He was struggling to work out the motives of the man in front of him. Was this genuine concern for the well being of his stable of athletes, or was there some hidden motive which was far less altruistic?

Jim refocused on the question and looked back at Gressley still waiting patiently for an answer. "Well," replied Jim, "let's take the example of an event which involves drinking during the competition. I could use my own sport of boxing, because we traditionally drink and spit most of it out during the minute between rounds. But a better example would be the marathon, where drinks are taken virtually throughout. Now I don't know if you have any marathoners in your stable, but at the top level, they all have their own water bottles set out and labelled so there is no confusion. Each one contains individual rehydration products, usually made up by team nutritionist and based on a combination of personal preference and sound physiological know-how. Now say one of these was made up incorrectly and contained products which could be damaging, say something as unsubtle as a laxative, within half an hour that athlete is in real trouble. Of course, as I said earlier, the athlete has to work in partnership with someone they trust to produce the drink, which is usually the case. The alternative, with something as crucial as this is to prepare your own drink, but very few athletes have access to the chemicals which could be an important part of it. So with diligence and trust, the chances of a drink used in a race like this being contaminated, 'in house' so to speak, is pretty remote. However, another competitor or official, who is determined to undermine a fellow athletes chances... well that would be a different matter. Just imagine a crooked coach making a copy of one of your athlete's water bottles in advance of the race, putting in the mixture a very small quantity of a banned drug. Simply switching the bottles and hey bingo, drug test after the race comes out positive, you know the rest of the story."

"Yes, but surely Jim there are security checks surrounding all these events, how could that happen in practice?"

"A lot easier than you think, Nigel, there isn't the manpower to cover every eventuality. In my sport, the drink looks kosher. It apparently comes sealed, but anyone could inject rubbish through the seal. Get real, Nigel, if someone is really determined, they can make it happen. It would take a bit of bravado, typical conman stuff, but you could almost always find a way to either switch or contaminate a drink or foodstuff with potentially devastating results."

There was a lengthy pause as Nigel Gressley took in what Jim had been saying. He appeared distracted, drumming his fingers on the table between them and then scratching his right ear. Jim spotted this and recalled a lecture from his first year as a student. A retired policeman had said that this action of scratching your ear or the top of the head was a sure fire indication of not exactly guilt, but personal involvement. The example the officer gave was when a police car had been following another car, then they could always tell when they had been spotted by this very action. It worked every time. It was happening right now, and Jim noted it with interest.

"OK," said Gressley as he made eye contact with Jim again, "tell me what else you've been working on."

"Well, the next area is sort of related, but instead of food and drink as the noxious agent, we are talking about infection."

"And?" questioned Gressley, now starting to warm to the options being outlined by Jim.

"Infection, or disease in general, would clearly be damaging to an athlete at almost any time, but just prior to or during a major event, it could be devastating. Your athletes just have to remain disease free, but the situation in the athletes' village, for example, with hundreds of athletes from numerous countries is an infection waiting to happen."

"So I should keep all my athletes out of the village?" suggested Gressley.

"Well, yes and no. You'll be cutting down on the risk of cross infection from other athletes, but depriving them of the benefits and experience of the camaraderie of the team. Once again, will your people be the aloof prima donnas who parachute in for their races and get out fast or will they be involved in team support and being more of a role model for less experienced athletes coming through?"

"My ultimate concern is to get them to the start line in perfect condition. I can't let sentiment overcome those risks."

"I recognise that," replied Jim, "and, as I don't have an agent to look after my interests, I can quite see the distinction, but the risks are pretty low."

"I would hope so," Gressley interjected, "but we are talking about casual infection levels and risk. The whole issue alters dramatically if we start to consider deliberate infection of an athlete, perhaps even from another athlete."

"OK," said Jim, "one could envisage, however unlikely, an athlete suffering from say 'flu and deliberately making close contact with another competitor to try to infect him and affect his performance. The trouble with this scenario is that the timing would need to be critical. Most common diseases of the type that will have a big impact on performance are fairly short lived, but of uncertain length. Take 'flu. You could have an athlete suffering from it for say two weeks before a major meeting, deliberately pass it on to a rival by airborne contact or even just by shaking hands and recover sufficiently to compete. This could leave the unfortunate rival totally wiped out and either unable to compete or perform badly, weakened by the disease. The trouble with this speculation is that it is a very unlikely set of circumstances and impossible to plan. Your real concern, Nigel, is not this scenario at all, but one where the infection is transmitted artificially, without the involvement of another athlete."

Nigel Gressley remained to the untrained eye impassive, but once again made that very small movement of scratching his right ear. Jim, as before, made due mental note and waited for Nigel's comment.

"Jim, you are starting to lose me again. What do you mean by 'transmitted artificially'?"

"Well, let's assume that the sort of person you seem to be concerned about is out to infect one of your athletes. Moving the infection threat away from another rival athlete, to say a coach or official, would mean having a suitable pathogen at their disposal and infecting your athlete directly."

"But how is that done?" enquired Gressley, trying desperately to disguise his rising level of interest.

"Not easy, but very feasible," Jim replied, being all too aware of Gressley's unhealthy interest in the topic. "Viruses and bacteria are being produced for all sorts of research into infection control. Pharmaceutical labs up and down the country have massive deposits of the stuff, mainly low grade, but some pretty nasty ones including TB, hepatitis, typhoid, tetanus and yellow fever. The thing is most athletes as a result of international travel will be well immunised against all these. It's the more recent viruses such as swine flu and bird flu that could be a threat to your athletes. Imagine the devastating effect of swine flu on one of your athletes. A company like Baxter Healthcare, who produce the antivirus, will have high levels of protection, but imagine if some of the viruses were stolen from the company and were released near an athlete. You can kiss goodbye to that athlete's chances for a week or two."

"I think I get the picture, Jim. You have a knack of putting things most graphically. Let's move on to any other threats your research has turned up."

"Well as I said at our first meeting with the Prof, another possibility is physical assault. Realistically the likelihood of that happening is pretty remote, particularly when you get close to the event, because security will be at the highest level possible. I suppose in theory someone could attack an athlete, either directly or using a weapon or even a vehicle. The problem is with this type of threat is that it would be known well before the race and all bets would be off. So these betting syndicates which seem to be worrying you Nigel, couldn't benefit from such a thing as I see it."

"Absolutely," said Gressley, not wanting to pursue this potentially distasteful line of discussion.

"A far more potent threat and one that could be hidden from the outside world would be psychological assault."

"Meaning?" enquired Gressley, returning to the topic with renewed interest.

"Meaning," echoed Jim, "the use of some form of, say, communication with the athlete, which would cause him concern, anxiety or even fear. Let's take a hypothetical example of an athlete close to the race who receives a phone call or text message saying that their mother is very ill and is likely to die. Think of the impact that could have, particularly in a sport that requires a high level of skill such as shooting or even golf."

"Yes," Gressley agreed, "but surely something like that could easily be checked. The athlete will obviously make a phone call to other relatives or friends for confirmation."

"Exactly," said Jim, anticipating this response, "but there are numerous ways of intercepting calls or having them diverted so that the athlete would find it very difficult to get verification, especially when time was limited."

"I have to admit, I am not very technological, so you will have to explain this in more detail for me to fully understand. But not now, especially as I have no evidence to date that this is a serious prospect. However I would welcome a fuller briefing in due course. Can you arrange that?"

"It would mean me talking to a few guys at Uni doing IT, but

I am sure that I can find out the main principles and even the method."

"Fine, but Jim, please be very cautious. The more people that get involved, the greater the chance of leakage. Remember my primary concern is for my athletes. At all costs, I need to prevent those people determined to find ways of wrecking their chances."

"Nigel, I appreciate that you're concerned for your athletes, but aren't you getting a little bit paranoid over the prospect of anything like this happening?"

Nigel anticipated this question coming sooner or later and was ready with his answer.

"Jim, what you have to realise is that apart from the prestige of a gold medal, the winning athlete with the right support structure could easily become a multimillionaire. Get it wrong and all they have to show their grandchildren is a piece of metal on a ribbon. Get it right and they're set up for life. But first they have to win. Just like the athlete prepares with absolute precision, my job is to cover all the bases and I intend to do it with the same precision the athlete will use. The reason you are here is that you can give me the detail and knowledge that, frankly, I do not have the time to obtain. It's all down to division of labour and I see you as part of a very important team."

Jim did a quick calculation and soon appreciated the significant additional income a gold medal would mean to an agent like Nigel Gressley. He could start to understand why this man would go to great lengths to ensure that nothing, absolutely nothing would be allowed to stop his athletes performing to their utmost on the day.

"Anyway Jim, going back to your original list, tell me about any developments in what you called the mechanics area."

"In track athletics the only possible influence is on the shoes. These days, as you are well aware with the sponsorship deals that you have arranged, all running shoes are tailor-made for the individual athlete. There's a lot of science in these shoes, but still room for personal adjustment coupled with the inevitable commercialism."

"It's no secret that all my sportsmen are contracted to Asics, with the exception of the three golfers in my stable. They are sponsored by Ping but I have far less concerns about them than the track athletes. They are the ones with the most to lose at least from now to the Games. All my athletes' shoes are delivered through a UK agent of Asics, mainly to get the publicity associated with the handover. Any new styling or special touches like the Olympic rings stitched into the tongue flap will always involve the athlete and a minor press conference. This will often be the first time the athlete has actually seen the new design in the flesh so to speak."

"But what if the athlete doesn't like the new shoes? How does that work?" asked Jim slightly perplexed.

"Very unlikely," said Gressley, because the athlete is always involved long before the official launch. My top athletes all go to Asics UK headquarters in Warrington for final fitting and testing, then the shoes are delivered by courier."

"So really the only way to have any influence on the shoe is some form of interception during the delivery stage," asked Jim.

"Exactly. In spite of this being unlikely, what type of influence are you talking about?"

Jim hadn't excelled at mechanics, but knew that the key to shoe design was the cushioning and the positioning of the internal orthotics.

"Every specialist running shoe is designed to suit a particular type of runner. I won't bore you with the science but it's largely to do with the position of the internal high pressure foam around the instep. This can alter the dynamics of the foot fall slightly, changing the angle of the lower leg relative to the ground. Even altering the density of this foam can have a dramatic effect on foot strike which over a relatively short period of time will cause discomfort and even pain. Even the slightly abnormal feel of a shoe which has been 'doctored' like this would worry an athlete sufficiently to affect his performance. Less experienced runners have even been known to put these instep orthotics on the wrong side of the shoe and cause real problems with their gait. This isn't going to happen to your people because Asics will do it all for them, but if someone were to intercept the shoe and doctor it, then you are talking about a serious loss of running efficiency."

"As you say, Jim, this type of intervention is pretty unlikely because of the care taken by Asics to work with the athlete and avoid any disruption to the delivery process. Still, I appreciate your comments and something I will have to double check in my planning. So does that bring us to the last method, what you mysteriously called sociological when we last met?"

"Yes Nigel. I couldn't think of a better term at the time and as I said it's a bit of a catch-all. Every athlete has external influences, often unrelated to their training, coaching and specific preparation for the event on the day. If I, God forbid, wanted to reduce an athlete's chances of success, I would be looking for any weakness in their make-up, their personality, their overall lifestyle. Once you know the athlete, as you must do, then you can see if there are ways to influence him for better or, more concerning for you, for worse. The GB team sports psychologist is doing this all the time. He will be constantly monitoring anxiety levels, attitude, personal issues and finding ways to bring the athlete to perfection for the major events. You don't leave these things to chance any more like you used to do in the old days. Coaches now know that the pre-match talk cannot be the same for every performer. In the past, the coach would go into the dressing room and whip the whole team up into a frenzy before they got onto the pitch. It worked for some players, but not for all. Some were so over the top that they performed really badly at first and only hit their true form when some of the hype had dissipated. If it's like that for team games, imagine the difference the right psychological approach would make to an individual athlete."

"Yeah, sure, but aren't you coming back to the same old psychological stuff that you talked about earlier with illicit phone calls etc?"

"To a degree, but I see this as slightly different. Top athletes live in a bubble of their own making, but to a greater or lesser extent, they have to live in society as well. Many of them are big stars and have the media chasing them, potential sponsors after them, and even members of the opposite sex trying it on. You know as well as I do how many footballers succumb to the sexual encounters which the press love to report in all its tawdry detail. Sportsmen and women who are in long term relationships are particularly open to exposure by the media. Any infidelity which is made public is bound to cause upset with devastating consequences on the relationship and ultimately their sporting performance. Of course the extreme case was Colin Montgomery. It took him over 12 months to get back to anything like his true form after his infidelities were exposed. Let's face it Nigel, there are women out there who could easily be bought to perform sexual favours if the athlete was susceptible. I know it takes two to tango, but can you be absolutely sure that all your athletes could remain squeaky clean if a beautiful woman were in the right place at the right time?"

"To be honest, Jim, I have one or two of my group who could be highly susceptible and already show, shall we say, worrying signs of over indulgence."

"I'm not absolutely sure what you mean by that Nigel, but you know as well as I do that opportunity is the greatest seducer. If you want to take a guy off his athletic focus, then nothing better than a pretty girl at the right time. Men can do crazy things with all that testosterone flying around. Channelling their precious energy into the wrong direction is a sure-fire loser."

"Yes but I'm only their agent, Jim. I can't control their romantic interests or love life."

"Of course you can't, but at least a strong warning from you might help to put your athletes on their guard."

"So tell me, Jim, put yourself in the place of some unscrupulous operator trying to use a woman to upset the training or competitive programme of one of my athletes. How would you set about it?"

"Christ, Nigel, use your imagination. I don't have a strategy worked out, but pay certain women well enough and they will seduce one of your athletes without any problem. Of course your people have to be the type, seducible you could say, but you've already said that a couple of your athletes could be in that category. Anyway to answer your question, I would check out the ones that are not in a long term and stable relationship, or even if they are, those that have the potential to wander. Contact a classy girl from one of these upmarket escort agencies and offer her a financial deal that pays up front to do the business and double the fee if she delivers."

"Delivers?" enquired Gressley, now starting to feel a surge of excitement from the prospect of another method of ruining an athlete's chances of success.

"Oh come on, Nigel, which century were you born in? Many an athlete has missed an early morning training session because he was enjoying the new found charms of a young lady. Get an athlete involved in a good looking girl who is way out of his normal class for a week or two at a critical time and his mind will permanently be on her and he can kiss goodbye to his next world record. You know as well as I do that the final weeks before a major competition are all about routine, discipline and one hundred percent focus. Destroy that with a sexy girl and he has lost it. You don't even have to pay her to be around all the time, in fact just the opposite. Your athlete will expend more energy in the chase than in the act. Basically I would contrive to have my target, one of your athletes, actually think he is in love with your...well let's be blunt, prostitute. The poor guy will be so mixed up emotionally that his performance is bound to suffer. And let's not forget if our unfortunate hero happens to be in a stable relationship and he still succumbs, even for one night, then you have the whole guilt thing and the very real prospect of media exposure. Of course to put that slant on it, an actual media exposure would double the harm. It would be a tough cookie who could cope with that just before an Olympic Games and not have it affect his performance."

"Jim, you paint a very convincing picture, but putting such a thing into practice would be virtually impossible. Especially the bit about an athlete actually thinking he was in love with one of these girls."

As Nigel said this, he suddenly realised that he was giving away far too much of his own personal agenda and tried desperately to correct himself.

"Of course, Jim, this is all hypothetical, but I can see from what you've said that a very much higher level of vigilance will be needed with one or two of my athletes. I appreciate your thoughts on this and would welcome any other scenarios that might come to mind. It's no secret that my athletes are worth a lot to me. Any way I can help them avoid anything that could be detrimental to top performance is absolutely critical. Jim, unless there is anything else from your research, we must talk seriously about contact with these Eastern syndicates."

"I've been thinking about this for some time, Nigel, and now reckon the time is right to try and make contact with those individuals that you seem to be worrying about. I'm a little concerned that any trip abroad will take me away from studying for my thesis, but you seem to be convinced this is necessary. Are you still sure that direct contact will be productive, or is this just some Gressley paranoia without any solid foundation?"

"Of course I have no first-hand evidence," Nigel replied, in total honesty, "but it's absolutely critical to explore this part of the jigsaw. If you find any indication of either a betting coup or plans to limit the performance of any of my athletes, then it's essential I know. You know I'll cover all reasonable expenses and what's more you'll have a great trip. You've never been to the Far East, so think of it as a working holiday. As long as you come up with the goods, I'll be more than happy for you to have a bit of a 'jolly'. Just don't push it because the benign Nigel Gressley you see today can turn pretty nasty if he thinks anyone is putting one over him."

Jim had no doubt that this was true and resolved to keep just the right side of Nigel as long as was necessary.

"I can't say I relish the idea of mixing with any of the unsavoury gangs of the Far East. I've heard some pretty nasty stories from that part of the world, the Triads etc."

"Jim, you're a Moss Side boy. Unless you were brought up in a convent, I'm pretty confident you're streetwise enough to handle most things. If you ever feel you're getting out of your depth, then I'll pull you out. No worries."

Jim was not totally convinced that a trip like this was absolutely necessary, but had to concede that few students would have an opportunity like this as a semi-legitimate part of their studies. It was also true that being brought up in Moss Side prepared him well for life on the edge of criminal activity and some of his past experiences could just give him the edge if anything became awkward. Not only that, but if a situation got too close for comfort, then his fists could soon become his friend.

"OK," said Jim, trying his best to sound convincing, "I've done some research in the grey literature and reckon that Hong Kong would be the best option. It's mainly because of the number of betting websites based in Hong Kong, but also the more practical reason that many more people speak English there."

"Sounds a good choice and could be a good stepping stone to other places, especially mainland China. But tell me Jim, how did you manage to establish the origin of these websites?"

"It's far from easy, Nigel, but in the student community at Loughborough there are some pretty smart cookies who like nothing more than a challenge like this. They've developed some very clever software which digs really deep into website developers' strategies and compares them with a major database culled from thousands of websites. The successful hit rate is already up to 87% and improving every week as more sites are added to the database. The two guys working on the software are getting very near to releasing it commercially and expect police forces worldwide to be interested. Pornographic websites are the main target, with the expectation of being able to literally pinpoint the website developer to a specific PC at a given address. Using this system I could literally knock on the door of the guy who is still in the process of developing a website."

"Good grief," Nigel retorted, "I trust you wouldn't do anything as stupid as that!"

"Come on, Nigel. I wasn't born yesterday, but it's a great way to validate information that I may get by more indirect means. Which reminds me, you talked earlier about reasonable expenses. You can't expect me to infiltrate betting gangs without some cash. I've got to be seen, at least initially, as someone who can literally roll the dice with the rest of them."

"Yeah," responded Nigel, with a wry smile. "I saw that coming miles ago and I've already made provision. I transferred £1,000 into your current account this morning for just such eventualities. I suggest very strongly that you trade it for cash well before you go and get yourself a secure money belt. If you need more I can arrange a bank transfer, but I'll expect a detailed report and full justification before you get another penny out of me."

"Sounds reasonable to me, but just one thing more, Nigel, can I have an advance for some decent clothes? You can see my style is jeans and T-shirt, mainly for reasons of economy, but I doubt if I'll even get into a decent casino dressed like this."

"Are you telling me that you don't possess a suit or some smart clothes, Jim?"

"Got it in one, Nigel, I really could do with some decent gear if I'm going to be anything like plausible."

"OK, OK, I get your drift, poor student needs to look the part and you're absolutely right. I'll advance you a further £500, but I'll expect receipts."

"Thanks, Nigel," said Jim cheerily. "It'll be an interesting trip for sure and I'll be in touch as soon as I get any leads. I expect to be gone for about three weeks, so don't worry if I stay out of phone contact. I'll make sure I text you from time to time."

With that the two departed, Jim looking forward with anticipation to what he described as a bit of an adventure. Nigel, on the other hand, harbouring somewhat darker thoughts about how to build on his knew knowledge to maximum effect. It was on that same drive home that Jim started to wonder just how far he could trust Nigel Gressley. Was he simply the sports agent who had a genuine concern for his athletes and prepared to invest significant sums of money in their protection? Or was there a more sinister side to his interest, even to the extent of ensuring that his athletes had an unfair advantage. Jim himself could not be detached from the moral dilemma because above all he knew this funded PhD was probably his one and only chance. Jim resolved to proceed with caution and start to build up a dossier on Mr Nigel Gressley. Jim sat back in his car seat, straightened his arms, and gripped the steering wheel with new found determination. He couldn't predict the future with any accuracy, but he was beginning to realise that the future could well be more complicated than he had ever imagined. Jim felt enlivened by the prospect. He welcomed living on the edge, but knew that every edge has its abyss. He had no intention of getting too near to this particular abyss, but was well prepared to trek to the very edge. He knew that it was likely to need exceptional mental and physical endurance. He smiled. He could have been thinking about boxing.

CHAPTER 7

July 23rd, 2010
Marlow, UK

Nigel Gressley was now ready. He knew enough. He had the resolve. He needed to act. And he knew exactly where to start. The dossier he had on each athlete gave him important clues to their character and lifestyle. First he considered Ngeny, the affable Kenyan, who had come back to prominence since holding the world record four years ago. This man was hot and on current form was a serious contender for a medal. He trained with the same group of runners in the high veldt of Kenya, not only Kipruto and Chortop who were by now past their best, but a new cadre of Kenyan runners who were undoubtedly stars of the future. Ngeny had one great asset – experience. He had been fifth in Beijing, the youngest and best of the Kenyan runners at the time, but now he had raced at international level for two years and had learned how to deal with the big boys of the track. Affable off the track yes, but he now knew exactly how to handle the rough and tumble of top flight competition. He was not built for the pushing and jostling of a compact field of runners and usually kept his tiny frame out of the risk zone. Contact with one swinging arm was all it took to upset an athlete's natural rhythm and Ngeny wanted none of it. In domestic events or European Team Championships he could set the pace by being a front runner, but at world and Olympic level his strategy would change to be the quiet one at the back of the leading pack. Then at the decisive moment, the famous Ngeny kick would take him round the outside of the leading runners and into the final straight to crucify the opposition. Gressley's dossier on Ngeny produced nothing of interest outside of his phenomenal running record. His wife and young family always accompanied him on the European tour and during the winter training season, they all returned home, living in a small village in the Mount Kenya National Park. His house was by far the biggest in the village and when away on tour, his mother looked after the small-holding at the back helped by his father who was a warden in the National Park. Gressley had painstakingly compiled Ngeny's dossier over the last three years, using all his contacts in the sports agency business combined with reports from coaches, other athletes and even a few shady characters from the Mombasa underworld. The fact is that Ngeny was clean. No suggestion of drug taking, philandering, gambling or anything which could be used against him. Gressley reviewed his options. It would have to be infection or contaminating his food with some illegal performance-enhancing drug. He decided to go for erythropoietin, commonly known as EPO. This was a favourite amongst endurance athletes, and Nigel needed to find a way to ensure that Ngeny had some in his blood stream about a week before the Olympic final. His action plan was still vague, but he knew the first stage was to get a quantity of EPO at precisely the right time. He knew that Ngeny always used the athlete's village, so Gressley had to find a way to overcome the anticipated security and smuggle the drug inside the accommodation block being used by the Kenyan team. Finally he needed to find a way to get Ngeny to ingest the EPO, but this last phase of his plan would have to wait. Stage one was the priority and even this would require some very careful and certainly illegal planning. Gressley made a few notes in Ngeny's file using a style of speedwriting he had developed over time and which anyone else would find difficult to interpret. He closed the file with a sigh of satisfaction and anticipation. Nigel Gressley felt he was always at his best when making plans but these plans were to move him clearly into unchartered territory. Gressley knew the risks, but, as is often the case, he allowed personal gain to dominate his questionable moral judgment.

Gressley now turned his attention to Benito, the current European record holder. Benito had a consistency which marked him as a certain finalist for the Olympics and one that could easily make the award rostrum. Benito's file was somewhat thicker than Ngeny's, not by virtue of his running performances, but his string of indiscretions with a variety of women all over the world. Benito was good-looking in a rugged, earthy way that was clearly attractive to numerous women. For a man so committed to his running, many commentators, usually journalists from the tabloid press, found it difficult to understand how he could maintain his elite position in the world of running and still find time for his womanising. Benito trained harder than most, which was guaranteed to reduce the libido of mere mortals, but not so with Benito. If he had been a professional footballer or a high profile basketball player then his name would have been in the celebrity press more than the sporting pages. Middle distance running rarely appealed to the mass audience, at least those who dictate newspaper and magazine sales, so much of his extra-marital activities went unnoticed. It was only when he was involved with film stars, pop singers and television personalities that the media considered his liaisons 'in the public interest'. In spite of this, Gressley's file, culled from media agencies around the world, gave vent to one very clear conclusion. Benito could not help himself when it came to a pretty face or lissom body. This, thought Gressley, is his major weakness and one that could bring him down. As Angelo Benito was unmarried at the time, there was little to be gained from exposing his past affairs. In his own country they were tolerated and even admired. There was some media interest when Benito was caught on camera enjoying the company of a high-ranking politician's wife, but it soon became yesterday's news. The exposure clearly had little impact on Benito's running because three days later he won the Athletics Grand Prix event in Copenhagen in a personal best time. A few newspapers spared two column inches on the speculation that for Benito love making made him run faster, but little came of it as Benito, true to form, moved rapidly on to another attractive woman.

Coming to the end of Benito's file, Gressley was stunned to see a press cutting which could change everything. The final cutting revealed that three months ago, Benito had got married. It must have been a very quiet ceremony, as the press cutting was from a local paper in Pienza, Benito's home town in Tuscany and certainly had not hit the national or athletic press. Thank God for the efficiency of the press agency thought Gressley, as this change in Benito's marital status now meant that further indiscretions could be damaging. The short press cutting indicated that Benito had married his childhood sweetheart who had waited patiently for him and the usual platitudes about being a changed man were part of the local reporter's exclusive interview. This major change in Benito's life gave Gressley real optimism. He knew that people like Benito, who had tasted the joys of numerous women, were very unlikely to settle for a life of married and faithful bliss. Gressley now turned his attention with confidence to arranging a very unsuitable sexual liaison for Benito. Once exposed, it would cause sufficient publicity that the outcome would without doubt cause Benito many a sleepless night. Even a man with Benito's track record should be sufficiently disturbed that his running would be bound to suffer. Benito would doubtless still run but with the press antagonism surrounding him, his performance would almost certainly be below par. This was sufficient for Gressley. Athletes in the 1500 metre final in the London Olympics running below their best was all Gressley needed. He closed his eyes and could see Josh Silverman on the winner's rostrum and 15 percent of the Olympic champion's income coming to him, Nigel Gressley, agent to the elite.

Gressley's day dreaming came to a rapid halt as his wife bustled in with afternoon tea. Christine Gressley was once an attractive woman but in recent years had allowed herself to go the way of many middle-aged women. She was now two stone overweight, yet remarkably had kept a lively, rather pretty face. She always maintained that were she to lose weight she would begin to look haggard and this could well have been true. She actually had ample evidence for this because over the years she had lost and gained huge amounts of weight, having subscribed to most of the diet companies and reduction schemes available. Gressley, if he were honest, would prefer a slimmer version of his wife, but this was dangerous ground and was rarely discussed. Christine carried her excess weight well, mainly because of her stylish and expensive clothes. She seemed content in her domestic role, putting her energies into the house and their two children, often in that order. Christine placed the tea tray laden with two home made scones, cream and jam from the local farmers' market carefully on the only space on Nigel's desk.

"Thanks, darling," said Nigel bringing his focus back to domesticity. "You really do spoil me. I trust these scones are your own."

Christine just smiled. She knew full well that Nigel wouldn't even contemplate any other type of scones. It was just one of his many quirks, but in this case it was at least complimentary.

"How's it going?" she enquired, not really understanding any of the details of the business he had built up over the years. Nigel kept his work, his family life and social activities well apart. Christine knew that he negotiated deals for top sportsmen and even knew some of their names, especially the ones that made the daily papers. Beyond that, his work was a mystery. They kept separate bank accounts. She received a more than satisfactory monthly allowance, and as Nigel paid for all major items of expenditure, the arrangement was in Christine's opinion, very satisfactory.

"I'm planning the lead up to the Olympics, mainly for Josh. I'm desperate to maximise the Silverman brand before and especially after when he gets Olympic gold."

Christine, who could not quite grasp how a person became a brand, replied "You sound really confident in Josh's chances, particularly with two years to go. Surely all the other big names will be just as confident of their chances."

"Yes, but..." Nigel began, but then thought better of it. "One has to remain confident on behalf of my own athlete. But you're right, it will be a strong field and anything could happen on the day."

"I'll leave you to your tea and scones. There is more in the pot if you need it." With that, Nigel Gressley was left to his files and his plans to give Josh Silverman every chance of success.

Gressley next took out the file on Jose Carrera, the Cuban and Pan-American champion at 1500 metres. Carrera was unusually big for a middle distance runner, but his raw power had won him many races because of his speed over the last 100 metres. The pack usually left Carrera apparently dead because he could never maintain the pace set by the lighter runners. But in that final straight, if Carrera was in touch with the pack, you could expect fireworks. It was said that he rarely ever ran more than 400 metres in training and that he could easily make the Cuban team in the 800 metre event. Such was the depth in Cuban running that the national coach could regularly find runners of Carrera's quality to run the shorter race. So Carrera ran in the 1500 metres and ran it exceedingly well. Although he never held a world record, he was consistently posting times which made all other athletes fear him. Strangely, he rarely competed out of South America, which always aroused suspicion in people's minds as to whether or not he was on drugs. Out-of-competition drug testing never happened in

Cuba and when Carrera competed, even in the USA, he was always clean. Gressley pondered Carrera's case and was surprised to find that he had never deviated from Nike being his shoe and clothing sponsor. Could this be the opportunity Gressley was looking for? Was there a way that his shoes could be doctored to force Carrera to run differently, alter his natural cadence and slow him down? From what Jim Stringer had said, it would take little more than a small orthotic inserted into the shoe to have a potentially devastating impact. But how to achieve that? Gressley had no immediate answer but knew that his inventive mind would find a solution and more importantly a way to implement it.

Khalid Gabet was a different animal altogether. He was home-loving and a very committed family man. Gabet had no obvious weaknesses for Gressley to exploit so he decided psychological pressure was the best option. Gressley's fertile and unsavoury mind went to sending a text or phone message at a critical time in Gabet's preparation. Ideally this would be just before the final to give Gabet no time to confirm its authenticity. Gressley thought long and hard over the text of such a message. He decided that the most damage would be done by telling Gabet that his family back home was in mortal danger. The details could wait, but Gressley now felt that he could tick Gabet off his mental checklist. At least with this plan, he could operate alone. There was no need to involve anyone else in this particular act of malevolence. Including others added to the risk and would be costly. Gressley was comforted by this fact.

Gressley now turned his attention to Lui Ho. Ho was the Chinese 1500 metre champion who was a something of a mystery, due largely to his lack of appearance outside of his home country. Most pundits put this down to a well organised drug regime which prevented him competing on the normal European and World circuit. They were confident that when Ho appeared at the Olympics, the Chinese doctors and supporting pharmacists would have made sure he was utterly clean. Gressley saw Ho as a real threat and would need some fairly aggressive action to slow him down. Gressley pondered the options, recognising that a contrived accident was probably too risky and uncertain. It would have to be something which still left Ho capable of running but had seriously compromised his health. His mind, now freewheeling, kept coming back to some sort of injection of the type that professional footballers often had to keep them in the game that little bit longer. Any injection, even apparently beneficial, is bound to cause temporary trauma. This would almost certainly be enough to bring Ho back to the level of a mere mortal. Gressley added 'injection' to Ho's file and left the detail to later.

The final file on Gressley's desk was on the American trio of Erchard, Fradley and Delves. These three had performed with distinction in 2008, but weren't even guaranteed selection for 2012. Gressley anticipated a strong American presence, especially as five Americans had already achieved the Olympic standard. He was not especially worried at this stage who they might be because he was confident that they would stick closely together in the weeks before the Games. This was the American ethos of teamsmanship and played directly into his hands. A squad that stayed together could be attacked together and Gressley, thinking back to Jim Stringer's research into infections, pencilled this in as the method of choice.

It was now late and Nigel Gressley closed the files on the likely finalists for the 1500 metres. He moved them to the bottom drawer of his antique walnut desk, locked the drawer and replaced the key in his wallet. His plan was without doubt taking shape and he had two years to implement it to its ultimate conclusion. Josh Silverman would be on the winners' podium, whatever it took, and Nigel Gressley had every intention that the British flag would be on the central pole.

Chapter 8

August 23rd, 2010
Baxter Healthcare, High Wycombe, UK

As a sports agent, Nigel Gressley had many reasons to visit the Commonwealth Games, but none would have suspected that his main reason was to ruin the chances of success of the British swimming team. Nigel saw this purely as an experiment to test whether or not he could make a group of athletes ill by infecting them with bacteria. This was to be no easy task as it required not only obtaining the bacterium in a suitable form, but also to find a way to introduce it to the athletes. In many ways the first task was the most difficult. Bacteria were not the sort of thing that you could buy over the counter. Nigel, however, had extensive contacts and one of these put him in the right place. The right place for infections was Baxter Healthcare which had become the government's main research establishment since Porton Down was closed. Baxter Healthcare had a poor public image and because of this, bi-monthly tours were organised for the general public. Gressley had been on one of these tours and it was clear that there were sections of the company that were totally off limits to the general public. Gressley noted, during his visit, that the security level was high, with all experimental areas protected by swipe cards in combination with a five digit alpha-numeric code. These codes were surprisingly easy to crack, largely because the actual sequence of the four alpha digits was unimportant. Once the digits were known then they could be input in any order and the lock would release. With four alpha options from A-D, this still left a huge number of variables to explore, but a piece of hardware available from pseudo-spy operations in the States could easily crack the code in a maximum of ten minutes. Baxter Healthcare's website conveniently gave the names of all the senior executives and tracing their home addresses was in most cases not difficult, especially if they had teenage children on facebook. Nigel's experience had taught him that senior executives were often the most careless with security issues such as swipe cards, mainly because such staff are well known in the company and security officers are likely to let them into the building without the usual controls. Set against that observation was the fact that their homes were likely to be more secure than those of junior personnel. This was largely because high value insurance policies insisted on high quality alarms. Obstacles like this were not going to deter Nigel Gressley.

In the past, Nigel had employed a special investigator to watch the movements of big name football players and keep track of any meetings they may be having with rival clubs. He soon found that the work was being outsourced to individuals with a colourful past and a proven ability for breaking and entering. Nigel simply bypassed the middle man, who was charging far too much for their services, and worked directly with these unsavoury characters. The cost of between £500-£1000 for a night's work seemed excessive, but compared with the fortune to be made when the transfer market was active, it was without question a wise investment. It was time for Nigel to re-invest. Using a mobile phone he kept exclusively for such calls, contact was soon made with a certain Jed Burnage, who appeared by all to be a reformed character after his six year spell in Wormwood Scrubs. By Jed's standards, Nigel's request was a fairly straightforward task. Jed's mission was to obtain the swipe card belonging to the CEO of Baxter Healthcare, by chance recently moved into a five-bedroomed house in Seer Green, South Buckinghamshire.

Jed Burnage had made a science out of being a private investigator and an art of breaking and entering. Above all he knew human nature. Estate agents, he had found, provide extremely useful information on the layout of houses on their website and often left such information on the web for up to a month after purchase. Jed could simply download the plans of the house and study the images of each room until he had a working knowledge of the home he was about to break into. Jed was particularly pleased to see that the house had a south facing conservatory. This meant one important bit of information to Jed. South facing conservatories were almost impossible to keep cool in the summer and at night most people would leave the windows on night vent, making his task of forced entry considerably easier. He knew from experience that only ten percent of home owners switched their burglar alarms on at night, when they were in the house. Armed with this additional information and the likelihood of the swipe card being either in the CEO's suit pocket or more likely his laptop bag, Jed opted for the distraction routine. He had already noted that the CEO kept his car on the drive in front of his house. Jed's skills allowed him to activate the alarm without damage to the vehicle by using a simple multiple transponder which acted like a series of electronic keys. Within 10 seconds one of these hit the right frequency for the CEO's BMW and set off its alarm. Jed waited in the shadows of the garden and watched for the usual scenario to unfold. The upstairs window at the back opened, telling Jed this was where the CEO slept. Hushed voices also told him that his wife slept in the same room. The front door opened and once the CEO confirmed it was his own car's burglar alarm causing the disturbance, he hurriedly went back inside to find his keys. This was the critical moment for Jed as he watched. Human nature told him that people either kept their keys near the front door or with their other work possessions. A light went on in a downstairs room near the front of the house and the CEO soon returned with his keys. He unlocked his car, checked for any sign of forced entry, muttered curses under his breath and finally locked and unlocked his car twice more to check for any obvious fault in the setting mechanism. Satisfied, yet annoyed, he returned to the house and back to the room at the back. After a few minutes discussion with his wife, the house returned to its normal somnolent state. Jed waited 20 minutes and repeated the process. This time he used the noise from the car's alarm to cover the sound of him forcing an entry through one of the windows in the conservatory left conveniently on night vent. Once again Jed patiently waited until the house quietened down, although he noted with interest that the discussion from the bedroom was more animated than before. Jed climbed dexterously through the now open window in the conservatory, was relieved to find the door from the conservatory to the main part of the house was unlocked, and made noiselessly for the room at the front. Jed could see from numerous sensors that the house had the capacity to alarm different parts of the house, but as he predicted this option had, even in the circumstances of repeated disturbances, not been used. Switching his muted flashlight on, Jed could see the keys that had previously been retrieved from this room were no longer there. Carefully unzipping the front pocket of the laptop bag revealed the prize. Jed was always amazed at how predictable people were. He had been in the house for less than a minute and in his hand was the precious swipe card. After zipping up the bag, a small but necessary action, Jed left the house via the conservatory making sure that his forced entry would be virtually undetectable.

The reason Jed Burnage, nominally a private investigator, was so successful in his illicit extracurricular activities was down to one feature. He simply looked the part. He basically looked normal, unremarkable, not an easy person to describe. He could slip into a role as required for the task and had two important characteristics, his ability to think ahead and talk himself out of tricky situations. Nigel Gressley, following Jed's successful robbery, now offered him a more challenging theft. Jed adjusted his fee accordingly and Nigel, recognising the futility of bartering, accepted the deal. It was agreed that the 'procurement' as Nigel called it, he was never one to admit to theft, would be attempted later the next day, before the loss of the swipe card caused too much inconvenience.

Jed just loved these missions. Although he was well paid for such enterprises, the adrenaline rush he got from these operations was like an addictive drug. He, above anyone, could understand the mentality of teenage joy riding. It just gave him a buzz that he couldn't get from any other situation. It was just as much the planning as the implementation that excited him, but he also recognised that even the best planning needed a set of contingencies. Nigel Gressley obtained a list of five staff members in the Baxter Healthcare building and this gave Jed the leverage to move around, simply asking for directions. He strode up to the security desk at about five o'clock and informed the security guard that he had a meeting with Dr Sanderson, one of the staff members on Nigel's list. The guard scanned his list and saw no record of such a meeting.

"I'm sorry, sir, but I have no record of such a meeting. Shall I ring Dr Sanderson to say that you are here?"

"Yes it's rather unexpected," said Jed, "I'd prefer you to keep it to yourself, but he was involved in a motor accident this morning and I'm here on behalf of the insurance company. It's a bit tricky as it appears to have been Dr Sanderson's fault so I need an urgent word to sort things out."

"I see," said the security guard, turning the multi-layered pass book towards Jed, "would you be so kind as to fill in the visitors' book and I can issue your visitor's pass." Jed breathed a sigh of relief and leaning over the book completed all the details, adding while the guard was distracted, a leaving time of 6.15pm in the final column. The guard removed the first section of the horizontal strip from the book, folded it and slipped it inside a plastic cover.

"There you are sir, now I'd be happy to ring him to say you're on your way up."

"Honestly, no need," said Jed, "I know the way, and please keep the reason for my visit under wraps. These things can be a bit tricky."

Jed took the lift just one level, got out and now fully authorised with his prominent badge, started to investigate the layout of each level of the building. Baxter Healthcare had been more than helpful by signing each floor with its activities and Jed took until floor four before he saw the key name. Microbiology Department, Bacteriology Section was listed along with Biochemistry, Tissue Cultures and the rather worrying sounding Embryonic Culture Laboratory. Jed had hit the jackpot and continued to the top of the building to wait patiently in a locked cubicle in the gents' toilet until staff would have left the building to go home. His instinct for human nature told him that Friday night was the most unlikely evening for even the keenest researcher to stay too late.

"Goodnight, sir," said the security guard to Dr Sanderson with a smile, "your visitor found you alright?"

"Haven't seen anyone all afternoon," Sanderson replied, "must have been a mistake."

"If you've got a moment," said the now concerned guard, "I'm pretty sure he asked for you. Something to do with an insurance claim," was the deliberately vague comment.

"It's Friday night, Jackson, just show me the entry," retorted a somewhat exasperated Sanderson.

"Here you are sir," said Jackson, now questioning his own competence and he turned the book around to face Sanderson.

"The entry is far from clear Jackson, even you should admit that. It could easily have been for Sanders in biological statistics, and anyway, the guy left at 6.15 pm. Look he's signed out."

"I'm sorry to trouble you sir. It's just that I could have sworn that he asked for you. I must have missed him on the way out."

"No problem, Jackson, and have a good weekend."

But Jackson was troubled. Something didn't seem quite right. He made a note to mention it at the shift change later in the evening.

By seven o'clock the building resonated with little more than the faint hum of air conditioning and Jed decided it was time to act. Using the stairs again he returned to the fourth floor. He attached his digital lock code breaker to the bottom of the lock and the four digit LEDs showed him the numeric code. As he removed the code breaker, Jed heard a click from the other side of the door and could barely compose himself before it opened. A good con man takes the initiative and Jed was a good con man.

"Excuse me," said Jed, "but I'm a visitor here just on my way out. Can you tell me where the nearest gents is?"

"Down one level," came the reply. "You'd better be quick, the Gestapo down in security do their rounds at seven thirty and woe betide anyone left up here without a damn good reason."

"Thanks," replied Jed, now realising that his mission had less than half an hour to run before nosey security staff would be on the warpath. He went down a level to the toilet, waited five minutes to give the late leaver time to go and returned to the fourth floor. He had memorised the four digits, but had to guess the letter of the code. For some reason the letter C was always chosen more than any other in digital locks. Jed's logic told him that people associated C with 'clear' and that's why it was used most often. As frequently happened with Jed, his logic worked and the lock clicked with C1893. He swiped the card reader with the stolen card and gently pushed open the heavy door. The corridor ahead of him was long and dark. With Jed's muted flashlight, he soon found the door marked Bacteriology Section and to save time tried the same alpha numeric code on the lock. Jed was far from surprised to find that it worked, once again knowing full well from his studies of human nature, that even top scientists cannot be bothered to learn more than one code for a building. So much for high level security thought Jed, checking his watch and realising he'd less than fifteen minutes to get out.

He soon found the freezer units and scanning the shelves it took less than two minutes to locate the dishes labelled *e.coli* and *salmonella enterica*. Slipping on the latex gloves, which Nigel had told him were essential, two petri dishes from each culture were sealed in ziplock bags and carefully placed in Jed's empty laptop bag. Jed knew that simply walking out of the building was not an option at this time of night, but had already planned an alternative route made possible by the company's no smoking policy. Jed had spotted a covered open area designated for smokers, but conveniently outside the building at the top of a fire escape. It was on the third floor, so he noiselessly headed that way, eased the door open and quietly exited the building down a rarely used spiral staircase. He phoned Nigel Gressley later that evening, keen to get rid of his special cargo. Gressley was equally keen to have it safely stored in his spare freezer and told his wife that the mysterious packet in the bottom of the freezer was a new type of carp bait. Knowing his wife as he did, Gressley was totally convinced that she would have nothing to do with Nigel's revolting fishing equipment. This was especially since the time she opened an unlabelled tin in the fridge, to find it full of maggots.

CHAPTER 9

October 2nd, 2010
Commonwealth Games, New Delhi, India

Nigel Gressley had one final and dangerous task to perform before he was fully prepared for his assault on specific athletes at the Commonwealth Games. He first bought a cheap spray bottle similar to the ones his wife used to squirt disinfectant and half filled it with water. Wearing a protective face mask and latex gloves, he opened the dish of salmonella and using a wooden spatula transferred a minute amount of the bacterium into the bottle. He sealed the spatula in a ziplock bag and discarded it. The bottle was topped up with water and also sealed in two ziplock bags. The dish of salmonella was returned to the freezer, labelled as before as carp bait. Nigel packed his suitcase with extreme care, ensuring that his personal weapon of infection was well cushioned in a foam container. He was well satisfied with his handiwork and left from Heathrow on the 08.30 Jet Airways flight non-stop to New Delhi. Getting through New Delhi airport's immigration was as tortuous as ever but Nigel was impressed with how the Indian government had improved parts of the airport in preparation for the Games. He stayed at the Radisson, mainly because this was one of the hotels used for registration of athletes and officials. His credentials as a sports agent allowed him to get accreditation for the Games, but limited access to the athletes' village, which rumour had it was still in the final stages of construction. He bought tickets for the badminton and swimming, changed sufficient money into Indian rupees, and spent the rest of the day visiting the site of Ghandi's assassination, a macabre but interesting experience. Most of the athletes staying in Delhi had arrived several days earlier to get acclimatised and over their jet lag. A few of the medal prospects had been in the time zone for over two weeks, coming from training camps in Sri Lanka or The Maldives. Nigel always made a point when arriving from abroad of never giving in to fatigue but staying up until night time locally. This usually ensured a good night's sleep and this occasion was no exception. Nigel woke the next day refreshed and ready to plan his attack on the British swimming team. With the first swimming event 48 hours away, he knew that he had to move fairly quickly, so he took a taxi to the newly constructed Commonwealth pool. He learned that driving in Delhi was the nearest thing to planned suicide and was constantly amazed at how each driver had a sixth sense which seemed to convert every certain head-on collision into a near miss.

At the pool he recognised a couple of the triathletes who had finished their session and joined them in the friendly banter that accompanies a meeting such as this. It didn't take long to learn that the whole British swimming and triathlete squad had been invited to a reception that evening at the British Embassy. Not everyone was keen to go, but the chef-de-mission had laid down a three line whip and in spite of the dissent Nigel soon learned that almost all of the swimmers would be there. Those that weren't would need a damned good excuse. Nigel had fully expected that any attempt by him to get into the athletes' accommodation would have to be at night, but this news now gave him the option of the early part of that very evening. Nigel returned to his hotel, carefully re-packed his potent spray bottle into his laptop bag along with latex gloves and a mask and took a taxi out to the athletes' village. As by now it was getting dark, he chose a local coffee bar overlooking the only route buses could use from the athletes' village and read the Indian Times while waiting patiently for the exodus to the British embassy. Shortly after seven, three buses wound their way past him, clearly occupied with athletes in the red, blue and white uniforms of the games. He waited a further ten minutes then made his way to the front gate of the heavily guarded accommodation block. At the entrance hall the guard demanded his pass which Nigel showed him in as casual a way as possible. As the guard was comparing the pass with those specified on his printed sheet, Nigel added with a level of authority that he had been sent to check no more athletes were left behind. Nigel added that the British ambassador would be very annoyed if this were the case. The mention of the British ambassador was sufficient for the guard to overcome his duty in deference to his respect of high rank and Nigel's pass was returned without further comment.

"The swimmers are usually the worst," Nigel commented gruffly, "which floor will I find them?"

"Most are on floor three, sir, with just four rooms also used by swimmers on floor four."

"Thank you for your help," said Nigel and set off towards the lifts.

"Good luck, sir," he heard, as the lift doors opened.

Nigel had no fully formed plan from here. The important thing was to get within range of the athletes and then spray the noxious bacteria and wait for it to do its inevitable damage. He clearly wouldn't be able to get into their rooms and he was uncertain whether spraying the doors would be sufficiently effective. He was disappointed to see that the design of the rooms meant that there were no door handles, because these would have been excellent targets. He had also hoped that there would have been communal bathrooms in the corridors, but once again he was foiled as the design provided en suite facilities. Getting slightly exasperated and very nervous of his illicit role, Nigel suddenly saw his opportunity. In each corridor was a trolley used by the cleaner with a range of replacement toilet items. Included in these was a pile of towels and Nigel was quick to appreciate this stroke of luck. Checking that no one was around, he put on his mask and gloves and lifting each towel individually, he sprayed them from his noxious bottle. Just as the pile was complete, he was horrified to find a cleaner turn the corner and approach him from the far end of the corridor. She came directly towards him demanding to know why he was dressed in gloves and mask. Nigel broke into a sweat, but managed to stutter: "The British Government has been informed that cockroaches have been seen in the rooms above. I have been sent by the British Government to spray the area to ensure that there is no contamination in your corridor. Will you please inform the house manager if you see any vermin of this type in the rooms under your control? It is most important for the health of our athletes."

"Of course, sir," was the shocked reply, "I can assure your government that I have seen no insects in the rooms. I have been most vigilant."

"Thank you," Nigel added, "the British Government appreciates your cooperation in this matter."

With that Nigel carefully put away his bottle, stripped off his gloves and mask, turned on his heel and walked briskly to the lift.

Nigel first returned to the cafe across the street, went immediately to the gents toilet, dumped his laptop bag in a waste bin and washed his hands and face a full three times before he was fully satisfied.

The next day, as most swimmers were completing a light, relaxed session prior to the first heats the next day, there was no apparent difference in the behaviour of the squad. Nigel took his time to see if he could detect any obvious concern amongst the swimmers and seeing nothing untoward, soon left to watch some of the badminton preliminaries in the main hall. That evening as Nigel sat in the hotel restaurant the first news started to circulate. He was sitting with a group of sports scientists and other ancillary staff that now seemed to populate the national teams.

"It's now six down and another three are feeling a little off," he overheard one of the nutritionists say at the other side of the table.

"They reckon it was dodgy food at that blasted embassy bash," said a leading land training coach.

"The docs are with them now trying to isolate things as much as possible, but it doesn't look good."

"Strangely it only seems to be the girls at the moment, but if it's anything contagious, it's bound to be spreading like wildfire knowing what they were up to after they left the embassy."

"The ones affected are not going to give up, however groggy they feel. You don't train for all this time to fall at the last hurdle."

"It's all very well you saying that, but if it is food poisoning they are going to perform well below their best."

"The worst thing is they'll push themselves to the absolute limit in the pool and have no capacity for recovery."

"We'll have to see, but some may not even make it to the starting blocks the way it's going."

Nigel Gressley had heard enough and took a walk to clear his head before heading back to his room. If only there could have been another way he reasoned. God, I may have overstepped the mark this time and to think this was just a trial. The real thing's not for another two years. At that moment, he passed a small group of low caste Indians living in a makeshift camp by the side of the road. They were filling water bottles from a hosepipe that seemed to be coming out of nowhere. It hit Nigel with a jolt.

"Bloody hell," he said to himself and for that matter anyone else who cared to listen. "Why on earth didn't I think of this option? Instead of all that ridiculous high risk operation to infect these kids with God knows what consequences, I could have simply brought home water from a place like this and virtually guarantee a result." A new resolve settled in Nigel's mind. He would at least use this opportunity in India to take back what must be contaminated water. This would be his strike against one or other of the finalists in two years time. He headed back to the hotel, but hardly at peace with himself. Nigel Gressley was far from a contented man. His drive for control and the satisfaction he gained from achieving his ultimate goal dominated his philosophy. Back at the hotel the group of people at the lift included those he'd seen at dinner. He decided to walk up the two flights of stairs to his room. He blamed the rather rare steak on the slight chest pain he felt as he went into his room. He always carried a pack of indigestion tablets and knew that a couple of those would do the trick. He took over two hours to get to sleep, turning over in his mind the events of the day. When he eventually fell asleep it was to doze fitfully, dreaming of young swimmers lying motionless on the bottom of the pool.

The next morning at breakfast, the British swimming camp was in uproar. Two swimmers were too ill to get out of bed and at least nine of the others were in no shape to compete. As the heats followed throughout the day it became clear that a number of the swimmers shouldn't even be in the pool. Their dogged determination had clearly exceeded their physical ability. One was physically sick by the side of the pool at the end of her race and two had to be lifted out of the pool semi-conscious. Another six who actually competed, reported unexplained listlessness, stomach cramps and diarrhoea. The team doctors were doing everything in their power to stem the tide and reckoned it was at least isolated to one floor of the athletes' village. As all the swimmers had been at the embassy party and had pretty much eaten the same, this was ruled out as the source. There were various conspiracy theories circulating but none seemed to stick. Swabs were taken from them all, but as it would take at least a week for the results to come back, the team doctors operated a damage limitation policy by giving everyone a heavy dose of antibiotics.

Nigel Gressley made his excuses, switched his ticket for a flight three days earlier than planned and headed for home. He took in his hold luggage three bottles of water collected late at night from that same hosepipe out in the street. In spite of the usual spoken sympathies, he showed no remorse. To Nigel Gressley this was all part of the master plan that would get his man, Josh Silverman, on the winning podium in 2012.

CHAPTER 10

July 8th 2011
330 Cowley Road, Uxbridge, UK

The ingredients for high explosives have been known for centuries. There are many options, but these are reduced markedly with the need to detonate electronically and cause maximum damage with a small quantity of chemicals. Malik Gandapur and Rahim Kichlu, two second year electrical engineering students at Brunel University, had researched the best options for a little over twelve months. They came to Brunel fresh from training camps in Pakistan and appeared highly committed to the cause. There were, however, some concerns over their zeal and those in ultimate control had deemed them 'unready for the ultimate sacrifice'. They were tasked with producing a number of small, deadly bombs, to be detonated remotely, but there was for them, no expectation of suicide. The two took to the task with enthusiasm, impressed their lecturers at the University with their academic commitment and made sure that they kept a low profile, especially with regard to political and religious activity. They attended the mosque in north Slough, which had a relatively moderate reputation and arranged specialised religious and historical training once a week with trusted colleagues. They paid their bills on time, avoided any level of conflict, were careful not to be associated with fanaticism and generally kept themselves to themselves. In an area with a high ethnic population, they aimed for now to be the norm, the unnoticed, even nonentities. Above all they were cautious, knowing full well that it was essential to avoid any suspicion of hostile intent. They committed nothing to paper. They kept all their notes, calculations and drawings on a pen drive, which was kept permanently around their necks and could be physically destroyed should it ever become necessary. Their explosive device had not only to be small and detonated remotely, but it needed to be acceptable to security guards at the Olympic Park. They had, after exploring a number of options, decided on the appearance of a thermos flask. It had the benefit of a strong metal casing, a good internal capacity to hold the explosive and the ability to insert a false chamber to hold the coffee or tea as would be expected in such a container. Additionally, it could be vacuum sealed, which should be sufficient to prevent any smell exciting the interest of any sniffer dogs employed at the stadium. Over a period of about six months, the two fanatics produced four prototype devices, each one a major improvement on previous versions. They were careful only to obtain the chemicals for the explosive at lengthy intervals and always from different suppliers, this being the major reason for taking so long in production. Testing each device was the most problematic and they always chose a different location from the previous time. Remote settings were the obvious choice, but this caused concern as their ethnicity made them stand out in such places. Although not absolute, it was rare to see Muslims of student age in places like the Yorkshire Dales or the Lake District, especially away from the popular tourist areas. To reach such places under the cover of darkness was one option, but they both lacked confidence in the map reading skills needed for such a venture. Disused quarries were considered, but even they needed to be far enough away from any centres of population, however small, to ensure that explosions would not be suspicious. An explosion from an active quarry would be accepted by locals, but most were well secured when not in use.

After much searching and exploration, the two decided

that a remote rocky shoreline which was constantly pounded by waves would suit their purpose best. It had the benefit of being permanently noisy from the waves crashing on the rocks and the seas would quickly remove any detritus caused by the explosion. Such a place was found on the west Wales coastline, a few miles south of Cardigan. They found that by leaving after lectures on Friday, the long drive to the west Wales coast would take them until about three o'clock in the morning. The minor road out of the town of Cardigan came within a mile of the coast and it was easy to park the car just off the road. In the unlikely event of any passing car seeing them, it would be reasonably assumed that it was a couple enjoying a bit of privacy. The trek across the fields to the cliff top was difficult without the use of a flashlight, but with care and a degree of fortitude it took them no longer than twenty minutes to reach their goal. The spot they had chosen did not provide any access to the beach, but this was acceptable as they only had to lower the flask over the cliff to sea level to achieve their objective. The cord they used extended for 45 metres before it either reached the beach or was stuck on the way down.

They wasted little time in detonating the bomb by keying in the critical number from a mobile phone. The expected explosion failed to materialise and their first reaction was that the detonator and explosive must have been incompatible. Running through the options, they soon assessed that the real problem was the network provision in this remote corner of Wales. This was something they had anticipated and Malik pulled another mobile phone from his pack using a different network. In spite of the cold night, they were alarmed to feel sweat on their faces and hands and it was with some difficulty that they keyed in the number a second time. The result was spectacular with a loud boom echoing around the remote bay, soon to be followed by the more regular sound of waves smashing on the rocks below. They briefly shook hands, dropped the cord over the edge and headed back to the car. They were both awash with a huge feeling of relief, combined with joy and excitement. "Allah be praised," they intoned under their breath as they retraced the route they had trod so cautiously not thirty minutes before. Back at the car they had little time to celebrate. To be on the road in the small hours of the morning would raise suspicions for anyone, let alone two Muslim students so far from home.

The drive back to Uxbridge was tedious and tiring, but they were buoyed up by the adrenaline of satisfaction that they were one step nearer their ultimate goal. They both now knew they could produce a bomb of the type, size and devastation that was needed for "Operation OG." It was not until they reached the Severn Bridge that the first light of dawn filtered through the easterly clouds. Their utter fatigue brought with it the realisation that they had been awake for over 21 hours, but they felt unable to rest until they reached the security of their home. As they hit the M4, they now routinely stopped at service stations. They stretched their legs as they bought sweets from the shops and coffee at the cafes, but as importantly they switched drivers at every stop. This strategy, in spite of slowing their progress, brought them safely back to Uxbridge by eight o'clock in the morning, confident in the knowledge that their part of the mission was achievable. Their immediate priority was sleep; they could report on progress later.

At precisely four o'clock in the afternoon both Malik and Rahim were awakened from the sleep of the dead by the shrill ring tone of a mobile phone. Their caution, drummed into them constantly at the training camp, dictated that they had a separate mobile phone for communication from their team leader.

"Success?" came the single-word question down the line.

Rahim was the first to answer. "Absolute," he said, trying his best to sound casual in spite of his understandable pride in the operation.

"Well done. You will be rewarded when it is the moment. We need a technical modification." Rahim's euphoria was momentarily suspended.

"You do? Is it major? It took us six months to achieve this version and last night we proved its capability." Rahim replied in a state of shock.

"It is necessary. The device needs to be fitted with a pressure transducer. It will be set with precision so that any removal of the phone chip which is the first phase detonation will activate the pressure transducer. This will also engage the detonator if it is moved downwards by more than ten metres. Can this be achieved?"

"Of course, but we will need time. The theory is well known, but the mechanism untried. How much time do we have?"

"Nine months."

"It will be ready."

"No, not it, them. I need at least fifteen."

"Fifteen?"

"Yes, fifteen, in nine months. Be cautious. Allah be praised."

And with that the phone clicked and their contact was gone. Rahim looked at the timer on his phone. The call had lasted precisely 41 seconds. These calls were never longer than 45 seconds and never from the same mobile. Untraceable.

Malik and Rahim were both trying to absorb the impact of the message. A major modification was needed which required a totally different technology. And then once perfected, fifteen copies were needed. The implications of this were potentially dangerous. Once you started to buy supplies in bulk then questions are likely to be asked. Obtaining a single pressure transducer is relatively straight forward, but when you need fifteen, it would need a convincing explanation. The words from the phone resonated with them both. "Be cautious. Allah be praised."

CHAPTER 11

August 23rd, 2011
Dubai, United Arab Emirates

Jim took Emirates flight EK0030 to Hong Kong via Dubai. The transfer at Dubai was inconvenient but it meant that Jim could keep within Nigel's pre-arranged budget. Jim's foreign travel experience was limited to the odd stag party in places like Prague where the beer was cheap, holidays in the rave spots of Cyprus such as Ayia Napa and short visits to France and Germany as part of the British Universities' boxing team. The Far East was for Jim a totally new experience and he looked forward to it with a sense of both positive anticipation and real concern. His mission was to make links with Asian gambling networks and brief Nigel Gressley on any plans to fix the odds on runners in the Olympic Games. As he settled into seat 21A of the Boeing 777 heading out of Heathrow, Jim wondered whether he had taken on too big a task. Surely this was the province of international police agencies, not a Manchester lad who had only been on a long haul flight once before, yet alone gambled on anything beyond the annual Grand National. As the soft drinks were being distributed before the packaged evening meal, Jim once again went over the plan that he had discussed with Nigel. Two days orientation, behaving like a conventional tourist, then heading for the casinos or other gambling operations as a way of finding a possible link to the twilight world of organised crime. Nigel had sanctioned a two day stopover in Dubai although he'd initially balked at the idea as being an unnecessary expense. Nigel was won over as Emirates were offering a deal in association with Tourism Dubai giving Jim two days in the five star Empress Beach hotel on a room only basis. The truth was that Jim and Nigel had no plan beyond trying to be in the right place at the right time. Nigel was being necessarily cautious in saying too much of his true intention and Jim didn't have the experience to go much beyond his own intuition – an instinct which had served him well to date.

Jim had no illusions that to get information on organised betting strategies was way out of his league, but Nigel seemed to think that the investment could be worthwhile. He relaxed in the knowledge that, whatever the outcome, this was an opportunity to see a part of the world which was to him totally unfamiliar and potentially very exciting. Jim scanned the range of in-house movies, and finding them incredibly bland, turned his attention to the camera he had bought while waiting at Heathrow. He was not by nature impulsive, but had been planning to upgrade his compact camera to something with a wider range of features for some time. Jim fancied the notion of getting high quality action shots from within his own sport of boxing but had found his compact camera not quite up to the mark. Security at Heathrow's number three terminal had been surprisingly quick leaving him with over 90 minutes before his flight was called.

The array of cameras in Dixons air side was vast and he had sought advice from a determined but knowledgeable member of staff within the shop. Jim wanted to avoid the full SLR paraphernalia which usually involved interchangeable lenses and a large bag to carry around all the extra items. He settled on a hybrid which had a 35 times zoom lens, a feature Jim thought would be especially useful in the boxing arena where access to front row seats was usually denied to all but those with the serious money. As the salesman had patiently explained, the zoom was incredible for a camera of this size but usually needed either a very steady hand or a tripod to eliminate vibration. The great feature of this camera, he explained, was the image stabiliser which froze the image temporarily, thus capturing the close up shots with minimum distortion. Jim was never planning to pay quite this amount for a semi-professional camera but was sufficiently convinced that this was the right investment for his needs. After enjoying a tasty dinner of salad, chicken tikka royale and chocolate mousse, washed down with rather disgusting coffee, Jim settled down to master the complexities of his new purchase. In spite of being frustrated by the limited documentation, Jim easily occupied an hour getting an insight into the different modes offered by the camera. He considered the time well spent compared with the innocuous family entertainment provided by the airline.

Jim's thoughts turned to the task ahead, but as he had limited insight into what the next few days might bring, he soon found himself able to doze, perhaps somewhat fitfully, until the lights in the cabin were switched on indicating little over an hour before landing in Dubai. His limited flying experience had taught him one thing that he could never forget. Unlike most people, he suffered very badly from ear and head pain during the plane's descent. He blamed 13 years of boxing but blame wasn't going to lessen the pain. Jim had tried everything from pills and sprays to ear filters and chewing gum. Nothing seemed to work and as the plane dropped from 35,000 feet to 10,000 feet Jim experienced the familiar excruciating pain in the temple and in both ear drums. He was sweating all over as the pain gripped him like a giant vice around his head, seemingly squeezing the life blood out of his upper body. Jim's only consolation was that it would only last until about an hour after landing, although the ensuing deafness could remain for up to 24 hours. He spent a miserable 30 minutes as the plane made its final approach to Dubai and was relieved to hear the grinding noise of the wheels being lowered to indicate the last few minutes of the flight.

On leaving the arrivals hall, Jim felt he had walked fully clothed into a sauna. The heat was phenomenal and he now realised why the Dubai Tourism deal was currently available. Who in their right mind would come here in August with the temperature hitting over 40 degrees on a daily basis? He was relieved to find a minibus bound for the Empress Beach, and settled into the relative luxury of air conditioning for the 40 minute drive to the hotel.

The Empress Beach was on the newly constructed road out of town which meant Jim had a fair distance to travel before reaching the old town of Dubai including the picturesque creek. He decided that in the limited time available, he would enjoy all the hotel had to offer and leave the rest of Dubai for another, perhaps more relaxed, visit. Registration in the hotel's sumptuous atrium was to Jim an experience in itself. The combination of beautiful, smiling women, showing him a level of courtesy and apparent interest was something he rarely experienced. He enjoyed spending time with the attractive concierge who used a DVD presentation to talk him through the variety of restaurants, gymnasia and even the walk-through aquarium. When Jim eventually opened the door to his room on the 16th floor, he was amazed at its sheer luxury and size. As he drew the curtains, he was astounded by the view across the bay to downtown Dubai in the distance and gave a short prayer of thanks, not to God, but to Nigel Gressley for making this happen. In all his travels, Jim never truly unpacked his case and didn't mean to start now. He simply found it more convenient to keep things in one place and saw no reason why that one place should not be his suitcase. Dragging himself away from the view was not easy and Jim spent a few happy minutes pottering around the room like a youngster just moving into a new house. He laid out his toiletries in the vast bathroom, took a much needed shower and enjoyed wearing the white towelling robe he found behind the bathroom door. He checked his watch, recently adjusted to Dubai time, and reckoned he had about three hours before he would next need anything to eat. He knew that to survive jet lag in the best possible shape, it was essential to take on all aspects of local time immediately and also to exercise as soon as possible. The hotel directory listed three gymnasia and what he'd seen at reception convinced Jim that the fitness suite on floor eight would be ideal, especially the immediate access to a sauna and steam room. Jim's workout of ten minutes on the cross trainer, ten minutes on the rowing ergometer, ten minutes on the inclined cycle and finishing with ten minutes on the stepper was tough but rewarding. The sauna and steam room were quiet but Jim lost interest in this enforced inactivity after fifteen minutes in each. Starting with a hot shower he cooled down by slowly reducing the temperature until the shower was an exhilarating stream of freezing water. Jim had never been a great fan of sitting in an ice-filled bath following extreme exercise and, although he could see the benefits, he was content that this cold shower would be a more than satisfactory compromise. He towelled down using the hotel's luxurious royal blue bath towels and now felt totally refreshed and ready to face the uncertainty of the next few days. On his way back to his room he passed an unmarked door and felt a strange compulsion to go in, in spite of this being far from his natural inclination.

The room was poorly lit and it took Jim several minutes for his eyes to adjust to light levels designed to give the appearance of a constant environment, whatever the actual time of day or night. To Jim's utter amazement, he now realised he was in a small casino, which Jim knew to be illegal in Dubai. The fruit machines and gaming tables themselves were well lit and few were already occupied at this time in the afternoon. Jim was surprised to see the number of people dressed in the local clothing of long white dishdasha and the typical Arabian keffiyeh head cloth. He assumed that the local culture and religion would have actively discouraged this particular form of recreation. Jim watched both poker and blackjack from a distance, noting with increasing interest the value of the chips being placed on each game. A notice adjacent to each table advised a minimum stake of $25, and it was clear that these Arab locals were consistently using chips worth $1,000, often placing between five and ten chips per game.

"Want to join us?" enquired one of the younger players at the poker table. "You can take my place as I'm out."

"It's kind of you," Jim replied, "but poker's not my game."

"I see," responded the Arab, shaking Jim by a hand laden with an excessive amount of gold rings and bracelets. "The name's Abi El Hoummani, but feel free to call me Abi as I realise how you westerners find it difficult with our lengthy names." Jim was somewhat taken aback by the informality and apparent friendliness of the poker player, as his perception of Arabs was for them to be austere and unfriendly, especially to strangers.

"Jim, Jim Stringer," came the reply, "can I get you a drink?"

"Why not," said Abi, "poker can be thirsty work. Gin and tonic, please."

Jim noted that another of his perceptions had just been shattered, having assumed that Arabian nationals rarely drank alcohol.

Abi picked up on Jim's surprise. "A habit I got into when at Harvard, but best in this country to be discreet."

Jim signed the barman's bill with his room number and Abi, noting this, said "So you are staying here, how long for?"

"Oh, just a couple of nights, I'm on my way to Hong Kong."

"And the purpose of your visit?" Abi enquired.

"I'm trying to raise a million dollars for a sort of project," said Jim, not really knowing where this was leading and wishing he could have thought things through properly long before this.

"A sort of project," Abi echoed, "tell me more."

"I'm working, along with others, to train a British athlete to be the best in the world. We believe we have a revolutionary system which will bring him from being a medal contender to win gold at next year's Olympics."

"Tell me more," said Abi, clearly showing a controlled, but developing interest in Jim's story.

"The trouble is that I can't divulge more because the system is untested. Not only that but the process is only good for 24 hours, so it's virtually impossible to test it on the world stage as the opportunities between now and the Olympics are very limited."

"I see," said Abi, "or rather I think I see. You're suggesting that you know a group of people who are secretly developing a novel system of training which will put your athlete ahead of all others on the day."

"I know it sounds rather vague, but I'm sure you understand that if this system became common knowledge then there would be no advantage to our athlete."

"That I appreciate, but what I do not understand is why you are telling this all to me, a complete stranger."

Jim tried to remain calm. He had already strayed into territory which was well out of his comfort zone, divulging information which was nothing more than a rumour amongst the Loughborough University students. "The team working on this is looking for some return on their investment. All this work is highly controlled by the University authorities and students get a pretty shabby deal out of it all. We just want to see our efforts rewarded in some way."

"And what is the way you propose, Jim?" probed Abi.

Jim now realised that there was no going back so cautiously played out the only option he could think of to fit the story he was developing.

"We want to 'invest' a large amount of money in betting on our man winning gold – it's as simple as that."

"And you're looking for 'investors', you mentioned a million dollars, to finance your stake."

"Put crudely, that's about it. We believe that we have a winning product, untested, yet with the potential to make a lot of money from a one off betting syndicate."

"Two things, Jim, you might like to consider. Firstly, the odds on your man winning Olympic gold are going to be very low, because his chances of success have got to be reasonably high otherwise he wouldn't even make it to the final. Not only that, but the semi-final times will virtually fix the odds. Secondly why on earth should anyone invest through you when they could just as easily place bets directly? Betting odds are very transparent."

"OK, Abi, both points are well made and I will try to answer as best I can. The odds will be low on any outright favourite, but remember the final will be a field of twelve, all known 48 hours before the event. The odds on Rashid, who was easily the favourite at the last Olympics, were short at two to seven. This would only bring a profit of about $285,000 on a million dollar investment. Even for an investment of a few days, you could argue that it's a poor return, especially as it could go horribly wrong. Poor tactics, such as being boxed in with 400 metres to go, could be devastating. No the real gain is when one of the lesser runners achieve well above their expectation and then the odds lengthen considerably. In Beijing, Ngeny was second favourite at two to one and Benito, Carrera and Silverman were longer odds at either three or four to one. Now you are really talking big money, but only admittedly if you can get one of these to win. Silverman as you probably appreciate is our man and my colleagues at Loughborough are convinced they have the know-how to give him two seconds extra per lap on the day."

"Interesting, but a risky investment in an unproven field. But more importantly, you haven't answered my second question."

"Sorry, Abi, I was coming to that. Of course anyone can

bet directly and there is no way that I can influence that. The winning card I have, if you'll forgive the horrible pun for a poker player, is that I will know whether or not our process is going to work. By the date of the Olympic final we will know with absolute certainty and I will reveal the outcome 24 hours before the race. It will be a simple 'yes' or 'no'. 'Yes' you invest and 'no' you don't."

"And are you planning to take a proportion of the winnings, once again a difficult option for someone betting from abroad?"

"Absolutely not. I have no control over that. I will charge £10,000, cleared through my bank at least a week before the Olympic final to give the definitive yes-no information."

"And why a figure like £10,000 when an investor could be making three million?"

"Big enough to make a major difference to me, yet small enough to avoid any major bank warnings. I'm also working on the basis that, at only one percent of a typical investment of one million, most punters would view the 'fee' as acceptable."

"Interesting, but for me purely hypothetical. I'll keep my investment to the poker table. Nonetheless you could leave me your card and I may talk to one or two people and they may get back to you."

Jim relaxed slightly, feeling drained from this conversation and relieved that Abi was not pursuing the discussion any further. One thing Jim had prepared carefully was his business card. He had produced them using the home address of a trusted friend and an email address set up especially for this work, deliberately avoiding his University site. He had bought a mobile phone from a supermarket using cash and set it permanently to answer-phone. Having checked he had good reception, he switched the phone to silent, and taped it to the back of a toilet cistern in the University's pavilion changing rooms. Jim casually handed over his card, knowing full well that he could only be contacted by email, his preferred method of communication and the most difficult to trace.

Abi responded by selecting a card from a gold-plated case, gave it to Jim and with a quick shake of the bejewelled hand, left the casino. Jim took a careful look at the card in his hand and was amazed to see that the person he had been talking to was none other than the CEO of Emirates Airline, the very carrier that had brought him here to Dubai. Jim returned to his room, this time without diversion, and stretched out on the comfortable settee to reflect on the extraordinary meeting he had just experienced. Jim felt uncomfortable having relied far too much on his wits than thorough preparation. He was honest enough to appreciate this was very much his style, but one that in these situations he wished he could avoid. He took comfort from the view that he now had a story which seemed acceptable, but a random meeting like today was a very different prospect from the professional gamblers he was hoping to meet in Hong Kong

CHAPTER 12

August 25th, 2011
Macau

Emirates flight EK0043 landed at the new Hong Kong airport on Lan Tau Island a few minutes ahead of schedule from where Jim took the airbus shuttle to central Kowloon. The vibrancy of the city, which was until recently virtually a country in its own right, was impressive and Jim soon started to absorb the atmosphere of China's hugely influential economic zone. He chose to avoid the quality hotels on the waterfront and to stay in one of the backpackers' hostels a block to the east of Nathan Street. These tenement buildings were a century old and constructed predominantly of wood making them a major fire risk. Two years previously a devastating fire had destroyed a complete tenement block with the loss of 106 known lives and many more unknown as actual occupancy was never recorded. Jim paid $10 for a shared room, lit by a single 40 watt bulb, and with a filthy toilet some 40 metres along a dingy corridor. Jim cared little for the trappings of luxury, although he did admit to enjoying the short stopover in Dubai. To Jim the important thing was to achieve his goal and to do it in the most effective and efficient manner. The sport of boxing had taught him this approach and the training environment of seedy gyms was as far from luxury as you would ever be likely to get. Jim's logic in choosing such dubious accommodation was that it could be close to any illegal gambling dens. This might be the springboard to the major players of the betting fraternity.

Jim took the precaution of taping his passport and credit

cards to the underside of the wooden bunk which masqueraded as a bed, selected a long-sleeved base layer in anticipation of the evening chill, and placed his locked suitcase on the top of the flimsy wardrobe. Armed with a map he had picked up at the airport, Jim set off north on Nathan Street aiming to find the night market, famed for its bargains, especially for casual clothing. After half a mile Jim took a right turn and soon found himself amongst closely packed stalls selling a range of products from fake watches to sportswear. The space between the stalls was packed with tourists all keen to find a bargain and although progress was slow, there was an atmosphere which can only come with big crowds. Jim was reminded of the first time his father had taken him to watch his beloved Manchester City play at the Maine Road ground and how the combination of the crowds, the noise, the colour and the enthusiasm had been utterly bewitching to a young boy. Jim chose two Lacoste polo shirts and although knowing full well they were not the real thing, the quality was impressive and he was happy to part with $10 for the pair. At the far end of the market, the streets to the left and right were only lit by the occasional bulb in the front of houses and the only activity of note were stalls selling simple food, mainly deep fried with noodles. Jim had some difficulty in recognising the food being fried in a large metal pan, but suddenly felt surprisingly hungry and pointing to the dish being prepared, sat down at a low table while it was served. He had been warned to be careful when eating in Hong Kong and especially to avoid street food, but Jim took the view that deep frying the food was as safe as it was likely to get. As he sat at a simple plastic table, the sort sold at home as garden furniture, Jim reviewed the purpose of this trip. To make contact with major betting operations, especially illegal ones, was clearly not going to be easy. The chance meeting in Dubai had been sheer luck and may come to absolutely nothing. He could see that living over here for some months might prove fruitful, but clearly this was not an option. He needed to get where the action was and apart from the famous Hong Kong race tracks at either Happy Valley on Hong Kong Island or the new race course at Sha Tin, he really didn't know where to go. As Jim finished his meal, he noticed deep into a passageway between two buildings to his left that something was attracting a small and increasingly noisy crowd. He paid his bill, left the table and sauntered towards the melee now growing more excitable by the minute. Although Jim was only slight, he was able to see over the heads of those following what turned out to be an intense board game resembling mahjong but the tiles having been replaced by coloured stones. As the game reached its climax, Jim was watching the spectators to see if money was changing hands. It took him a little time to work out that one of the spectators, somewhat better dressed than the others, was switching short bamboo sticks with others in the crowd and the colour of the sticks seemed to denote their value. The game came to a sudden and abrupt end with one of the players slapping the board as a sign of submission. This was followed immediately by a variety of cheers or groans, depending on which player was being supported. This was equally quickly followed by the distribution of the short sticks to a limited number of the eager spectators. Jim noted that the man distributing the coloured sticks had the majority left in his hand and Jim recognised the parallel between this individual and the average bookmaker back home. A low whistle sounded from back in the direction of the street market and the crowd enjoying the game simply melted away within a matter of seconds. Jim was left looking at an empty passageway which a moment ago had been host to a thriving and purposeful game. Two policemen appeared with their white gloved hands fingering lethal looking truncheons and stopped alongside Jim, showing specific interest in the passageway that a moment ago was so densely packed. "I suggest you head back to the market, sir." said one of the policemen.

"It's probably a bit safer than in here and you're less likely to meet trouble." Jim nodded and headed back to the market, where by now many of the stall-holders were packing away both their wares and the collection of bamboo poles and tarpaulin that had made up the brightly coloured stalls. As the stalls were dismantled Jim noticed with interest and some concern how the electrical wiring which looped just above the heads of the crowd was little more than a series of precarious extension leads. All too frequently bare wires protruded from the numerous plugs and connections and he made a mental note to have a good look at the wiring back in his room in the hostel. Jim walked slowly back to the intersection with Nathan Street and initially walked one block north away from the hostel. As most of the activity seemed to be centred on fast food, souvenir and jewellery shops, he soon headed back to his lodgings. In doing so, he wondered whether his efforts to source the gambling fraternity was going to prove in the slightest way a feasible option.

On returning to his room, he was surprised at first to find someone in the other bunk, but recognised that in a place like this, privacy was a privilege not an expectation.

"Hi," grunted the stranger who in the dim light seemed to be dark and with a wild beard, probably the product of rough backpacking more than sartorial intent.

"I hope I haven't disturbed you," Jim responded, "I guess it's a bit late."

"No problem," came the reply with a distinctive antipodean drawl, "just settling in for the night. Where you from?"

"England." Jim replied.

"Christ, I'd worked that out. Which part?"

"Manchester, but I now live in Loughborough."

"Don't know it. I was over in London for two years, but didn't get far. Went to the Lake District and Scotland once, but mainly headed to the continent in my free time. Now there's a place! Anyway what you doing here?"

"I'm doing a thesis on gambling in sport and thought I'd come to the home of the biggest gambling nation in the world. Do a bit of action research."

"Waste of time, here mate. Hong Kong has it all sewn up. You can gamble your house at the race tracks, but it's still illegal anywhere else. You'll find stuff in the back streets and there are plenty of gambling dens about town, but they all have lookouts. The fuzz rarely catch them at it, unless they infiltrate the gangs and they haven't the manpower to cope."

"You seem very well informed, if you don't mind me saying so. How come?"

"Simple mate, I was in the game, right up to my neck in it. If you want to lose money, I'm your expert. Been clean for two years now and intend to keep it that way. Forget Hong Kong, mate, go to Macau. That's where the action is."

"Macau?" Jim enquired.

"Sure. Take the ferry from pier six. Fifteen minutes walk from here at Tsim Sha Tsui. You can be there in forty minutes. Casinos galore. Don't know anything about gambling in sport, but those guys would bet on your grandmother's next meal. Best place to be. Don't eat breakfast here. I'll show you the best place. See you in the morning."

"Goodnight."

There was no answer. Realising that the two now sharing a room hadn't even exchanged names, Jim thought it was prudent to leave it at that and turned towards the wall trying to make sense of this part of his trip. He knew that without any clear strategy, he might just as well let things take their course and at least he now had some advice for the next day. Why not, thought Jim, and in spite of his unfamiliar surroundings, he found his eyes getting increasingly heavy and very soon gave in to a more than welcome sleep.

Jim slept heavily and slowly became conscious of some movement in the room. He struggled to keep his eyes open, which was made doubly difficult by the fact that this room had no window. The only light was coming from outside in the corridor as the door briefly opened and shut. By the time his room-mate had returned Jim was up and half dressed.

"Hi," said Jim, as cheerily as he was able at this stage in the day, "the name's Jim by the way, we didn't get round to a proper introduction last night."

"Sorry, mate. I'm Sean, from King Country, New Zealand, good to meet you."

"You may not remember, but you offered to show me the best place for breakfast last night. Are you still on?"

"Sure. I'm ready when you are. What's more I'll let you pay!"

"Sounds a deal," said Jim, warming to the idea of a good breakfast after his modest meal last night, "give me ten minutes."

Jim slipped on a pair of trainers and grabbing a towel, walked slowly down the corridor looking for the wash room. It was at the end of the corridor and still empty. The shower was stone cold, so Jim splashed warm water from the sink over his upper body before shaving, more carefully than normal, with a safety razor. Jim had long believed that shaving gel or even soap was an unnecessary luxury for shaving and returned to his room refreshed and ready to face the day.

Sean was fastening his rucksack, prompting Jim to enquire over his plans.

"I'm heading into the New Territories this morning. There's a half marathon race at the end of the subway line going north and I fancy having a crack at it. Then I plan to hook up with anyone going into mainland China to get up to Shanghai by the end of the week."

"Wow," said Jim, "you seem to have your plans pretty much settled, and here am I just going on a random hunt with no particular direction, at least for today."

"So you're not taking my advice to go to Macau?" Sean enquired.

"Oh, sure, I'll certainly be doing that."

"So you have a plan."

"Well as much as taking a ferry boat is a plan, I guess so. How it will go from there is anyone's guess."

"Let's go and eat," said Sean, "I'm as ready as I'll ever be." And with that Jim grabbed his day sack and followed Sean down the stairs – stairs that had he seen them in daylight, would be classified as a serious hazard to ones health.

Sean took Jim to an American diner three blocks west of the tenement block they were staying in. The owner had made a big effort to give it an air of authenticity with a combination of stainless steel, cosy screened-off areas for more intimate dining and open areas for parties. The front half of a 1950s Studebaker graced the entrance lobby, but above all the menu was typical of the mid west. Strangely the owner was from Leeds in England and had set up the diner primarily for the expat community in Hong Kong. It had evidently taken time to get established, but was now gaining popularity with the local Chinese as an alternative to the burgeoning fast food industry such as McDonalds and Kentucky Fried Chicken. In truth the food was not that different from the well-known brands, the difference being the presentation and service which was second to none. Even with space at a premium, the owner had managed to attract local live bands and this added to the ambience of the place at least five times a week. Sean ordered the full American breakfast for them both. Jim considered this pre-race meal somewhat unconventional, but Sean, sensing Jim's unsaid surprise, assured him that the half marathon was not for another six hours.

The breakfast, when it arrived was lavish and both ate in silence, enjoying the cacophony of flavours that can only be achieved by this combination of fried foods.

"Look Jim," said Sean, wiping his lips with a white tissue, "if you are really serious about gambling in sport, I can give you a name. I wouldn't trust him for a moment and he's unlikely to give anything away unless it's self interest."

"What have I got to lose?" Jim replied, "one thing I've learned so far is that without contacts I won't get anywhere beyond stuff already in the public domain and that's pretty flimsy."

"Your call Jim, but just be careful. They call him Bonzo – seems he was a big fan of the Bonzo Dog Doo Dah band back in the 60s and the name just stuck. His real name is Eduardo Vieira. He's of Portuguese stock and runs the Macau Charity Casino – the biggest privately-owned casino on the island. The charity name is genuine enough because he does give huge amounts to local charities, but in so doing gets a huge tax break. They say that he pays virtually no taxes because of the charity label but don't be fooled by his apparent generosity. He's rich and tough in equal proportions, and he is seriously rich. One last thing, he married into the Chinese community, a very beautiful girl so they say, and this gives him family connections to both Macau and mainland China. Don't forget that the Macau Charity Casino is the biggest employer on the island. They run three shifts of 150 croupiers, which with management puts the numbers employed at over 600 at the casino alone. Add in the drink and catering services, plus everything else associated with the casino, and Bonzo is providing for over a thousand families. Macau needs him, so he is pretty untouchable. Good luck my friend."

With that, Sean swung his rucksack over his shoulder and headed off. Jim finished his third cup of coffee, paid the bill, consulted his map and set off for the ferry terminal. This could be a long but interesting day. The nine o'clock hydrofoil service to Macau was surprisingly full and Jim took time to find a seat. He was surrounded by a great raft of Hong Kong Chinese, many reading the morning paper, a few eating from plastic pots, and some chatting with friends. It was as though they were all on a morning commute to work and it took time for Jim to appreciate that this was how a nation of gamblers spent their leisure time. This ferry was simply the transportation from a place of restricted gambling to the free world of casinos and slot machines. Forty minutes later the hydrofoil docked and the ferry disgorged like a nest of ants being disturbed by a gardener's trowel. Jim was unsure about directions so chose to keep with the crowds slightly uphill to the town centre. He spent two hours following a walking trail recommended by the tourist office, which took in the magnificent facade of the earthquake damaged St Paul's Cathedral. From there he headed into the heart of the island with its skyscrapers and impressive hotels, each one vying to outdo the others with their lavish casinos. As Jim approached the Macau Charity Casino he was surprised to see what looked like a tour party of well over a hundred chattering Chinese women all dressed alike in a bright purple jacket over black trousers. As the party dispersed, Jim then realised that this must be a group of croupiers just finishing their shift and making their way home from a single casino.

The main door to the Macau Charity was held open by a smartly dressed and very attractive young lady and Jim wondered whether this was all she did all day, every day, or whether she had other responsibilities in the casino. In the dimly lit entrance foyer he was welcomed by a polite but thorough search of his day sack and an invitation to leave it in the adjacent cloak room. The lighting level dropped even lower as he moved into the bowels of the casino and as his eyes adjusted to the relative darkness he could see that the place was subdivided into four major areas. The main area housed about 150 gaming tables offering games such as poker, roulette, blackjack and baccarat. Jim, although inexperienced in games such as these, at least recognised the tables, but was intrigued to see other games which were totally new to him. On enquiry through one of the ever present drinks hostesses, these games had names like boule, Sic Bo, Fan Tan and keno, all especially popular with the Chinese. The next major area housed hundreds of slot machines, with only about half of them occupied, and all considerably more complicated than the ones Jim remembered from his youth. The third major area was the food and drinks hall which served a variety of fast foods at what Jim considered very reasonable prices. The final area seemed to be a general administrative complex where staff would exchange chips, get instructions and ensure that the smooth running of the casino was maintained. To one side of this area were a series of lifts and Jim speculated that these not only took staff to the back room areas of the casino but also took the high rollers to private suites, well away from the melee of the main hall. As Jim started to get oriented to the complexity of the casino, he noticed that most of the staff had bluetooth ear pieces and were constantly in touch with people unknown, well away from those bent on making money.

Jim bought $500 worth of chips and, not being too familiar with the details of roulette, placed $100 worth of chips on red. He lost, but undeterred, he then placed $100 on both red and even. After all, he affirmed, he was playing with Nigel Gressley's money, so on this occasion could afford to take risks. The ball spun fast at first, then slowed to finally slot in red 12. Jim let the next spin go by without becoming involved and then placed $200 worth of chips on both red and even. As he waited for the ball to rock up and down the roulette wheel, he found himself gripping the side of the table as if his life depended on it. Suddenly recognising this unusual state, he forced himself to relax and as he did so the ball dropped neatly into red 32. He picked up his chips as casually as he could and returned to the nearby exchange area to retrieve his now substantial winnings.

Jim saw little point in delaying things. He had a clear mission and playing a few games of roulette were never going to help his cause. He strode purposefully up to the person who, based on his uniform, seemed the most senior.

"Good morning," said Jim almost as if he was about to interview someone important for local radio, "I would like to speak to Mr Vieira on a personal matter."

"Do you have an appointment with Mr Vieira?"

"Unfortunately not, but I can assure you that our meeting will be of considerable mutual benefit."

"And your name sir?"

"Jim Stringer. Here is my card."

The official placed Jim's card in his top pocket without a glance.

"And the purpose of this proposed meeting?"

"I have a proposal for Mr Vieira which I believe he will find of interest."

"Do you represent a charity, because if so we only accept written submissions? In fact why don't you email Mr Vieira with your proposal?"

"I do not represent a charity and the nature of my proposal is such that I am only prepared to discuss it personally with Mr Vieira."

"I see. Please give me a moment and I will establish Mr Vieira's availability."

With that the official turned away and, using his mobile phone, had a brief conversation lasting no more than ninety seconds.

"I am sorry but Mr Vieira is away on business today and is therefore unavailable. He should be returning next week if you would like to try again."

"I assume that Mr Vieira has someone to deputise for him when away. Would it be possible to speak to him?"

"I very much doubt it, but I will do you the honour of trying. We try to be helpful to our customers."

A further brief mobile phone conversation took place and to Jim's surprise he was invited into a glass-fronted lift, closely accompanied by the official who from his name badge, Jim could now address as Mr Fu.

"Mr Fu, as Mr Vieira is away, I would be grateful to know the name of the person I am to meet."

"I apologise, please understand that we receive many requests as a charitable organisation and it is not always easy to arrange meetings at such notice. You will be meeting Mr Run Sho who is one of Mr Vieira's personal staff. He is available between meetings for ten minutes, so I suggest you conduct your business speedily. I must also request that I conduct a body search before we proceed. Simply a matter of precaution you understand, but sadly necessary."

Jim raised his arms as Mr Fu undertook a thoroughly professional search. When satisfied he punched four digits to open a heavy door to an inner sanctum.

Jim was escorted along a plush corridor and rooms on either side were undoubtedly private gaming rooms. It was clear from the security staff at some of the doors that those were in use, but in cases where the doors were open, Jim could see the opulent style of these rooms. His casual glance into one room suggested that an interior designer with a fetish for snakeskin had been let loose, yet in another the theme was clearly that of a hunting lodge where animal heads would be peering down on the players as if they had a mild interest in the activities below.

Having passed at least a dozen of these rooms, Jim was asked to wait in a small ante-room but was quickly invited into an office decorated in a minimalistic style. This struck Jim as being somewhat incongruent as the hub of a Portuguese operation in South East Asia. A middle-aged Chinaman was sitting at a glass topped desk in a black chair somewhat reminiscent of the Habitat style of the 1980s. He was on the phone and signalled Jim to sit down with a waft of an open hand in the direction of the only other chair in the room. He then dismissed Mr Fu in a similar manner, finished his phone conversation, and switched his attention to his guest.

"Mr Stringer, how can I help you?"

Jim decided to take the initiative and replied coolly, "I think it is me who can help you and your organisation," and with that Jim produced his card, presenting it in the formal way that the Chinese expect. He placed the card carefully between the thumb and forefinger of both hands, stood up, flexed slightly at the waist and proffered the card to Run Sho. It was accepted and more than by habit than forethought, the introduction was reciprocated, although Run Sho remained seated throughout the exchange.

"I am working closely with a British athlete, who I believe can win a gold medal at the Olympic Games in twelve months time as a result of a revolutionary training programme that we have developed. He is currently ranked fourth in the world and this presents an ideal betting opportunity for your organisation, particularly as his win will be somewhat unexpected."

"I'm listening, Mr Stringer, but I must warn you that I have very little time between now and my next appointment."

"We will not know for certain of the success of our training method until within 48 hours of the race. I will be happy to tell you whether or not you should place your bet at that time."

"For which, presumably, you will charge a substantial fee?"

"Not substantial considering the outcome for those placing the bets. My fee will be £10,000 for a simple yes or no, paid in advance."

"And my guarantee?"

"Mr Sho, nothing in this world is guaranteed, but if the answer is no, you will lose £10,000. If the answer is yes and my runner wins, then you stand to gain up to three times your investment."

"An interesting proposition, Mr Stringer and one that I and my colleagues will consider carefully. We will of course require more verification of you and your team."

"My contact details are on my card. We cannot disclose our

training methods for fear that they may get into the hands of our opponents, but I will remain in contact should you wish to pursue this further."

"Thank you for visiting us Mr Stringer. Please excuse me but I need to bring this meeting to an end." With that Mr Sho stood up, stretched across the table and shook Jim's hand with surprising vigour. A button was pressed, the door opened and Mr Fu was waiting to escort Jim back to the main gaming hall.

"Is it your wish to continue playing?" Mr Fu enquired of Jim.

"Thank you, but no," Jim replied. "I will happily quit while ahead."

Jim was escorted to the reception area, retrieved his day sack from the cloak room and stepped into the fresh air. He winced from the heat and squinted because of the intense sunlight. As he stopped suddenly to retrieve his sunglasses, he failed to notice that someone close behind had to alter course rapidly to avoid bumping into him. As Jim walked casually back to the jetfoil landing stage, he had no idea he was being followed, by now at a discrete but manageable distance.

Back at the Macau Charity Casino, Fu had already placed a copy of Jim's facebook details on the glass topped desk.

"He claims to be an amateur boxer, quite promising by student standards," said Fu.

"Check that one out, will you Fu," was the response from Run Sho. "Nothing too heavy, just see if at least the boxing is genuine. Usual way."

Jim's return to Hong Kong appeared, to him, uneventful. The man sitting two rows behind Jim on the hydrofoil looked like any of the many others returning from a morning at the casinos in Macau. The difference was that this man, now talking into his mobile phone, was no gambler. He was far more adept at using his hands and feet in the ancient art of reikinjo. This fighting style originated in the Buddhist temples of central China and was developed with the sole aim of defeating enemies who used multiple weapons. Ideal to test someone who claimed to be a boxer, but could also be carrying a knife or even a handgun.

Jim stopped at the harbour side restaurant which outwardly looked nothing more than a large tin shack, barely capable of withstanding the strong winds of the monsoon season. This place was known throughout Hong Kong as the place to go for dim sum and after the excitement of the morning Jim was more than ready to enjoy the variety of small dishes on offer. The place was as basic inside as it appeared from the outside with long plastic tables and the same white plastic chairs he had seen near the night market. There was no menu, just a regular circulation of waiters coming from the kitchen and bringing out trays of food, delightfully served in small bamboo or clay pots. Jim sampled nine different types of dim sum, washed down with liberal amounts of green tea, before he felt more than satiated. He paid the bill, which he considered modest, and strolled along the waterfront until he reached the Star Ferry, the popular transfer to Hong Kong Island. As Jim sat on the ferry he was intrigued by its peculiar but very logical seating arrangement, so that the backrest could be moved through 90 degrees, allowing the seats to switch direction. Passengers were moving the backrests to suit their preference for facing either forward or backwards, but one passenger moved his to ensure that he was facing Jim. It was a short crossing of just seven minutes, but Jim was deep in thought over the consequences of his actions over the last few days. Where was this leading; what would he tell Nigel on his return; what would he learn about gambling cartels as a result of this costly investment of his time? All he had gained was two business cards - two very uncertain contacts. Both were probably treating him as some struggling student who was punching way above his weight in a world which needed a lifetime of experience to become a real part of the action. On reflection, Jim decided this was really a fool's errand, but he at least could enjoy visiting a part of the world which was totally new to him. He took a tram to the funicular station at the bottom of The Peak and was soon enjoying the views from the highest point on the island. Now feeling the effects of the high levels of salt in his lunchtime dim sum meal, he bought a bottle of water and opted to walk down from the funicular station at the top of The Peak. Jim was impressed with the residences up here, some boasting lush gardens, occasionally seen through main gates, often the only break in the defensive walls around these exclusive properties. By the time he had strolled back into the main commercial centre of Hong Kong, Jim had decided on one further plan of action. One of his friends back home, whose father had escaped from Tibet with the Dalai Lama during the Chinese purge of the late 1950s, had developed an incredibly useful talent for hacking into telephones and emails. What started as an academic exercise, had on very few occasions become a tool of some magnitude in the continuing struggle for the Tibetan people to reclaim their homeland. Tenzin Gephel was a person of strong morals, as were many Buddhists, and he would only use this particular skill to spy on his sworn enemy, the Chinese. Jim needed this talent to stand any hope of making progress with this project. Hard evidence was essential and Jim could think of no other way to obtain it. He resolved at least to approach Tenzin to see whether he would even consider helping to get this crucial information.

Jim took the precaution of walking into the largest hotel on the waterfront of Hong Kong island and after scanning the entrance lobby took a side passage to the ground floor toilets. He entered a cubicle, took out his phone and started to dial his old friend. As he did, he detected a door opening and closing in the next cubicle. Not normally a problem, but this was to be no normal phone call. He snapped his mobile shut, left the cubicle and headed out to the busier and noisy public lounge, where people were starting to gather for afternoon tea, a highly regarded feature of the Hong Kong Mandarin. Choosing a seat facing into the lounge and with no possibility of anyone eavesdropping from behind, he once again dialled Tenzin's number.

"It's Jim, and I need help," he whispered into the phone.

"Is that you Jim, you're very faint and do you know what time it is?"

"Look Ten, I'm sorry to wake you so early, but I really need a big favour."

"I hardly think you would get me out of bed at six thirty in the morning to talk about training programmes. What's the problem?"

"I'm in Hong Kong and in a bit of trouble and I need a phone tapped."

"What. Are you crazy? You know I only do that sort of thing to support the Tibetan people and anyway with me in my final year it's too big a risk. If ever I got caught, I'd be out, no questions asked, and probably deported."

"Ten, I know it's a big ask, but it really is important. It involves a group of Chinese businessmen who may well be planning to wreck the chances of some runners in the Olympic Games in a betting scam. I need to know because it could involve a British runner we've been working with for three and a half years. I'd have thought you would be keen to get one back at the Chinese thugs."

"Look, Jim, I'll give it some thought. When are you back?"

"I plan to stay for a few days longer so should be around for the weekend."

"Fine, call me when you're back and I'll give you an answer. Oh just one thing. Do you have any email addresses for these guys?"

"Yes, but not sure if they're active."

"OK, that could be really promising. I've developed some new software to hack into emails and it's proving really useful in obstructing some of the ant-Tibetan developments in Lhasa."

"Ten, I'm going to hang up, it's getting too busy here and I want to keep this call to ourselves."

"No problem, Jim, see you soon."

And with that the call was cut. Jim, now surrounded by diners all jostling for the best seats in the lounge, made a hasty exit to the warm and humid conditions outside and headed for the Star Ferry back to Kowloon.

Jim, now back in his decrepit room at the backpackers' hostel, was browsing the tourist brochures to find some places to visit over the next few days. The only light in the room was from a small bedside lamp and Jim found some difficulty in reading with such poor light. A firm knock on the door surprised him and he sauntered over to see who the unexpected visitor might be. He took the precaution of using the spy hole put into the centre of each door and could see a Chinese man of modest height and smartly dressed in casual clothes. Jim knew it wouldn't be room service because places like this had no such luxury, so took the precaution of putting the chain on the lock before opening the door a few inches. As he did, the door burst open with such force that the lock disintegrated and the door smashed into his left knee. Caught totally by surprise, Jim reacted to the pain in his knee by bending to hold it and as he did so a right hook caught him hard on his left ear. Immediately the adrenaline kicked in and Jim reacted with a flurry of punches to his assailant's head. Each one was parried with professional skill and Jim responded by moving further back into the room keeping his guard high to avoid further contact. Jim's brain was rapidly assessing the options when another blow, this time to the ribcage, nearly knocked him off his feet. All Jim could feel was a searing pain in the ribs, but summoning all his ability even to stay upright, he again aimed punch after punch at the shadow dancing ahead of him. In the general gloom of the room, Jim was suddenly aware of another figure rushing through the door and immediately went on the defensive, fully anticipating a further vicious attack. The second assailant swung what seemed like a small bag at Jim. It checked in mid-flight and the arc of the bag now changed to fly towards the shoulder of Jim's initial attacker. As the bag accelerated, Jim saw with amazement that his attacker redirected his attention in a split second towards the bag. He swung a clenched fist to parry the projectile but with a sickening thud it caught him a glancing blow on the side of his head. The crunching sound of metal on bone was like a butcher's cleaver severing a hip joint. This was followed immediately by a muted howl and Jim's assailant fled out of the door and rapidly retreated down the corridor.

Jim collapsed on the bed, curled up to get respite from the pain of his ribs. As his breathing slowly returned to normal, he now looked cautiously across the room to the stranger who had so thankfully intervened. As Jim refocused from the pain in his ribs to the person now searching the bag that did all the damage, he heard a familiar voice.

"Christ Jim, you soon manage to make friends."

"Sean. Thank God you came by. What the hell was in that bag you hit him with?"

"Ah, Jim, my secret weapon. None other than my steel-cased laptop. And what's more apparently undamaged."

"But, Sean, I thought you were heading off after the race."

"That was the plan, but fortunately I had an intuition that you may have overstretched things with your plans. Came back to check on you and, from what I saw, just in time."

By now the pain in Jim's ribs had started to subside, but he was still finding each breath was an effort. "Sean, have you got any painkillers?"

"Very few. Hopefully I have some ibuprofen left over. I usually take a couple before a race. Helps to combat muscle fatigue." And with that Sean unzipped an outside pocket in his rucksack and produced a small strip of ibuprofen. "Just four left, have them all now and we'll get some more on the way out of here."

"I don't feel much like moving," said Jim, still curled up on the bed, but he made the effort to turn sufficiently to swallow the pain killers.

"There's one thing for sure; we need to be out of here fast. Whatever that fight was all about, I don't know, but we're not staying to wait for reinforcements to arrive."

Jim carefully rolled to the edge of the bed and gingerly stood up clearly still in pain. With Sean's help he retrieved his suitcase from the top of the wardrobe, packed the clothing scattered around the room and snapped the case shut.

"Do me a favour, Sean," Jim said, "just check the room to see if anything's left."

Sean scanned the room, checked the small bedside chest of drawers and under the beds. "Good job you asked me to do that," he said, "your mobile is down here under the bed."

"I don't think so," Jim replied, "I always keep it in a zipped pocket for security."

"Must have come out during the fight," Sean volunteered, retrieving it from under the bed, "anyway, here it is."

"Not mine," Jim confirmed, "must have been dropped during our little altercation."

At this point Jim's thoughts, which had been dulled by the pain in his ribs, started to become clearer and he recognised the need for immediate action.

"Sean, you're right. We need to be out of here right now. Let's just get to a more public place and think things through."

Sean threw his own rucksack on his back, grabbed Jim's suitcase with one hand and his precious computer bag with the other. "Ok let's go. Can you manage the stairs, Jim?" Without waiting for an answer, Sean led the way out of the building and Jim, holding on to the flimsy banister, followed him down the stairs and out into the street.

"Shit," said Jim, "that phone under the bed totally distracted me. My passport and credit cards are still taped there. Do me a favour Sean and get them will you? I don't think my ribs could stand another go at those stairs." Sean ran back and found Jim's documents and cards just where he said, still taped firmly under the bunk. Soon they were back in the same American diner they had enjoyed in more comfortable circumstances earlier that day. This time Jim settled for a straight coffee as the events of the last hour had been too unsettling to contemplate a meal. Sean ordered a large plate of French fries and was pleased when Jim helped himself to the odd one, showing signs of being on the mend.

"So what's your plan now?" Sean enquired in between mouthfuls of fries.

"Regrettably, I see no option than to get out of here fast, but I'm still not sure what all that was about back there."

"I've been thinking about that myself," Sean added, "the guy could obviously do serious damage if he wanted to. You can defend yourself pretty well, but he was in a different league."

"Yeah, but strangely, after the initial punch to my ear, which kicked the whole thing off, he seemed more interested in testing my ability than getting total control. The way he was dealing with my attack was leaving me punching at shadows. I reckon he could have finished me off completely if he had a mind to. That punch to the ribs was one of the hardest I've ever taken."

"I don't know," said Sean, "perhaps you're right, he was just assessing you. What did you tell the fellow you met in Macau?"

"I can't remember the details, but yes I'm pretty sure I did mention I boxed."

"So at best it could have been a quick test of your honesty. Checking up that you were not bullshitting them."

"And some form of warning, I guess, that you don't mess with the likes of him without knowing the consequences."

"Exactly. And the consequences at the moment are sore ribs on the minus side, but his mobile phone on the plus side."

Jim had momentarily forgotten he had his assailant's mobile phone. "Christ, the mobile phone, best to get rid of that."

"You're still not thinking straight." said Sean. "Give it to me." With that Sean stripped out the SIM card, and placed it carefully in Jim's hand. "That SIM card could be your passport to the core of the gambling fraternity you seem so keen to study. But one further word of advice. Once your friendly attacker has searched your room back there in the hostel, he'll be after it. I suggest we go from here straight to the airport. We can pick up a new SIM card there."

"But," protested Jim weakly, "I planned to stay in Hong Kong for a few days, see some of the sights."

"Forget it Jim. Just get out of here fast. On balance I would say you're just ahead. Your attacker seems to have been testing you so far, to see if you're the real deal. Things have changed since you got his mobile. You'd be crazy to stay any longer unless you want more bruised ribs."

Jim didn't need any further reminding. "OK, point taken, let's go before we meet any more of his friends."

With that they called a taxi and made the 10 mile trip out to Lan Tau Island and straight to the Emirates ticketing office in departures. Jim switched his ticket for a flight in three hours time and visibly relaxed at the thought of leaving later that day. Even so, both men were now increasingly vigilant and made sure that they kept to the busiest part of the concourse. There Jim was able to buy and fit a new SIM card and stock up with a variety of pain killers. Sean had suggested that Jim's own phone was packed in the checked in luggage, leaving his assailant's phone to take through security.

As the line for security snaked into the innards of the terminal building, Jim and Sean parted company with a cautious hug which even then caused Jim to wince.

"Thanks for everything," said Jim as they parted, "hope the travels work out. We'll be in touch" Two men standing in the next line immediately separated, one to follow Sean and the other keeping a discrete, but watchful eye on Jim. Jim put his coat and day sack in the large baskets provided for the scanning machine and carefully placed his coins, watch and the problematic mobile phone in one of the smaller containers. Jim was called to the passenger screening frame and although he did not appear to set off any alarms was body searched thoroughly. Behind Jim, the conveyer belt into the x-ray machine had been stopped for a few seconds, the mobile phone was quickly removed and the man following Jim was now heading back to the main ticket hall. Jim retrieved his watch and coins, noticed the phone was missing more with interest than concern, and went straight to gate 18. He pulled out his notebook, and, once again on this trip, tried to make sense of the whole affair. He was not looking forward to the uncomfortable flight back to London via Dubai and particularly how much he would say to Nigel Gressley. It was literally going to be a long haul.

Chapter 13

September 25th, 2011
Little Chef, A1, UK

Nigel Gressley had no cyclists in his agency stable, but through the National Association of Sports Agents he had powerful contacts. The timing was perfect as the Tour de France had recently finished and EPO would have been used by at least half the teams in the tour. EPO, a synthetic hormone which stimulates more red blood cells, increases muscle endurance dramatically. Its use was commonplace in cycling but also known in athletics with the Kenyan runner Lagat and the Russian Yegorova both testing positive. Nigel made contact with Serge Bouillon of the Rapobank team, who had just had their most successful tour ever with seven stage wins. Nigel flew out to Paris on the Monday morning after the Tour de France had swept along the Champs–Elysees in Paris. Rapobank's star sprinter, Hans Van Weber of Belgium had taken the overall green jersey in a dramatic last gasp sprint and the celebrations had gone on well into the night. Serge was understandably cautious when Nigel made a direct approach and denied having ever used EPO with any of his athletes. This was no surprise to Nigel, but one thing he was able to learn from Serge, after drinking a whole bottle of calvados between them, was the source of the drug. Somewhat surprisingly for Nigel, the source was very close to home. EPO was being produced by a small pharmaceutical company by the name of Propharm, just north of Milton Keynes. On Nigel's return from France he made immediate contact with George Hyde, the marketing manager of Propharm. By Wednesday of the same week, Nigel was sitting in Hyde's modest office behind the single story manufacturing plant on the north Milton Keynes industrial estate.

Nigel considered passing himself off as an academic or clinician with legitimate interest in EPO, but knowing that a quick look at Google could confirm or deny any inaccuracies in his story, he truthfully introduced himself as a sports agent. He expressed concern that EPO was part of the culture of certain sporting events, especially cycling. He took the line that he was seriously considering extending his agency into that sport and was seeking advice as to the movement of the drug from manufacturer to athlete. George Hyde had been in the marketing business for most of his career and with Propharm for over ten years. He was well aware of the pitfalls of admitting to anything outside of the legitimate uses of EPO. He was more than happy to extol the medical benefits of the drug but could never be drawn into any discussion on its use in sport. He did concede that there were very few randomised controlled trials on the use of EPO in athletes, so its validity was still being questioned in spite of its apparent widespread use. But then came the piece of information that made Nigel's visit so worthwhile.

"The only current trial of EPO I am aware of is at Loughborough University. We are supplying a limited quantity for their trial and I am told that the outcome will be published next year. I understand that they are working with cyclists and middle distance runners, but the full protocol is only available to our medical director. Until it is published, I would imagine that the results will be kept under lock and key, or these days in a password protected computer. The results, once published, may be of interest to you, but I am sorry that I have not been helpful with your initial question."

Nigel left Propharm with renewed optimism. He now knew where EPO was stored outside of the manufacturing base and he already had an existing contact at the University. The pieces of the jigsaw were being assembled; it was a question of how they could start to lock together. Nigel could hardly walk into the lab at Loughborough and help himself to a vial of EPO. He needed someone on the inside who could get him the drug and then he would need to find a way to administer it unknowingly to one of Josh Silverman's strongest opponents. Nigel worked in logical steps and he concentrated solely on obtaining the EPO. He decided that although risky, he would have to involve Jim Stringer. He could think of no other method of gaining access to the labs.

Nigel's bi-monthly meeting with Jim was held towards the end of September and once again on the pretext of convenience for both parties, they met in a Little Chef on the A1 to the north east of Bedford. The two, as usual, sat in a quiet part of the cafe and ordered a cafetiere of coffee, a panini for Jim and the Olympic breakfast for Nigel. Jim recounted his experiences in Dubai, Hong Kong and Macau to the very real concern of Nigel, especially when it came to the assault in the hostel.

"The worst of it all," said Jim, "is that I've had to modify my training dramatically while my ribs heal. It couldn't have come at a worst time with the final Olympic trials coming up just before Christmas."

"But what I don't fully understand," said Nigel, after listening intently to Jim's account, "was how you managed to get these guys interested in even talking to you."

"The truth is, Nigel, I was flying by the seat of my pants. I just came out with this story about training one of the Olympic contenders in a unique way and how this would increase the chances of success dramatically. I offered, for a fee, to provide them with inside information on the success of the trials. Of course I wasn't specific about which athlete we were working with, but clearly Silverman has to be in the frame as he is one of the few British athletes of Olympic standard."

"And did they fall for it?" Nigel enquired. "Without hard

evidence or proof, I wouldn't put big money on someone just showing up and claiming to have a magic formula for success."

"Hard to say," Jim replied, "but at least I now have contact details and this could lead to further intelligence. If there is any suggestion that these guys are showing interest in Josh Silverman, you will be the first to know."

"OK," said Nigel, "we will have to take the trip as being work in progress. At least we know that there are people out there who could bet heavily on my boys. I'll now have to redouble my efforts to protect them from any form of interference."

Nigel took this as the lead he was looking for and hesitantly turned to Jim. "Part of my problem, Jim, is that I have always kept at arm's length from any form of drug involvement. As far as I am aware all my athletes are clean and I constantly reiterate the importance of keeping it that way. But I feel now we're stepping up to the Games, I need to emphasise the warnings. I need to engage more fully in drug awareness, but I'm limited because I cannot even show them the sort of equipment and substances that may be around. I need your help in getting hold of some stuff so that I can at least show my athletes what there is out there."

"Oh come on Nigel, they will know all about this stuff. The UK anti-doping agencies will have briefed them thoroughly. It will all be on the web. You'll be telling your grandmother to suckle eggs."

Nigel started to flounder a little, not expecting quite such a reaction from Jim.

"Yes, I am aware of this, but I am thinking specifically of EPO, used widely by professional cyclists, but still pretty rare in athletics. My boys don't seem to have much specific information on its appearance, method of administration etc. I need to keep them fully informed."

"So what you are saying is that you want me to get you some EPO, just so you can show your guys to ensure they avoid it.

Sounds a bit shaky to me Nigel. If I didn't know you better, I would suspect that you want to use it to improve the chances of your athletes and you're asking me to be the supplier to cover your own back."

Nigel was now getting both frustrated and a little angry and was aware of the slight pain in his chest. He now recognised the Olympic breakfast was hardly the ideal meal to have during a difficult discussion like this.

"And anyway," continued Jim, "I don't have any access to EPO. It's just not part of my life."

"I fully appreciate that," said Nigel, now finding the pain in his chest easing a little, "but I am reliably informed that EPO is being used in a legitimate experiment in the physiology labs at Loughborough. Couldn't you talk to some of the students involved in that project?"

Jim took a deep breath as he ruminated on the implications of Nigel's request. On the one hand he would be taking a huge risk in trying to obtain any EPO from the labs but Jim also realised that Nigel was the sponsor of his PhD and without this he wouldn't be able to continue his studies. He knew exactly what to do and that was to buy time. This was not a request that needed an immediate answer.

"I'll give it some thought, Nigel. Leave it with me and I'll come back to you."

Jim's drive back to Loughborough gave him time to contemplate the options. He was starting to become even more concerned about Nigel Gressley's motives. Nigel consistently gave the impression of being genuinely concerned for the well being of his stable of athletes. Yet Jim was increasingly aware of the possibility of Nigel using information, and now products, as a means of harming other athletes. Jim was not a great believer in conspiracy theory, but for the first time he was torn between his own self interest and a niggling doubt that Nigel was acting irrationally. He found it hard to accept that Nigel needed a sample of EPO just to warn his own athletes of the dangers, especially as he knew that for EPO to be beneficial it had to be injected. By the time Jim had turned off the A1 towards Leicester and then on to Loughborough, he had decided on his plan of action. He would provide Nigel with a placebo in place of EPO, probably a weak saline solution, and then monitor Nigel's activities with considerable care.

On returning to his room in Gaviot Hall, Jim immediately rang Tenzin Gephel, his Tibetan friend.

"Ten, how's it going?" said Jim, "Anything to report?"

"I assume you're not talking about the boxing training," Tenzin replied, "I'd be happier if we talked somewhere privately, face to face."

"Sure," said Jim, "meet me at the Foresters at eight, in the back bar."

"Make it eight-thirty to give me time for a shower after training."

"Sorry Ten, I was losing track of the days and with me unable to train right now. Eight-thirty it is."

As agreed the two met in the quiet back bar of the Foresters Arms, an unpretentious estate pub favoured by students living locally. Shipstones, the brewery owning the pub, had seen little need to refurbish the pub in recent times and it had a tired feeling which seemed to suit the locals. The back bar had a pool table, a darts board and a scattering of old tables and chairs on a well-worn carpet, its main function being to soak up spilt beer during riotous student drinking games.

Tenzin took a sip of the orange and lemonade put in front of him. "It took me a couple of days to get through the various firewalls and pass codes, but today was a breakthrough. That's why I've not been in touch. The Chinese gentleman who roughed you up made a number of calls before he realised that the SIM card had been switched. The most important one was to the guy you met at the casino, so that saved me a lot of time trawling through the info on the SIM card you brought home with you. He's definitely a big cog in the wheel and seems to work pretty independently of the Portuguese owner of the casino. In some ways I think it was lucky that he was away because I don't think he would have been interested in you at all. On the other hand you wouldn't have sore ribs now if you had met the top man. His name is Run Sho, just as he said when he was with you. He informed the Portuguese owner, a Mr Vieira, of your visit, but said it was a request for extended credit which he refused. Vieira didn't seem very interested, so the real purpose of your meeting has been kept between you and Run Sho. I managed to trace a series of calls to and from Run Sho from the time that you met him. There is no doubt that he organised the visit you received back at the hostel and the guy who damaged your ribs also went away with a serious headache thanks to your friend's laptop. From what I could gather, they were just testing your claims to be a boxer, possibly as a way of validating your other statements. I think it was also meant as a bit of a warning that you were dealing with serious players. But the most important information I picked up was a call to some sort of sporting agency in Shanghai. Run Sho requested a thorough briefing of all the likely finalists in the 1500 metres, including Josh Silverman. If my translations are correct, and remember my Cantonese is getting a little rusty, there was a clear intent to reduce the chances of success of other runners apart from Silverman. No details as yet, but the request went out in the form of 'What would it take to stop the others from competing at their best'."

"Christ," said Jim, "I seem to have started something which could turn nasty. I wish to God that I'd thought of a different ruse to get them interested."

"Well," said Tenzin, somewhat thoughtfully, "The hard work has been done. I can monitor his phone calls from now on but it will take me time to trawl through all the rubbish to pick out the relevant stuff."

"How about, Ten, if you just taught me how to do it. Give me the codes and procedures for hacking in and that will cut you out of the action completely."

"That's possible, Jim, but I would have to install the software onto your PC. I guess it would get me out of the loop and I would appreciate that. What you get up to is your business, but I have to be very careful I don't get caught being involved."

"Look, Ten, I appreciate that your only real interest in hacking is to bring about a better deal for your own people, especially the displaced ones from Tibet. What you've done for me so far has been great, but I agree it is time for you to back off. If you can give me the software, then leave me to carry on where you left off."

"OK, Jim, it's a deal. Bring your laptop over on Monday and we'll sort it. I'll tell you what, Jim, as this is all getting pretty interesting right now, I'll take a lower profile, but be on hand if you need any specifics. I would hate to see you get this far but be unable to deliver for the sake of a little eavesdropping, so to speak. Changing the subject, Jim, when can we expect you back in training?"

"I've got the Olympic trials in eleven weeks time and these ribs are slowly on the mend. Which reminds me, you'll keep the damage I suffered in Hong Kong to yourself, won't you? I don't want anyone at the trials to get wind of it, otherwise my ribs will be well and truly targeted."

"No problem, we Tibetans have a long history of keeping secrets. The Himalaya have always given us a pretty good protection from the actions of others and I guess it's now part of our psyche."

With that, Tenzin drained his drink and left, leaving Jim to ponder his next move. By the time he had finished a pint of the month's guest bitter, a real ale called 'Southern Glory' from the Chilterns Brewery, he'd decided that his concerns about Nigel Gressley needed positive action. With Tenzin's software, he could hack into Nigel's phone and find out exactly what he was up to. Cheered up by this resolve, Jim left the pub and headed home, feeling for the first time that he could stride out and breathe more deeply without the recent discomfort from his ribs. With just eleven weeks to the Olympic trials, Jim knew it would be a close call to get fit, but he now had a further reason to be in that Olympic village. To see this whole business through, he needed to be at the heart of things and where better than the Olympic Park itself.

Jim's next task was to respond to Nigel's worrying request for EPO. Over the next few days he took an empty vial used for blood analysis from the physiology labs, created a very professional looking label on his computer with Propharm's logo and the word Erythropoietin 10cl. He then filled the vial with a ten percent salt solution and packaged it in a small polystyrene box, giving every impression of the real thing. Having checked with Nigel that he would be at home to receive the package, Jim then sent it by overnight recorded delivery to his home address. Nigel, receiving the package the next morning, followed Jim's instructions to keep the vial in a fridge, and relaxed in the knowledge that he now had the armoury to cause immense damage to Ngeny. The first phase had been achieved for Gressley. He now had to find a method to administer the drug without Ngeny's knowledge. This needed just one opportunity and Nigel Gressley planned to find that opportunity.

CHAPTER 14

January 21st. 2012
Portland, Oregon, USA

Nigel Gressley could find no weakness in Jose Carrera's lifestyle. He wasn't a philanderer like Benito. He wasn't a conscientious family man like Gabet. The only thing Nigel had to work on was Carrera's commitment to one clothing company. Nike had sponsored Carrera since he was a junior champion and despite many attempts from other sponsors, Carrera had stayed with the same company ever since. He had stuck with Nike through thick and thin, largely because he genuinely liked the product. Nike looked after him as a potential Olympic champion and Carrera, as their premier ambassador, was more than happy to promote the company strongly. Nigel's plan was simple in design but complex in implementation. The only way he could conceive of slowing Carrera down was to make some minor adjustments to his running shoes. This should be sufficient to alter his running gait, cause little discomfort and be just enough to slow him down by a few seconds. A few seconds is the difference between a place on the podium or watching from the stands. Nigel just needed to get to those running shoes. The challenge was just how. Carrera wore Nike's Goldswoop RX2012 and no other runner in the world had these shoes. Their promotion was all targeted at Carrera winning the Olympic gold medal. Full page promotions in every health and running magazine, on TV and in selected tabloid weekend supplements was the approach used by the Nike marketing department. But the clever part was that the shoes were not available until the day after the Olympic final. It was the old trick of getting the buyer psyched up to a product which is apparently in short supply. The floodgates would open when Carrera wins gold and the product gets a second wave of promotion, following all the hype about its lack of availability.

Nigel Gressley was a past master at negotiating sportswear deals for his stable of athletes and was considered one of the best in the business. His skill had been in anticipating the up and coming companies and getting modest deals for his athletes which would then improve dramatically as the company took off. He had done this with Asics for two of his marathon runners. Now that Asics shoes were used by more runners than any other manufacturer in the London Marathon, Gressley was reaping the rewards of deals linked to sales.

It was relatively easy for Nigel to arrange a meeting with the Nike marketing department on the pretext of a potential deal with Josh Silverman. He knew that the level of meeting was crucial and he had little choice but to fly to the Nike headquarters in Portland, Oregon, a journey which would take a full day of travel. Nigel hated flying. He hated the way passengers were treated at Heathrow; he hated the boredom of the flight itself with the second rate family movies being the only means of entertainment; he hated the consequences of crossing time zones; but most of all he was a nervous passenger when it came to take-off and landing. Nigel always flew business class, which at least increased the comfort level when flying. Even so, as the engines wound up to full thrust at the start of the runway, Nigel found himself wiping a trickle of sweat from his brow and that tightness in the chest which seemed to reoccur in moments of stress was starting to cause concern, but quickly dismissed as a symptom of his fear of flying.

The Nike Company had arranged a limousine to take him from the airport to the vast building which was now the Nike empire. The building reminded Nigel of either a five star hotel or a luxury cruise liner with its central atrium and impressive glass cage lifts, one of which soon whisked him up to the sixteenth floor. Nigel knew that the briefing paper he had sent in advance was key to the level of management he would meet and was relieved to be introduced to the senior vice-president of marketing, with two aides, one of whom was the company lawyer. They met in a small committee room overlooking an urban park and freshly ground coffee was dispensed from a small Italian machine. Always one for quality coffee, Nigel was immediately impressed and looked forward to the meeting with renewed interest. The senior vice-president, Walter Hammond, wore a blue suit with the Nike swoop in his buttonhole, a white shirt and a striped tie with the alternate light and dark blues of Cambridge and Oxford Universities. The company lawyer, a Mr Swarbrick, wore a dark grey suit, a cream shirt with a red and black bow tie and a serious face as if his whole being depended on the contracts he administered on behalf of Nike. Nigel had the distinct feeling that this was a man who was very experienced and whose knowledge should be respected. The other aide, James Barclay, was younger, appeared more relaxed, and from his posture seemed to be keen to please the older men. He was the one to prepare the coffee, to make notes and generally fulfil the role of a personal assistant to the others. He kept quiet unless asked for an opinion and Nigel noted that his opinion was often little more than an embellishment of what had been said before.

After the introductions and obligatory exchange of cards, Hammond cleared his throat and said "Gentlemen, let's get down to business. I appreciate that Mr Gressley has travelled a long way to see us, so I am sure that his time is valuable. We have all read his proposal with interest and I can say with absolute confidence that Nike would be very pleased to have an athlete of the stature of Josh Silverman on its books, so to speak. We recognise that he is currently under contract elsewhere, but this is up for renewal or renegotiation at the end of the Olympic Games in six months time. As Mr Gressley is well aware, Nike is putting great store in Jose Carrera's chances of winning gold in London and has developed its marketing strategy around this expectation. We are not sufficiently naive to recognise that nothing is certain in this game. Should Carrera not win gold it will be a minor embarrassment, but we believe that the publicity of failure can often be incredibly positive. Athletes don't win or lose races because of their shoes, but we can make great mileage out of winning and sometimes make even more mileage from the sporting press when they comment on how our pre-publicity got it wrong. Clearly if your man, Silverman, were to take the gold then we could gain a huge amount of publicity from him switching to Nike shoes. Clearly it's a little premature for that decision to be made right now."

There was a slight pause in this statement which was clearly well prepared, so Nigel took it as an opportunity for comment.

"Well thank you Mr Hammond," Gressley started to say.

"Please, call me Wally," interjected the Nike veteran.

"Thank you, Wally, for an excellent summary of the position. Could you give me some indication of timing, should you decide to go with Silverman following the Games and, from what you have just said, following his unqualified success in the 1500 meters final?"

"Of course. Should the contract we are proposing be satisfactory, we would relaunch the Goldswoop RX2012 with Silverman as Olympic champion on the day of the closing ceremony, effectively 36 hours after his win. How does that sound?"

"As I would expect, but I do have one slight concern. Should this happen on the timescale that you propose, my athlete will have no prior use and experience of the shoe. Above all I need to look after my athletes' health and I would be a little unhappy to launch a shoe which Silverman had not even worn in training."

"In view of Silverman's current contract, I can't see a way to resolve this particular dilemma. What's your suggestion Nigel?"

"Although I take total responsibility for all contract negotiations, the one item of clothing that I insist my athletes find totally acceptable must be their shoes. I fully appreciate that a company like Nike will personalise the shoes to the athlete but the basic model will be identical to the one on sale to the general public. To put it bluntly, I need to have Silverman test the shoe and be totally happy that this is a shoe he wants to promote."

"Of course, of course," interjected Hammond showing a little irritation, "this is essential for us as well. We want all our sponsored athletes to be totally committed to our product. James, what arrangements can be made to satisfy Nigel here?"

"Could I come in here?" said Warbrick, the company lawyer, fingering his bow tie nervously, "We can produce the standard contract with the usual exclusions, plus a strict press embargo until after the Olympic final and have it ready to be couriered back here to Portland on the Friday night. No one will be interested in anything but the final day and the closing ceremony, so a Monday launch would be perfect. Should Silverman fail then all options are off, at least at the figure that we will be proposing."

Wally Hammond nodded his assent and then added looking at James, "To go back to what I was saying earlier, what resources do we have this end to get Silverman a trial pair?"

"Current manufacturing base is in China and first delivery is expected next week. We do have four extra pairs here in Portland, but they are all in Carrera's size of eight and a half or 42 European."

"Perfect," interjected Gressley, "Silverman's size exactly. Can you get two pairs of those to the airport in time for my flight?"

"Better than that, sir," said James, "I can personally bring the two pairs to your hotel this evening and then you'll be free to focus on your travelling options tomorrow."

"Excellent," said Gressley, very satisfied that he was about to achieve his objective, "would it be expecting too much for the proposed contract to be delivered at the same time?"

"I can but try," said Warbrick, once again toying with his bow tie, "but for the sort of figures we are talking about, I will need to contact at least three board members for endorsement and that could be difficult. Failing that the contract should be in your hands by early next week."

"I appreciate you trying," said Gressley standing up, "and unless there is any other business, I will leave you to deal with the actions from today's meeting. This is my first visit to Portland and I am looking forward to seeing something of your city."

"I certainly hope you will," said Hammond, extending a hand, "I particularly recommend that you see the waterfront and the Japanese gardens."

With that the meeting broke up and Nigel was escorted to the ground floor. As the glass lift descended, Nigel turned away from James, his escort, removed his visitor's pass and casually placed it in his jacket pocket. At the lavish reception desk he shook hands with James and headed out into the low winter sun. It all seemed too easy, mused Nigel as he hailed a taxi from those parked at the rank outside the Nike building. By tomorrow I will have a pair of shoes matching those worn by Carrera. I only have to make sure he wears them in the semis or final because by then they will be a little different. Sufficiently different to upset the natural cadence of this great athlete. Sufficiently different to lose just a few seconds a lap. Sufficiently different even to take him off the podium.

Nigel Gressley returned to his hotel as dusk fell, having been totally absorbed in the variety of buildings and parks in Portland. He had taken Hammond's advice and stopped off at the Japanese gardens which were undoubtedly an oasis of calm in the centre of a thriving metropolis. As he strolled past reception, the concierge, called out "Mr Gressley, there's a package for you. It will require a signature."

"No problem," said Gressley, trying to suppress a feeling of excitement like a small boy getting a present from a thoughtful uncle, and he took the package up to his room on the second floor. Unusually for Gressley, he took the stairs instead of the lift and was surprised to find himself a little out of breath. Strange he thought; when I played squash last time everything appeared normal. Must be that rather oversize steak I'd eaten at lunchtime, sticking to my ribs. With that thought in his mind he toasted success with a small bottle of champagne from the mini bar and began carefully to unwrap the running shoes. Along with the shoes was a well constructed publicity statement, carefully worded so any top athlete could be Nike's lead performer. The shoes themselves were certainly elegant. The Goldswoop was a thing of beauty, an object of desire. The uppers were of reflective gold latex with the Nike swoop embossed in a slightly darker gold, reminding Nigel of the old gold colouring of the shirts his players wore at Wolverhampton Wanderers. Nigel found it hard to believe how light they were. It was like handling a pair of delicate gloves, but manufactured to the exacting demands of one of the world's top athletes. Nigel felt inside and found on the instep exactly what he'd hoped to find. He located a small wedge, clearly required in response to Carrera's running style. Nigel recalled the information Jim Stringer had given him on the importance of the mechanics of the shoe design. He now knew that a small change could be devastating for the athlete. He carefully worked the wedge free using the handle of a spoon and having got both free, he then rotated them and replaced them on the opposite side. The wedges clearly didn't fit true in this new position but by both switching sides and shoes, Nigel found that they fitted well in their new position. He had anticipated this alteration and had bought a tube of superglue and two small clamps from a hardware store in town. Having been totally satisfied that the new position of the wedges was a robust fit, Nigel glued them in place and clamped them so that they would be solidly fixed in their new position by the morning.

Highly satisfied with his unorthodox handiwork, he placed the shoes out of sight in a cupboard, took a single malt from the mini bar, ordered a club sandwich through room service and settled down to watch basketball on channel 23. He thought about ringing home, but realising it would be about four o'clock in the morning, settled for a text message to send his love and his flight plans. For Nigel, everything was slowly fitting into place. His task now was to get these doctored shoes onto the feet of Carrera. He had two plans to achieve this, one purely opportunistic and the other to impersonate a Nike employee. He went to his jacket pocket to retrieve the Nike visitors badge and carefully put it at the bottom of his hand luggage. This could be a valuable part of his plans and he wanted to make sure it was always with him. The incessant commercials during the basketball game on TV were starting to irritate Nigel so he switched to the pay TV adult channel and spent $9.95 on a tawdry movie involving a group of bisexual college students bearing little resemblance to any of Nigel's experiences as an undergraduate.

Nigel was careful in the morning to pack the shoes, with their newly positioned wedges firmly in place, in his hand luggage. He discarded the two clamps and the superglue in a bin next to the ice machine on the floor above, checked his room carefully and ordered a taxi to Portland airport in good time. His final task was to use the in-house internet connection to Google firearm suppliers. He found two close together and phoned the first one to find that it only dealt in small arms and hunting rifles. The second had a much bigger range and he was surprised how his British driving licence was sufficient ID to obtain a black cobra taser with a number of spare darts. These items were carefully secured with bubble wrap and repacked in his suitcase to go in the hold. At the airport he phoned his wife and having established her commitments, arranged to be picked up at Heathrow shortly after his arrival. He had been out of the country for less than 48 hours but now had the capability to bring Carrera from being the best in the world to a gallant loser. His plan for the taser was the requirement to immobilise Lui Ho when the time was right. Nigel Gressley had always been a fixer, but this and other plans were to give him the biggest payoff in his life. He relished the prospect, but knew all too well that it would require a cool head when it came to the final part of each plan. As he tried to relax in business class, the anticipation caused him to sweat and he was grateful of the cool flannel provided by the stewardess. Nigel noticed a distinct thudding in his chest with each heart beat and resolved to drink less strong coffee, a habit he found increasingly difficult to resist.

CHAPTER 15

March 8th, 2012
Marlow, UK

Angelo Benito was certainly no angel. Nigel Gressley's file on Benito was extensive and consistently pointed to his philandering as being his weak spot. But Benito was discreet and always came across as a loving family man with an adoring and not unattractive wife. Since Gressley had made his initial plans for Benito two years ago, he had fathered two children and appeared to be a reformed character. The press had photographed him in the company of attractive women, but this was considered par for the course in the world of corporate entertainment. It was only the insiders, and Nigel was one of these, that knew that Benito had a particular interest in Asian girls, especially young Asian girls and even more salaciously, very young Asian girls. Nigel was frankly surprised that this had yet to hit the media, but apart from Benito's remarkable talent as a runner, he now kept a fairly low profile. Benito was not a man to be seen at night clubs in the early hours like so many of the premier league footballers. He apparently divided his time between his family, his altitude camps and his intensive training schedule most often based around Naples or the hills inland from the Amalfi coast. Those who followed his movements as closely as Nigel could see just two periods of time in every year when Benito simply disappeared. It was never with his family or coach or even his agent. He simply went away. Some said he went away to meditate, to refresh, some even suggested he was on a retreat to revitalise his spiritual life. It was just accepted that this was Benito's style, his thing, his way and they left it at that. The truth was that Benito, covering his tracks with remarkable skill, spent a week or more twice every year in a remote part of Thailand where he engaged in an orgy of sexual activity with young girls. These things were not difficult to arrange if you had the money and the right contacts and Benito had both. It was a sordid little bi-annual adventure for the Italian. As so few knew about it, and those that did could never provide hard evidence, it remained a well kept secret compared with Benito's otherwise exemplary lifestyle. Importantly, Nigel Gressley was one of those who knew about Benito's sexual predilection and had every intention of exploiting it to the full. He was to arrange for a very young Asian girl to meet Benito ideally on the night before the 1500 metre final, and for events to take their natural course. Nigel had already established that the stars of the Italian team were not staying in the Olympic village and would be in the luxurious Hampton Lodge near Virginia Water. This would make the task considerably easier for Nigel as there would be no possibility of getting anyone, especially an attractive, young Asian girl, into the Olympic village. As soon as Nigel had confirmation of the Italian team plans, he booked a room at Hampton Lodge for three nights. Fortunately the Italian chef de mission was moving his prestige athletes progressively from the privacy of Hampton Lodge to the Olympic village as their events concluded. Nigel assumed this was to provide moral support for lesser members of the team, but whatever the reason, it meant that rooms became available at precisely the time that he needed one. The room he booked was certainly not for himself.

A large part of Nigel's success as a sports agent was down to his network of contacts. Some of his acquaintances were very long standing, a few even back to Nigel's schooldays at Shipton. Bryn Perry was one of these and although Nigel would never consider him a friend, they had kept in touch ever since. The reason Nigel had kept Bryn at arm's length was because

Bryn had become the owner and CEO of a number of highly successful escort agencies. These were not the sort of agencies that advertised in local papers or worse still on cards in telephone boxes. Bryn's empire, which stretched from his home town of Cardiff in the west, London in the east and Edinburgh in the north was run exclusively through the management of top class hotels. It only catered for the rich and the ladies and men who worked for the agency were top class in every way. Clients ranged from ladies who needed male company for some event or function in town to foreign businessmen who wanted a woman for far more than pleasant company when away from home. It worked because discretion was guaranteed and it made Bryn a very rich man. The whole operation worked on the basis of phone transactions between the client and Bryn and between Bryn and the escort. Bryn never kept a mobile phone for longer than a month and had never been tempted to get greedy with any sort of 'kiss and tell' operation, photographic evidence or blackmail. For such a sordid profession, in which he was little more than a pimp, Bryn justified his actions on the basis of providing a need and not actually knowing any of the more lurid details of his clients' requirements. He had one problematic case in Cardiff when a client had expected more than his escort could manage and the hotel manager had to intervene. In another unfortunate incident in Edinburgh a Scottish MP had gone into anaphylactic shock following a hornet sting and the escort, having called the paramedics, had to stay with him to administer adrenaline from the client's own epipen which in fact saved his life.

"Bryn, it's Nigel Gressley."

"Nigel, what's new? I trust you don't need my services at this time in the morning or has the mid-life crisis finally hit you where it hurts most."

"No Bryn, that part of the ageing process is still intact and anyway I think I would go the Viagra route before succumbing to your company's charming but expensive services."

"OK, Nigel, enough of the banter. You don't ring me after three years of only Christmas cards without a reason. Out with it."

"I need a special lady for a special job, Bryn."

"Don't we all my boy. Sounds intriguing, but I am not one to be intrigued. You know my rules. Never ask questions and then I can't be held responsible in a court of law. Give me the request, no reasons, and I shall try my best to help an old school friend."

"Dateline, August 9th; location Hampton Lodge, Surrey – I already have a room booked; requirement, young Asian girl to seduce my contact."

"I like the brevity of your requirements, Nigel, but I have to say slightly unusual. Especially the bit about seduction. My experience is that clients who need escorts don't usually need seduction."

"Agreed Bryn, but this is a slightly unusual case. The client isn't exactly looking for or expecting company that evening. I just want him to have that company and the more, shall I say, robust the evening the better."

"Hey Nigel, I've just clicked. That date you gave me is the last week of the Olympic Games. You want someone shagged out just before they race. Am I right?"

"Well, you needn't have put it quite so crudely, but you're on the right track."

"For something special like this I usually charge more, but for an old friend, let's say £500 non returnable for an escort to be there, a further £500 if she's successful. How does that sound?"

"Just within my budget, Bryn. One other thing, any chance of getting any evidence?"

"Good God man, what do you expect? Bloodied sheets hanging out the window. This isn't the Middle Ages you know."

"I had something like a photo in mind."

"No can do, mate. I'm not prepared to go down that route.

I've built my questionable reputation on discretion and photos don't work for either party. Sorry but I draw the line at that one."

"OK, point made. So it's settled. Room 23, ground floor. Room booked in the name of Mr and Mrs Tom Murray. I'll get you the client's room number nearer the time. Anything else Bryn?"

"Sounds as if you've got all bases covered, Nigel. Good to be of service, Ciao."

Nigel Gressley heard the phone click dead and put his mobile down on his leather topped desk. He found himself humming that old Sunday school hymn, 'One step at a time, Lord Jesus, one step at a time' and wondered what Lord Jesus would make of his little schemes. He was certainly taking one step at a time and so far each step was bringing him closer to his ultimate aim. To bring Benito's downfall needed a little fine tuning, but Nigel could wait until exactly the right time for that part of his plan to come to fruition. He made a diary note to be in room 23 at the Hampton Lodge at lunchtime on August 9th. It would be interesting to see what Bryn had procured.

Chapter 16

April 7th, 2012
Brunel University, UK

Malik Gandapur and Rahim Kichlu were now in the final year of their electrical engineering degree and had considerably more freedom than in the first two years. They had both opted to write a thesis on mobile communication devices and had been meticulous in their research.

Malik was investigating the coverage by mobile providers and had selected two geographical areas. The first was Slough, the area around Brunel University, and the other was East Stratford, a demographically similar area which had received full approval from his thesis supervisor. His supervisor had even commented that with the huge increase in mobile users for the period of the Olympics in East Stratford, his research may be of some practical as well as academic benefit.

Rahim had selected a topic which was of particular interest to his supervisor, that of remote operation of household equipment. The University had in recent years gained quite a reputation in household sensing devices, largely through the work of Max Woolf. It was agreed that Professor Woolf would be a joint supervisor on this work with the aim that mobile phone technology could be the method of activating household systems such as heating and lighting remotely. As a great deal was already known on this topic, it took little for Rahim to persuade his supervisors that pressure measurement was a critical element, especially in relation to domestic boilers and sudden changes in water pressure.

These two projects gave the two students full access to equipment and expertise associated with the critical areas of their evil task, the production of the fifteen bombs and especially the modifications required beyond the one tested so successfully last July. From October 2011, when the two students returned to the University, they had been assiduously working on their academic research. In parallel they spent most of their free time on the design of the small bombs which would wreak such havoc the following summer.

The area which challenged these students the most was sourcing the various ingredients for the bombs. They had decided from the outset that the quantities needed would be bought in very small amounts and from different suppliers to allay any suspicion. They had worked out a buying schedule so that every month an order would be placed but that the seller would never be repeated. It was well recognised that with certain chemicals, software was built in to the ordering process to recognise any unusual sales trends. Repeat orders were always treated as suspicious. Their training in Pakistan had made this very clear and they knew that slipshod practices could result in questions being asked by the Home Office. Malik and Rahim had invested a great deal to be seen as exemplary students and they had every intention of keeping it that way. They knew that the production of these bombs was Al-Qaeda's way of testing their ability and their resolve. They had no intention of failing on either account.

The two students bought an old Morris Minor for £300 and installed it in a lock-up garage just half a mile away from where they lived in Cowley Road. They took out the engine and removed the wheels and it soon gave every appearance of a long term restoration project. They chose their friends with care and avoided any that had the remotest interest in car mechanics. This avoided the prospect of any unwelcome visitors to their lock-up, a place that was an ideal store for the products needed to furnish their wicked intent. Not only was it a store, but the car restoration was an ideal cover for the production process. This, by necessity, needed to be a slow process as the delivery of the bombs' ingredients was by their nature going to take time. It would have been so easy to organise bulk delivery and this would have almost inevitably led to suspicion and detection.

The other aspect which challenged the two students was how to get the ingredients delivered. The fact that they both had the typical Middle Eastern appearance made over the counter purchases a risk, so their preference was to use mail order. Even so, with Pakistani names, coupled with the type of products being purchased, mail order was potentially suspect. Fortunately for them both the opportunity to resolve this issue came from an unexpected source. When doing their weekly shopping in Tesco, they noticed that one week there was a huge drive to get customers to register for a Tesco credit card. The commitment of the sales team to hit their target numbers was such that little notice was taken of the unlikely names that Rahim and Malik gave as they filled in the credit card application form. Rahim became Jack London, one of his favourite authors, and Malik became Robert Stephenson, in deference to an engineer second only to Brunel in importance. Thus within two weeks, both students had in their possession a legitimate credit card, with the minor exception of the anglicised names they had chosen. They both now had the ability to order on-line without risking the sort of questions that their Middle Eastern names could initiate.

The specialised camp both students had attended in Pakistan over the summer recess was given over, in part, to the detailed construction of highly dangerous explosives. The training covered the use of Semtex, dynamite, TNT and other explosive mixtures, but the one that they both found of greatest interest was the use of readily available components. These, if mixed correctly, could be equally devastating and the ingredients would be relatively easy to obtain on the open market. The key ingredients were hexamine, hydrogen peroxide and citric acid, all of them a departure from the explosive they had developed earlier from the readily available ammonium nitrate fertilizer. Privately they were both annoyed by the changes required following all the work they had put in to the tried and tested method of last July. They daren't even show their displeasure to each other as this could be reported as lacking faith in the cause. It all came down to the new requirement to include a pressure transducer, which needed a friction primer. Fifteen pressure transducers were easy to obtain through the Radiospares catalogue, but they still stayed with their original plan of ordering a few at a time over several months. This precaution was probably unnecessary in view of Rahim's genuine research work on pressure measurement, but they had been taught well to be ultra cautious in every aspect of their work. They started with the friction primer, which needed potassium chlorate and antimony sulphate in a wet 5% gum arabic solution. These chemicals were not readily available but the car restoration project was an ideal front to get hold of such things.

Taking great care to link every request with the work they appeared to be doing on the car, the two students befriended chemistry graduates with access to every item they needed. Over a matter of months, Malik and Rahim had obtained all that was required for the friction primer. To make it more stable, they added sulphur, ground glass and calcium carbonate. The latter was the easiest to source as it was the main component of indigestion tablets, causing some amusement to the otherwise serious bomb-makers.

The hexamine for the main explosive was the main component of solid fuel camping tablets and, as Uxbridge had two camping shops in the Pavilions shopping centre, it was easy to obtain a large quantity. Malik and Rahim took the precaution of always buying another low cost camping item so that it appeared a more natural purchase. From the camping season of March onwards, Halfords, on the outskirts of the town, also sold these solid fuel tablets, so it was not long before they had ample supplies of this key ingredient. Hydrogen peroxide was available on the internet through hairdressing suppliers and their home address of 330 Cowley Road was renamed 'Cutz' for the purpose of the delivery. The final ingredient was citric acid, known as sour salt in the bakery trade and was obtained in a similar fashion through the internet. Once again, a false name the 'Uxbridge Cheesecake Factory' was added to the delivery address, a precaution which both students thought absolutely necessary.

As the ingredients were delivered, they were taken to the lock up garage, which now also housed a substantial refrigerator. This was crucial as once the explosive was prepared it needed to be kept cool. Malik and Rahim knew that there was no room for experimentation. They needed to get it right every time. The two students had only followed this intricate and dangerous procedure twice before in their summer training camps in Pakistan and then with expert tuition. This was different. No guiding hand to get the proportions just right. No one to give them the confidence to move steadily on to the next stage in the complex process. Both students knew that the smallest error could make the explosive totally unstable. Lives were at risk. Their lives. Allah had chosen them for this task. Allah would guide. Allah would choose. But even Allah couldn't stop the fear in their hearts and the slight tremor in their hands. As they worked intensely and silently, they prayed ceaselessly. They had been chosen. They would obey. They must succeed.

The peroxide was dissolved with the hexamine in exactly the right proportions, to which the citric acid was then cautiously added. After 24 hours in the fridge, the whole solution was filtered through a conventional coffee filter to collect the solid particles which were then washed with distilled water and allowed to dry. This whole process was repeated fifteen times to supply each vacuum flask and these were also stored in the refrigerator until needed. The design of the mobile phone interface had been perfected during the previous summer, but they now had to install the pressure transducer as an additional component. The vacuum flasks were modified so that two USB ports were now part of the outer casing with the mobile phone dongle and the pressure transducer both ready to be attached at the last minute. The friction primer was activated by rapid movement and this was supplied by stripping down a small electronic dental flosser and using its inherent vibration mechanism.

The vacuum flasks themselves had been obtained from a number of BP garages which were running an Olympic promotion. Each flask was emblazoned with the union flag and the Olympic logo, something which the students thought would give some credibility when they were taken into the Olympic stadium. The adjustments needed for the flasks were difficult and it was only on the third attempt that they were satisfied. The friction primer had its own compartment, as had the main explosive, and it was essential to retain a separate section above them both for a hot drink. Soldering these all in place was an intricate task but Malik and Rahim had been well rehearsed over the summer months in Pakistan and the skills needed were soon honed to perfection.

After several weeks of evening work, both students were satisfied with the final modifications to the original bomb and returned once again to West Wales. They travelled with renewed confidence, buoyed up by their knowledge of the area and eagerly anticipating the final test of all their efforts. As before they parked their car just off the road out of Cardigan towards the coast and set off excitedly across the fields towards the coast. The weather was threatening at this time of year with a strong wind and no moon to give them any additional light beyond their flashlights. Within 20 minutes they reached the spot they had used before and carefully took the two vacuum flasks from their rucksack. Both were soon primed with the mobile phone dongle by the simple act of plugging them in to one of the double USB ports. One of them was additionally primed by plugging in the pressure transducer to the other USB port. On the previous expedition to these parts, they had used a length of cord to lower the bomb, but now they had brought with them a telescopic fishing rod. The first flask they lowered over the edge of the cliff until the fishing line went slack. Malik dialed the crucial 11 digits and within six seconds they could just hear the explosion above the sound of the crashing waves. With considerable care they now attached the second vacuum flask to the fishing line they had retrieved from the first bomb. The pressure transducer had been set to detonate the friction primer at a pressure difference of exactly 30 metres. Laying the flask on the ground at the top of the cliff, and in spite of the wind, they marked the line to measure the 30 metres using a short piece of white cotton. Once satisfied the line was wound in again with the fishing reel fixed to the rod. This was now the big test and slowly they reversed the reel and released the line at a rate of about a metre every few seconds, looking intently for their marking cotton. As Rahim shone a light on the reel, the time it took to spot the cotton marker seemed endless. Within two minutes, it appeared and with bated breath they let it slip through the guides on the rod until it reached the end. Within a metre of the cotton marker descending beyond the end of the rod, they both heard the explosion muffled by the roar of the wind and waves hitting the rocks at the base of the cliff. They turned to each other with a look of great satisfaction on their faces.

"We did it," they said in unison and briefly embraced before packing the rod away and heading back to the car. They were both so satisfied with the successful task, that they'd relaxed their normal level of caution. They were almost on top of their car when to their utter shock they saw a police car parked not ten metres way.

"Shit," intoned Malik under his breath, but it was now too late to take any evasive action. As they approached their car, the doors of the police car opened and two policemen slowly emerged from the darkened interior.

"And what brings you two to this part of the world at this inhospitable hour?" enquired the taller of the two.

Rahim and Malik were stunned into silence, not knowing how to respond. The wind continued to howl and in a sarcastic tone, the shorter of the two policemen added, "I'm sorry, I didn't quite catch that. Perhaps you'd like to show me what's in your rucksack."

The reference to the rucksack gave Rahim unexpected inspiration and he now responded with little confidence but at least a level of coherence.

"We were looking for a spot to do a little night fishing," said Rahim, the words coming out with a distinct lack of conviction.

"I see. Something you do often?" enquired the same policeman, who by now was shining a powerful flashlight directly at the two students.

"No sir, this was the first time, and we have to say rather unsuccessfully." Rahim continued.

"That's no surprise around here. Perhaps you'd be kind enough to show us your fishing equipment," said the taller policeman, warming to his task.

Malik, who until now had been utterly silent, terrified by the unexpected encounter, opened the rucksack and took out the fishing rod and a flashlight.

"I see," continued the same policeman a little surprised, "you'd better show me your licence."

"What," said Malik, annoyed that this detail had slipped their otherwise meticulous preparation, "I thought a licence was only required for inland fishing."

"Gentleman," said the policeman wearily, "we're not talking about bloody fishing, show us your driving licence."

With relief, Rahim produced his driving licence from the front section of his wallet. The policemen both took their time looking at it and then asked, "And is this your car Mr Kichlu?"

Rahim, now feeling slightly more in control replied "Yes sir, I've had it for two years."

"So you'll know the registration number."

Rahim's confidence started to grow, while Malik, still feeling insecure, was happy to stay in the background.

"V354LDN" Rahim intoned.

The policeman sauntered round to the front of the car to confirm what had been said.

"Be so kind as to wait in the vehicle, while I run a couple of checks," said the same policeman, the other one having by now returned to the comfort of the police car. The two policemen, both enjoying the benefit of a very efficient heater, took their time checking on the validity of the registration details.

"What do you make of these two?" said one to the other.

"Highly suspicious to me, but unless we can label them with a specific, I guess there's little we can do. I bet the car's not taxed or insured."

"I'm patched through to DVLC, so we'll soon know."

Five uncomfortable minutes passed for the two students as they waited. Although sheltered from the biting wind, they both felt chilled to the bone, but knew starting the engine to get the heater going would be a big mistake. One of the policemen returned with his notebook now opened and indicated to open the window.

"You both seem to be a long way from home, gentlemen, perhaps you could confirm your home address?"

"330, Cowley Road, Uxbridge," said Rahim.

"Hmm. It seems to fit with DVLC records. Tell me gentlemen,

when did you come out here?"

Malik, now relieved that the checks seemed to be over, saw no good reason to lie. "We came yesterday, last evening that is. We drove straight here for the night fishing."

"Night fishing on one of the wildest coasts in West Wales?"

"Yes, we seemed to have been rather badly informed," Malik commented, now feeling that this interrogation could be coming to a close.

"My recommendation, gentlemen, is that if you want to go night fishing again, you go much further south from here. Try some of the bays in Pembrokeshire and keep away from this part. OK, you're free to go. Have a good Easter."

Rahim started the engine, turned the heater fan to maximum and slowly inched the car onto the road. He drove steadily for a few miles before stopping again to consult the map. "We take the next right into Cardigan and then pick up the main road from there," he confirmed.

Malik, who had been silent from the time the engine started, now felt able to speak.

"Allah was with us tonight. His protection is all we need."

Rahim said nothing; he was watching his rear view mirror with continuing concern.

CHAPTER 17

July 17th, 2012
Bisham Abbey, UK

Sometimes in life, two unrelated events or activities collide in an unexpected manner. Some call this coincidence, others fate and yet others fortune. The importance is not that it happens but the outcome. Nigel could hardly believe it when he learned that the American track squad was to be based at Bisham Abbey, just two miles from where he lived in Marlow. Not only that, but they were using the sumptuously equipped sports centre where Nigel had been a member for several years. The Americans had always had a mistrust of the athletes' village ever since the assassination of eleven Israeli athletes by the Black September group back in 1972. Bisham Abbey was far from ideal as a final training venue. The rooms were sparse and it afforded few of the luxuries of a five star hotel. The major disadvantage was its distance from the Games site in East London, but the squad planned to move their athletes into the newly-opened Olympic Hilton, just two stops north of Stratford International station, two days before competition began. The Americans had probably been seduced by the historical associations of Bisham Abbey and its glorious location on the banks of the River Thames. It was also easy to make secure, had a nine hole golf course and provided the key elements of excellent outdoor and indoor training facilities. In spite of requests from the American team for exclusivity, the management of Bisham Abbey had only permitted the American team use of the Abbey as long as its regular members could continue to use the sports centre. The management knew that the Americans would only be around for two weeks and membership retention was top of their agenda. This played directly into Nigel Gressley's hands as he could legitimately be on the same premises as three of the athletes he was aiming to infect.

Nigel's exercise regime, which at best was sporadic, took on a new impetus during this time. He would arrive at the club on a daily basis and at different times so that he could observe the nature of the training regime of the American's 1500 metre runners. It took little time to establish that they would routinely take a gentle slow, continuous run, mainly using the perimeter of the Abbey grounds, for about 40 minutes, starting promptly at 10 o'clock every morning. Coaches would then insist on them drinking from a crate of Gatorade bottles, always brought out from an external refrigerator minutes before the end of their session. Nigel saw this as being his one and only opportunity to get these athletes to drink the foul water he had kept in cold store since his visit to India two years previously.

Having established the Americans' routine, Nigel picked up four Gatorade bottles in two sizes from a health food shop in Marlow and took them to the cash desk.

"Thank you sir," said the young student on the till, "were you aware that Gatorade's doing a promotion this week. If you buy four more bottles, any size, you can get a Gatorade rainproof jacket for just £5.99? Nigel's initial reaction was to refuse but a sixth sense told him otherwise and he uncharacteristically accepted the offer. At home, Nigel replaced some of the Gatorade in each bottle with the infected water and was ready to return to Bisham Abbey with his noxious weaponry. He had already noted with interest that the coaches from the American team had a regular routine of motivating the runners before they set off and then using the forty minutes while the athletes were out for a late and relaxed breakfast. During this time, Nigel could easily walk to the refrigerator, which was at the back of the sports hall, add his own adulterated Gatorade and get away from the area totally undetected.

The next day he was back at Bisham Abbey and in position just before ten o'clock. He waited ten minutes until the athletes were well out of site and grabbing the four infected bottles, headed for the refrigerator. Nigel spun round in alarm as a voice behind demanded "Hey buddy, what you doin'?" For a fraction of a second Nigel was paralysed, but then recovered enough to respond.

"Hi, just refilling the ice box. The company is pretty hot on this sort of thing. Use by dates need checking. That sort of thing."

"Well OK," said the stranger with resignation, "I can see you're with the company from your jacket. It's just you can't be too careful with our athletes. If we're gonna beat the Russians at this meet, we gotta cover every base."

Nigel smiled, mainly with relief, shut the refrigerator door firmly, shook the stranger's hand, wished the American team good luck and left at a pace he thought was appropriate for a Gatorade employee. Back in his car for the short drive home, he started to relax for the first time, but even then he noted his hands were gripping the wheel far too tightly.

Twenty minutes later the three American athletes sprinted the last 400 metres just for the fun of it. Each one kept a little in reserve because even amongst friends, they knew that once racing, friendship meant nothing. As had happened every time, the coaches trailed out from their late breakfast and joined the athletes as they came to a halt.

"Coach, do we have to drink this crap every time? It's OK once in a while but every time is getting us all down."

"Come on guys you know the deal. It's good stuff, does the job and most importantly we have to be seen to use it as Gatorade is one of our biggest sponsors."

"Yes but coach, there's no one around here. Can we

163

supplement it with something else, just for a change?"

"Look guys, I know how you feel, let's cut a deal. At this stage in your training, now you're tapering, you're never going to go hypo. You've gotta keep your fluid level up, but good old fashioned water will do that. If there's anyone around, especially the press, at least look as though you're drinking it. Just put the bottle to your lips and tilt it right back. That should be enough for our sponsors. But guys, mark this down. This only applies until you start racing. Then it's back to normal business. Is that clear?"

"Thanks coach, every bit helps. It's a deal."

Nigel Gressley returned home in a state of self satisfaction of another job well done. He would have been sickened if he'd been party to the deal the three American athletes had just cut with their coach.

CHAPTER 18

July 23rd, 2012
Shardloes Hall, UK

Nigel Gressley had limited options with his outrageous plan to inject corticosteroids into Lui Ho's Achilles tendon. It was high risk, but he had paid good money to the leader of a known gang in East London who had every reason to hate the Chinese. Nigel had always recognised that people need a strong incentive to act maliciously and there was none better than people who had a strong antagonism to other countries or religions. Such things often occurred many years before, and you needed to look no further than the Irish situation to appreciate that. A festering ill will was often quite sufficient to make people behave in unacceptable ways. Nigel had chosen well because, in spite of the financial rewards, the notion that Chinese athletes could be pre-eminent caused most Taiwanese to hate that nation even more. Nigel's links with the Taiwanese underworld stretched back many years to the time when he had started his questionable career trading in fake shirts. He managed to move on from this at a time that things started to get too hot, but fortunately for Nigel he was able to tip off the big boys that the police were closing in and saved them certain prison sentences. The Taiwanese, for all their faults, were grateful for his timely intervention. Nigel ensured that the 'phone numbers of such contacts were never loaded onto his mobile. These contacts, of which he had a number, were kept in a special book in his locked desk. He even took the precaution of coding the contact numbers, not in a particularly sophisticated way, but sufficient for any prying eyes to pass them over as being irrelevant. The big mistake that Nigel made was to use his mobile phone to ring the gang leader whose name he dredged up from all that time ago. The deal had been conducted swiftly and without the unnecessary questions which often accompanied such transactions. The fee had been set at £1000; £500 up front and the rest on successful completion. Nigel undertook to supply his contact with exactly where Lui Ho was staying in the weeks leading up to the 1500 metre final and also to hand over the taser well in advance. Nigel was consistent in his choice of venue for the exchange, using once again the gents' toilet in Costa Coffee at the Premier Inn by the side of King's Cross station. He arranged to place the taser on the floor behind the toilet in the far cubicle at exactly three o'clock. Fifteen minutes later an Asian in a cheap suit entered the gents' toilet. Finding the far cubicle occupied, he spent time washing his hands and face, using the mirror to watch the locked door. Eventually the door opened and an elderly man, who looked as though he had been sleeping rough, emerged carrying a well-wrapped parcel. Within a split second the Asian turned, hit him with unbelievable force throwing him off balance and projecting him back into the cubicle where he slumped semi-conscious into the corner. The parcel was quickly retrieved, the cubicle door slammed and the Asian made a swift but unobtrusive exit into York Way, disappearing into the forecourt of King's Cross station.

The Chinese team had split their training base between Roehampton University in Wimbledon and Shardloes Hall near Amersham. The track athletes were mainly at Roehampton where they could train on Wimbledon Common and use the extensive sports science facilities. Lui Ho had been given special dispensation to stay with the equestrian and shooting teams at Shardloes because his wife was in the Chinese dressage squad. This dispensation only applied up to the stage of the semi-finals at which point, Ho was required to be back in the Olympic village. Nigel knew that his best chance of getting Ho alone was at Shardloes Hall. Once in the Olympic village Ho would be under constant surveillance and the chance of a stranger getting into the accommodation block was virtually zero. Security was tight at Shardloes Hall, but was restricted to the three entrances at different points on the estate. The Chinese had hired a private security firm to patrol the grounds and perimeter fence, but the company wasn't able to cope with staff absences due to genuine holidays and the British habit of simply not turning up for work. It was clear, even to the casual observer, that security was stretched, particularly in the remote areas of the grounds, away from the main gates. For someone with the necessary experience and who was sufficiently determined to get into the grounds, especially under the cover of dark, it was no difficult challenge. Chen Tsou, a notorious member of the Nakamura brotherhood, was a man with this experience and skill. He had been involved in a number of hits over the years and was known to be effective and highly successful. This particular task he accepted with relish, considering it to be as straight forward as he was likely to get in his specialised line of business.

It took him the early part of one night, once darkness had fallen, to establish a route into the part of the hall used by the Chinese equestrian team for their accommodation. A hastily erected fence had been placed around the perimeter of the park, but Chen's wire cutters soon dealt with this obstruction. He was careful to replace all elements of the fence and, as it was up against a substantial rhododendron plantation, he rightly assumed that the perimeter guards were unlikely to be patrolling this particular part of the fence. His appearance was sufficiently similar to the Chinese to raise little concern once he was inside the building. Chen moved cautiously around the single story accommodation block, somewhat surprised that the Chinese had no form of obvious security in place except a number of CCTV cameras which were easy to see and if necessary eliminate. This form of security was only of value retrospectively and even if they used night vision technology his image would be of little value after the event. His task this first night was to establish the exact bedroom of Lui Ho and his wife and this was made considerably easier because their room was the only one with a dual Chinese character attached to the door. He tried the door and finding it locked left the building by another route, making a note to bring the necessary tools to force the lock next time. Once outside the building, Chen confirmed that none of the bedroom windows had been left open. After all, why attack from inside when an open window made an attack from outside a much easier task. Chen took the direct route over the fields to Amersham where he was met in the car park of a conveniently situated 24-hour Tesco store by another member of the brotherhood. This was going to be one of the easier tasks he had undertaken over the years and he was relaxed as he laid his final plans to follow the strange instructions he had been given not 48 hours earlier. Chen pondered the merit of giving an injection to an Olympic athlete as opposed to simply eliminating him, but it was not for him to question, just to perform. He knew full well that unless he undertook his task to the exact specifications he would receive no fee for the job. Chen was confident. The plan was clear. Get into the bedroom, taser both occupants rendering them helpless for sufficient time to inject Lui Ho in the Achilles tendon and then get out without being seen or heard. Simple. Back in the south east of London, after a late start due to his night time foray into the Buckinghamshire countryside, Chen picked up the supplies he would need that night. A single black cobra taser, tested and fully charged with two additional battery packs, a syringe with microscopic needle containing the corticosteroid betacoxib, a head torch to leave his hands free at all times and importantly a master key combination set for quiet and rapid access to the room. As an afterthought, Chen packed two small stun guns and a stun pen, both ideal if he could get close to Ho and his wife. The taser is a well proven weapon and ideal when you need to stay fifteen feet from the target, but the stun guns and stun pens are easier to use if you can get close up. Chen was not sure how the assignment would develop so he took the precaution of the more extensive incapacitating armoury.

As before, he was dropped off in the supermarket car park and under the cover of darkness made his way across fields to the perimeter of Shardloes Hall. Tonight was considerably warmer than last night with a high level of humidity which sometimes hit the British summer. This could make sleeping more difficult, but Chen was comforted by the knowledge that Ho and his wife would be well used to high humidity. They were unlikely to be affected by such changes in the atmosphere and should by now be sleeping soundly. All his equipment was safely stored in a small black rucksack, leaving his hands free to make it easier when entering the grounds and buildings. Chen made for the rhododendron plantation, removed the sector of wire fence he had prepared the night before, evaded the sparse security cameras and soon found himself outside Ho's room. He took his master keys from his rucksack and quickly and silently worked his ways through the options. To his horror and self-criticism of his professional standard, he noticed for the first time that the door was deadlocked. It was no wonder he hadn't spotted this earlier because the lock was almost at floor level. He cursed, knowing that this needed a different style of entry which, although he could do it, would inevitably be noisier than picking a conventional lock. This was a risk too great and as he pondered the options, his highly developed senses noticed something slightly different from his previous visit. The sounds and smells were the same, but something about the environment had changed. It was as he bent to examine the deadlock at the base of the door that he realised what was different. There was a slight but perceptible movement of air coming from under the door which had not previously been there. Chen's immediate thoughts were that a fan had been switched on but he dismissed that option as so few houses in Britain had them fitted. Then it struck him. The air movement was coming from an open window. With such an unusually humid night, Lui Ho had opened a window, breaching every security protocol but giving Chen the perfect opportunity to get into the room. He retraced his steps and within minutes was back outside the low accommodation block, quite probably former stables, now tastefully converted to provide rooms for delegates to the conference trade. Thank God, thought Chen, with the English obsession of maintaining the original appearance, because the whole floor had simple sash windows. Ho's window, as Chen anticipated, was open a few inches and Chen had little trouble in silently lifting it enough to squeeze inside the room. With his head torch on the low setting, Chen surveyed the scene rapidly and efficiently, taking note of the key information needed for his immediate task. Ho and his wife were in twin beds, with Ho by the door and his wife nearest the window. He slipped off his rucksack and took out the taser, battery packs, the stun guns and syringe. He prepared for the injection by placing the needle into the vial of corticosteroid and slowly extracted the fluid into the syringe. A little pressure ensured there was no air bubble between the fluid and the needle and he was ready. He was tempted to leave Ho's wife sleeping while he dealt with Ho, but knew from experience that the reaction to the taser can be variable, some recipients falling noiselessly, others screaming with the pain of the 50,000 volts. As he moved noiselessly around the room, the only sound was the gentle breathing of the two sleeping competitors. Chen selected the stun guns as he was confident of being able to make direct contact with his targets. He slowly drew the covers back from Ho's wife, pausing to admire her shapely form and pressed the stun gun firmly to her exposed shoulder. As he pulled the inbuilt trigger, the gun instantly fired over 50,000 volts totally incapacitating her nervous system. She convulsed once causing the bed to creak alarmingly but then lay totally still. He was tempted to spend more time admiring her prone body as the convulsion had exposed her left breast, but he knew that he had very little time before the devastating effect of the stun gun wore off. Lo was stirring, woken by the noise from his wife's bed and Chen, now realising that he had to work very fast, turned his attention to him. Pressing the other stun gun firmly to Ho's chest he fired another noxious charge into the now fully awake athlete. Ho felt the full effect of the voltage and screamed, but Chen, anticipating this, quickly slammed a hand over his mouth to quell the noise. Ho slumped back on the bed, his eyes wide open but totally unable to move. Chen had no more than 30 seconds to finish the job, knowing full well that Ho's wife could easily regain consciousness in that time. Turning Ho on his side he picked up the syringe and felt for the clear raised surface of the Achilles tendon on Ho's right leg. At that precise moment, Chen jumped back as all around him alarm bells and sirens filled the room and the corridor outside. Within seconds people started running and doors were banging. Chen was temporarily paralysed not knowing what to do. Then he heard the unmistakable sound of a key in the lock and Ho's name being called. He knew he had little time before both locks would be opened and someone would be in the room. Ho's wife was stirring and rubbing her shoulder. He grabbed his syringe and stun guns, threw them into his rucksack and squeezed through the open window as the door burst open. Waiting on the outside, Chen could see Ho being shaken and half carried in a groggy state into the corridor. At the end of the building, people were gathering, using flashlights and assembling in rows directed by someone in a fluorescent jacket. As Chen headed back into the garden shrubbery he cursed repeatedly. So close to finishing the job and thwarted by nothing more than a fire alarm practice. His best hope now was another humid night with the window left open again. At least he was now confident that his approach would work. No one had a fire alarm practice two nights running. Chen's rendezvous back at the car park was far from what he'd hoped. Tonight he planned to celebrate a job well done. The celebrations would need to wait for a further 24 hours. Chen was annoyed and when Chen was annoyed it was best to keep clear. The journey back to London was dominated by silence. As Chen morosely went through the items in his rucksack he knew that something was wrong. He checked again and with utter dismay and frustration he realised that one item was missing. The vial which contained the corticosteroid had been left in Ho's room. Chen, the ultimate professional, had failed to meet his rigorous standards and the consequences could be dire.

Chen returned the next night, totally unsure how his error would have changed things at Shardloes Hall. It was clear from his approach to the perimeter fence that security had been increased dramatically. Nonetheless his caution in restoring the fence each time had paid off handsomely. He had to wait longer than usual as the security patrols were now more frequent, but he eventually gained access in his usual way. Making his way for the third time to the single story accommodation block, Chen was disappointed to find no windows open in spite of the humid evening. He had no alternative than to get to the Ho's room from the inside. Now he knew he would have to break through a deadlock, he came prepared with the right tools and was confident of success. Unsurprisingly there was now a security guard at the end of the corridor leading to Ho's bedroom. Chen contemplated the options which he summarised as distraction, immobilisation or death. The latter was way outside his brief although he was quite capable of it. Chen had been told quite clearly that he was to do nothing more than inject Ho and in doing so to arouse no suspicion of it actually taking place. He had already failed in that task by leaving the vial behind so Chen had much to make up. Immobilising the guard using the taser was a real option but the length of time before recovery was always uncertain. Distraction was more risky because the outcome was unknown. Chen had little choice so retreated from his vantage point to a nearby room which looked as though it was used for recreation and relaxation. It had low chairs, a TV, a coffee table littered with newspapers and magazines and most importantly a waste bin against the far wall. Chen first removed the battery from the smoke detector in the ceiling, then having quietly moved some newspapers from the table into the bin, he lit them with the cigarette lighter he'd retrieved from his rucksack. As they started to smoulder, he ran down the corridor alerting the security guard to the fire. The guard ran back into the smoke-filled room. The fire had by now had taken hold, but still within the bin. His training had taught him to close all doors and this was Chen's opportunity to break into Ho's room. He ran down the main corridor looking for the double character on the bedroom door indicating Ho and his wife. He thought he knew which room it was but there were now no characters on the door. The door was blank. He was about to force the two locks when to his surprise the door opened easily and Chen almost stumbled in, having fully expecting to meet the resistance of the locks. Once in the room he snapped on his head torch to reveal to his horror two empty beds. He cursed, knew that he couldn't go back to the corridor with the possibility of security back up for the fire, and escaped out of the sash window into the darkness. Chen Tsou was enraged he'd not been kept informed of Ho's movements and it took all of his professional self control not to go back and cause mayhem. As he made his way back to his car park rendezvous, Chen was particularly annoyed that he wouldn't receive the second instalment of his fee. His boss only paid fifty percent up front and he had spent three nights in relative discomfort, achieving absolutely nothing. Chen decided to negotiate a bigger percentage in advance next time. After all, his work was highly specialised and he deserved more for all that effort. On reflection, thought Chen, who would know that he'd failed. Chen Tsou resolved to keep failure to himself. He would report a resounding success and collect his full fee.

CHAPTER 19

July 24th, 2012
Premier Lodge, King's Cross, UK

Jim Stringer was very concerned about his appointment with Rachel as his moral compass was being seriously challenged. Jim had been brought up in a society where giving evidence against a friend was totally unacceptable and was likely to result in serious reprisal. Not that Jim ever considered Nigel Gressley a friend, but he felt he owed a certain measure of allegiance as Nigel was funding his research. Nonetheless Jim felt he had sufficient grounds to share his concerns with others and there was no one better in the business than Rachel Rosen. Jim had been a fan of Rachel's since the Beijing Olympics, when she had reported with some distinction on the use of prisoners to build the stadium. At the same time she had reviewed the final preparation for the British athletics team, so would have worked closely with many of the GB squad, including Josh Silverman. Rachel was slight in appearance, with a waspish waist and a pretty, rather engaging face. She had deep brown eyes with a dark skin tone that was still tanned following the three weeks she'd spent working in a kibbutz in her beloved Israel.

Jim had specifically asked that the meeting was held in a neutral spot well away from Rachel's office in Fleet Street and she had suggested Costa coffee in the Premier Lodge just behind King's Cross Station. Jim was early, having travelled down to London from Loughborough on the 05.30 train, mainly because it was substantially cheaper than later trains. He had enjoyed a breakfast of egg and bacon rolls on the train but by mid morning was starting to feel hungry after his early start. He ordered a large cappuccino and two slices of what Costa called millionaire's shortcake, but was in fact a rather bland version of what his mother had often cooked as a special treat for the family. He sat at the back of the coffee bar facing the only entrance and ran over in his mind just what he could tell an investigative reporter like Rachel. As he was contemplating the options, Rachel, who looked every bit as young as her photo in the Evening Standard, strode in, stopped and looked around expectantly. Jim stood up to greet her, half waved and she was soon seated next to him at his table. She had a latte with an extra shot, a glass of Perrier water, declined the offer of any cookies and, with professional ease, took out her notebook. The introductions were brief and the usual pleasantries about travelling and the weather were concluded swiftly. Jim and Rachel sensed that they were both being assessed and first impressions were positive and self-assured.

"Jim, your phone call was a little mysterious but as a reporter I just love a mystery. Tell me more."

"To be honest, Rachel it is somewhat difficult for me. Where I come from you never rat on a friend."

"This I understand, but sometimes the public good exceeds friendship."

"One of the reasons I called you Rachel is because the individual concerned could not exactly be called a friend, but he has given me support and this I respect."

"As you say, Jim, a difficult call. Anyway like it or not, you've asked me to meet you because I assume you have some information that is not only worrying you, but you consider newsworthy."

"Well, yes and no. I am certainly worried and I believe that the public should be aware of it. I will have to leave you to judge its importance relative to other news stories. My big worry is how much I will be implicated in it all. Can it remain anonymous or will I be named as your source?"

"No, a journalist is not required to give her source, except in a court of law when under oath and even then only if it is guaranteed not to cause more harm. It becomes my judgement as to whether or not the source is reliable. Of course in some cases it adds more credibility to a story if I can reveal the source, but if you wish I can leave your name out of it."

"Thanks, Rachel that would be appreciated. I've been supported through my PhD studies to date by a well known sports agent. He has used me to give him information on methods to ensure that athletes under perform. He has always stuck to the line that it enables him to protect his own athletes from sharp practice. Knowledge gives him an edge against anyone who might be trying to harm his stable of sportsmen and women. He claims he's particularly concerned about betting cartels in Asia who might be finding ways of slowing athletes down. Not sufficiently to stop them running, but enough for them to lose a few seconds and therefore significantly change the betting odds. My very real concern is I now believe he could be the one damaging the chances for other athletes. There have been a couple of occasions when he has asked me to do things which could easily result in him having the ability to act against other athletes. Obviously I am very concerned for the athletes and any damage he may cause them. As importantly, I am concerned about the hollow victory that his athlete could achieve as a result of his illegal actions. Potentially it could be a very dirty business all round."

"Jim, you say potentially. What hard evidence do you have that could back up your concerns?"

"This is where it gets a bit tricky, because to bring me to this point I've had to resort to somewhat illegal methods. Based on what I've heard and seen, I'm now pretty confident that he has plans to reduce the chances of a number of key athletes, all likely to make the Olympic 1500 metre final."

"Jim, you've got my interest, but so far you haven't given anything away which I could use. Are you going to give me names or am I to play a guessing game with you?"

"I'm sorry Rachel, but I just find this whole thing sort of difficult. I realise that once I give you names then the whole thing gets out of my control."

"Jim," said Rachel, putting a reassuring hand on his arm, "I know where you're coming from. Why don't you just drip feed me a bit more information, leaving out names at this stage. Then if it becomes necessary, you can commit or not at that point?"

"OK," said Jim, "that sounds very reasonable. I've known this sports agent for over two years, ever since starting my PhD studies. My thesis was concerned with methods of cheating in sports, covering the range from drug control, mechanical aids and perfectly legal enhancements such as the use of probiotics. I expected my research to uncover a number of sharp practices and even to move into the realms of those who could gain from it outside of the athletes themselves. I certainly wasn't aware of the massive involvement of the betting fraternity. Perhaps it shouldn't have been too much of a surprise when you consider the activities of some members of the South African and Pakistani cricket teams. Anyway my Prof didn't seem that interested in my work apart from a regular update on his pet subject of drugs in sport and most of my dealings have been with the sports agent I mentioned earlier."

"Sorry to interject, Jim, but you haven't actually mentioned the agent by name as yet."

"No, sorry Rachel, but let me come to that. This guy has a fairly large stable of athletes from a number of different sports, mainly football and athletics. His key athlete is a middle distance runner, currently number one in Britain and pushing for a medal in August. The other athletes in his event have done it all. They are much more experienced in the major events, having won Olympic and world medals. But the names on the podium and the order are still a lottery. There has rarely been an Olympic event where the outcome is so uncertain. I would estimate that any one of five athletes could take gold and you know as well as me what that could mean."

"Yes, but surely Jim this is all in the public domain," said Rachel, somewhat exasperated. "You're not telling me anything new."

"OK, sorry. The truth is that I now believe that this person is deliberately planning to use methods to slow down all the other expected finalists so that his own athlete will have a major advantage. His methods may be subtle or direct, ingenious or blatant, but if they come off then Britain could have a new Olympic champion who has won unfairly. That sort of sticks in the gullet."

"Of course, of course," said Rachel, beginning to wonder if she would ever get a story out of this seemingly reluctant young man. "Tell me why you have these concerns."

"The agent's name is Nigel Gressley and the athlete who is by far his biggest prospect is Josh Silverman, the British 1500 metre champion."

Rachel could hardly contain herself at this revelation. Although at this stage the apparently innocuous statement had no substance, the name Josh Silverman hit her like a sledgehammer. She visibly blanched at the mention of Josh's name and had difficulty in maintaining her focus on what was being said.

"Jim, you said Josh Silverman was involved in this suspected scandal?"

"No Rachel, far from it. Silverman is likely to be the last person to know. My intelligence suggests that Gressley is working alone, or potentially using a few other people. It has been for some months now that I've suspected that Gressley was not just using information to protect his own athletes from external threat. He may even have started to use me with that in mind but I'm confident that the situation has changed."

"You talk about intelligence, Jim, what exactly do you mean?"

"I can't claim to be very proud of my methods, Rachel, in fact I'm somewhat ashamed. I've been using phone tapping to confirm my intuition."

"But Jim, surely you know the impact if this was ever exposed?"

"Absolutely and I'm not prepared to reveal my source."

"Easily said, Jim, easily said. As a journalist I would adopt exactly the same stance. But you have to be aware that in a court of law, you may have to reveal your source when under oath."

"God, I hope it doesn't come to that, and anyway if you use the story, I would cover for my source and claim it was me doing the hacking."

"Jim, moving on. If I'm to take this story, you've got to give me a lot more than an intuition and a bit of phone hacking. What is this guy Nigel Gressley up to?"

"OK, let's go through Silverman's main competitors. Jamil Ngeny is a real threat and I'm convinced that Gressley plans to somehow get him to take EPO."

"And what's his source of EPO, Jim?"

"Hmm, that's somewhat embarrassing. Gressley asked me to get some for him, in the guise that he wanted to be able to show his athletes what it actually looks like. What I ended up giving him was a vial of harmless saline, made to look like the real thing and even if injected would do no damage. I assume that his plan is to find a way to get Ngeny to drink it and get him disqualified immediately prior or after the Olympic final. This would very much depend on how he can get access to Ngeny's meals or drinks."

"But beyond that nothing?"

"Not in the case of Ngeny and EPO. He doesn't seem to find

it necessary to share this with anyone, at least not by phone. This rather suggests that if he is going to act, it will be alone."

"So you've been monitoring Gressley's phone for some time?"

"Actually, Rachel, only since I returned from Hong Kong and started to suspect his motives were not as he described them."

"And are you the one doing the hacking?"

"Not up to now. As I was saying earlier, it's best to keep things one stage removed. The truth is, Rachel, I've now got the software to do the hacking myself, but have yet to use it."

"OK, to be honest I don't really want to know. The term 'a reliable source' ought to cover this well enough. So let's recap. You have one athlete potentially under threat, a major opponent of Josh Silverman. You suspect, based on a request from Nigel Gressley for a sample of EPO, that he could be banned if Gressley manages to get this EPO into him. The only snag is that Gressley believes he has EPO and if he did succeed in getting Ngeny to take it, nothing will happen because you cannot be banned for having salt in your body. Come on Jim, you haven't really got a story at all. If you had given Gressley EPO and he was caught in the act of trying to administer it in some way to Ngeny, then you do have a story. Do you get my drift? It's not just speculative; it just isn't going to happen, because of what you've done."

"Rachel, I accept what you're saying, but there is much more to tell. Another real possibility for a medal is Angelo Benito, the Italian. As you know he had a pretty good reputation for womanising, some high profile and many less so. Nigel Gressley plans to set him up with a woman on the night before the 1500 metre final and has chosen with care Benito's personal predilection for young Asian girls."

"Interesting," Rachel replied, "and is this speculation or can you give me some solid evidence?"

"My source, based on hacking into Gressley's phone, is a transcript with a certain owner of an escort agency by the name of Bryn Perry. Gressley has organised for a suitable girl to be available and very willing at the Hampton Lodge, Surrey, which is where the Italian team will be staying right up to the day they compete."

"And this phone transcript, it makes this clear and could not be interpreted any differently?"

"Absolutely," said Jim with renewed confidence, "even for someone like Nigel Gressley it's difficult to organise something like that without making it very clear."

"Fine," said Rachel, now showing more interest in a potential story, "and do you have more?"

"Absolutely," Jim replied, now warming to the task and starting to feel his personal concerns lighten as he offloaded to Rachel. "The next athlete Gressley's attacking is Khalid Gabet."

"I know all about him," Rachel interjected, "he often trains with Josh Silverman when he's on the European circuit."

"Exactly, and a nicer guy you couldn't wish to meet from what I hear."

"So what's Gressley up to with Gabet. He sounds a difficult nut to crack short of direct assault or does he plan to poison him?" Rachel said with an element of sarcasm.

"No Gressley's plan is more subtle for Gabet. He plans to send him a text message on his personal mobile a few hours before the final. The message will claim that two of his children back home have been kidnapped. It will cause Gabet absolute devastation and is bound to cause him to lose focus entirely. Especially as he'll try to get confirmation of it right up to the point he has to race – assuming he is even able to race. With his family back in the Atlas Mountains in some remote ranch he will be in an impossible situation."

"Sounds pretty sinister, Jim, so what's your evidence on this one?"

"Gressley was stupid enough to prepare the text now and leave it in his messages file on his mobile. My hacker friend found it there and it's clear it's ready to launch at precisely the right time."

"And can I assume that you have a transcript of this as well, Jim?"

"Of course, although I accept that Gressley could delete it at any time."

"That's not a problem," said Rachel with a knowing smile, "there are always methods of getting back to the original, whatever Gressley thinks he's done. Right Jim, you're starting to seriously interest me. Do you have more?"

"There are eight athletes all capable of getting a medal in the 1500 metre Olympic final. I've covered three of them in Gabet, Benito and Ngeny. Fortunately Gressley is using a single mobile. My contact is monitoring all his calls so it's fairly straight forward to obtain incriminating evidence. Apart from Josh Silverman, who'd be the last person to be tampered with as Gressley's his agent, that only leaves Jose Carrera, Lui Ho and the three Americans. I've got relatively little on Carrera as such, except a very mysterious email from Gressley to Carrera's sponsors in Portland."

"Hey slow down, Jim, you're now talking about emails. Don't tell me you're hacking into those as well?"

"Not me entirely, Rachel. As I told you this isn't really my scene, but yes my contact has also been hacking into Gressley's emails and a damn good job too. Gressley recently took a flying trip to Portland, to the Nike headquarters. The extent of what he did there is largely unknown, but my suspicions were raised as not a single one of Gressley's athletes, including the footballers, use Nike kit. Anyway the gist of the email was to thank the vice-president of Nike, basically the head of marketing, for letting him have Nike running shoes for Josh Silverman."

At Jim's second mention of Josh Silverman, Rachel once again felt her throat go dry and the skin at the back of her neck go uncomfortably clammy. She took a sip of her Perrier water and involuntarily wiped the back of her neck with a delicate white handkerchief she took from her sleeve.

"So," she hesitated, leaning forward slightly as if guarding a secret, "what do you think this is all about?"

"Goodness only knows, "said Jim, "I'm pretty sure that Silverman is under contract to Asics at the moment and I find it hard to believe that his contract would not extend to way beyond the Olympic Games, especially if he got a medal."

"That's easy to check, Jim, you can leave that one with me. But more importantly, what's the significance of Gressley being involved with Nike and Josh Silverman?"

"Well clearly I'm not privy to Silverman's contract arrangements, but my real concern is that these shoes are not meant for Silverman at all."

"Jim, you're losing me again. You just said that you've an email thanking Nike for giving shoes to Josh Silverman and now you're saying they're not for him."

"OK, Rachel, it's pure speculation, but one of the ways that any unscrupulous individual could slow someone down would be to doctor their shoes. At this level a small change could be enough to slow an athlete down by a few seconds and lose him a medal. I feel somewhat responsible for this possibility because I actually suggested this course of action to Nigel Gressley as part of my briefing to him. You have to understand that my PhD topic has to cover any method possible to decrease an athlete's chances of success. This was one I put to Gressley some time ago and he now has the potential to do just that. You see Rachel, with Carrera being under contract to Nike, it is now possible for Gressley to find a away to alter the shoes he has obtained on the pretext of them being for Silverman. Basically the doctored shoes only have to change Carerra's running style by a fraction, even if they still feel reasonably comfortable, and the damage is done. Carrera is out of contention. Problem solved and once again it increases his own athlete's chances of success dramatically."

"And of course," said Rachel, her voice noticeably unsteady, "Gressley's athlete is Josh Silverman."

"Exactly, Rachel. You must by now be starting to see the way this is all going. Nigel Gressley is systematically finding ways to influence all serious competitors for Silverman, so his man wins gold. It's a frightening prospect and frankly it stinks."

Rachel felt physically sick, but just managed to retain her composure sufficiently to look up at Jim, who by now felt he was at least winning the battle of acceptance over Rachel's initial reluctance to hear him out.

"Is there more?" enquired Rachel in a soft tone, very different from her more demanding attitude earlier in the meeting.

"I'm afraid there is," said Jim, now not wanting to lose the initiative, "in the top six this only leaves Lui Ho the Chinese champion. He's a bit of an unknown on the international scene but he's been posting some phenomenal times at home. He'll be coming to the Games with very little high level competitive experience, but based on his times, a real prospect for a medal. It just happens that my contact, who is hacking into Gressley's phone and computer, has very good reason to hate the Chinese and will do anything to attack their regime. To be honest with you, Rachel, without him on board, I doubt if I could give you much information at all."

"So what can your contact tell us about what Gressley is up to with Ho?" said Rachel, pleased that the discussion had moved away from Josh Silverman.

"This is potentially the most serious of all," said Jim, "because this is the only case that Gressley seems to be planning a direct physical assault. Once again by hacking into his mobile phone I have strong evidence that Gressley is planning to inject something into Ho's leg which will be damaging without necessarily stopping him running."

"And how do you suppose this is going to happen?" enquired

Rachel with a hint of scepticism, "I cannot imagine a situation where Ho or any of his coaching squad are going to leave him unattended."

"Sure," said Jim, recognising this obvious limitation, "I've only got evidence of his intent, not the details of when and where. The phone messages and texts that have been intercepted cover a series of guarded arrangements between Gressley and what appears to be a Taiwanese gang leader, based somewhere in London. It's pretty clear from what's been said that Gressley has hired someone to do his dirty work and a deal has been struck."

"A deal?" Rachel prompted "What exactly do you mean by a deal?"

"It appears that at some stage during the Games, a hit man arranged by this gang leader is going to incapacitate Ho with a taser. While he is unconscious, which is no more than a minute or two, Ho will be injected with something like hydrocortisone into his Achilles tendon. It is bound to cause at the very least local swelling and will make his tendon pretty stiff for a day or two. He certainly won't be able to train properly, but will probably have recovered sufficiently to compete. Even assuming my analysis is correct then any load on the tendon will cause him not so much pain, but discomfort. If he races, he will be conscious of it the whole time, a perfect scenario for a poor race performance. The success or otherwise of this particular assault will be timing. Too early and Ho could recover completely, too late and he would have to withdraw. You see what's clever about all these scenarios, Rachel, is that Gressley isn't preventing them from competing, he's just finding ways to slow them down."

"Jim, I need to be absolutely clear on this one. Can you show me transcripts of these texts, phone messages and emails which will incontrovertibly support what you're saying?"

"Rachel, remember I chose to meet you, not the other way round. I'd expect you to check everything I've told you using your media contacts. I'm desperately trying to walk away from this and would be more than happy to hand everything over to you."

"Jim, you've got to realise it's not that easy. Much of your critical information has come by illegal means. Since the furore over the hacking by News International last year, my editor would never sanction any of our people doing the same, even for a story of this importance. If I ran this, I would just have to trust my source which is you and your contact. It's you guys who are providing the crucial evidence. For all I know your hacker may have some deep seated antagonism for, say, 1500 metre runners and is making the whole thing up."

"Trust me Rachel. My contact is very reluctant to get involved in this whole business, but he, like me, now sees the importance of what's going on. I think in truth you do too. I appreciate your caution, but time is running out. I don't even know the best way to play the whole thing. I honestly thought of taking it to the police, but felt that there was still some reasonable doubt. I've really come to you for a second opinion."

"Jim, I appreciate everything you've done and especially talking to me. You understand that I'll have to take advice myself for a story of this magnitude but I'll keep you fully informed."

"But Rachel, we haven't finished yet. You're giving me the impression that this meeting is almost over, but you're forgetting the three Americans who could easily make the final."

"I'm sorry, Jim. I was getting distracted by the implications of the whole thing. Don't tell me that Gressley has worked out a way of stopping them perform to their optimum?"

"I suspect so, but once again it's fairly speculative and there's certainly not sufficient evidence to pull in the police." Jim paused, not sure whether he should continue with his considerably weaker evidence against Nigel Gressley.

"Jim you cannot go this far without giving me the full picture. Even if you're in some doubt about Gressley's involvement, it needs to be said."

"OK. You'll recall that in the Commonwealth Games two years ago in New Delhi, the British swimming team was severely compromised by a mysterious bug that hit many of our top swimmers. Some of our best prospects for medals underperformed and were even sick following their races. They blamed food poisoning; the traditional 'Delhi belly' got the blame. Well Gressley was there for the Games and had easy access to our swim team. He was supposedly setting up agent's rights with some up and coming swimmers, although interestingly nothing ever came of it. Now that in itself is no crime and it's quite possible that the bug that hit our swimming team was a local issue as is often the case in India. However, and this is where it really becomes interesting, my contact has picked up an email from Gressley to a guy called Jed Burnage, which starts to suggest that something much more sinister could be going on."

Rachel leaned forward and scratched the side of her head, a sure sign that her full interest had returned. She was not going to cut this particular meeting short, whatever else she planned to do that day.

"Jed Burnage has some form, six years in Wormwood scrubs to be exact. Gressley used him as the front man to break into Baxter Healthcare, a drugs trials company based in High Wycombe. They use a private suite in a local hospital to trial drugs once they move to the human testing stage. Rachel, you're well aware of these companies because you covered the so called 'elephant man' story when the trials company Paraxel was involved in some near fatalities a few years back."

"Of course I do. That story kept me on the front page for over a week."

"Baxter Healthcare operates in the same way but is much smaller and most of their work involves out patients only, mainly working through GP practices. Anyway this company seems to deal mainly in low level infections, 'flu and the like. Once again, based on a combination of emails, texts and phone conversations, I've established that Gressley has managed to get hold of a virulent strain of bacteria and I'm convinced that he plans to infect the Americans, causing them to suffer symptoms just like food poisoning. The Americans always stick together at international meetings. It's part of their supportive culture. So Gressley only has to find the right time and place to release the bacteria and bingo, you have a group of American athletes all down with what looks like food poisoning. Another case of underperforming without the Americans being sufficiently ill to withdraw totally. Just like happened in New Delhi. The dress rehearsal worked perfectly with no one suspecting anything but a nasty case of local food poisoning. It was clear that Gressley got the stuff before the Commonwealth Games. How he will obtain more is open to speculation, but I suppose one option is to go back to Jed Burnage and Baxter Healthcare. The odd thing is I've got no evidence of him doing so. It's possible that he has some of it left over from 2010 and plans to use that. It's the one thing that can hit a group of people at once and is totally logical that the Americans are his target."

"I accept the logic, Jim, but proof is quite another thing," said Rachel.

"Rachel, I can't offer you any more proof at this time. In fact, I have a strong suspicion that Gressley may only be using this bacterial infection as a back up to something else. For all I know, he may already have dealt with the Americans. Let's face it, this week is absolutely critical. Gressley is playing for very high stakes. He's investing a huge amount of both cash and risk to his reputation in what I'm convinced is one of the most despicable scams imaginable. There'll be billions of people worldwide watching the 1500 metre final on TV and the whole thing could be a sham with the odds heavily weighed on the only athlete who has not been tampered with, namely Josh

Silverman."

Rachel could hardly breathe. She felt a constriction in her throat and had to concentrate hard to force a single swallow. The name Josh Silverman, one she had taken for granted for the last three years of her life, was now so closely associated with every element of this incredible story that she almost collapsed. Summoning every ounce of her resolve she slowly turned to Jim Stringer and weakly uttered "Jim, forgive my initial reluctance to accept what you were saying. I'm happy to accept everything you say in good faith and fully appreciate what you have been through to bring this all to my attention. Clearly I'll need to run a few checks and talk to my editor before taking any action. You can appreciate that just like Gressley, timing is everything. If I act too quickly he could cover his tracks and the whole case could evaporate. If anything further comes up I would appreciate you letting me know day or night."

Rachel retrieved a personal card from her purse and gave it to Jim. "This is my direct line. I reiterate, Jim, day or night." Using the arms of her chair to get unsteadily to her feet, Rachel slowly stood up and smiled weakly at Jim. She held out a hand, but then felt impelled to move closer and kissed Jim lightly on the cheek.

"Thank you," she whispered, "thank you."

Rachel turned, placed her notebook in her bag with unusual care, and headed out to the still bright sunlight of York Way. She strode quickly into King's Cross station wondering how and when she was going to share this incredible story with her fiancé, Josh Silverman.

Chapter 20

Rachel was excited at the prospect of seeing James Clancy, her editor, a man with a fearsome reputation, yet one who was clearly comfortable in his own skin. He had been the editor-in-chief of the Evening Standard for 15 years, had survived numerous changes of ownership and had overseen the difficult transition from being London's main evening paper to one of many free broadsheets now littering the underground and streets of the city. Rachel's excitement was somewhat modulated by her concerns regarding the source of her copy, especially the use of 'phone and computer hacking.

"Rachel, do come in," welcomed Clancy, "I really liked your piece on Oryxoil and their shady dealings with the Libyan government."

"Thank you, sir," Rachel replied, not quite sure how to address one of the most respected men in Fleet Street. Rachel had met Clancy before and the man never seemed to change. His clothing and physical appearance usually gave the impression he had dressed in a hurry. He was always dressed in corduroy slacks, summer or winter, a shirt with his tie permanently knotted a few inches below the neck and an open waistcoat of an indistinguishable colour.

"How do you enjoy investigative journalism, Rachel? You know it's where I started in the trade, although they probably called it something else back then."

"I like it very much, but it does seem to bring with it some ethical dilemmas which I sometimes find quite tough."

"Making the right call can be difficult at times, especially when the future of careers or families can be at stake. I pride myself that here at the Evening Standard we get it right ninety five percent of the time, but we still have to live with the five percent we get wrong. Anyway, I'm sure you're not here to discuss my troubles, what can I do for you?"

"Mr Clancy, I think I'm on to a massive story. It concerns a deliberate and highly organised attempt to substantially influence the outcome of the 1500 metre final which is now only days away. The sports agent representing our British hope, Josh Silverman, is planning to influence all the other finalists so they cannot run their best on the day. He intends for them all to be in the race, but each one will have been tampered with sufficiently to be incapable of their best performance."

James Clancy moved from his usual position of resting one buttock on the front edge of his desk to sitting in his well-worn chair. He waved his hand indicating for Rachel to sit on the only other chair in the cramped office.

"Sounds interesting," said Clancy, "what's the quality rating of your sources?"

"About B2," Rachel replied. "The main source has no grudge, just honest Joe doing his duty. The big problem, Mr Clancy, and why I wanted to speak to you directly, is that my source has been hacking into both a 'phone and the internet."

"But not you Rachel, you've not checked the information this way yourself?"

"No way, sir, not after the News of the World fiasco last year."

"So what's your back up, Rachel, or is it all word of mouth?"

"I have transcripts of all the relevant phone calls and emails. I've also got a video of an exchange taking place. It's pretty solid."

"And all this is one removed from us – you're sure about that?"

"Better than that really sir. My source is not technically capable of doing this himself, so he uses a friend to gather the information."

"OK. It sounds solid enough to me. Give me the copy and half an hour to make a few checks with our legal boys. Go and grab a coffee and we'll talk again, right here. If it's as big as you suggest we'll need to discuss timing."

Rachel left the room, glad that the meeting was over. Feeling the sweat on her brow and neck, she headed to the toilet wanting to freshen up before meeting Clancy again. It seemed like the longest thirty minutes of her life and although the canteen was full and the coffee good, she could concentrate on neither colleagues nor her drink.

"Hey Rachel," said a friendly voice, "you with us today?" Rachel was startled by the sudden intrusion into her private thoughts.

"Sorry Dick, I was miles away. I have to see James Clancy in ten minutes and I was a little out of it."

"No probs," said Dick cheerfully, "they say his bark is worse than his bite, but knowing you Rachel, it'll be some devilish project he wants you to tackle. He seems to trust you with stirring up hornets' nests."

"Could be," said Rachel, not wanting to give anything away, "I guess I'll know my fate soon enough." She looked at her watch as she spoke.

"Dick, sorry to appear rude, but I need to get along." And then to try not to offend too much, she added "You still covering track and field?"

"Of course I am, Rachel. That's why you rarely see me here. Got the big one soon, 1500 metre final. Hey that reminds me, are you still seeing Silverman? Can you get me an exclusive after the final?" Rachel just smiled.

"Call his agent, Dick," but added as an afterthought, "If I see him, I'll put in a good word."

"Best of luck with Clancy," was the final riposte as Rachel headed out of the door. Five minutes later, Rachel Rosen was back outside the editor's office. Through the glass door she could see that he was back to his usual position sitting on the edge of his desk, telephone clamped to his left ear. He saw Rachel and beckoned her in. She stood waiting patiently, but Clancy waved her to a seat.

"Just do it," he finally said and placed the 'phone firmly on the handset.

"Rachel, this is very special. I'm going to run a couple of extra checks but best you're not involved. It will authenticate not add a thing to your piece. The copy is fine, very professional. The question is when exactly to publish? Your evidence is incredibly compelling but the one flaw in the whole piece is that we have no evidence that anything Gressley planned has actually taken place."

"But, Mr Clancy..................."

"But," interrupted Clancy, "the piece is strong enough as it stands. I've checked with our lawyers. We are definitely going to print. The question is when. When it goes public, this story will go viral. We've got to be ready for the backlash, with follow ups on all the athletes involved. I may even decide to run the piece without naming Gressley and then hit him with the next edition. Sorry Rachel, I'm getting carried away. What's your take on this?"

"Mr Clancy, timing is critical. Some of the planned activities by Gressley are literally hours before the event. Anything prior to this would blow it out of the water. Basically it's got to be after the final, so we've got to let events take place as planned. The final is on Thursday at 3.00pm. We could make the evening edition of the paper if everything is in place. The papers will be hitting the streets as the award ceremony is being held late in the afternoon."

"OK, Rachel. I'll buy that. So barring a major terrorist attack, we'll run it as the top story, hopefully in parallel with the gold medal success of our own athlete."

"Terrorist attack, Mr Clancy?"

"A joke, Rachel, a joke. Oh Rachel, one last thing. I need a copy of the full details of your investigation, transcripts, the lot. No need to reveal your sources just yet. I trust you."

Rachel left the building troubled. There were times in her job when personal and professional issues clashed dangerously. This was without question one of them and she was torn. She saw no immediate resolution. She trusted that God, in his own time, would guide her. It remained to see just how.

CHAPTER 21

July 30th, 2012
Olympic Village, London, UK

Jim Stringer's selection for the British boxing squad was both a surprise to himself and a testimony to his restorative powers. After the damage to his ribs in Hong Kong, Jim thought that his chances were minimal. The combination of his physiotherapist's skills, the cocktail of anti-inflammatory drugs and a punishing training routine brought him back to a level of fitness that was unexpected, even to the most optimistic individual. The GB boxing squad had been pencilled in since the ABA championships, but in Jim's weight category, the final decision was made late in the day, largely as a result of his injury. He had fought over three rounds in a gruelling contest where his opponent had tried his best to work on his weakened ribs. Perversely that had worked to Jim's advantage, because it was expected. Jim had been able to counter the offensive in the lower thorax with some excellent blows to the head that were scoring points with comparative ease. The outcome was a unanimous decision and Jim's reward was a place in the Olympic squad. Having shared his concerns about Nigel Gressley with Rachel, Jim felt freer to concentrate on the early rounds of the Olympic boxing tournament and to bring himself to peak fitness for the event. One thing was for certain, after all the issues surrounding his trip to Hong Kong and the anguish associated with Gressley, Jim had every intention of enjoying the camaraderie of the Olympic village.

It was therefore with considerable shock that Jim spotted

none other than Nigel Gressley going into one of the other accommodation blocks in the Olympic village. Jim was in his room overlooking the short causeway which led up to the next block. He was enjoying a cup of coffee and idly watching the coming and going from the nearby railway station. Jim was amazed when Nigel, carrying a small parcel, entered the next block. Jim's initial reaction was to do nothing; frankly he had enough of Gressley and would have been happy never to see him again. Something deep down made Jim uncomfortable and he felt impelled to act. Finishing his coffee in one gulp, Jim raced down the stairs and into the next block. The security guard at the turnstile stopped Jim dead in his tracks, demanding his pass. It was clear that Jim could get no further so ran back to his room to collect his pass. Returning with this, Jim still needed to go through the lengthy process of registration as this was not his allotted residence. After a delay of five minutes he was able to get into the building and, assuming that Gressley was aiming for Jose Carrera's room, he headed up the stairs to the Cuban team's floor. Arriving slightly out of breath at the third floor, Jim turned towards the lift to find Gressley waiting for the doors to open.

"Nigel, what on earth are you doing here?" Jim exclaimed, perhaps a little more aggressively than intended.

Gressley turned, took a moment to regain his composure and looking at Jim, stuttered "I was just delivering something."

"But how on earth did you get in here?" said Jim, "Security is incredibly tight. I know that. Anyway what do you mean by delivering something? It sounds pretty mysterious."

"Oh, I am simply acting as a messenger for a colleague in America. Could have used the post of course, but in this case speed was of the essence. Nothing to hide Jim, it was some essential kit for one of the Cuban team. And I don't mind admitting I was paid well for the task. Anyway Jim, must go. Good to see you again."

The lift arrived and Nigel Gressley turned away soon to be engulfed in the chasm of the lift shaft.

Jim turned around and headed straight for Jose Carerra's room. He banged his fist on the door and didn't stop until Carerra opened it.

"Mr Carrera," said Jim, "I'm sorry to trouble you but I need to tell you something."

"Hey calm down young man." was Carrera's reply. "What's on your mind?"

"It's just that I understand that you've just had a delivery, a box of some type."

"Sure," said Carrera, "some guy just gave me a new pair of shoes, straight from Nike. Fabulous. They're over here. Let me show you."

The package was already unwrapped and Carrera showed Jim the new shoes with obvious pride.

"What do you think," he said, "gold medal material I'd say."

"Would you mind if I had a closer look," Jim said, picking up the shoes with evident care.

"Sure, they're classic."

"Mr Carrera, would you allow me to compare these with your current shoes just for a minute?"

"I can't quite see why, young man, but sure. My regular pair are in my bag over there. Can I get you a drink or anything?"

"No thanks, Mr Carrera, if you don't mind I just want to look closely at the inside of these shoes. To be honest I'm really concerned that your shoes may have been tampered with. If you feel inside carefully, Mr Carrera, you should be able to detect a clear difference between the inserts in the instep."

Carrera felt inside the shoes and probed the exact position of the instep with considerable care. He soon noticed the way the instep supports had been switched from left to right.

"Hey you're right. How on earth did you know about this?"

"It's a long story, too long really, but the important thing is you needed to check out those shoes very carefully before you ever consider wearing them."

"Oh don't worry. I had no intention whatever of using those new ones, in spite of the insistence of the guy from Nike who delivered them."

"The guy from Nike?"

"Yes the fat guy who brought these over for me from the States. He made a big play about the importance of using them in the final. Something about the new branding and a massive commercial strategy. Claimed it would be worth a huge sum of money both to Nike and me. I can tell you no way. He must have been stupid. I never wear a new pair of shoes until I've trained in them for quite some time. This close to the Olympic final, it would be most unlikely for me to even consider them. They're a beautiful pair of shoes and my plan was to take them to the track and carry them in the award ceremony. Nike would love that. Admittedly there was a slim chance I would wear them, depending on my training programme from now on in. I've still no idea how you came by this information but really appreciate your intervention. Say, I've just realised, you haven't even given me your name."

"Jim Stringer, on the British boxing squad. Good to meet you."

"Well thanks, Jim, you've done me a great service. After the final, I'll report back to Nike and see what the heck was going on here."

Jim could easily have stayed but was increasingly uncomfortable about Gressley's ability to move around the athletes' village at will. What if he was planning any other malicious activity? Jim shook Carrera's hand warmly and headed back down to the ground floor. As Jim entered the dining hall, he was alarmed to see Gressley on the far side of the hall near the main servery. Stepping back behind a column so as not to be seen, Jim watched Gressley with care.

Somehow Gressley then contrived to sit close to Jamil Ngeny, on the opposite side of the long wooden tables used in this section of the hall. Gressley had three glasses of water on his tray along with a pile of pasta and two bananas. Gressley sat quietly playing with the pasta, but watching Ngeny's every movement. Jim watched, anticipating that Gressley would find some way of doctoring Ngeny's drink. Most of the athlete's were leaving their food on the trays and Ngeny looked as though he would do the same. Gressley placed his food and glasses on the table and seemed to suggest to Ngeny that he did the same, presumably suggesting that it would give both diners more room. Ngeny shrugged his shoulders as though it didn't matter much to him. Gressley smiled and even started to lift Ngeny's food off his tray. Then Jim saw the switch, worthy of a professional magician. Gressley lifted the near edge of Ngeny's tray obscuring the glasses of water. He rapidly moved one of his water glasses away from him while pulling Ngeny's glass close to his own dish of pasta. He then lifted the tray and propped it against his chair along with his own. Straightening the glasses up completed the switch and Jim observed with concern that Ngeny was almost bound to drink the one placed there by Gressley. Jim had little doubt in his mind that Ngeny was about to drink water well laced with EPO and would unwittingly be disqualified for using an illegal drug. Jim quickly considered the options and was relieved to see that Gressley appeared to be leaving. Jim assumed that Gressley was satisfied with his illicit handiwork and was getting out before arousing any suspicion. As Gressley left the dining hall, Jim grabbed a tray from the nearest trolley and went swiftly over to Gressley's abandoned food. He stacked Gressley's pasta, bananas and drinks on to the tray and then added Ngeny's drink to the tray, turning away as he did so. Ngeny's response was rapid and he demanded his drink back. Jim apologised profusely and returned a different glass to the bemused athlete. Jim walked away, keeping a finger touching the one that Gressley had switched. He returned to the servery, collected one of the empty plastic bottles emblazoned with the logo of the games sponsor, Coca Cola. The offending drink was carefully poured into the flask and Jim left the dining hall, well satisfied with his second intervention of the day. The drink would be sent to Rachel for analysis, providing further evidence of Gressley's treachery. As Jim left the building he checked the visitors' book and was relieved to see that the Nike representative, signed in under the name of N.Crossley, had already left the building.

Jim returned to his own room feeling exhausted from the emotional involvement of the morning. He checked the email account he had established solely to deal with the two characters he had met in Macau and Dubai when researching the gambling cartels. To date there had been no traffic at all on this account, so Jim was somewhat surprised to receive emails from both sources within 24 hours. He guessed that as it was now just days before the Olympic final and all the favourites were in contention, the gambling fraternity would be reaching fever pitch. Jim had a serious dilemma. He knew that Nigel Gressley's plans to ruin the prospects of most of the finalists in the 1500 metres placed Josh Silverman in a strong position. He also knew that the highly secret work at Loughborough University had the potential to make Silverman go faster than ever before. The cocktail of totally legal substances that were being tested on Silverman included common products such as bicarbonate of soda, propolis, probiotics and epicatechin found in dark chocolate. The balanced combination of these products was designed to delay the time in the race when Josh would run out of fuel. But they would only work under true racing conditions. The research in the laboratory had been encouraging, but the scientists at Loughborough could not replicate the extreme conditions of an international race and its massive disruption to stress hormones. Jim was in a no win situation, brought upon by his own naivety and not preparing himself adequately for his meetings abroad. He now had £20,000, safely banked away from the prying eyes of anyone who may be interested in such an amount. He mulled over the notion of returning the money and quitting his whole involvement with such unsavoury characters, but the temptation was too great. He was unlikely to earn this amount of money in a whole year for a long time, yet there were clear risks of reprisals if things went wrong. Jim shuddered as he recalled what happened in Hong Kong and how near it was to losing him a place in the GB team. Jim knew that his double intervention that morning had swung the pendulum further away from Josh Silverman's ultimate success. Both Ngeny and Carrera could easily have been eliminated from serious contention had Jim not spotted Gressley in the athletes' village. The bookmakers' odds on Silverman winning the final were still modest and there was potential for a huge amount of money to be made if he did. Jim for the second time that day had to weigh up the options. If he predicted Silverman to win, and he did, then the overseas gamblers would make a killing. If he said Silverman was unlikely to win, then the betting would switch to the other finalists with the Asian gamblers probably favouring Ho. The trouble was that Jim now had inside information that Ho had either been, or would be assaulted by Gressley or one of his less desirable contacts. The options for the Arabian gamblers were more uncertain, but in a way that didn't matter. It was really down to whether or not Silverman would outperform the others on the day. Jim rationalised that the likely medalists were Ngeny, Carrera, Gabet, Ho, Benito and the Americans. In spite of Gressley's best efforts, two of them were now known to be in great shape, the semi-finals proved that. Due to Jim's intervention, they were still very much on top of their game and Gressley had lost his chance to change things. The situation for the others was unknown. Gressley could have had far more success in stopping them perform. On balance the chance of Silverman winning the gold medal was still slight. His semi-final performance only put him in sixth place and he had persisted in his style of leading from the gun. Jim's understanding from the Loughborough scientists was that this had to change. If their theory of maintaining the fuel supply to those precious legs until the last 200 metres was correct, then Silverman could no longer approach the final in his usual style. Jim decided that the risk was too great. He emailed his contacts in Dubai and Macau, stating that in his opinion the experiment was unproven and his confidence in Silverman even getting a medal was weak. In the end, he said, it was their choice, but he couldn't recommend from what he had seen or heard that Silverman was the best prospect. He had few regrets in life, but getting involved in betting syndicates was one of them. He knew that regret was a wasted emotion, but it leant heavily on him. As often with such feelings, he had a temporary solution. Jim Stringer headed for the practice ring and was soon prepared for some serious sparring. After 60 minutes of concentrated aggression, Jim started to feel more relaxed. Josh Silverman could not be forgotten, but Jim had his own schedule to consider and he knew that this was where his undivided attention should lie. Even so he kept coming back to his meeting with Rachel Rosen. Where would it all lead?

Chapter 22

Karl Jenkins froze momentarily as he quickly absorbed the impact of what he had seen on his screen. His training at the Army School of Languages outside Beaconsfield gave him an awareness of imminent danger. His job required more than just rapid and accurate translation, but a thorough appreciation of importance and urgency. Jenkins knew that the message on the jihadist website he had been monitoring for days was ranked critical. He instantly hit three key buttons to guarantee immediate action. The deputy head of GCHQ was the first to react, followed by a nameless senior officer in MI6's inner sanctum in Whitehall. The third response was slower, but within thirty seconds he had patched in all three to his monitor via a secure network using his unique password.

An imminent terror alert at the Olympic Stadium was to unfold in precisely one hour with a bomb to be detonated at the base of the Olympic flame. There was enough information in the stark message for all three officials to know that this was no hoax. The codes shared by Al-Qaeda's most dangerous cells were all buried in the message. The bomb itself would be sufficient to cause maximum impact. The only part that didn't add up was why the warning. The answer was simple; terror is amplified when the terrorists have control. At 4:45 in the afternoon, as the stadium was almost full to capacity, Al-Qaeda had total control.

The anti-terrorist squad put together specifically for the

Games had started their shift one hour earlier and were casually recalling last night's varied recreational activities. Their job was to prepare, to wait and to respond. At this stage, some two weeks into the Games, members of the squad were finding this posting progressively tedious. Their base was an underground bunker built within the stadium and leading off from a single door within the drug testing suite. It showed little signs of the homeliness you might associate with an army barracks or even a fire fighters' dormitory. They saw little point in adding any personal touches to a room which after the Games would be consigned to a store for the next occupants. As the emergency phones rang in the windowless room kept at precisely 20 degrees centigrade, twelve highly experienced personnel moved as one into action. Within minutes they had sufficient detail to execute a rudimentary plan which would be refined as they gained more solid information. Banks of CCTV cameras, combined with computer images of seating plans, architects' drawings and crowd movement modelling were hurriedly scanned.

"Could be interesting," understated the squad leader for the watch, a commander with 23 years experience in war zones stretching from Bosnia to Afghanistan. "The royal box, stuffed with a load of the great, the good and the wanabees is right next to the Olympic flame. It'll be fun if that lot gets blasted."

Names were never used by this elite group, partly to maintain security, but more importantly for reasons of speed. Why use four names when one colour code prompted immediate action.

"Blue to the bomb site and disarm, green to clear the royal box first and then everyone within 40 metres of the flame, red stay right here and maintain communications and back up. Switch to emergency wavelength three for all comms."

Within 60 seconds the three teams were deployed. Red team's leader was talking calmly, but urgently to key personnel within the stadium. The Metropolitan Police head of security for the Games, Assistant Commissioner James Roth, was in the stadium and was instantly summonsed. He alerted all police officers on the site and within a one kilometre zone of an imminent incident using the pre-prepared codeword, 'Cardinal'. The senior security officer for the Games organising committee, Jenny Jones, was sitting in the royal box but with her mobile phone temporarily switched off. As green team moved into position she was quickly identified and briefed. In spite of her clear concerns, there was no time for lengthy explanations. She knew that the level of authority of green team's leader was sufficient for her to cooperate without asking too many questions. Anyone watching the orderly, if reluctant, departure of the forty people from this prestigious area of the stadium could easily assume that they had been invited to the hospitality suite for a sponsorship banquet. Such an assumption was right in terms of location, but this was to be no banquet.

Blue team had by now formed a close wedge right in front of the Olympic flame, having taken just three minutes to collect essential equipment for both protection and investigation. Blue one was rapidly reviewing the tools needed, although a high level of guesswork was needed for a bomb which could be of any size and type. Blue two was now fully protected with a kevlar armour suit, a ballistic helmet reminiscent of a motorbike courier and a one inch thick visor from the peak of his helmet to the top of his breastplate. Blue two's experience with defusing improvised land-mines in Helmand Province in Afghanistan was essential, as this was likely to be the work of well trained amateurs. He knew that the first priority was to find the device in amongst the mechanism at the base of the Olympic flame. Then to establish the type of detonation mechanism, before the highly skilled and dangerous task of defusing it. As he quickly reviewed the options, he could see out of the corner of his eye that nearby spectators were slowly being moved to the exits. His focus rapidly returned and the task of removing the metal cover to the base of the flame was extremely challenging. In spite of this being a temporary structure, it had clearly been made to a very high specification. No wonder, he thought, when you consider that it held a gas pipe of some twenty millimetres and under sufficient pressure to keep a two metre flame alight for seventeen days. Blue three, who was by now kneeling just behind his colleagues was maintaining communication with red squad back in the bunker under the main stand. He was desperately trying to get confirmation that the gas to the flame was being cut off. He visibly relaxed as he saw the Olympic flame, a symbolic icon of the Games itself, first wavering, then growing smaller and eventually going out. The extinguished flame caused an audible gasp amongst the 80,000 people still remaining in the stadium. This flame, the culmination of a torch relay which had taken three months to get to this very spot, was now no more. One could sense the confusion, disbelief, anger and even resentment in the crowd. They saw the flame, quite rightly, as the centrepiece of the stadium; the one element of continuity in an ever changing maelstrom of sporting endeavour. And now it was snuffed out with no explanation or warning. The emotions associated with the extinguished flame started to gather pace and the crowd needed and deserved an explanation. Jenny Jones had now recovered her composure and was soon in a position to take decisive action. She phoned the stadium studio, the nerve centre for all internal communications. "I need a clear, slow announcement over the complete PA. Announce that there is an incident in progress and that for the time being there is no need to leave the stadium. The incident appears to be related to the gas supply to the Olympic flame. We are in the process of moving spectators nearest the flame so the repair team can continue without fear of compromising the safety of people nearby. No change that. Replace 'compromising the safety' with 'affecting the safety'. There will be a delay of 30 minutes in the athletics competition. I repeat, there is no need to leave the stadium at this time and we will keep you fully informed of progress. Read the announcement back to me please."

The duty announcer, who had been chosen from a select list of experienced staff working for BBC Sport, repeated the announcement to Ms Jones.

"Fine," she said, "go."

Within seconds the terse, worrying and partially untruthful statement was relayed throughout the stadium. Immediately the noise level, which had been muted during the announcement, increased to an unprecedented level. Not the high-pitched tone of panic or fear, more a rumble of serious debate and concern. Quickly this was followed by a different sound when all those with mobiles were phoning family or friends to report the ongoing situation.

Blue two had located the bolts embedded in the metal cover to the base of the flame. The fitters had used deep set, recessed locking nuts which needed a specialised allen key to extract them. Blue one improvised the right sized allen key by filing off the head of a socket set and handed it to blue two. Cautiously he unscrewed the bolts, taking care that they were loosened in sequence before carefully removing them from the cover.

The crew members from red squad, back in the bunker, were linked to individual communication networks. Everyone was equipped with noise-reduction headphones to guarantee maximum concentration on the incoming messages. Red one was linked by scrambled short wave to blue two to give him constant advice and support. Red two was desperately trying to make contact with the site engineer and human resources simultaneously. He was making every effort to gain intelligence on those involved in the construction of this part of the stadium, especially the base cylinder for the Olympic flame. Leaving a message on the site engineers' mobile, he eventually contacted Joan Patefield, PA to the director of human resources. She promised to ring him back with staffing details as soon as possible.

As politely as possible in the circumstances, red two spoke

into the mouthpiece. "This is urgent, seriously urgent. Please understand that we have a category A incident in the stadium and any information about the construction team associated with the flame could make a difference to the outcome."

"Understood, sir," came the sharp reply. "I shall try my best."

"Great," said red two, "remember that you can use the emergency IT system and send me any docs straight to my PC."

While red two was ringing the office and home phones of the site engineer, he was surprised by a bleep from human resources.

"Hi, it's Joan Patefield. I've got some details from the files. The fitters were all employed by British Gas, standard screening procedure, all done by British Gas, nothing from this end."

"Joan," interjected red two, with an increasing level of frustration, "it's names I need, give me names."

"The list is on its way to you. Look on your computer screen. I'm sorry but this is all I can do without higher authority."

"Joan, that's great. Thanks, I can sort things from this end."

Red two was already running a profile scan on each name, a mixture of Eastern European and British, but with one that caused the hairs on the back of red two's neck to rise inexorably. Ahmed Ghambir had a profile which was at first sight of real concern. But this information was largely circumstantial. It was only when red two punched in the code for 'detailed profile' that his initial concern was confirmed. A gas fitter employed by British Gas and installing the Olympic flame, was unbelievably a member of a known terrorist cell based in Luton.

"Shit, shit, shit," said red two, not quite under his breath, "this means we have a highly trained terrorist quite capable of making high quality bombs."

Blue two took a deep breath as he worked the cover loose now that the holding bolts had been removed. He knew that this was the trickiest part of the operation as any potential device was exposed for the first time since it was planted. He also knew that removal of the outer covering could trigger a booby trap which would detonate the bomb immediately. Blue three, in his support position immediately behind blue two, had heard red two's comments about the terrorist cell over his open line. He passed the information to his colleague working on the outer covering of the flame stanchion. Blue two nodded to indicate he had heard but didn't take his eyes off the intricate mechanism inside the cover. The primary gas pipe was clearly visible and there was a series of valves, switches and pressure gauges which blue two had already anticipated. Blue four, who until now had been standing two metres back, now moved up alongside blue one so that the three men formed a chevron around the base of the flame. His helmet was fitted with a camera and digital recorder so that every move was recorded for future analysis and training. The three men switched on powerful LED torches, also attached to their helmets, and giving them the best possible view of the inner workings of the flame stanchion. Blue one, still acting as support, carefully handed the two men in the second row of the tight knit group a full length plexiglass shield, each with a narrow slit for the eyes. Blue two, who was known for his cool in these extreme situations, could feel his heart pounding as he spotted what looked like a small thermos flask strapped behind the main gas pipe.

"Blue two to control," he said, his faltering tone giving some indication of his concern, "I have located what could be the target and at this stage and can see no secondaries. Progress on the local evacuation please?"

Green one's team had by now cleared the royal box and they were now shepherding all spectators within 40 metres of the flame to the exits.

"Green one to blue two. All spectators clear for at least 35 metres. We will hit the 40 metre zone in sixty seconds."

"Thank you green one," said blue two, now regaining his composure as he started to assess the task. He used the 60 second interval to plan his attack on the bomb and to get a scalpel and electrical pliers from blue one who was now positioned close to the other three.

"I plan to strip the tape which looks like conventional electrical tape from the left hand side of the flask. I have to assume this is the bomb. I can see no alternative and it is clearly not a component part of the mechanism for the flame. There is no space to get a mirror behind the device, so I cannot see what is at the back of it. This is likely to be the area for detonating it, but I have no choice."

"Red one here," came through blue two's cams, "We've done a search on likely weaponry for a terrorist cell of this nature but haven't a lot to go on. The only consistent feature seems to be the use of phone technology so this may be the method of detonation."

"Understood," replied blue two, who by now was slowly trimming the tape from the left side of the device. He was making very fine incisions and peeling back the tape rather as a surgeon would trim excess cartilage on the inside of a knee to relieve pressure on a joint. He ensured that the tape at the top and bottom of the flask remained in place to keep it in position while he removed the rest. It needed precision, skill and strength, because, as with many of these tasks, his arms were fully extended while he worked. He sliced away the tape from the bottom of the flask, leaving it suspended from the top only. Transferring the scalpel to his left hand, he now reached round the pipe with his right. While supporting the flask, he deftly trimmed the final piece of tape at the top of the flask. The device was now free on one side and blue two very slowly and cautiously rotated the device around the back of the pipe so that its only method of support was the tape on the right hand side. With sufficient rotation he was now able to see the back of the bomb. To his utter concern and increasing confusion he reported what this movement had now revealed.

"It appears to have a small electronic circuit attached. Coming from that is a wire which looks to have a standard USB connector into the flask."

"Any identifying marks?" interrupted red one. "Can you see anything on the circuit which we can run a search on?"

"My best guess is that it's the innards of a mobile phone. There is a battery similar to a mobile phone and what could be a SIM card in the circuitry. Standard practice is to disarm the battery in the hope that it will cut all power supply, but it's pretty well embedded. Battery may have one corner at an angle, but it's virtually impossible to see."

"Sounds more like a camera battery, which would ramp up the power," said red one, "but that doesn't help you remove it."

High in the terraces to the north of the stadium Ahmed Ghambir dialled 11 digits on his mobile phone.

CHAPTER 23

Thursday August 9th 2012, 5:00 pm
Olympic Stadium, London, UK

The eruption from the blast at the base of Olympic flame could be heard and seen from every seat in the stadium. The four soldiers from blue team were lifted three metres upwards and backwards to be dumped in a crumpled heap. At first there was no movement from anyone. Then a slow, laborious untangling of limbs could be seen, coupled with a low guttural collective moan as excruciating pain hit deep and hard. Bits of human flesh and bone were spewed in a jagged arc some ten metres around the base of the Olympic flame. The sheer horror of the blast was being played out in real time to every spectator in the stadium and to a TV audience of millions across the world. Unlike the tragedy at Hillsborough, when football fans were slowly crushed to death, this catastrophe was both concentrated and instantaneous.

Three teams of paramedics arrived within thirty seconds, having been briefed earlier by red two and on local standby. Their immediate task was to restrain movement to prevent spinal damage, to stem the now visible bleeding from gaping wounds and to prepare what was left of blue squad for airlift to hospital.

Red two, still in the bunker, had heard and seen the explosion from the camera on blue four's helmet and had immediately ordered the emergency helicopter. The air ambulance was normally stationed at Northolt but re-assigned for the period of the Games to waste ground near to East Stratford station.

It was airborne in minutes and the drone of its rotor was the only thing to be heard above the rising clamour and disjointed reaction of 80,000 spectators.

Jenny Jones and James Roth, the two most senior security staff on site, agreed rapidly on decisive action. "It is with regret that the stadium is to be emptied immediately of all spectators, volunteers and athletes," came the measured statement across the public address system. "Please remain calm and follow the instructions given to you by stewards or volunteers wearing high visibility jackets. Only staff who have received rapid response training are to remain and are to report to sector 35 as soon as the stadium is clear of all nonessential personnel. I repeat, please remain calm. Leave the stadium as instructed by the steward nearest to you and move quickly to the exit areas and away from the Olympic site. There will be no further events in the Olympic stadium today." After a few seconds, the announcer then added, almost as an afterthought, "Please give special consideration to those with children or mobility issues."

The paramedic team showed their usual high level of efficiency and skill. Even so it was clear that injuries from the bomb blast were a distasteful and unwelcome sight. Only one of them had seen such injuries before, having been on first call during the terrorist attack on a bus in Tavistock Square in 2005. A rapid review of the situation showed that blue two, who was handling the bomb as it exploded, was already dead. Blue one and three, who were immediately behind him and protected by Plexiglas shields as well as their Kevlar suits, were both in a critical state. This was where the paramedics focused their attention. They applied tourniquets to limbs where hands and feet had been ripped to shreds and rapidly set up lines to provide morphine and essential fluids Their bloodied heads were swiftly braced and at the exact moment they were being gently placed on rolling stretchers, the air ambulance landed on the centre of the track. The roar of the rotor blades just added to the intensity of the drama now unfolding to the world and it seemed strangely to give the crowds leaving the stadium a new focus away from their own personal fears and concerns. Time was the killer with injuries like this and the paramedics sped across the track to the waiting helicopter. They lifted the stretchers clear of their wheeled undercarriages to avoid the step from the track to the central grassed area. The pilot was keeping the rotors fully engaged to ensure the fastest possible exit from this localised yet vivid scene of carnage. As soon as the two stretchers were loaded, the change in the pitch of the engine signalled it was lifting off to touch down as rapidly as safety would allow on the helipad at St Thomas' hospital in Lambeth.

Blue four, slowly recovering from the shock of the blast, was being attended on the side of the track. His face was covered in the pock marks of shrapnel and his left eye was little more than an empty socket. The paramedics tried desperately to get him to hospital but in spite of the pain and deeply wounded face, he was equally desperate to remain operational. Blue four knew that with three of his team out of action, the intelligence he could provide would be essential to the ongoing situation. Having assessed his vital organs, the paramedics handed him over with considerable reluctance to James Roth who was now taking control of the bombing incident, leaving Jenny Jones the responsibility for safe evacuation of the stadium. James Roth with his 30 years experience in policing and the last ten in the Met was responsible for the emergency strategy for the Games. It was he that had planned the critical venue for category A situations and knew that he needed to assemble his team immediately. He needed to make one call only to pull all the key players together in one place. A well rehearsed cascade using the one term 'Chalfont 20' mandated Lord Cooke, Rt. Hon. Jeremy Huntingdon, Brigadier Charles Babb and Jenny Jones to all be at Chalfont Manor by eight o'clock that evening. James wanted to be there with blue four and red two and was commissioning a police helicopter to remove all three of them rapidly from the Olympic stadium. It was essential to get blue two treated by a surgical team and to work on all the options before the eight o'clock evening deadline. No one pulls in the big boys without good reason and he needed that reason and he needed it fast.

The test events for the Olympic Games had been thorough and the timing of sectors of the crowd leaving the stadium had been measured and recorded. It was not until the Games itself that the stadium had been anything like full capacity, so it had never been possible to trial an evacuation on this scale. Fortunately because the blast had been localised and spectators had been moved from the immediate area, the evacuation had caused no general panic. There were isolated incidents of people desperate to locate friends and family within the stadium, but the highly-trained stewards had total control and were firmly and politely shepherding people out of the main and emergency exits.

High up in the stands, twelve young men, all bar one with Middle East features, took what looked like a vacuum flask from an innocuous bag and carefully taped them to their seats. The seats were then tipped up, concealing each device totally from view. These men, many in the company of their families, slowly made their way to the exits, knowing that their part in the mission of devastation was over. Twelve bombs were now securely in place. Twelve bombs, twelve hours, twelve disciples of Christ, twelve sons of Jacob, twelve tribes of Israel. Vengeance comes in twelves.

CHAPTER 24

August 9th, 2012, 8.00 pm
Chalfont Manor, South Buckinghamshire, UK

Chalfont Manor was the venue where that evening the most senior and important individuals in organising the Olympic Games were to meet. Its location in the leafy lanes of South Buckinghamshire was nondescript and deliberately so. Originally a country hall of some eminence, it had one distinguishing feature which made it highly suitable for critical communications. Only the occasional dog walker, treading the paths at the rear of the site, would be aware of the four huge satellite dishes, each one oriented to different sectors of the sky. These dishes were some twenty metres in diameter and could, by a series of pneumatic valves, be positioned to transmit and receive throughout the world. Their original purpose was to broadcast to the troops via the BBC on such programmes as 'Forces Favourites' in the 1960s. In recent years their only use had been working with a charity committed to maintaining contact with overseas troops, but they were nonetheless fully functional and could still become operational within 15 minutes. It was rumoured that when a certain Beatles song was broadcast from Chalfont Manor, this was the signal for the start of the Gulf War. Another feature of the site was a concealed, but high key and ever-present level of security. The perimeter fence was a modest, chain link fence just two metres in height, but within that had been planted extensive shrubbery and woodland concealing a four metre fence, topped with razor wire. The grounds were regularly patrolled by a private security firm and CCTV cameras added to a level of security worthy of its status as a key government installation. Cost reductions by successive governments had meant the site needed to capitalise on its commercial value and to generate income.

In addition to the broadcasting charity, it was used three times a week as the National Lottery HQ, utilising a mid-sized studio to draw the lottery numbers amidst a level of security worthy of the military. Within the past two years two attempts had been made to break in and tamper with the machines which selected the numbered balls, but in both cases the intruders were detained by the well-trained security team long before reaching their target. The staff and minor celebrities who arrived every Wednesday, Friday and Saturday to operate the national lottery draw were always escorted from the front gates directly to the studio and were never permitted to venture beyond a narrow, well lit corridor once within the building. A further reason for Chalfont Manor being selected as the venue for highest level meetings was its geographical position. It was just fifteen minutes drive from RAF Northolt which not only housed the Queens Flight, but more importantly was the military command centre for the Ministry of Defence. A fifteen minute drive due west from Chalfont Manor was Chequers, so the Prime Minister himself could join any meeting within a very short time if in residence at his weekend retreat. The site had invested heavily in recent years in fibre optic cabling so contact with GCHQ in Cheltenham was assured and was permanently active.

Assistant Commissioner James Roth's priority was to get blue four's injuries treated before expecting him to assist in the decision making process which was inevitably to follow. The police helicopter took James Roth, blue four and a paramedic to Wexham Park Hospital, the nearest emergency unit to Chalfont Manor, while a theatre was cleared for facial surgery. The services of two ophthalmic surgeons from Moorfields

Eye Hospital in East London were requested directly from the Home Office. One was pulled out of a meeting and the other was stopped just before entering Old Street station. Both were given a police escort to Wexham Park and thoroughly briefed on the 45 minute journey through the heavy traffic leaving London going west. By six thirty, blue four was surrounded by the best ophthalmic team that could be mustered at this short notice and he was just a few minutes from the all important Chalfont Manor venue.

"How much time do we have?" requested Professor David Nash, the surgical lead.

"I need him in a coherent state by seven thirty latest," replied James Roth.

"Not ideal," responded Professor Nash, with a deep sigh. He was more used to putting the patient first, not political and commercial interests.

"Can you achieve that?" said Nash, addressing his anaesthetist who would be central to the procedure.

"I'll sedate him to the absolute minimum giving you 45 minutes surgery time. What state he'll be in when he comes round I cannot say, but he looks pretty tough to me. Let's just do it."

The pre-med had already been given and it was with some relief that blue four tried to count to ten as the propofol in the general anaesthetic took effect. The collective commitment of the next 45 minutes was a model of concentrated expertise. The two surgeons, working in tandem with the support team, knew that a man's sight depended on their skill and experience. The left eye was beyond repair, so the team worked with precision on the right eye, cautiously removing tissue which by now was starting to degrade. They paid little attention to the myriad of superficial shrapnel wounds, knowing that this could be dealt with later when time was not at a premium.

"I think there's hope," said Prof Nash, "the right eye should recover in time, now that we have stabilised his injury, but he cannot use it for a minimum of 48 hours. The pad and bandages will have to remain in place for that time, but with luck he'll be fit to talk very soon after we bring him round. I am happy to hand him over to a general recovery team for two days, but insist on seeing him personally after that. You can get a trauma surgeon working on the more superficial wounds before then, but on no account must his eye be touched. I suggest that after you finish with the poor blighter this evening, you admit him to St Thomas' and I will see him there. At least he will be with his colleagues, if they survive the night."

James Roth had heard this directive from behind the theatre's observation window and acknowledged it over the link phone.

"Thanks to all of you for your work and I hope we haven't spoilt your evening entirely."

The anaesthetist soon brought blue four back to consciousness and was surprised how little the procedure seemed to affect him. Blue four, in spite of still being in a state of semi shock, seemed to be ready for action and it was James Roth who was soon briefing him on the short journey to Chalfont Manor.

By seven forty five that evening, the small but powerful group was assembled and, more out of necessity than hospitality, were helping themselves to the adequate buffet supplied by the three members of the catering staff who were permanently on standby for such an event. None of the members of this distinguished company had found time to eat and there was every chance that it would be a long night. The room was well-proportioned with an impressively high ceiling, most likely the drawing room of the original hall. The oak panels had been replaced by high quality beech to give it a lighter, more modern feel. The large central table and chairs were in the same light beech as were the more utilitarian carousels, each containing a computer screen. The original fireplace had been replaced with bookshelves containing nothing but legal tomes and the heating was provided by an underfloor system, guaranteed to maintain the room at 22 degrees Celsius. The once beautiful windows, overlooking gardens originally designed by Gertrude Jekyll, had been replaced with a large projector screen on one side and a plasma television screen on the other. The whole effect was hardly an interior designer's dream, but somehow the room maintained a balance of comfort, elegance and gravitas. It was fundamentally a place of work and of serious decisions. Everything had been arranged to ensure the minimum of distraction.

In spite of being well-known figures in their areas of work, few were household names so introductions were needed. Brigadier Charles Babb was still in his military fatigues, so was easily distinguished. Lord Cooke had been appearing almost nightly on television leading up to the Games so was well known to everyone present. He wore a light-coloured suit, a pale blue shirt and the Olympic tie. Jeremy Huntingdon, the Olympic Minister, in spite of his occasional foray into programmes like 'Question Time', was less well known and felt obliged to introduce himself to all present. He was wearing a dark blue, herring bone suit, a white shirt and a predominantly yellow tie reflecting his allegiance to the Liberal Democrat party.

Jenny Jones, the senior security officer for the Games organising committee, was only known to Lord Cooke so introduced herself to all. Jenny was a planner and a fixer and was quickly finding herself out of her depth in such august company. This was mainly because of the intensity of the situation, something which was never her style. Jenny's maxim had always been to buy time before making the big decisions and she had moved distinctly out of her comfort zone as the afternoon progressed. Jenny wore a dark tailored suit but her ample figure accentuated the limitations of the style. She was never one to give time to her looks and although respectable in appearance, most people took the view that she needed some form of a makeover to make the best of herself.

Red four remained on the periphery of the group. He concentrated exclusively on the three computer screens angled so that he could focus on each one with a minimum of movement from his leather-bound swivel chair. He avoided eye contact with any of the distinguished company, perfectly content to play a supportive role in the proceedings to follow. He above all recognised the dynamics of communication and the distinction between the team around a table and electronic access to the outside world. The team around the table needed him and he would provide all information needed swiftly, effectively and with minimum intrusion. He converted decisions into action and did it well.

James Roth was also still in his police uniform bearing the distinctive ribbon of the Queen's Police Medal, awarded to him in 1998 for distinguished service. He, as the person nearest to the incident, took it upon himself to chair the meeting and had prepared a hurried agenda which he was now placing carefully in the places around the table. The table had no decoration, floral or otherwise, but was suitably supplied with a variety of soft drinks. As none of the assembled company had ever been to this room before, James made them aware that there was a well stocked bar in one corner and led the way by mixing himself a long, but weak gin and tonic.

Since his arrival with James Roth, blue four had been steadying himself on the arm of a pretty lance corporal who had been assigned to the role. She had arrived from RAF Northolt with the Brigadier and was clearly somewhat overawed by the status of the group in the room. She made sure blue four was offered a meal, but the after effects of the anaesthetic, and the recognition that his colleagues were either dead or seriously injured had dulled his appetite. She gently chided him knowing that his sugar level would be dangerously low, and was at least comforted by his willingness to drink steadily. She made him a large mug of strong coffee, adding two heaped spoonfuls of sugar, and having seated him at one end of the main table, put a variety of soft drinks within reach. She held his hand, not out of affection but to show him where each drink was placed. Now confident that he could cope with the situation, she withdrew quietly from the room. Once blue four had been seated amongst this small and secure company and his helper had left the room, he felt able to reveal his identity. The others, picking up on the cues, shook his hand warmly and introduced themselves before taking their places at the table. His response to each introduction was a quiet "Jake Dorney, Special Forces." With the exception of Jenny Jones, the others knew the significance of this simple statement. Special Forces was a generic term which could include the SAS, the marines and other elite regiments. Most commonly it was a cover for special missions, often deep into enemy territory. The man sitting beside them had clearly been recruited from the best of the best.

James Roth interrupted the subdued fragments of conversation. "Lady and gentlemen, could we start by skipping item one on the agenda, that of introductions, as we have had ample opportunity to do the rounds so to speak. The position to date is that a single, low impact bomb was detonated in the Olympic Stadium at 17.00 hours following a single warning from the Al-Qaeda website. Sadly one of the bomb disposal team was fatally injured, two are critical but stable in hospital and the fourth, Jake Dorney, is with us this evening, following eye surgery. After the warning, all spectators within a 40 metre radius of the site were immediately evacuated and following the detonation, all spectators, athletes and officials left the stadium. There were no further casualties. It has been established that one of the British Gas employees who fitted the supply to the Olympic flame was in fact a member of a known terrorist cell based in Luton. GCHQ in Cheltenham is on high alert to monitor all known terrorist cells in the UK for any unusual activity, but to date none has been observed. Should anything change, I will be informed directly."

As if on cue, James Roth's flow was interrupted and he paused for 15 seconds while he focussed on a message being relayed through a well concealed earpiece. As he tilted his head to one side with his left hand cupped over his ear and his elbow resting casually on the table, the others in the room waited in anticipation. James Roth had seen service in Northern Ireland and Bosnia, but the implications of what he now heard drained all colour from his face. He knew that he needed to keep calm and in control. He was a man who recognised the benefit of involving trusted colleagues and he had them all around this table.

"Colleagues, I've just received a message from GCHQ. From 6:00 am tomorrow, twelve bombs will be detonated at hourly intervals within the Olympic stadium. The only condition which will prevent this happening is the cancellation of the remaining two days of the Games including the closing ceremony. I am assured that this is a genuine threat and one that we have no option but to assume is real."

For a full 60 seconds no one moved a muscle. Each person present was taking in the enormity of the statement. Lord Cooke's neck was arched forward with his chin on his chest, his elbows on the table and both hands with fingers interlocked were forming a skull cap at the back of his head. As he slowly looked up, he was the first to speak.

"Without question this is a serious issue and the safety of the athletes and the public must be paramount. However the cancellation of the remaining part of the Games, which now includes the sessions lost today, would be ruinous. Apart from the total loss of international credibility, the major sponsors are dependent on a successful and complete Games, with millions of pounds of investment in these final stages. Loss of television coverage alone for the closing ceremony is the difference between the Games showing any chance of meeting its costs and huge amounts of irrecoverable debt. We must find a solution which will restore the full integrity of the Games as soon as is physically possible."

Brigadier Charles Babb was the next to speak and either for effect or from habit, he rose from his seat to address the group.

"I fully recognise the concerns of Lord Cooke, but we all need to be equally aware of the humanitarian impact of this threat. We have already lost one of our finest soldiers, with another two still in a critical state. It would be unacceptable to risk any further lives of individual members of our armed forces, who would clearly be front line in any bomb dispersal role. But, as importantly, it would be intolerable to contemplate putting the general public at risk just to satisfy the commercial interests of the Games. I cannot see any viable option then to suspend the Games until we are absolutely confident that there is no risk of further disruption." With that, Brigadier Babb, who by now had been striding repeatedly around one end of the table, sat down forcefully as if to emphasise his conclusion.

James Roth now took the lead back from the first two speakers before giving others an opportunity to speak.

"Until we can confirm the veracity of these threats, I believe we have little option than to postpone all activities within the Olympic stadium. Al-Qaeda has already achieved its primary objective of generating a level of terror which is already making headlines around the world. Our task must be to restore international confidence in our ability to deliver the Games but to do so with minimal risk to any person, athlete or spectator. Can I remind you all that we now have less than ninety minutes before the main evening news is broadcast and we should endeavour to have a clear statement prepared by then. I suggest that we have a ten minute recess while we all review the situation with anyone outside of this room. This will at least give time for me to receive updates from GCHQ. Jenny can I suggest that you use the time to contact the stadium, that you Jeremy bring the Home Office into the equation unless powers have been delegated to you and that others here use the time to update on any aspect which is relevant to the situation. Agreed?"

Without waiting for assent James Roth turned to red four who had been scanning between a bank of three terminals trying to retrieve information from recognised international sources.

"How's it going, Gary?" said Roth, now happy to drop the formality of security by using his Christian name. "Anything new to report?"

"Three main things to consider, sir. First, the only intelligence we have on the bomb itself is that it is not a known device with any particular hallmark the security forces recognise. We have a forensic team at the Stadium trying to piece together any shrapnel from the device. The timing mechanism is crucial and forensics at this stage believe that it could have been triggered remotely, most likely from a mobile phone. This emphasises the importance of any recall that blue four, sorry Jake, can give us. Second, the information on the gas fitter who is most likely to have installed the device is solid. Ahmed Ghambir is confirmed as a member of a known, but until now, low profile cell. Special branch had knowledge of the cell, but tracking was fairly low key. Clearly a false address was given to get work with British Gas and no link was made with any of the other members of the cell. The Luton location was abandoned several weeks ago with all members apparently going to ground. Ghambir has worked for British Gas for two years with an unblemished record. He went on planned and legitimate leave, presumed holiday, one week ago and has not been seen since. Thirdly, and I guess most importantly, sir, GCHQ reckon that the threat is genuine. Senior intelligence gathering staff at Cheltenham believe that the feasibility of a number of bombs in the Olympic Stadium is more than a possibility, in fact a probability. Small devices, probably in the region of 500 grams of high explosive could have been introduced by persons unknown to key locations in the stadium. With airport level security and scanners for everyone, and in spite of bag searches, it would have been possible for final assembly to have taken place in the stadium and items hidden successfully. With 80,000 spectators, and a further 2,000 staff in locations ranging from track side officials to catering, a determined person, or more likely persons, should be able to assemble items and locate them at any time before today. Let's not forget, that this is the twelfth day of the games and these devices could have been positioned before today and primed later. This is pure speculation, sir, but my guess is that if these bombs do exist, then they were probably introduced today and primed immediately after the first bomb went off. All the attention would have been on the activity around the base of the Olympic flame. The perpetrators could easily have secreted them at that time and left the stadium with everyone else. The threat of detonation at hourly intervals is utterly logical from the terrorist perspective. It effectively increases the threat as time goes on and makes it more difficult for the organisers to reinstate any activity until one of two things happens."

"And those two things are either agree to their demands or disable all the bombs," said Roth somewhat cautiously, not being absolutely sure that these were the only options.

"Exactly," added Gary Wheeler, who during this time was constantly scanning the screens in front of him in anticipation of fresh information.

"But," added James Roth, giving away his concern by the slight change in tone of his voice, "how can we be sure that the number of bombs is limited to twelve and this isn't just a smokescreen for carnage on a massive scale?"

"We can't," replied Wheeler, "but my experience, based on a combination of probability theory and knowing the mindset and culture of such terrorists, tells me that this specific threat is likely. What I mean by that is if we do not meet their demands, lives will be lost in significant numbers. Loss of life to date has been horrific but in relative terms small. Our men were as well protected as they could be for the operational role. Ordinary spectators will have no protection and could be literally sitting on twelve bombs. Today we had a head start because we knew the location and could evacuate accordingly. Following the very first bomb to explode tomorrow, assuming it is among the spectators and not in some isolated part of the stadium, there is likely to be mass panic. This could precipitate numerous deaths by this alone."

"So what are our options, in your view?" interrupted Roth.

"Put very bluntly, option one is to concede to the terrorists' demands and cancel the rest of the Games including the closing ceremony. Option two is to put every resource available into locating the remaining twelve bombs and disarm them. This, at the very best, will take until tomorrow morning, probably later. If we are successful, today's athletics programme will have to be re-scheduled for Friday, meaning that some events will still have to move to Saturday. I'm not the right man to advise on the details of this, but I would very much doubt if the closing ceremony could remain unaffected without a guaranteed bomb clearance by lunchtime tomorrow at the latest."

"And other options?"

"Frankly, sir, at this stage I cannot see any other options."

"OK, thanks, most helpful. Please feel free to interrupt the rest of the meeting at any stage should it be necessary."

With that Assistant Commissioner James Roth poured himself another small gin with a double tonic, liberally iced, and returned to his seat at the main table. Other members of the group, who had either been making calls to more senior colleagues or talking in hushed tones in small groups, now returned to their respective seats.

"Thank you all for keeping to time over the recess." said Roth. "There have been no developments over the last few minutes, so I suggest that we continue exactly where we left off. We are faced with what appears to be the very real prospect of twelve devices within the stadium, primed or in some way to be detonated externally throughout the day tomorrow. It is impossible to know whether this is the full extent of the terrorist intrusion. However my advisors consider that it is a reasonable assumption that this is the limit of the Al-Qaeda activity in the Olympic Park. It has already caused maximal disruption to the Games and clearly will have major repercussions for the rest of the Games. We have little time before the 10 O'clock News so we must move fast. I will invite you in turn to brief the group before we have to go live with our strategy, however temporary. Mr Huntingdon, as the representative of the government, would you please go first?"

"Colleagues, I have spoken to the PM and the Home Office during the last few minutes and her majesty's government is adamant that we should not permit terrorism to gain any further advantage from the situation. We will do everything in our power to continue the Games as planned and will not agree to any form of cancellation of any component of it. This statement is clearly dependent on achieving no further loss of life and in not placing the public at any increased risk."

"Thank you for that clarity, Mr Huntingdon. Lord Cooke, as chairman of the organising committee, please can I have your perspective."

"It was difficult within the recess to speak to many of my colleagues, but we have run emergency scenarios regularly as part of our preparation for the Games. Clearly there was never the expectation of this specific situation. However I can say with confidence that the committee would wish to complete the Games, including every aspect of the closing ceremony. After four years of preparation and such a successful outcome until today, any change in plans would be devastating both for the Olympic Movement and the UK."

"Thank you. Brigadier Babb, could you please summarise your view?"

Charles Babb once again stood up as if to address a much larger audience.

"As you would expect, my overriding concern is for the safety of any of my men involved in this barbaric act of terrorism. Every life lost in the cause of duty, especially those that are preventable, has a dramatic effect on families, on other members of the forces and on the national psyche. My men accept that they need to be front line in this operation. However we have to find a balance between the pressures from government and national pride. Significant risks will be required to deal with this unfolding situation. I am prepared to order my special forces into defusing known devices, but I am not prepared to put my men's lives at unnecessary risk because of undue time pressures. Do I make myself clear?"

"Thank you, Brigadier, very clear. We now need to hear from the operational side of the Games. Jenny would you like to speak first?"

"Thank you James. I understand completely the concerns of our previous speakers and don't wish to add anything to that debate. From an operational aspect, we have to date lost one entire athletics session from today and the tail end of another. This included the finals of the men's 200m, the 800m, and the triple jump. We lost the women's 800m semis and the first round of the 4 by 100m relay as well as the javelin final. This is possibly the most problematic because of the time it takes. We also lost six victory ceremonies, but these are of less concern because they take far less time and can easily be re-scheduled."

"If we were able to get back on track by say tomorrow afternoon at the latest," interjected Lord Cooke, "what are the chances of completing all the athletics events by Saturday evening?"

"I can only give you approximations at this stage, Lord Cooke," Jenny responded, "but with a lot of goodwill on behalf of the athletes and a massive truncation of the victory ceremonies, it would just about be possible. If we lose the whole of tomorrow, then I would say it is virtually impossible."

"I am concerned that we are getting ahead of ourselves here," said James Roth. "Our absolute priority must be to discover and defuse or disarm any remaining bombs and this is where the critical intelligence from Jake Dorney here could be invaluable."

Jake Dorney had been sitting quietly throughout the discussions. Partly because of the residue of his anaesthetic and the continuing pain from his injuries, but mainly because he was absorbed in trying to remember details from the attempt to defuse the bomb.

"As you are all aware, my role was what we call sub. It's short for substitute and not unlike a football match my job is to take over if for any reason one of the others is incapable of continuing. In our business, reasons can range from injury, fatigue or sometimes even temporary paralysis. Of course this happens rarely, but has been known when an operator just cannot decide on the right option. This is why my position is at the base of the diamond to give me extra protection should anything go wrong. The consequence is that my vision is impaired somewhat. Luckily we keep in contact verbally throughout any operation so I can at least hear what is being seen by blue two who was leading the shout today. The extent of the blast does suggest a small quantity of high explosive, unlikely to be more than a kilogramme, probably nearer half. We were not able to move the device before it exploded so it must have been detonated remotely. I saw no laser beam and high frequency detonation is fairly unlikely in view of the size of the device. Blue two had the impression, although sadly he had no time to confirm, that the detonator was associated with some form of mobile chip or SIM card. This was based on very limited observation because the device was strapped behind the main fuel pipe. As I am fairly certain that movement was not a factor, detonation from a remote mobile phone seems an increasingly likely option. The timing of the blast would help confirm this as the bomb was detonated at the point when we were close to checking it out in more detail. Although it was taped to the back of the pipe, we would have been able to get a flexible probe based on fibre optic technology to give us much more detail. Sadly the explosion occurred before we got to that stage, with the outcome you're all aware of......"

At this point Jake's voice weakened as he recalled with considerable vividness the death and injuries to his colleagues. Jake gave a small cough, cleared his throat and continued.

"If my analysis is correct and similar bombs have already been placed in the stadium, then the precise hourly detonation can be achieved without any timing mechanism within the bombs. This will not only simplify them but also mean they will be considerably smaller than devices needing internal timing mechanisms. There would be little to be gained by the terrorists exploding them in an empty stadium, so unless they are found and disposed of they could be activated remotely at any time. This puts into perspective the demand to cancel the Games, especially the closing ceremony."

"Thank you Jake," said James Roth, now becoming acutely aware of time pressures, "your contribution is invaluable. If I could try to summarise the situation to date. It seems to me that our absolute priority is to locate and dispose of 12 bombs which could still be located in the stadium. Failure to do this would put the general public at considerable risk and could lead to further loss of life. Cancellation or even curtailment of the Games is an option that no one wants, but this has to be balanced against the dire consequences of further terrorist activity. Our priority must be to locate and negate each of the remaining twelve bombs. Until this has been achieved, the Games are effectively suspended. Should we be successful in locating and destroying these twelve bombs, and there is no indication from Al-Qaeda of any further terrorist activity, the Games will restart with the aim of completing all athletic activity by Saturday evening. I fully accept that there are shades of agreement over this issue, but can I report unanimous acceptance of this strategy?"

James Roth looked around the table, deliberately making eye contact with everyone involved. There was little enthusiasm, mainly due to the gravity of the situation, but each person in their own individual way nodded assent. For some it was by pushing forward a bottom lip, turning down the corner of their mouths and a slight bob of the head. Almost an act of resignation. For others it was a slow and more deliberate nodding of the head with no discernible movement of the mouth. For one it was a more enthusiastic show of agreement coupled with a half smile.

"Thank you," said James with some relief, "I trust that you will all be happy for me to make a statement to the media? I will, of course, keep you all fully informed through the usual channels. We will reconvene if the situation demands it, but in the meanwhile I wish you all a safe journey home."

James stood up, shook hands briefly as each person left the room and rapidly returned to his laptop. He now concentrated on the delicate task of writing the press release which would headline the Ten O'clock News in a few minutes time.

CHAPTER 25

August 9th 2012
10:00 pm news

The familiar opening credits rolled on both BBC and ITV before each presenter opened the news with a twenty second summary of what was to come. The Olympic Games explosion headlined both channels with the BBC moving to the uprising in Oman followed by a minor earthquake in the Philippines. ITV followed the news of the bomb at the Games with the arrest of a serial killer in the West Midlands and then the civil war in Oman. Both presenters knew they had a full update on the Olympic Games situation from James Roth but it was limited to a thirty second statement without any chance to interview or ask for comment. Both channels had live footage of the explosion from their respective sports channels covering the events in the stadium. The usual warning about the following pictures causing upset to viewers delayed the process fractionally. ITV opted to play the drama sequentially, with the BBC going straight to the press release from James Roth.

Tricia Hughes, who had presented the Ten O'clock News for the last six months, leaned slightly forward, took a deep breath and focused her full attention on the autocue.

"Following the dramatic events of the day at the Olympic Stadium, when a bomb at the base of the Olympic flame caused the death of at least one member of the Special Forces, we can now bring you an update on the situation from Assistant Commissioner James Roth who has overall responsibility for the Olympic Park in London." Tricia clicked the mouse just out of camera shot on her desk, instantly starting the DVD relayed from Chalfont Manor a few minutes earlier.

"It is with considerable regret that I confirm the death of a member of the Special Forces who was attempting to defuse a bomb within the Olympic Stadium. His wife and family have been informed, and our sympathies are with them at this difficult time. His commanding officer, Brigadier Charles Babb, considered him to be a soldier of outstanding abilities, highly respected within the Force and someone who will be sorely missed by all his colleagues. The Olympic Stadium was partially evacuated when the explosion took place and thankfully there were no further injuries to competitors or spectators due to the incident. Although unconfirmed at this stage, the atrocity is believed to be the work of the terrorist organisation Al-Qaeda as a deliberate strategy to disrupt the remaining part of the Games. It is possible that further explosive devices have been placed in the stadium and Special Forces are currently engaged in locating and disarming these so the Games can continue uninterrupted. The situation is constantly under review and we have every hope that once the stadium is known to be safe, all activities will re-commence including that of the closing ceremony. We are constantly in touch with Her Majesty's Government, the London Games Organising Committee, the armed forces and others at a very senior level to ensure that the safety of all those involved is the highest priority. We cannot state with any degree of certainty the impact of the device or devices on tomorrow's events, but will inform the public through the London2012 website and the media. Thank you."

"The bomb went off at exactly 5:00 pm this afternoon. The explosion can be seen at the top left of your screen from cameras covering the long jump which was taking place within the track. As you heard in the statement from Commissioner Roth, one member of the Special Forces dealing with the bomb was killed and a further two soldiers are believed to be in a critical but stable state in hospital. The Olympic Stadium is currently closed but we are now going over to our Olympic correspondent, Darren Gilbey, who is outside the stadium."

"Thank you Tricia. Following the bomb blast this afternoon and the immediate evacuation and closure of the stadium, the Olympic schedule has been considerably disrupted with a number of events and medal presentations currently postponed. I use the term postponed quite deliberately because I understand the Olympic authorities have every intention of rescheduling the programme as soon as it is safe to return to the stadium. Since the closure of the stadium, we have witnessed the arrival of a number of police and other vehicles, presumably trying to establish every detail of the explosion and searching for further bombs. As you heard earlier in your report, there appears to be considerable evidence that more bombs are still located within the stadium, but this is as yet unconfirmed. Details are still sketchy but I did note that two vehicles entering the stadium contained dogs and it is likely that these were sniffer dogs trained to detect explosives. You can also see behind me that all the stadium floodlights are still on which would not normally be the case at this time of night. This indicates that there must be considerable activity within the stadium and we all hope and pray that it will not result in further loss of life as the investigation continues."

"Darren, do you have any information on tomorrow's programme within the stadium?"

"No, Tricia, not at this stage. Clearly this will be of interest and some concern for all the athletes and also the 80,000 people that we were expecting here for all sessions tomorrow. The organising committee will give a press conference tomorrow morning at 10am and we hope that the situation will become much clearer by then."

"Darren, I anticipate that this will be a long night for you and your crew, so I wish you well and understand that you will be providing hourly updates on our BBC News 24 Service."

"Yes Trish, although we cannot yet get access to the stadium, I hope to interview key personnel as the situation develops and will report, as you say, on a regular basis throughout the night."

"That was Darren Gilbey, our Olympic correspondent, outside the Olympic stadium. In the studio here we have David Sartor who is Professor of Forensic Ordnance at University College London and an expert on explosive devices. Professor Sartor, what can you tell us about the bomb which has caused this outrage at the Olympic Stadium?"

"Well, specific evidence will be being collected as we speak by forensic staff within the stadium and the information provided by the member of the Special Forces who was present will be critical to help answer this question. However the TV pictures we have seen certainly give us clues to the type of bomb. The extent of the blast suggests that it contained a high explosive of less than a kilogramme, most probably sealed in a metal container. The most interesting aspect is that although the device was fully exposed, it was not apparently moved before it was detonated. It is unlikely that a timing device was used because the terrorists could not know the exact time of discovering the bomb. This suggests, therefore, that the device was detonated remotely. There are limited options for this and the most likely is using a mobile phone signal. If this supposition is correct, then this would only require a relatively small piece of solid state circuitry about the size of a mobile phone battery and detonation could even be caused by the vibrating mechanism used in all mobile phones."

"So, Professor Sartor, what are the implications of this for any other bombs which may still remain in the stadium?"

"If my supposition is correct and the bombs can be detonated remotely using mobile phone technology, then the terrorists clearly have the upper hand. Any remaining bombs can be detonated at will and at a time schedule to suit the terrorists' intention to cause maximum damage or loss of life. The only solution, frankly, is to be absolutely sure that no bombs remain in the stadium before the public can be readmitted. I am sure the stadium security staff are working on this as we speak."

"Thank you, Professor Sartor for giving us your insight into this particularly worrying situation. We now go to our Westminster correspondent, Harold Portman, who has in the last few minutes been speaking to the Deputy Minister for Sport and Culture, James Leddingham, MP. Harold, what can the government tell us as this incident develops?"

"Hello Tricia. This clearly is not easy for the government as I understand that the key ministry officials have been at a top level meeting until a few minutes ago and have yet to return to Westminster. However, I did speak to James Leddingham, who is deputising for the Minister and he assures me that an extra-ordinary cabinet meeting has been called for 08.30 tomorrow to review the ongoing situation. He reiterated the earlier statement from the government that it will not bow to any pressure from terrorists and that every effort is being made to continue the Games programme as soon as possible. This will involve continual contact between the Olympic Stadium and the government throughout the night and the public will be made aware of any developments as soon as is possible."

"Thank you Harold, I'm going to interrupt you there because I have just heard that we have made contact with Lord Cooke, chairman of the organising committee, and I now need to maintain this link."

Tricia Hughes, whose professionalism and poise was renowned throughout the industry, was starting to show signs of the strain of this dynamic and ever-changing story line. She was well used to coping with breaking news, but this succession of interviews all within a space of a few minutes at the top of the news was starting to make her feel considerably more uncomfortable than the normal effect of the studio lights. As she sipped a glass of ice cold water, the movement made her increasingly aware of the sweat now trickling down her back and arms. "Just stay focused," she thought to herself and the calming voice of the producer in her earpiece jolted her concentration back to the reality of live television. "Green telephone and camera one, Trish" came the distant voice and she automatically lifted the handset on her desk.

"Lord Cooke, this is Tricia Hughes speaking to you live on BBC News at Ten. I realise that this is a very difficult time for you and your team, but the nation is desperate to know how you are planning to resolve this frightening situation."

"First of all myself and the organising committee wish to send our condolences to the family of the officer who was killed in the explosion and to wish a speedy recovery to the others injured this afternoon. I can assure the general public, and especially those attending the Games, that it is our every intention to continue the Games as soon as possible. We will not, however, compromise public safety and our task at present is to ensure that the stadium is completely risk free before the Games can continue. All other venues are considered safe for public use and events scheduled in those will continue as planned."

"Lord Cooke, if I may interrupt, the question on everybody's lips is how did the organising committee allow a bomb to be placed in the Olympic Stadium in the first place?"

"Over 3,000 construction workers were used on the Olympic Park site and this included a large number of sub-contracted workers. Much of the site has been completed for over a year so this inevitably leaves a long time for incursions of this nature to take place. Every effort was made to provide high level security clearance for these workers, but with over 1,500 people on site at any one time, it is virtually impossible to cover every eventuality. We sadly live in a society where any determined terrorist can cause serious damage and loss of life as happened in London with the bombing of the underground and bus in Tavistock Square. The organising committee had security as a highly important part of our planning and yet clearly we were unsuccessful in preventing this atrocity. What we are doing now is to put all resources, our own, the government's, the police and armed forces' into a concerted effort to make the stadium safe to reopen as soon as possible. Clearly when we are able to reopen the stadium, we will need to reschedule events to complete the programme on time. Details of this will follow as soon as we are sure that the stadium is safe."

"James Roth, Head of Security for the Games, indicated that there may be further bombs in the stadium. Can you tell me what the organising committee is doing about this, Lord Cooke?"

"The organising committee is confident that the right people are in place to investigate this possibility. We have teams of people at the stadium right now examining every aspect of this venue with considerable diligence and I am confident that they will only commit to reopening the venue when it is safe. I have every intention of being at the press conference tomorrow and will report on any developments then."

"Trish," interrupted the producer through her earpiece, "Close him down, we need to move on."

"Lord Cooke, thank you for your time in such difficult circumstances and on behalf of the BBC, can I wish you and your team every success in bringing the Games to a satisfactory conclusion. And now to the rest of the news, I hand you over to my colleague, Roger Best who will bring you an update on the developing situation in Oman."

Tricia saw the red light on her camera switch off, took a deep breath and grabbed for the water. One of the make-up staff gave her a cool flannel and as she wrapped it gently around her face the tension of the last twelve minutes slowly ebbed away.

"Great stuff Trish," the ever-present voice of her producer

intoned, breaking her momentary reverie, "I want you back on to lead the item on the serial killer. Two minutes. You OK?"

Tricia Hughes, the consummate professional, gently removed the flannel, and signalled to make up for a quick facial powder. The makeup assistant knew the drill, and she quickly applied powder with a few deft strokes of her brush, making absolutely sure that Tricia's eyes were never covered, Tricia checked the first few lines of the autocue.

"In Gornal, just outside Wolverhampton, today, a 53-year-old man was arrested on suspicion of murdering a woman in her late thirties in the small hours of last Tuesday. Police believe that there could be a strong connection between this murder and a number of similar incidents in this part of the West Midlands over the last two years."

Josh Silverman and Rachel Rosen just stared at the screen with utter bewilderment, neither able to form any cohesive thoughts. After a few seconds of total paralysis, Josh hit the remote and the picture evaporated as did his normal confidence and utter control. He just slumped on his grandfather's old leather chair and became physically smaller and strangely distant. His distinctive determination and focus seemed to desert him totally and a mantle of despair ranged heavy on his shoulders. Rachel suffered with him, but showing a more decisive edge to her personality, hugged him lovingly round the neck, broke off and ran to get a bottle of Josh's favourite wine, a Rashi Joyvin.

"I know this is really for Shabbat, and you would never normally drink anything so close to a race" said Rachel, "but I think the situation calls for something special, even if only a drop, to help us think as a team."

She slowly and carefully uncorked the wine and poured it into a long stemmed glass, allowing the slight effervescence to infuse the wine before handing it to Josh. Josh, his eyes still devoid of their usual sparkle, turned to Rachel gratefully and slowly seemed to focus on an old photo of his parents on the far side of the room. Rachel, sensing the moment, walked over to the photo and picking it up gently, brought it over and placed it in Josh's free hand.

"I could do with a bit of their strength right now," said Josh. Rachel's instinct was to cuddle up close and rest her head on his shoulder as she often did when he needed her support. Right now something inside said to give him time and space, so she sat on the floor at his feet and just held tightly to one calf so he had the freedom to sip the wine and stare at the photo. As Josh looked again at the photo, he whispered "God doesn't make our journey easy is what they would have said. Trust Him to make the right decisions in His own time."

"Of course," said Rachel, "we must trust in the Lord, but one thing we have precious little of is time. Tomorrow should be your final. Your God-given chance to be the best in the world. As things stand right now, we don't even know when the race is to be scheduled!"

Josh took a sip of his wine, looked lovingly at the photo in his left hand, and placed it face down on the floor next to Rachel. He knew he could expect no help from a fading photograph. But he also knew that resolve in times of hardship was one of the many things his parents had gifted him. Now was the time for resolve, but resolve needed clear and decisive goals to achieve his ultimate aim. His lifetime aim of standing at the award ceremony to the strains of the British national anthem. Rachel detected a shift in Josh's posture, a small movement when the muscles contract slightly to prepare for action. She clung even tighter, subconsciously hoping that her warmth, closeness and energy would somehow flow into Josh's very being to give him the strength he needed. This strength was not to run fast, for this was a given and had been banked from the countless hours of physical punishment in the years before. Josh now needed the psychological strength to adjust to the shifting sands of events which started with the explosion earlier today and would impact without question on the days to come. Like a slowly uncoiling spring, Josh stretched his arms forward, fingers locked and knuckles cracking in a sort of ritualistic preparation for the final assault on a vertical and yet unclimbed rock face. He stood up, moving slowly at first, but then like a butterfly unfolding its wings for the very first time, the blood pumped into the big muscles of his arms and legs and the crumpled man became a powerful youth. He craved action, he wanted to race right now, and had half a mind to head for the treadmill in the air conditioned basement and drive the adrenaline screaming out of his perfectly tuned body. Rachel's quiet but determined voice brought him back to a locus of reality.

"Let's make supper together."

Such a simple statement, yet one with all the elemental needs of the moment. The call to action, the sharing of the deed, the simplicity, the opportunity to plan, the chance to enjoy, the noise of preparation, the silence of eating, the prayerful thanks before the meal. It was the perfect distraction from events yet to be unveiled. Josh and Rachel approached the simple task with harmony, purpose and a great deal of love.

Within a short time, the simple meal that they had planned for months was on the table. They had chosen a spinach and ricotta pasta dish with a mushroom sauce. Each organic ingredient had been carefully sourced and they had personally collected them from various suppliers. This was no time to take risks and in spite of the inconvenience of it all, they were both convinced that it was a prudent investment of their time. Nigel Gressley had warned Josh constantly of the risks associated with food from unknown sources and had even suggested on more than one occasion that food contamination was a serious threat to his due success. The bottle of Rashin Joyvin was recorked to await the lighting of the candles for the Sabbath tomorrow night. This, the great celebration of the Jewish week was planned as the greatest celebration of Josh's life with his family sharing the joy of winning that elusive Olympic gold. As the wine was being returned to the fridge, the awful realisation of the unfolding events resurfaced and Rachel, turning to Josh, said with utter simplicity, "We need to make plans."

"OK," said Josh, "let's explore the options. Clearly after today the organising committee will be desperate to accelerate the programme so that all the athletic events finish by Saturday evening. They will not contemplate any spill over to Sunday because the closing ceremony will have massive TV coverage and sponsorship income."

"Yes, but there are clearly more bombs in the stadium and absolutely nothing will happen until they are all removed or detonated," said Rachel.

"Of course, but the information is so thin that we do not even know if this is true or have any idea of the timetable."

"The truth is," added Rachel, "we are both second guessing, but at least we can prepare together for a number of options."

"OK, let's start with tomorrow and make an assumption that the stadium is considered fit for use, although I wouldn't want to be the one to make that call."

"Right," said Rachel encouragingly, "assuming that tomorrow's programme starts on time, or even earlier than planned, what options do we have?"

"Being totally selfish," said Josh, "the best possible scenario is that the 1500m final is held before sundown and I can compete as normal. Well hardly as normal in view of the situation, but with no more pressure than anyone else. The timing is bound to change, but I can adjust to that as well as anyone."

"And the worst possible scenario?" enquired Rachel, really not wanting to hear the answer.

"Any time after the start of the Sabbath clearly presents me with a major issue. I've never competed on the Sabbath and you know my faith just won't permit it."

Rachel remained silent and slowly moved the dishes to the work surface above the dishwasher. "Of course," she eventually replied, "so Al-Qaeda has not only brought terror to the games, but they could rob you of the one thing you had dreamed about for four years."

"That's exactly as it is if the 1500m is rescheduled to any time during the Sabbath. I totally accept this is nothing new. Eric Liddell took a similar stance in 1924 and Jonathan Edwards would not compete on a Sunday before he hit the big time. Rachel, I am not looking for martyrdom, it's just, well you know....."

"Can we do anything to get a more up to date fix on the schedules?" Rachel asked, feeling a rising surge of desperation yet impotence in the situation.

"I'm absolutely sure either the Chef de Mission or Nigel will be in touch just as soon as they hear anything new."

The mere mention of Nigel Gressley's name shocked Rachel to the core, but she hid her personal loathing to try to stay focused on Josh's needs. As if pre-ordained, the bleep of the phone cut into the tension like a knife through butter and Rachel, seeing Nigel Gressley's name on the handset, handed it without comment to Josh.

"Nigel, good to hear from you. I've seen the TV news. Do you know anything else? Any update?" Josh gripped the phone tightly as he listened to Nigel's reply.

"Josh, I cannot seem to get any information beyond the general news that everyone's heard. I've phoned the BOA as well as the Chef de Mission and they were virtually impossible to contact. There's just nothing coming out of the organising committee and I suspect they simply cannot make any plans until the stadium's been cleared. Frankly, we're just in limbo at present. But how are you coping? I guess like me you are reviewing all the options. I know what your feelings are concerning the Sabbath, but please do not make a hasty decision. Just talk to people – me, your family, especially Rabbi Levin. I know you're way past me giving advice, but do try to keep focused. I'll be in touch as soon as I get anything new, so try to get some sleep. Ciao"

"Anything new?" asked Rachel, barely able to keep her loathing for Nigel Gressley under control.

"Just nothing," said Josh disconsolately. "Nigel has been trying all his contacts without success. It looks as though our only option is to wait until morning and get the update from the media like everyone else. It's hard to accept that the athletes cannot be better informed, but I guess it's just an indication of the hiatus at the stadium."

"OK," said Rachel with resignation, "let's get back to the options. If the 1500m final is on Friday before the start of Sabbath, then we're good to go. We have until about seven in the evening and with today's programme to be included, I think it could be touch and go. Let's hope and pray that there's no delay beyond tomorrow morning, otherwise the prospect's incredibly bleak."

"Realistically," said Josh, "I cannot imagine any event going on beyond say eight o'clock anyway because of all the transportation issues that late at night. Getting up to 80,000 spectators plus competitors and officials out of the Olympic Park and home would be a massive undertaking. A headache the organisers could do without."

"So, as it would be virtually impossible to use Sunday for any athletics, this only leaves Saturday as the spillover day if they haven't caught up everything by tomorrow."

"Rachel, I know you're only being practical, but aren't we both in danger of forgetting the seriousness of the situation. We've already had one soldier killed, a further two badly maimed and a terrorist cell currently in total control. God knows what further havoc they could wreak over the next twenty four hours."

"Josh, I know it sounds clinical and almost calculating, but you know that preparation is all. Unlike the other athletes, you have your faith to consider and this is something that needs careful and prayerful thought right now. The situation is likely to change by the hour and you have to be ready with all the answers. I've always supported your stance on the Sabbath being a joyful celebration and a true day of rest, but we've never been confronted with this before. Even when the World Championships finished late on a Friday last year, you were able to compete and retain your spiritual standing. You've never veered from this course and I respect and love you for it."

"Rachel, I feel a 'but' coming on here. What's your reservation?"

Rachel moved to Josh's side, slipped her arms around him and put her head on his chest. She hugged him to the point where she could feel his massive heart pounding in his chest and sending shock waves through her whole frame.

"The truth is Josh, I want you to run. I want you to run for reasons way beyond comprehension right now. It's not just the four years of dedication and utter commitment. It goes way beyond that. Unless you run and win, then your true character cannot be defined. Josh, the next forty eight hours will be your destiny. It will define you for life. I honestly believe that to refuse to run will become secondary to winning. The consequences that will follow will, in God's eyes, be far greater than never standing on that podium. You will be a better disciple of God as Olympic champion than making a stand which will soon be forgotten in the sands of time. But Josh, it must be your decision. I will love you no less whatever you do. My only request is that you work it out so you are confident in your answer. Please talk to those you can trust, family, friends, Rabbi Levin. I know time is desperately short, but I beg you to share your every concern with the ones closest to you. And above all Josh, pray. I've heard you say so often that you will not pray to win, but pray to have the opportunity to win. I will pray with you, not for courage, but for the opportunity to practice courage."

With the word courage on her lips, Rachel fell silent. She felt Josh's heart beats speed up and slow down in rhythm with his breathing and sensed their joint energies ebbing and flowing as one body. They didn't move for what seemed like minutes and then slowly and lovingly Josh's hand gently raised Rachel's chin so that their lips met. For a moment the stress of the last hours was forgotten in the intimacy of their embrace and their eyes closed temporarily on a dark and dejected world.

CHAPTER 26

August 9th/10th, 2012
Olympic Stadium, London, UK

The warning had clearly specified that twelve bombs had been placed in the Olympic Stadium and there was intense pressure to locate and disarm each one. The task was vast with the huge amphitheatre, now eerily quiet, a home for weapons of death and destruction. Somewhere amongst the track, the green sward of the field events, the numerous spaces for storage and reception around the track and the silent rows of 80,000 seats stretching up to the sky, would be hidden twelve explosive devices, probably the size of a bag of sugar.

"For these bombs to cause maximum damage," intoned the head of southern region bomb disposal, Major John Little, "we have to assume that they've been placed in the public areas. We've little option than to do a sweep search of the entire seating area and failing that work on other areas more remote from the public. I've already demanded that all mobile providers for the whole of East Stratford are either switched off or blocked so there is little chance of the devices being activated from outside the stadium. Our information, based on the bomb that's already exploded, is that they'll be about the size of a thermos flask and likely to be fitted with some mobile-activated device to trigger the detonator. We've no idea if each one is fitted with tilt transducers to detect movement, but that has to be a possibility. Beyond that we cannot say, so we'll have to treat virtually anything unrecognizable as suspicious. As you know, there's huge pressure on us to clear the whole stadium by the morning, so I suggest we divide our disposal teams into four groups and take one side of the stadium each, working from top to bottom. Any questions? Good luck, gentlemen."

The sixteen strong Special Forces disposal unit, always on standby in the home counties were dressed in full Kevlar protection suits. They worked from behind a transparent, plexiglas shield which gave them limited protection, but at least they had the visibility needed for the task. They worked in pairs, with one acting as front man to detect items and take the lead in disposal while the other could supply specialist kit and watch his partner carefully. A huge amount had been learned within the bomb disposal fraternity by partner observation, especially when things go wrong. A dead or seriously injured colleague can never provide feedback but an observer can. The tried and tested method was now standard practice and was especially useful when tough decisions had to be made.

The floodlights around the stadium were all fully on, but their design was to light the track and events area not the seating. Each officer worked with a powerful head torch and slowly, carefully and methodically they checked on, around and behind every seat. The operation had been going for about fifteen minutes when the short wave radio crackled into life down in the central control at ground level.

"C2 calling. I've got a hit at seat 1848 top tier of the north stand. Over."

"I read you. Give me a position with your laser and I'll send up the cavalry. Over."

With that, out of the gloom of the vast array and massed ranks of the seating came a green shaft of light pinpointing the position of the possible bomb. Two other squad members made their way up to the top of the terracing and were soon alongside.

"It's looking likely," came the comment over the short wave. "Looks like a thermos flask, firmly taped to the top of the seat, but hidden from view with the seat retracted. You did well to spot it without tilting the seat. How come?"

"Looking from this angle, the seat is a fraction out of line with the others. Suggests something could be behind it."

"Brilliant, just need to ease the little baby out of its cot and that'll be one less to worry about."

"It feels like either electrical tape or something broader like ductape holding it in place. I'm not keen to take a Stanley knife to it without a good look, so we'll have to risk pulling the seat down."

"I'm not happy, because that'll trigger any movement detector, but I agree we've no option. Go for it."

The whole squad held their collective breath as the seat was slowly pulled forward using an extended rod not unlike a fishing pole. When horizontal, the device was clearly in view and was seen to be a thermos flask emblazoned with a union jack and with a tiny dongle about the size of a bottle top inserted in one side.

"There's your electronic detonator for you, very clever. Probably has its own SIM card and activated from a simple phone call. Thank God the boss wiped out that option. Still better leave everything in place and bring the little darling down. We can detonate it down in the centre of the track."

"Hang on let's consider the other options. Shouldn't we leave it in place, sandbag it and detonate it here?"

"Come on Pete, we've got eleven more of these little babies to find and destroy. It'll take us an age to get the gear and then bring it up here, far better to take it down, especially now we know there's no movement detector on board."

Pete shrugged, still uncertain, but accepted the logic. The bomb was cut free from the seat, placed in a protective, insulated box and moved slowly down the steep steps. Half way down there was an explosion that ricocheted around the stadium. The two officers carrying the bomb were blown sideways by the force of the blast and both landed ten feet away in a gut wrenching twisted heap. Paramedics arrived within minutes but could do little to save the arm of one officer which had been blown clean off and the other had hideous facial injuries despite his protective visor. They were strapped to stretchers and to the mournful sound of a siren were dispatched to the nearest hospital emergency unit.

At the command of the senior officer the small groups were rapidly being debriefed.

"OK, so we just learned a hard lesson. These bombs seem either to have a movement detector with a built in delay or alternatively have a highly sensitive pressure detector. That bomb was half way down when it went off which could be a result of either. It was about four minutes after it was originally moved and it dropped about 100 feet. The next one we find we'll move, then leave and see if the delay theory is correct. If it doesn't explode within say ten minutes, then we can assume it responds to pressure changes as it is brought down. If so, that provides us with a different problem. Any comments or suggestions?"

"If it's the pressure change which detonates it, what are our options, boss?"

"Far less straight forward, but I've already put a call out to our chief scientist at the ministry. He may not have the answer but he'll know someone who will. Leave that one with me for now and I'll get back to you as soon as poss. It's tough for me to say this gentlemen, in view of what you've all just experienced, but we've just got to get on with it. For Christ sake be vigilant and swop lead man with observer every ten minutes from now on in. That's all. Good luck."

Ten minutes later a call came in from QinetiQ, the old aviation research establishment at Farnborough.

"Seems you've got a problem with an explosive device possibly triggered by a pressure transducer. The trick is to find a way to maintain pressure while you bring it down. It's exactly what we're usually trying to do when either flying or up mountains. Maintaining the right pressure, so the human body can cope with the reduced pressure around them. The mountain is my only clue. The only thing I can think of is to get hold of a Gamow bag."

"I'm sorry you've lost me. All this talk of mountains and bags. This is a national emergency not a debate on mountain craft."

"Sorry, but I'm thinking aloud here. Don't forget you've got me out of bed to try to help. Anyway, the Gamow bag is probably your only answer. Get one of these. Put your bomb in it and as you descend pump the pressure up in the bag and hopefully it should keep the bomb at its original pressure and not trigger the transducer. Sounds pretty hit and miss to me but I can't think of another option right now."

"Thanks for the advice, but where do I get one of these bags?"

"Yeah, I thought you'd be asking me that. You rarely find them in this country, because we don't have high mountains, but there's a guy at University College who's doing a lot of work in this area. There's a chance he'll have one. Hang on a minute, I think I have his details. Yes here it is. His name's Floyd Montgomery, Professor of Environmental Medicine. I've only got a work number. Best I can do."

"That's fine. We'll find a way to get him through our home office contacts."

"Best of luck."

With that Professor Montgomery's number at University College was noted and Major Little used his pass code to contact the night staff at the home office. They took twenty minutes to find Montgomery's home number and Major Little dialled immediately despite it now being well past midnight. Professor Montgomery's wife answered the phone and it soon transpired that Montgomery was out of the country. She recommended two research students who she thought would both know how to use the bag and gave Major Little their numbers. One of them didn't answer but the other offered to help in the morning.

"I don't think you appreciate the importance of this request," stated Major Little, trying to remain calm. "This is nothing short of a national emergency and I want you to get this bag thing to me within the hour, two at the most."

"But I'll have to get to the College, retrieve the bag and then get out to the Olympic Park."

"I have one man killed and four men seriously injured by bombs which I believe could be made safe with the use of your blasted bag. I want you here with the bag and ready to show me how it works immediately. Do I make myself clear?"

"I guess so," replied the disgruntled researcher, still nursing a sore head from celebrating a recent grant success. "I'll do my best."

"Good. If you can get yourself to University College by taxi, I'll have police motorbikes standing by for you and the bag at the front entrance on Gower Street in 30 minutes."

With that Major Little returned to the job in hand, instructing his men to locate the remaining bombs but to leave them in place. By the time the Gamow bag arrived a further three bombs had been located, each one in similar thermos flasks and all at the top of the stadium. Two men volunteered to use the bag and were instructed in its use. It was crude as you might expect for something designed for extreme mountain use and required a small pump to increase the pressure as the bomb was lowered to the centre of the track. The gauge on the bag was imprecise, having been designed to pump the bag to high atmospheric pressure. The men had little choice than to pump in air to maintain the shape of the bag as it was brought down the steps. When the bag was safely at the bottom, Major Little realised the folly of this plan. Retrieving the bag for the next bomb meant opening it, thus reducing the pressure and triggering the bomb. The mysterious person providing the information from QinetiQ hadn't been told there was more than one bomb so wouldn't have anticipated the need for multiple Gamow bags. The researcher, now fully awake, could see the problem and suggested a solution.

"Sir, you may just get away with some simple form of self-sealing bag and increase the pressure using the pump from the Gamow bag."

"Well worth a try, but at this time of night where on earth can we get any of these self-sealing bags?" replied Major Little, fast running out of options

"Kitchens, sir," suggested the researcher. "They're used all the time for food storage."

Thirty minutes later a supply of suitable bags had been obtained from kitchen stores in the athletes' village and the bombs were being gingerly sealed and slowly carried down to ground level as constant pressure was maintained. Miraculously it worked and an hour later the three bombs were stacked in the end of the long jump pit. Major Little had meanwhile been frantically sourcing supplies of sand bags. Considering the fact that it was way past midnight, his rank and approach, coupled with the severity of the situation, had worked wonders. Three helicopters were at this moment ferrying the stock in from several local builders' merchants. As every bomb was located a crew of auxiliaries brought in from a nearby TA centre carried the bags up the stands and into position around the bombs. The bomb disposal crew supervised the operation ensuring that a small access hole was left through the sandbags. Using an electronic probe some three metres in length, each bomb was laboriously but successfully detonated. The noise from each one was deafening and many athletes in the nearby village had a disturbed night, no doubt wondering if the Games could ever resume.

By five in the morning, as dawn was breaking in the eastern sky, the disposal crew had successfully dealt with eleven bombs, all located high up in the stands around the stadium. The twelfth bomb was illusive. In spite of a renewed search, and drafting in a further bomb disposal squad from the eastern region based in Colchester, the final bomb could not be found. Despite the time, frantic phone calls were now coming through from the Olympic Organising Committee demanding a decision on the safety at the stadium. Major Little was unmoved. He knew that the final bomb had to be found before he could even contemplate re-opening the site. He promised to phone back every hour and as the squad renewed their efforts it was clear that the stands were now unlikely to be the location of the final bomb. Every seat had been checked and double checked. The controlled explosions in the stands had taken out about eight seats for each bomb, but a small price to pay compared with the devastation had the seats been full. The potential carnage was too horrific even to contemplate. But still that final bomb. The squad slowly descended from the stands and converged in front of the royal box. It was inconceivable for a bomb to be here, but essential to make one final check of this area, already screened by sniffer dogs on a daily basis. In front of the box was the royal coat of arms and there cleverly concealed between the gilded metal of the arms and the retaining wall was the final bomb. It was beyond comprehension that this bomb could have been detonated at any time and could have eliminated members of the royal family, who were certain to be there for the closing ceremony. The royal coat of arms was removed from the front of the wall, taken to the centre of the track and detonated along with the others that had been brought down earlier. With one final explosion, heard over the whole of East London, the job was deemed complete. Twelve bombs located and detonated. The consequence for the rest of the Games had yet to be assessed, but Major Little after thanking his men, was able to report that to the best of his knowledge the stadium had been made safe. Whether or not the Games should resume was not his responsibility. He, like many people, waited with anticipation for the decision to be made by those at the top. For now, more pressing things were on his mind, and these included a shower and sleep.

Chapter 27

Jeremy Huntingdon, MP and Minister for Sport and Culture, was the first to arrive at Downing Street and with his ministerial pass was quickly admitted to number 10. Assistant Commissioner Roth arrived a few minutes later with Brigadier Babb and they were initially not permitted beyond the gates at the end of Downing Street. There was some delay as their clearance status was confirmed and they were then escorted the final thirty metres along one of the most famous streets in the world. Lord Cooke, who was well known to the Prime Minister, had to go through a similar clearance procedure in spite of being one of the most well-known faces in Britain. At exactly 6.25am the four men were led by a private secretary from the downstairs reception room to the cabinet room dominated by its vast oak table, shaped rather like an elongated coffin. To one side of this distinctive table was a smaller one, on which rested an impressive ceremonial sword, some one and a half metres in length, and housed in a silver scabbard. Each of the four men, now sitting at the sunlit eastern end of the table, were individually reflecting on the impressive number of key decisions that must have been made in this very room over preceding generations. As a clock outside chimed once to indicate the half hour, the door opened and the Prime Minister, flanked by the Home Secretary, came in and walked the length of the room to greet his guests. The private secretary who had escorted the visitors shut the door behind him and sat a discrete distance from the others. The four men rose in unison and shook hands with the Prime Minister, the Home Secretary clearly indicating that he could dispense with such formalities. The Prime Minister was dressed in a mid grey suit, a white shirt and his traditional light blue tie. The suit bore none of the hallmarks of a bespoke tailor, seemingly more from the upper price range of the ready-made stores, in keeping with his intended image of being a man of the people.

"Good morning gentlemen. I've ordered coffee and croissants, but even I can't get them before seven," smiled the Prime Minister, "so please help yourselves to juice for now."

As the cut glass jug full of orange juice was passed around, he continued. "I've had regular briefings from the Home Secretary over the last fourteen hours. As I understand it today's meeting has one major purpose – to make an unequivocal decision over the continuation or otherwise of the Games. Do we all agree on this very simple, albeit difficult agenda?"

The Prime Minister paused and looked at each person in the room in turn. As expected there was no dissent. Everyone gave approval in their own way, ranging from a quick closure of the eyes, coupled with an almost imperceptible nod of the head, to an audible 'Yes, sir'.

"My latest briefing at 06.00 this morning indicates that overnight the security forces, in combination with the military have safely removed twelve explosive devices from the Olympic Stadium. I also understand, sadly, that this resulted in further serious injury to two of our bomb disposal officers. How are they Charles?"

"They are both still in intensive care, sir. One has very nasty facial injuries which will ultimately need plastic surgery and the other has lost his right arm. They both appear to be in good spirits, although I'm sure the implications of their injuries have yet to be appreciated."

"Thank you, Charles," interrupted the Prime Minister, and

turning to his private secretary, said, "Stephen, prepare me a letter for the injured and their immediate relatives and I'll sign it before the cabinet meeting later. It was only through the good offices of these men and others like them, that the twelve bombs were detected and detonated. Damage to the stadium is relatively light and subject to our intelligence being correct, there is no expectation of any more devices. Is this essentially correct, gentlemen?"

"It is," said James Roth and Charles Babb in unison and the other two just nodded.

"So we now have the crucial decision to make. Do we continue the Games, essentially where we left off on Thursday afternoon, do we bow to the terrorists wishes to abandon the Games or do we come to some typically British compromise and truncate the Games, even to the extent of aborting the closing ceremony? Jeremy, you're ultimately responsible on behalf of the government for the Games. What's your view?"

"The government's policy has always been never to give in to any form of terrorism. I see absolutely no reason why the situation here should change that approach."

"Jeremy, I consider that a given. I want your view on the decision we have to make."

"My ministry is firmly behind continuing the Games as planned. We should get back on track as soon as possible and demonstrate this government's ability to run the most prestigious sporting event in our lifetime in spite of what's happened."

"Fine. Charles, back to you again. Your people have suffered most over this. Do you share Jeremy's view?"

Brigadier Babb was looking concerned as he listened intently through an earpiece connected to a mobile phone. From long experience he could pick up on cues around him and, even when his attention seemed to be elsewhere, he very quickly responded to the question.

"Frankly Prime Minister, I think we should exhibit more diligence than Jeremy seems to suggest. We do appear to have dealt with the threat for now and I have no further intelligence to suggest that any further terrorist action is planned. However we do need to recognise that the Games have been compromised and that our security coverage has been seriously breached. Sadly, I have just heard that another of our bomb disposal officers from the original explosion has died. Nothing can replace the harm and the hurt for the families of these men and others seriously injured to date. Even if we assume that no further incidents occur, I feel that it shows little respect to my men if we just restart the Games, almost as if nothing has happened."

"Charles, I understand and sympathise with your view. Have you any specific alternative option from those I indicated earlier?"

"No Prime Minister, not as such. I just feel that we shouldn't rush into a decision with all the security issues still very much unresolved."

"James, you're head of security for the Games, do you share Charles' view?"

"In part, yes, Prime Minister, but I also appreciate the national pride which is at stake and the clear message we must send to international terrorism. One can never be a hundred percent certain, but all the evidence I have is that we have contained this particular terrorist incursion. I am confident that all the bombs have been found and dispensed with. Given time, we can alter the security arrangements to prevent any bags of any sort entering the stadium. The hundred or so seats we lost when detonating the remaining bombs, once again given time, can be replaced. Alternatively we can re-allocate those seats to unused ones in the sponsors' boxes. However inconvenient, I believe that we should maintain the mobile network embargo for the duration of the Games. Fortunately the media centre is all hard wired so they will be able to communicate to the outside world and all our security personnel use short wave."

Assistant Commissioner Roth was interrupted by a knock on the door and tea, coffee and croissants were brought in on a trolley. He waited while the light breakfast was distributed to all around the end of the table. The Prime Minister turned to the smartly-dressed attendant and asked him to thank the cook for organising things at such an early hour. The attendant bent down to the prime minister and whispered in his ear.

"Perfect," was the response, and the attendant withdrew discreetly.

"I'm sorry for that interruption, James, but I'm sure this will be most welcome. You were indicating that if the Games were to proceed, then you felt security was sufficient."

"More than sufficient, Prime Minister. I couldn't possibly recommend that the Games continue unless every element had been considered and brought up to a triple A rating."

"Thank you, James. Seb, what would be the implications for you of the three options I outlined earlier?"

Lord Cooke had been making notes throughout the meeting and placing his silver propelling pencil to one side, turned to the Prime Minister.

"Prime Minister, the organising committee has overnight been running some software on two of the options you suggested. Truncation of the Games, especially abandoning the closing ceremony would be an economic, political and even social disaster. We accept that the Games has cost considerably more than the original budget, but cancelling the closing ceremony would lose more than twenty percent of our overall budget. Most of our main sponsors have a contract clause which requires us to deliver every aspect of the Games. I am not saying they would all use this to avoid payment, but it is a possibility. I don't have to tell you about the massive impact on losing the television and other media coverage. That speaks for itself. The bottom line is that the Games would be a financial disaster, whereas right now everything is containable. The political and national embarrassment is also self evident. We made a big issue six months ago about the huge security investment. I believe this embarrassment can only be ameliorated by showing that, in spite of what happened, we can deliver every aspect of the track and field programme and the closing ceremony. The country as a whole has become enthused by the Games beyond my wildest dreams. Millions of people throughout the UK have become personally involved in ways that would be impossible to list right now. Prime Minister, let me give one simple example. The closing ceremony should be the day after tomorrow, a Sunday. I have been informed that over three thousand churches throughout Britain have changed their normal Sunday services so that their congregations can see the closing ceremony and then still attend church. The majority of these are organising large screen events so that they integrate with the local community. This is just one story. Any form of truncation or cancellation would by extremely damaging to the national psyche right now. Prime Minister, I have been charged with delivering these Games and I can deliver. Pre-empting your question, Prime Minister, I have nothing more to add."

"Thank you, Seb. Home Secretary do you have any questions or comments?"

"Not at this stage, Prime Minister."

"Home Secretary," exclaimed the Prime Minister, showing an increasing level of frustration, "we need to make a decision very soon. As you are well aware, we have a cabinet meeting in just over an hour. There will be little opportunity for questions or comments once the decision is made."

"Then perhaps we should move to the vote, Prime Minister."

"Home Secretary, I thought we might be able to avoid that as I was hoping we could reach a consensus. However, I sense there is a level of disagreement around the table and I therefore propose not a formal vote, but a final brief statement from each one of you. Before that, however, gentlemen, we will have a very short recess. During this time we can enjoy some bacon sandwiches, as I am reliably informed cook has kindly prepared some for us. I'm sure that the Home Secretary will confirm that this is the first time that bacon sandwiches have been served for a meeting in Downing Street, at least by this government."

The Prime Minister pressed a bell on the wall. Miraculously the door to the cabinet room opened and fresh tea, coffee and a large platter of deliciously smelling bacon sandwiches appeared, this time brought in by the Downing Street cook to universal approval.

Five minutes later, the Prime Minister called for the meeting to continue and invited everyone to make a final statement.

Lord Cooke and Assistant Commissioner Roth both indicated that the Games should continue as soon as possible. Brigadier Babb remained opposed to restarting the Games without further evidence that the security issues, and especially the safety of his men, had been totally eliminated. Recognising that should the decision need a vote, he would be a lone voice in support of the cancelling the Games, Charles Babb made a short but impassioned plea for an appropriate recognition of the lives that had been lost in the terrorist attack.

"Rest assured, Charles, that I will do everything in my power to show the country's debt to your men. James, as a minimum, I propose a one minute silence in homage to those who have died at the start of each remaining day."

"Of course, Prime Minister."

"So gentlemen, we do not have consensus, but as with Seb and James, I am in favour of the Games continuing as soon as possible. James, you said earlier that you would need time to re-arrange seat allocation and to organise the prevention of any bags entering the stadium. How much time?"

"We could reopen the stadium at lunchtime today, and

complete the full afternoon session. We could also run on a little later than planned with the light evenings at this time of year."

"Excellent. And Seb, working on this restart time, have your people been able to plan the rescheduling of the missed events?"

"We have, Prime Minister. It will be incredibly tight and it will need a huge amount of goodwill from the athletes. Some of the award ceremonies will have to run back to back and be shortened, but we can be confident that every event can be concluded thirty minutes before sunset on Saturday. This will inevitably leave less time for the final rehearsal for the closing ceremony, but I can guarantee it will start on time as planned."

"Thank you, I admire your confidence. So, gentlemen, I appreciate your candour over this difficult issue and accepting Charles' reservations, I will now propose to the cabinet this morning that the Games restarts at 12.30pm today and this will be formally announced at a press conference at 10.00am. Any final comments? Thank you. I will take silence as assent and appreciate that you all recognise in situations like this the important distinction between agreement and acceptance. I only wish more of my colleagues, who will sit around this table at 8.30 this morning, could appreciate the same. I call this meeting to a close and thank you all for your attendance."

With that the Prime Minister, stood up, shook hands briefly and left the cabinet room closely followed by his private secretary and the Home Secretary.

"You appreciate," said Lord Cooke to no one in particular and still consulting his notes, "that one of the many consequences of this decision is that Josh Silverman would now have to run on Saturday afternoon. Sadly his religion doesn't permit that."

Charles Babb and James Roth made no comment.

CHAPTER 28

August 10th, 2012
Golders Green, London, UK

Josh was utterly disconsolate. To run on the Sabbath was against the teachings of the holy book, yet this single race had been his life's ambition for four years. How could the God he loved, the God he had entrusted with everything, put him in this unbearable position? Only once before in his life had he suffered such a moral dilemma. This was when the first opportunity to be paid substantial money to race, so called appearance money, meant he had to run on the Sabbath. His agent was desperate for Josh to run, arguing that this provided the solid foundation for future earnings from the sport. Josh prayed then for guidance and eventually followed the embedded culture of him and his forefathers to rest on the Sabbath. But this was different. This was not some Scandinavian meeting where records could be broken but faith could be destroyed. This was the final of the Olympic Games, in his home country, with billions watching on TV. Probably his last chance ever to win the coveted gold medal. As he prayed once again, fervently, feverishly, with an almost unbearable anguish, kneeling with eyes closed and hands clasped over his ears, he failed to detect the shrill sound of his mobile ringing a few feet away. The ringing stopped and such was the intensity of his prayer that when Rachel came into the room he failed to notice her standing there watching his pain.

"Lord God, please show me the way," Josh implored. "Your way will be the right way, and I will trust your judgement." Josh stood, saw Rachel and smiled.

"There will be a way, Josh," said Rachel. "We are both confident in the Lord's purpose."

"I'm sorry Rachel." said Josh, moving closer to give her a hug, "I didn't hear you come in."

"I could hear your mobile ringing, so came up to find it."

Josh picked up his phone and clicked on his message box. "It's from Rabbi Levin, inviting us both for the Sabbath feast. Perhaps God is guiding me to share my problems with Rabbi Levin. I can't think of a better way just now. I'll ring him back."

"Josh, it's a lovely invitation and you must go, but would you mind if I stayed away tonight. I know Rabbi Levin will want to discuss the situation privately and honestly I have something pretty big on at the moment and I would really welcome an evening in alone."

"Rachel it's your choice, but you know you'll miss a rather special meal."

"Sadly, yes; it could have been your celebration meal, so don't get too carried away with Greta's cooking. And please Josh, don't be late. When you've talked with Rabbi Levin, I need some time with you."

Josh took Rachel in his arms and with her right cheek on his chest he held her tightly, his thoughts still scrambled and searching for an answer. Gently stroking the contours of her chin he lifted her mouth to his and their kiss sealed the shared resolve to find the answer. Not any answer, but the one that would honour their God and themselves in mutual agreement.

"It'll work out," said Rachel, "I know."

Josh squeezed her hand. "Together it will," he replied and after a few seconds he reluctantly released his grip to call the Rabbi he had known since childhood.

Josh arrived at Rabbi Levin's house promptly at seven o'clock. Rabbi Levin was clearly no gardener and it was quite a struggle working his way past overgrown bushes and trees that needed more regular pruning to get to the front door. Josh met Rabbi Levin when he was the PE teacher at Josh's school, long before he trained as a rabbi. It was David Levin who had seen his potential as an athlete and had persuaded him to give up his aspirations to play for Arsenal and concentrate on the track. Reluctant at first, David Levin's inspirational training methods had brought Josh from being a promising, but raw runner to win the English Schools 800 metres in a record time. When David Levin decided to retrain as a rabbi, he kept one thing from his earlier career. David Levin always kept his love of physical activity and personal fitness. In fact these days he was a veteran triathlete of county standard and retained the slim, wiry physique necessary for his sport.

As the solid front door swung open, Rabbi Levin greeted Josh with enthusiasm and with a powerful handshake almost dragged him into house. "Greta can't wait to try her latest culinary creation on you Josh, because you know she's always valued your opinion."

"I can't think why, David, you know that since I got serious about athletics my diet has been incredibly boring."

"Well just try a little and pretend to like it," said Rabbi Levin, with a big smile, "and anyway it should be right up your street as its some type of vegetarian pasta."

"So you're still not let into the secrets of Greta's specials." Josh teased. "You just enjoy everything placed in front of you."

"Of course, of course. I always say that my contribution to cooking is to keep out of the kitchen, and it's worked so far. And don't forget, young Josh, that so far it's been 26 years. The kids are dying to see you again. Sam is down from Cambridge and Becky is staying with us while she finds a new flat. I'm afraid her last set of flat mates didn't work out, but no doubt she'll tell you all about it. Sorry Rachel couldn't make it, but professional women these days seem to have to work all the time. Great shame. Great shame."

With that, Josh was ushered into the bowels of the house, a house he knew well from many visits over the years.

"A quick drink before dinner, Josh?"

"Of course, but just a soft one, please," was Josh's anticipated reply.

"Of course, but you'll take a small glass of the Sabbath wine with your meal?"

"David, how could I come to the Sabbath meal with your family and not take the wine, but please just a drop?"

The candles were lit, the prayers of thanks were intoned, hands were held and after the symbolic preliminaries, the Sabbath was welcomed. Soon, as the wine was enjoyed, Sam, Becky and Greta brought Josh up to date with their respective lives and activities, while Rabbi Levin patiently waited for the meal to conclude. He knew there were important issues to discuss and Josh couldn't wait too long.

"Greta, thank you for a lovely meal," said Rabbi Levin, "can I leave the children to clear up while Josh and I talk?"

"Of course, darling. Why don't you and Josh go to the study and I'll bring you both some fresh coffee?"

With that, the athlete and his mentor retired from the meal to Rabbi Levin's study. David's study was simple, almost to the point of being stark. It had a small bookcase, sparsely filled with not more than a dozen books. An old and rather cheap desk was littered with letters, papers, a phone and a large and well thumbed Torah. The most dominant items in the room were two identical chairs. They were well worn, comfortable and no different from those seen in many homes throughout the land. Sitting in these chairs seemed to put people at their ease. Rabbi Levin was aware of this in himself and made the reasonable assumption that others felt the same. He considered these chairs to be an essential part of his work and valued them as a way of helping those who occupied them to relax. This evening was as important an occasion as could be imagined. One of the occupants was here to get advice on what could be the most important decision in his life. The other was to give that advice.

"Josh, shall we start with prayer?"

Josh nodded assent, closed his eyes and allowed himself to relax with the tension starting to flow from his shoulders deep into the back of his chair. "Holy father, guide us in our thoughts and give us the confidence to make the right decisions and the strength to carry them through. Amen."

"David, I knew when you called that God had his hand on this whole venture. Can I summarise? Following the terrorist attack on the Olympic stadium, nothing has been finalised but it's looking almost 100 percent that the 1500 metre final will be tomorrow sometime. David you know my stance on this one. I've never been prepared to compromise our faith's view of the Sabbath, and it would be hard for me to act otherwise. But, David, I've worked so incredibly hard for this one opportunity to get a medal, even a gold medal. I'd be utterly devastated if I had to give this up. Four years of my life dedicated to one single objective. David, I need your help, my mind is in utter turmoil."

Rabbi Levin sat impassively, his eyes half closed. He gave the impression of meditation but was in fact thinking deeply of his response. His apparent reverie was interrupted when Greta came in with two steaming mugs of coffee and a plate of her home-made flapjacks. She placed them all within arms' reach on the old desk, having cleared a space for the tray by moving one of her husband's piles of papers. Josh thanked her profusely and as she left the room Greta squeezed his shoulder as she passed, showing her concern and support. Rabbi Levin noted the gesture, smiled approvingly, and turned to his visitor with renewed focus.

"Josh, let's try to put this difficult dilemma in perspective. Firstly this is nothing new. The Christian, Eric Liddell took exactly the same view in the 1924 Olympics and refused to run on the Christian Sabbath. More recently Jonathan Edwards, the triple jumper, would not compete on a Sunday but sadly he lost his faith along with his resolve. The Sabbath is without doubt an important day in our week and Leviticus commands us to 'do no manner of work'. For the Orthodox Jew this could be as extreme as setting lights on timers to avoid switching them on. Most Conservative Jews wouldn't worry about such things and would feel perfectly at ease driving to the synagogue. Many Reform Jews will ignore such restrictions entirely, but will try to attend the evening service on a Friday night. Our faith luckily for me, Josh, is broad in its interpretation. As you know there is little of the Orthodox in me, but I still love and respect those in our community who feel and act in the way they interpret the holy words. Remember, Josh, that the Sabbath restrictions do not prohibit everything that takes effort. Far from it. On the contrary, we are encouraged to play games, to exercise, study the Torah, sing, go to lectures, or make love with our wives on the Sabbath. It is work itself that is forbidden, but play and sport is encouraged. Josh let me ask you this simple question, Do you see your running as work?"

"It's undoubtedly my occupation, David, but I've only ever seen my running as a God given talent which for now occupies my time fully. It's certainly not a career and my only income is from bursaries and sponsorship. For this period of my life my running is something I'm prepared to give all my time to, simply to be the best that I can be."

"Well said, Josh. A somewhat erudite answer to a simple question if I may say so, but Josh, I'm looking for your true conviction, your soul. When you're training outside on a miserable day and you're exhausted and you know that you can only go back to a limited diet and more of the same, how do you feel then? Do you still feel this in your heart to be work, as others perceive work, or is it something else?"

"David, I really don't know. There are clearly times when it's incredibly hard, but many amateur sportsmen would say the same. You know that as a competitive triathlete. Your training's as tough as it gets, having to work at three disciplines. Let me turn the question round on you, David, do you consider your training and competing in triathlons to be work?"

"Of course not, Josh, but my situation is somewhat different. I do have a clear job description and my sport is a true recreation."

"OK, so let me ask you a different question, David. Would you compete in a triathlon on the Sabbath?"

"Josh, you're asking me a question which is truly hypothetical because by far the majority of my events are held on a Sunday and I always have the choice. Plus the fact that in my position I need to take account of the feelings of my Orthodox flock. But you ask a fair question and I shall give you an honest answer. If I were confident that taking part in a triathlon had no conventional element of work, then I would be happy to participate. The difference, Josh, is that if I were to get it wrong, the impact would be minimal. I may upset a few of my parishioners; some may even stop speaking to me for a while. But unlike you, my decision will not be headlining the sports pages of every newspaper in the land. If you choose not to race, then the impact will be nationwide and the sport loving British will be collectively disappointed. Many will understand your stance and will respect you for it. Some will interpret it as an illustration of how religion is an unnecessary controlling force in free will. One thing I can guarantee is that within a week it will all be forgotten. If it hadn't been for the film 'Chariots of Fire', Eric Liddell would hardly be remembered. Do you know, they even lost the whereabouts of his gravestone for almost thirty years? If, on the other hand you do race on the Sabbath, then it might merit an editorial in the Jewish Chronicle, little more. Those Jews with no love of sport may shun you for a while and you might expect some highly critical letters and emails. But this will all be temporary. Sadly, we are not a very forgiving nation, but time will heal, especially for someone with a gold medal in his hand. Josh, I didn't invite you here this evening to give you an opinion, just to share with you your own dilemma. Our God will guide you. My advice is to go home and talk to Rachel. Pray, sleep on it, pray some more and then you will be able to decide with absolute confidence. In fact you won't decide, God will do it for you."

Josh, looking at his watch and remembering Rachel's request for him not to stay late, sought out Greta, Sam and Becky, made his farewells and returned to the Rabbi's study. Rabbi Levin was back at his desk, scribbling a note on a piece of paper. Folding it carefully, he sealed it in an envelope and gave it to Josh.

"Open this when you are ready. Shalom," he said, shaking Josh's hand warmly. Josh placed the envelope in an inside pocket and headed out into the gathering gloom.

CHAPTER 29

August 10th, 2012
Thamesview, London, UK

Thirty minutes later, Josh turned the key in his flat on the twelfth floor. He and Rachel had been together for two and a half years and had managed to keep their relationship out of the media. This was in part because Josh never courted media attention. He was not the type to be seen falling out of night clubs at two in the morning or attending film premieres. He made the occasional appearance on TV programmes like 'A Question of Sport' but he was content with a close circle of old friends and a life well away from the wrong end of the paparazzi camera lens. The other reason that he and Rachel's partnership was kept out of the limelight was much more by chance. In the early days of their relationship they had coincidentally bought flats in the same large block in Brixton and found that they could see each other by simply using the stairs between flats. As no one else seemed to use the stairs, it was not difficult to visit each other both frequently and discreetly. As this worked so well, they both continued the arrangement as they upgraded their property. They now had identical flats, with almost identical views, separated by nothing more than three floors. Rachel's flat was on the ninth floor and Josh's on the twelfth. As their relationship developed and became more intimate, they had the choice of spending their time together in either of their respective flats. Depending on their working schedules, they could be found returning to their own flats after an evening together or increasingly since their engagement staying over at one or other of the flats which were so conveniently located. To them both, this was an ideal arrangement, especially as they had agreed to postpone even the discussion of wedding plans until after the Olympics. The other important discussion they had concerned their sexual relationship. Unusually for young people of the 21st century, they had both agreed that a full sexual relationship was to be kept for their wedding night. They were not sure about the whys and wherefores of such a decision, but it was one they found comfortable and somehow strengthened their personal bond. Neither of them was prudish or insecure sexually, they just felt that for them the right moment could be delayed. At the times when one of them stayed over they would happily share a bed and enjoy the intimacy of each other. It was just that full sexual union was something they preferred to look forward to at this stage in their lives and the strength of their joint will kept it this way.

On entering his flat, Josh found Rachel engrossed in her laptop, almost as he had left her hours earlier. She looked up, smiled, shut the laptop down and came over to kiss him.

"How did it go?" she enquired, "was David helpful?"

"Enormously," he replied, "he has that knack of listening well and always giving a deeper perspective. He's a real friend."

"And have you come to a decision?" said Rachel, as she poured them both a large tonic water with ice from the fridge and a slice of both lemon and lime.

"Not yet," replied Josh, "his advice was to pray and talk to you before taking any action."

"Josh," said Rachel with a tone of resignation in her voice, "we do need to talk, because I have some worrying news for you. I've been deliberately keeping it from you, but you need to know it all from me and it has to be now."

She took his hand in hers, led him to the low settee which faced the picture window overlooking the long embankment of the Thames. They had paid dearly for this view with the curved line of the river now lit by numerous street lights. It was their favourite place in both of their flats and they had taken great pleasure in making sure they both had the same view from the same picture window in either flat. There were times when if one of them was away, they could sit in their own flat in this very spot and feel a strong and enduring bond. It was their safe haven, their shelter in the storms of life, their 'still small voice of calm'.

Rachel curled her long legs up under her, took a long sip of her tonic. "Josh," she said, looking him straight in the eye, "I know you've had a miserable 24 hours and believe me I wish I could do more to help, but you need to hear me out. There are things going on in the background of the Games, especially around your event that you have to know. I would give anything to keep you in the dark, even for another day, but the situation has developed to the point that tomorrow would be too late. Sadly it concerns your agent Nigel Gressley. To put it bluntly, Josh, Nigel has been finding numerous ways to influence the outcome of the 1500 metre final. As far as I can see he has done nothing which affects you in any way. Then why should he? He has everything to gain from your success and everything to lose if you don't succeed. Nigel has systematically been finding methods to ruin the chances for most of the other finalists. It appears that he has been planning this for years and has even tested one of his methods at the Commonwealth Games meeting in 2010."

Josh felt a cold sweat engulf him as he sat and listened to this preposterous accusation.

"Are you trying to tell me that my friend, one of the few guys to stick with me for the last four years, is some type of crook?"

"Worse than that, Josh. I'm not talking about fiddling accounts or actions which result in a criminal sentence, I'm talking about very serious accusations which, if true, make Nigel Gressley one of the most untrustworthy and degenerate men I know."

Rachel then described in as much detail as she could the series of incidents in which Gressley had been planning to compromise the individual abilities of each finalist. She explained to a disbelieving listener the way he had manipulated the running shoes of Carrera, how he was planning to get Ngeny to drink EPO, the spurious text message for Gabet, the way he had organised a sexual liaison for Benito, his plan to inject Ho with corticosteroids and finally how he was intending to infect the three American athletes. Rachel was careful to explain in her narrative the basis for each accusation. How in some cases she had video evidence, in others transcripts of emails and for some little more than the word of Jim Stringer. Josh sat there stunned to the core. He could hardly function as he absorbed the level of barbarism described by Rachel. As he felt a pounding in his chest only associated with an extreme training session, he turned to Rachel and exclaimed in an anguished tone "Rachel, darling, what on earth are we going to do?"

"Josh," Rachel replied, "although the evidence is utterly damning, until Gressley plays his hand totally, or is actually caught in the act, everything I have told you is by definition speculation. It is possible, though in my view unlikely, that he could change his mind over any of the heinous actions he appears to have planned. Frankly, I cannot imagine having come this far, in so many ways, that he would not continue with even one of them. I mean if there was just one athlete he was trying to restrain, then you might imagine him having second thoughts and let his conscience get the better of him. But we're talking here about numerous athletes, all in one race."

"But Rachel, shouldn't the police become involved? Can't we warn these athletes to be on their guard? Can't we do something constructive instead of sitting here debating it?"

"I've tried to look at all the options, I really have. The police cannot act unless they have much stronger evidence.

I've spoken to my editor and he thinks that all athletes will be fully briefed about this type of thing in general, but Gressley is far too clever and specific in his threats to them all. He has specifically targeted the apparent weakness in each athlete in a most menacing way, using everything from physical assault to psychological abuse. Not only that, but some of his crimes must have already been committed. He is already likely to have attacked Ho with an injection and the Americans with bacteria. He will have switched the shoes for Carrera, somehow got EPO into Ngeny's system and at this very time I should imagine that Angelo Benito is being seduced. I guess the only thing we could do is to contact Gabet and warn him to expect a hoax phone call or text tomorrow. It's now ten o'clock and you know Gabet well enough to be sure he's in bed. I promise I will do that first thing in the morning, but it assumes he will pick up."

"Rachel are you sure there's nothing else we can do? It's just too horrific for words."

"I'm sorry, Josh, but at this stage we are stuck between a rock and a hard place. The paper should have gone to print with the whole story last night following the final, but I got the editor to hold off until after the race. It will be launched in the lunchtime addition tomorrow and continue into the evening editions."

"And does this sordid affair have to be printed?" said Josh, somewhat naively.

"Josh, how else can we bring this guy to any form of justice? We print stories which are predominantly in the public interest and this story is absolutely huge. You can see that. I'm convinced this is the right thing to do. I'm just so gutted that it involves you, my love, and that in the biggest race of your life you could be starting at a distinct advantage."

For the last hour as Rachel had recounted Nigel Gressley's malicious plans, Josh had given no thought to his own personal moral dilemma. Rachel's reference to tomorrow's race brought everything back into focus. Rabbi Levin had advised him to talk to Rachel, but the devastating news about Nigel Gressley had given no chance for the one thing he wanted to share with her.

"Rachel, a moment ago you used the expression 'between a rock and a hard place' and this is exactly how I feel about me running on the Sabbath."

"Oh Josh, I'm so sorry," said Rachel, moving closer to him and resting her back on his chest. "I've been so consumed by the issues over Gressley that I've failed you totally in your horrendous situation. Darling, please forgive me for being so selfish, but I honestly felt that this news about Gressley has to influence your own decision."

Josh pulled her tightly to him and as Rachel looked up their lips met. At last they slowly pulled apart and somehow their affection for each other generated mutual energy and created a new clarity of thought. Josh was the first to speak.

"Rachel, darling, if I choose to run it will be seen by some as dishonouring the Sabbath, the one our God designated as the day of rest. So in doing so I dishonour God, which would cause me great sadness. On the other hand, Rachel, by running and even by winning, I bring great honour to God. It is only He who has brought me to this critical stage in my life. To Him alone is the honour, the whole of my being is nothing without God."

"Josh, you know I share your faith, but why oh why has our God allowed people like Nigel Gressley to do the things he has done?"

"Rachel, Nigel is evil. The devil challenges our God frequently and in unimaginable ways. Surely the only way to challenge the devil is in God's name. You have done this by preparing your article for tomorrow's paper. If I fail to run, the whole exposé becomes almost irrelevant. My success is the counterbalance between every malevolent action that Nigel has engineered. I have to believe that God has His hand in all of this and our God must be greater than the prohibitions of our faith. The Sabbath was made a day of rest for a purpose and I love and respect that purpose. I just honestly think that I can honour God's ultimate purpose by running a great race in His name."

Rachel embraced Josh once more, snuggled closer, and the two in perfect harmony of thought and deed truly relaxed in each other's arms. Josh, enjoying the moment, allowed his mind to wander back over the events of the evening. As he recalled the wise words of Rabbi Levin, he suddenly remembered the envelope that he was given and David's words to 'open this when you are ready'. Josh gently unwrapped Rachel from him he took the envelope from his pocket.

"David gave me this when I was leaving, Rachel. He said to open it when I was ready and I think I'm now ready."

He opened the envelope with care using a knife his father had given him on his very first fishing trip. In the envelope was a single sheet of paper with two quotations. At the top, in David's distinctive handwriting, were the words:

Josh, I give you these passages with my love. The first is from our own bible and the second from the bible the Christians use. The order is important.

1 Samuel 2:30 Those who honour me, I will honour

Hebrews 12:1 Let us run the race that is before us and never give up.'

Josh showed the passages to Rachel, who was now back in his arms. She turned, smiled, kissed his cheek and whispered "Josh, it's time for bed."

She led him to the bedroom and that night, gently and in total harmony, they relaxed in each others' arms, exhausted from the tensions of the day. As they lay there together, lost in their own private thoughts, they knew that being together like this was all so right. They both felt a mutual level of contentment, which, with God's help, could sustain them for whatever tomorrow would bring.

CHAPTER 30

August 10th, 2012
Hampton Lodge, UK

The Hampton Lodge hotel was the perfect venue for the stars of the Italian team and only the potential medallists were invited to stay there. It provided a combination of untold luxury with all the support structure needed for the final stages of Olympic preparation. Benito spent his time between relaxed training, one to one sessions with his sports psychologist and last minute advice from the nutritionists and coaches dedicated to bringing him to peak performance for the 1500 metre final. In between all of these focussed activities, Benito relaxed with colleagues or alone, reading, playing cards or watching specially selected and somewhat bland DVDs, designed to be entertaining without causing any deep emotional impact. This was not the time to expose the prima donnas of the athletic world to films about the Holocaust or the horrors of global warming. The selected few from the Italian team were revered and lauded by a country obsessed with winning. They were not limited by convention or history. They revelled in the Italian notion of style and made sure that however they win, they win in style.

No one was sure if Jep Lu Song was her real name because professional hostesses were always kept anonymous. This was mainly to ensure that disaffected clients could not trace them, but in Jep's case this had never been an issue. Jep was the consummate professional and made a habit of always satisfying her clients. She was good and she knew it. The only slight concern for Nigel Gressley when employing Jep was that she rarely needed to encourage her clients. Normally Jep's clients were ready and willing and Jep, within reason, would follow their wishes. She had one or two experiences that she would rather forget, but as her clients usually came from the very rich, the famous or in a few cases the infamous, she always knew that disclosure of their extra-curricular activities could be very damaging. That said, the agency Jep worked for had an unblemished reputation for discretion, and this was particularly important for the delicate task required that evening. Jep had been relaxing in room 23 in the Hampton Lodge for two days, increasingly annoyed that the delay in the Olympic programme had spoiled her busy, somewheat unusual schedule.. She had enjoyed a hot bath and spent time deciding which of the two somewhat revealing dresses she would wear that evening. It was a long time since she had actually been required to seduce someone and the prospect excited her. From what she had been told, it all sounded very straightforward. Approach Angelo Benito without involving others, keep him thoroughly occupied and awake for the rest of the night and leave him in the morning exhausted but happy. It almost sounded fun. Jep chose the short black dress with the plunging neckline. The dress suited her slim, petite figure and following a lengthy appraisal in the room's full length mirror, Jep decided it was the perfect choice. She decided it was time to make herself more visible and taking one more look at Benito's photo, she strolled down to the restaurant to eat at the table prebooked to give her a good view of the whole room. The twelve athletes staying at Hampton Lodge, easily distinguished by their country's tracksuits, drifted into the dining room in twos and threes. Jep watched them carefully as they ordered their meals, mainly pasta and pizza, each one treating their food as though it was the most important thing in the world. Jep stole a glance at her photo of Benito and was concerned that he was nowhere to be seen. She decided that immediate action was necessary and, strolling over to the Italian athletes, she asked for their autographs. She was soon chatting amiably about their home towns and the Italian countryside as if she had lived there all her life.

"It's a big day tomorrow for some of you I guess," said Jep, appearing to be interested, "are you all competing tomorrow?"

"Only Angelo," came the answer, "and he always eats in his room the night before a final. It's his routine. From early evening before every final he locks the door and does his own thing. Knowing Angelo, it could be anything, probably involving some adult movies."

Jep had all the information she needed and soon made her excuses. "Good luck guys," she added as she left. A testosterone surge emanated from the remaining Italian diners and admiring glances followed her as she headed out. Jep returned to her room, with an ever increasing interest in the elusive Angelo Benito. She decided it was better to act now before Benito's team mates returned from their meal. She ordered two bottles of champagne from room service, insisting it arrived urgently. One of the bottles she left on ice in her room, and the other she placed on a tray with two champagne flutes. Jep smoothed her dress down, took a deep breath and walked the length of the corridor to room 43. She knocked on the door and waited with anticipation as Benito reacted to this unexpected intrusion.

"Who's there?" was the muffled response. Jep knocked again and waited, not wanting to give anything away. From inside she could hear the television being turned down and Benito moving across the floor. Eventually the door was cautiously opened, Benito keeping the chain in place as he looked out into the poorly lit corridor. Jep saw Benito in the flesh for the first time and was pleasantly surprised. This could be an enjoyable evening she thought with a real man. It would make a pleasant change from the usual rich, overweight punters she serviced on an all too regular basis.

"A big day tomorrow," she said, "thought you might enjoy a

nightcap."

"I'm sorry," said Benito, "do I know you?"

"I'm a guest in the hotel and was talking to the rest of the squad. You were missing and I thought you might need cheering up."

"Thanks, but I'm fine," was Benito's response, still peering through the crack in the door, "kind of you to offer."

Jep was not to be rebuffed so easily and added "At least take the champagne, I feel stupid standing here outside your room."

"I'm sorry," said Benito politely, "I'm forgetting my manners." With that he released the chain and opened the door cautiously. "Please leave the champagne on the table."

Jep strolled into the bedroom and surveyed the scene rapidly. She made sure that as the tray was placed on the table she faced Benito and leant forward. As Jep bent down she revealed a deep cleavage and Benito's eyes lingered on the upper surface of her pert breasts.

"Shall I pour you the champagne?" said Jep, still leaning forward and giving Benito a willing smile.

"Why don't you pour us both some champagne?" said Benito, "perhaps I do need cheering up after all."

Jep knew that she had to pace things this evening. This was no ordinary assignation where the conclusion was known well in advance. She opened the champagne with a flourish, a skill noted with interest by Benito, and poured them both a large glass. As she turned, cleverly concealing the glasses from Benito, Jep dropped half a pill of rohypnol into his glass. Just right, she thought. This will relax him totally but will keep him interested for a very long time.

Benito took a longer look at Jep and liked what he saw. An hour in her company would be a most pleasant way to spend the early part of the evening and should have little impact on his performance a day later. Jep had other ideas. Angelo Benito, one of the fastest middle distance runners in the world, found it almost impossible to take his eyes off the young Thai beauty. She now sat on the edge of the bed, crossing and uncrossing her legs in a most provocative manner and happy to sip her champagne while Benito stared at this vision in front of him.

"So what brings you to London?" Benito enquired, quite genuinely.

"I am here to see my parents. They both live in town and I plan to surprise them tomorrow when it's their wedding anniversary. I flew into Gatwick earlier and was recommended to this hotel."

"So how long have they been married?" said Benito, taking another sip of the quite excellent champagne.

"Seventeen years," Jep answered, "they had me a year after they were married."

Benito tried hard not to show his excitement at the notion of an Asian girl of this tender age sitting sipping champagne in his room, but the involuntary scratching of his left ear gave away his true thoughts. His predilection for young women was matched by his enthusiasm for women from places like Thailand, Cambodia and Malaysia. Christ he thought, this girl has arrived gift wrapped. A heterosexual's dream come true. Benito just sat enjoying the vision in front of him. Jep, not used to such inactivity found it difficult to read him. There was obvious interest in her but an undoubted level of restraint. She tried to rationalise this unusual situation, where a man didn't make a move on her, especially as she was always willing to cooperate with their demands. She took time to appreciate that Benito was torn between the prospect of sexual fulfillment and what could be the biggest day in his life. He needed some encouragement.

"Angelo," said Jep, "you haven't even asked me my name and I'm sitting here at your invitation drinking champagne with you."

"I'm sorry," he replied, "once again you've caught me out

with very poor manners."

"Jeplina, but everybody calls me Jep. It means little dancer."

"Little dancer," repeated Benito, "how would your parents know that when you were born?"

"Oh no," said Jep, "in my country you are only named properly when you show some clear characteristics to suit your temperament. I wasn't named until I was six. I just loved to dance and still do. Finish your champagne and I'll find some music."

As Jep moved across the room, she made a point of filling Benito's glass, once again bending in front of him to show her breasts. Benito was mesmerised and starting to enjoy the effect of the champagne. Jep found some slow dance music on one of the radio channels, took Benito by the hand and guided him to the space in the room by the picture window. From this second floor room, the views over parkland were fast receding in the gathering gloom of the August dusk, but the remaining light created a mood in the room which was sensual and alluring. For Jep this was business and for Benito it was pure folly but the combination of alcohol and the small hit of rohypnol was starting to work its dubious charms. Jep led Benito in a slow, passionate dance which transported him back to the carefree days in Naples before his life was dominated by running. Benito had always found that the most sexually charged act, apart from intercourse itself, was to undress a woman while dancing to a slow rhythmical beat. In the arms of this beguiling girl, Benito had totally abandoned all resolve. They moved to the bed and it was then that the rohypnol kicked in. Benito collapsed, tried once to take Jep to him, but within seconds lost total consciousness. Jep cursed. This was not the plan. She wanted the drug to overcome his resistance but never expected such an extreme and uncharacteristic response. She tried to wake him by shaking him, gently at first but then with increasingly force. It was useless. Benito was now lying on his back breathing deeply, almost comatose. Jep covered him with the duvet and considered her options. She saw no reason to stay here in a room with an unconscious man. At this stage in the evening, there was also the risk that his team mates might call by to wish him luck. She would give it time for him to recover, return and finish the job. In the half light she dressed, picked up his door key and, after checking the corridor, walked briskly to her room. Jep lay on her bed, set the alarm for three hours time, sipped a cool tonic water from the minibar and drifted off into a troubled sleep. Jep woke to the shrieking of the alarm and at first couldn't distinguish it from her tempestuous dream. Slowly gathering her senses, she hit the snooze button, dragged herself from under the covers, was shocked to find herself still fully clothed and resolved to get back to the joyless task of keeping Benito up all night. Jep grabbed the room key to Benito's room and once again headed back along the still dark corridor. She slid the key into the lock in Benito's door, removed it and waited for the light to turn green. Nothing happened so she tried again without success. She took the key to the nearest security light some ten metres down the corridor and was horrified to see the card in her hand was for American Express. This evening was turning into a disaster and Jep was at a total loss. Returning to her room, she considered the impact of her failed efforts. She had left Benito some three hours previously in an unconscious state and had no idea what the impact of the date rape drug could be having on a highly tuned athlete. He could stay like that all day sleeping it off, or worse could be near to death. She soon rationalised that her best option was to quit. She had failed in her instructions to keep Benito awake all night with a succession of sexual activities, but who would ever know? She would be paid handsomely for the evening and hopefully that would be the end of the affair. Although inclined to leave the hotel immediately, she had to avoid any suspicion, so decided to wait until early breakfast was served some five hours later.

Soon after six thirty she ordered a taxi, took a light breakfast and checked out at the slowly awakening reception.

"Are you planning to see anything of the Games, Miss?" asked an all too cheerful concierge.

"Sadly, not," came the reply, "but I hear that today is the 1500 metre final. I would love to be there."

"We're all supporting the Italian team. I shouldn't tell you this but we have their star athlete, Angelo Benito staying here."

"Really," Jep replied, trying her best to sound interested, "well I hope he does well."

"Thank you, Miss. Your taxi is by the front door. Do you want a hand with your case?"

"Very kind, but I'm fine." With that Jep, turned on her heel and headed out into the fresh air of the Surrey countryside.

One hour later at exactly eight o'clock, Angelo Benito woke, stretched, wondered initially why he was not wearing his usual boxer shorts and then saw an empty champagne bottle. He had slept the sleep of the dead. He had not enjoyed such deep and relaxing sleep for years. Angelo Benito felt totally rested. He felt energised. He felt so good he found himself singing in the shower. This was not the normally sluggish Benito who would never train until at least three cups of strong coffee had worked its stimulating charm. Benito was ready to take on the world. Benito was on fire. As he left the room he picked up his credit card from under the door. Careless he thought. Very careless.

CHAPTER 31

August 11th, 2012
Olympic Park, UK

Khalid Gabet was probably the best middle distance runner Morocco had ever produced. His training regime in the Atlas Mountains was the stuff of legend and he always arrived at a competition fresh and in great physical shape. Although naturally talented and conditioned to perfection, the main reason given for Gabet's success was his family support and his strong religious belief. He was convinced he had a God-given destiny to be the best of the best. One of the benefits of his fame was that the Moroccan government had given him a large house in the Toubkal National Park, big enough for Gabet and his extended family. His wife, three children and parents all lived together in a home that overlooked the High Atlas Mountains in the distance and at an altitude of 3,500 metres gave him a permanent high altitude training base. Gabet would return there as often as the world tour would permit. He liked nothing more than to spend his days training twice a day and sharing with his family the more homely activities of tending his garden, baking bread and relaxing with his children and dogs. For many the remote location of his home would be seen as a severe handicap, but for Gabet, who was brought up on a poor homestead to the east of the country, it was heaven on earth. The nearest town, which was little more than a general store, a small bar and fuel dump was 30 kilometres away, but with his trusty Landrover, a gift from his main sponsor, Gabet managed to keep the family well supplied with provisions on a weekly basis. When Gabet was away from home, which was about five months in every year, the store in town would deliver food and other essentials as required. At the request of his wife, Gabet had installed satellite television which worked surprisingly well in such a remote location. With no mobile phone coverage in the immediate area, he experimented with a satellite phone, but after a variety of problems gave it up as an unnecessary convenience. He always made sure to catch up with the news on his weekly trips to town and would enjoy a cool lemonade in the shade of the bar's veranda while phoning his coach, friends and family. Gabet always knew that if anything serious happened which needed his attention, the storekeeper in town would be more than happy to drive over. He was a man who needed little beyond his love of running and close family. He was a man at peace with himself and this, in no small part, contributed to his phenomenal success on the track.

Nigel Gressley didn't need his psychological training to know that such a man as Gabet, with his simple and ordered lifestyle, only needed a sudden shock to cause severe distress. Severe distress would throw his physiological balance into disarray and this would be quite enough to cause Gabet to underperform. Gressley was about to deliver some distressing and totally fictitious news to Gabet. In spite of modern telecommunications, Gabet would have no way of verifying the news. It would haunt him, cause him anguish, even despair. If he ran, he would be thinking about it every step of the way. Gabet was about to be pushed off the podium as easily as if Nigel Gressley was there to do the pushing.

Nigel had weeks ago prepared his text and in saving it for later transmission, had fallen into the trap set by Jim Stringer's Tibetan friend.

It read 'To Khalid Gabet form the Brotherhood of Udra. We have your children Hassan and Shada in captivity. They are unharmed but frightened. Our demands are simple. For their safe release, you will pay one million dirham in cash. The money will be handed over to our contact in Marrakesh by Tuesday August 14th. Arrangements will follow. If you involve the police you will never see your children again. Any delay in our demands will result in permanent damage to your children.'

Nigel knew that Gabet left the athletes' village for the short walk to the warm up track some two hours before the race, so he timed it for exactly three hours before the race.

Gabet decided to leave for the training track early that morning. This was to be the most important race in his illustrious career and he knew just how time seems to accelerate on these big occasions. He'd already deliberately ignored a missed call from some reporter called Rachel Rosen, and he made a conscious decision to leave his mobile phone in his room that day. It was always nice to hear from his wife just before a big race, but as she was here in London they'd already spoken at length. As Gabet pulled the door closed in his room he could hear his mobile ringing from inside. His immediate response was to let it ring but at the last minute he re-entered his room and hit the green button. The text had been converted into a voice message so it was totally devoid of accent or intonation. This gave it an impersonal quality which made the chilling message even more intense. Gabet immediately broke into a cold sweat and collapsed onto the bed. In total disbelief he forced his shaking hands to replay the message. There was no doubt, the message was clear but how could it be true? His two young children, his joy, his life outside of running, in the hands of common criminals. Still in shock, his world seemed to take on a shapeless form. His thoughts became confused, chaotic and he lay inactive, almost paralysed, for what seemed like hours but was in fact no more than a few minutes. Slowly the fog lifted from his brain and he recognised the futility of doing nothing. He grabbed his mobile and headed out the door for the second time that fateful morning. Unsteadily he made his way out of the athletes' village and walked slowly, but determinedly towards the warm up track. He had to share his horror with someone, but had no clear plan. His knew his wife, Salima, would be unable to cope with such horrendous news, so she could not be told. How could this be? How could his parents, who had always been so loving, so cautious, so protective and so careful, allow this to happen? As his mind raced through the options, he was ashamed that he was even considering his parents were to blame. He had no details; they could have been injured protecting his children. Conceivably they could have been killed. As he continued to walk, he was totally unaware of his surroundings, of other athletes smiling and wishing him luck. He was acting like an automaton, a zombie, a walking ghost. He was in motion, moving towards the track, his limbs responding but his brain in neutral. His eyes could see, but nothing focussed; as his tongue passed over his lips it registered the salt of his sweat but he tasted nothing; the cacophony of sounds from around the park were hitting his eardrums but he heard nothing. His mobile phone, still in his hand, rang and vibrated in unison, but the dual sensation simply could not penetrate his deficient nervous system. The ringing stopped. Gabet sensed a small change in his immediate environment, but couldn't register the exact cause. He glanced at his phone and saw with horror the words 'one missed call'. That was it, he realised to his utter dismay. His phone, the one contact he had with his children's captors had been ringing. In his devastation, he now realised his senses hadn't even registered the call, such had been the state of his mind over the last half hour. The phone rang again and this time with the feeling of doom more suited to a man going to the gallows, he struggled to give his name.

"Khalid. Is that you? You sound strange. Khalid, Khalid."

Gabet knew the voice, but in his devastated state, couldn't get it into context. He saw confusing images of his children, home, mountains and his family. Family that was it. The voice

– his father

"Khalid, it's me, Dad. Just ringing to wish you all the best for the race."

Gabet's jumbled mind cleared sufficiently to babble a few disjointed phrases as he half collapsed behind a stall selling the day's programmes.

"Where are they? Are they alright? Any injuries? The children?"

"Khalid, the line's bad. What injuries? Are you injured Khalid?"

"The children, Dad, where are they?"

"Hassan and Shada are just fine. Here with me now. I'll put them on."

"Hi Dada. All the best for the race. We're going to watch it on the TV in town. Everyone's here. We can't wait."

"Are you alright Hassan?"

"Missing you Dada, but Grampa says you'll be home soon. Here's Shada."

"Hi Dada. Grampa has bought us an ice cream and says we can have another one if you win."

"Shada. Are you alright my little one? Are you alright?"

"Yes Dada. Missing you lots but Grampa says I've been a really good girl."

"Of course you have my love. I'll tell Mama what a good girl you've been. Can I speak to Grampa?"

"Khalid, what's this about an injury. You OK?"

"Dad. The children. How are they?"

"Just fine, Khalid. They've been as good as gold."

"And they've been with you all the time?"

"Of course. Where else would they be? I never let them out of my sight."

"Thanks, Dad. I was just worried. Being so far away. It's not easy."

"Of course not son, but you needn't worry about these two.

They're the centre of attraction in town just now. Until you come on that is. Tell me about the injury, son."

"No injury, Dad. You must have misheard on the line. I'm fine. Just fine."

"Well that's good son. You just do your best. Love to Salima."

"She'll be in the stadium now. Probably as nervous as me. Take care."

"And you son. Now don't you worry about Hassan and Shada. They're doing fine."

"Thanks, Dad. Thanks for the call."

With a surge of relief tempered with confusion and a degree of anger, Gabet straightened himself up from his crouched position behind the stall. He slowly stretched and felt a renewed surge of energy. Like a butterfly emerging from its pupa, the blood slowly pumping from the core to the periphery, Gabet felt the tingling of renewal in his feet and hands. Still dazed from the events of the last hour, he now had a renewed purpose. Whoever had sent that message must be sick. Gabet knew that had he left his room without his phone, a distinct possibility in the state he was in, he would have been in no state to run. His new resolve was simple. He would show the cowards behind such atrocities that Gabet was above them. Nothing could stop him from being in the awards ceremony. The Moroccan flag would be fluttering proudly above the Olympic Stadium. Gabet was back.

CHAPTER 32

August 11th, 2012
Warm up track for the Olympic Stadium, UK

The warm up track next to the Olympic Stadium was heavily guarded and only those athletes with authority for the day were allowed entry. A bar-coded entry permit was issued daily by the chef de mission for each team and came with a brightly coloured lanyard to hang the permit around each athlete's neck. No permit, no entry was a strictly enforced rule and any athlete forgetting their permit had little option than to return to the athletes' village to collect it. In the stress of the forthcoming events this happened surprisingly often and even if the athlete's face was emblazoned across the sports pages for a week, they would be turned away.

After the revelations from Rachel the night before, Josh Silverman looked around desperate to see for himself the outcomes of Gressley's fiendish schemes. First to join him on the warm up track was Ho, the Chinese champion. Ho was accompanied by his coach, who was carrying a sports holdall over his shoulder with the bulk of it between Ho and himself. As the two walked together, the bag bumped between them and to Josh's surprise they made light of the inconvenience. Josh watched Ho like a hawk about to descend on its prey and was amazed to see no sign at all of the expected injury. Ho's movements, far from being restricted, were positively lithe. He seemed to Josh to have the motion more of a gymnast or dancer than a runner and was clearly in superb physical shape. Josh's initial reaction was that the illicit injection must have caused minimal damage and would only show up during the stress of running fast. This notion was soon dispelled when Josh saw Ho prepare with 50 metre warm up sprints. Ho was bouncing along like a racquet ball in a squash court. If anything was to test his Achilles tendon then this routine of high stepping, not unlike a triple jump athlete, would surely do so. Josh was amazed. No one would consider this warm up sequence if he was trying to protect his Achilles. There was only one conclusion. Ho was totally uninjured. Nigel Gressley had failed with this one.

As Josh was contemplating the contradiction of Ho, he saw Angelo Benito on the far side of the track. Benito stripped off his tracksuit trousers, folded them carefully and put them in the basket provided for all athletes. At that moment he looked up and seeing Josh, waved and jogged over. In his excellent English, Benito wished Josh well with a genuine smile.

"Best to be sociable now before the heat's on," said Benito.

"How are you feeling, Angelo?" Josh asked cautiously.

"Great," came the reply. "I normally never sleep well before a final, but for some reason I slept like a bambino – baby, last night."

"That's good," was Josh's somewhat quizzical response, not certain whether Benito was bluffing to gain psychological advantage. Josh was unsure but Benito certainly looked in great shape. His overall demeanour was far from being that of someone who had been up all night enjoying the charms of the opposite sex. Benito either had the capacity for superb recovery from exhausting bedroom adventures or it never happened. Josh couldn't say which was most likely, but had to admit to the possibility that Gressley had failed again. Josh instinctively and quite genuinely wished Benito good luck and the two parted, each to his own preparation.

Josh plugged in his ipod and started his routine of stretches, keeping time with the beat of the music as he had done so many times before. His stretching was interrupted by Khalid Gabet loping over in his normal relaxed way. Josh was astounded to see Gabet so relaxed in view of the devastating news that should have reached him only hours before.

"How you doing, Khalid?" Josh enquired, trying to comprehend the inconsistency between Gabet's appearance and his own knowledge.

"Just fine," he replied, "I've just spoken to the family back home and they're all in great shape. Really strange because I had this weird threatening text which scared the shit out of me, but it must have been some sick hoax."

"What do mean, Khalid, someone threatening you?"

"No, not me. Some sick individual claimed to have kidnapped my kids back home. Stopped me dead in my tracks better than the recall gun. Turned out to be a lie because minutes later my dad came through on my mobile and I was chatting to them all in turn. It was truly joyous."

"But Khalid, who would do a thing like that? Has it ever happened before?"

"Too many questions, Josh, and no answers. You need to watch out, there's some crazy guys out there who'll do anything to disrupt your preparation. Could be anyone, even some of the guys in the race. Now you look out Josh. You know as well as me that this race is worth a fortune. For us its gotta be run fair, but don't assume the other guys are seeing it that way. Win at any cost is their motto."

With that, Gabet stretched out a sunburnt hand and shook Josh's with genuine warmth. "No point in wishing you luck, Josh. It's all about hard work and you and I've both done all of that stuff. Carrera's the guy to watch. Rumours say he's got new shoes, worth a second a lap. Crap I say. Pure psych. We'll know soon enough. See you at the start."

Gabet turned and loped off without glancing back. Josh was both relieved and confused. He wanted his friend to be in the best psychological state and thanked God that Gressley's scheme had totally failed to dent Gabet's infectious enthusiasm. His comment about Carrera's shoes was a worry as this was exactly what Rachel had predicted. It was then he saw Carrera lacing his shoes not forty metres away and they certainly looked special. Carrera looked up and saw Josh staring at his shoes.

"You like them Silverman?" he asked with a directness which matched his reputation.

"Had them long?" Josh found himself saying and regretted the enquiry immediately.

"No secret," Carrera replied, "they're the latest Nike wonder shoe. Had them about two months and they're fast."

"Two months?" Josh enquired, trying hard to show no emotion. Nigel Gressley hadn't even been to Portland two months ago, so Carrera couldn't be wearing the doctored shoes.

"Sure. Nike sent me their latest model two weeks ago and wanted me to wear them today but, although they break them in for me, I couldn't be bothered to change. It'll probably blow my contract with them, but I'm thinking of switching after today."

"I thought you were contracted to Nike long term," said Josh, cautiously probing into Carrera's plans.

"They wanted me to, but a win today puts me in a different league and I've had some pretty tasty offers. Keeping those on the boil could have been really dodgy if I'd won in the latest Nike offering, so I just ignored the directive. As I say, it might come back to bite me but I've grown used to these and I'll fly, mark my words. Anyway, Josh, good to chat, but we've got a race in less than 60 minutes and I need time to myself. See you."

With that curt dismissal, Josh nodded an acknowledgement and shuffled away deep in thought. It was clear that in spite of Gressley's unforgivable actions in trying to doctor Carrera's shoes, he wasn't using them. Gressley had once again failed to handicap another runner. Josh was starting to question Rachel's assertions, but even the act of thinking this way made him uncomfortable. How could he not believe the one person he trusted above all?

On the far side of the track Josh could see the group surrounding Jamil Ngeny. He had brought with him three athletes from the 400 metre relay team who, although they were going through a controlled stretching routine, were also quite capable of nonstop banter amongst themselves. This was the athlete that Josh feared most and feared most for. Ngeny had the best form coming into the final. He had the best time in the semi-final by two seconds and looked relaxed and in total control. But Josh feared most for him because if Nigel had somehow got him to drink EPO, as Rachel had said, then he would be disqualified irrespective of his innocence.

Josh now turned his attention to the American trio of Fradley, Erchard and Delves. They were the last to arrive at the warm up track and as usual were keeping well away from the others, surrounded by a posse of coaches, trainers and medical staff. It was difficult for Josh to see any external signs of infection but they were far from lethargic or in any way quiescent. In fact just the opposite. Somewhat like the Kenyans, they were chatting with each other and there almost seemed to be a jocular mood amongst them. Someone was telling a story and they were unanimous in their spontaneous laughter. This was not the expected reaction to serious food poisoning and once again Josh had cause to question the information he'd been given only the night before. Here he was, less than an hour away from the biggest race of his life, and Josh was starting to question his own sanity. He was led to believe that every one of the finalists had been subject to an assault perpetrated by his own agent, Nigel Gressley. That each one of them would be suffering injury or illness, fatigue or psychological stress, which would put him, Josh Silverman, at considerable advantage. None of them would have suffered enough to pull out of the race, but every one of them could not possibly perform to their expected level. Theoretically this could still be the case, but the evidence of Josh's own eyes and the conversations he'd had over the last hour made such a scenario extremely unlikely. Josh took a deep breath, mentally summarised the situation and came to only one conclusion. He was about to enter a race with the best in the world. Not only the best in the world, but to a man they were all in perfect shape. Nigel Gressley had failed; Josh Silverman must now succeed.

Chapter 33

August 11th, 2012, 3:00 pm
Olympic Stadium, UK

At exactly 3:00 pm on August 11th, the twelve athletes who had been spending the last ninety minutes preparing their bodies and minds for this classic race stood a few metres back from the start line. The introductions were all over, each athlete raising an arm as their names were called and then re-focussing on the race before them. Each one was lost in his own private thoughts. Race plans were being rehearsed. They could anticipate the exact point in the race when the gear would change. It was different for each one. They knew the colour of the vest they would overtake. They knew when. It had been visualised again and again. Their communal reverie was disrupted by the command 'Take your marks'. Each one had an involuntary response to those three words. A final shake of a wrist, the sign of the cross, a couple of deep breaths, a flattened hand on the left chest, a glance at the sky, a wipe of sweaty palms on the side of the shorts, bending to flick imaginary sand from the toe of a shoe, a touch of hands between the three Americans, a tongue licking an upper lip and from Josh Silverman a silent but deeply meaningful 'Amen'.

Twelve athletes spread across the track, a slight crouch with twelve pairs of eyes focussed some forty metres ahead. 'Get set'. A pause. The gun fires and the crowd erupt.

Within forty metres the line across the track funnels into the inside lane, each athlete jockeying for position, but not any position. They know where they want to be. Where they think they should be. But they also know that the pace dictates. They finish the first lap and know immediately there is something wrong. The clock on eight million television sets around the world stops at 58.48, way too slow for any sort of record. Silverman is not leading the pack. Silverman, the front runner who never dies is not to be seen. Silverman, the one who always sets the pace, the one to beat in the final sprint is not ahead. The pack is unsettled, perplexed, confused. The tempo is strong but the order is wrong. Silverman should be out front, with others planning the chase. The breakaway hasn't broken away. The three Americans confer as they work together and one reluctantly takes the lead. The big Cuban, Carrera, tracks the American closely and tucks in behind him. The rest of the field is bunched behind but the pace now increases and the field spreads out covering a good twenty metres. The order doesn't change for the rest of lap two but the pace is hotting up. Eight hundred commentators from the media centre watch for the time and at two laps it is 1.57.10. Still well off a record pace but a fast lap and Ngeny, Gabet and Benito, the clear favourites, still to make their move. The field glance up at the big screen as they take the next bend and Gabet sweeps past Carrera to the shoulder of the lead American. The other Americans sense danger and move up in turn to position themselves behind Gabet but on the inside of the track, forcing Gabet to the outside and dropping Carrera to fifth place. Benito now makes his move and quickly settles in behind Gabet. The American trio still hold the inside track and Benito has no option but to run in the wake of Gabet, adding valuable inches to every step. Ho now shows his frustration at the group in front, especially the American trio who are dictating the quality of the race. He drifts past Carrera and moves effortlessly up to Benito. The second and third Americans are fading fast and Gabet and Benito can now command the inside of the track with Ho right on their heels. The bell sounds for the last lap and Jamil Ngeny, who has kept his usual rhythm and style throughout, sees that the lead American is fading. As Gabet, Benito and Ho overtake the spent American, and concentrate their attentions on each other, Ngeny takes a wide line and pulls ahead of them all. He stamps his authority on the race in the last 200 metres and takes a three metre lead to the palpable excitement of the crowd who just love to see the positions change by the second. Lap three has been unbelievably fast and the commentary boxes here and around the world are now starting to talk of records. In middle distance races there is only the illusion of athletes running faster as they overtake in the home straight. But this time it is for real. The split over the last 200 metres showed a time more reminiscent of an 800 metre race and still the leading athletes were moving at an astonishing speed. Ngeny holds his lead for another 50 metres and first Ho then Gabet and Benito, pumping their arms like the piston rods of a steam engine, vie for the lead. Ngeny maintains his place for no more than another ten metres before Gabet, the Moroccan inches ahead. The final 50 metres and the cheering from around the stadium builds to a mighty crescendo. The Olympic track seems to pulsate with a wall of sound on a scale never heard before. Benito goes wide to get on terms with Gabet and they seem to trade step for step, both straining for the line now 30 metres away. The deafening roar around the track is not for Benito or Gabet, who can only focus on each other waiting to see who will break in the final strides. No, every person in the crowd is now standing and screaming for the athlete wide out in lane four. Josh Silverman is finishing fast like a man possessed. On Benito's blind side, Silverman is gaining those precious centimetres on every stride and the three dip to the tape as one. The crowd is in absolute uproar as the British athlete collapses to the ground in total exhaustion. Concerned officials gather round but Silverman is soon on his feet as he, Benito and Gabet each turn to the giant screen to see a repeat of the final stride. The crowd is hushed as the final 10 metres is played in slow motion. Gabet's foot crosses the line first but Silverman's lunge was perfection and his chest clearly crosses the line ahead of the others. A separation of ten centimetres is more than enough. As Josh Silverman's name is announced the crowd erupts like a volcano with a noise that could be heard for miles around the Olympic Stadium. Before the sound had time to abate another roar went up as the time was flashed on the giant screen with the magic words 'world record' alongside. An unbelievable last lap had given Josh Silverman and Britain a time of 3 minutes and 25 seconds which had destroyed El Guerrouj's record by a full second. It was over ten minutes before the noise of the crowd in the Olympic Stadium started to abate and Josh Silverman, now fully recovered, was enjoying every moment of his magnificent achievement. He jogged not once but twice around the track, stopping to pick a Union Jack from the crowd and waving it with such enthusiasm that the pole broke to great amusement from the still cheering supporters. On the second circuit he sought out Rachel. Hugging her like a skinny bear, Rachel was crying with relief and delight at his incredible achievement. Josh's sweat left a stain on her new dress and this was not lost on the posse of reporters who were desperate for the personal angle from this enigmatic and newly crowned Olympic champion and world record holder. As Josh was escorted away to be interviewed by the world's media, the troubling news that Rachel had shared with him resurfaced in his brain. He knew that his name would not be the only one featured in tonight's press. One thing was sure. Whatever had been planned by Nigel Gressley to give him the edge, it was clear that a new world record by three men was vindication of its outright failure. He knew the paper had its story. He knew that Nigel Gressley had to be discredited. He still hoped that somehow the sour taste of exposing the tragic story of greed could be written in some other way. Deep down he felt a hopelessness of being a pawn in Gressley's awful plan. He thanked God for his success and thanked God again that it was achieved by his own ability and not through the evil intent of his agent. It was with a degree of sadness that Josh accepted that Gressley and he could no longer be a partnership. As his thoughts raced to the implications of it all, his escort steered him towards the track side media centre. Josh, even now still breathing heavily, gave his first interview as Olympic champion. Josh Silverman was transported into a new world of greatness.

Chapter 34

August 11th, 2012, 5:00 pm
Oasis Squash Club, London, UK

Nigel Gressley was on a personal high having just witnessed Josh Silverman, not only winning Olympic gold, but in a world record time. As he headed toward Westminster Bridge, he felt as though he was walking on air, already anticipating the massive income his athlete would be generating for him over the next few years. Nigel was on his way to play his weekly game of squash when he saw the headline poster outside the news stand on the Victoria Embankment. He was handed a copy of the early evening edition of the Evening Standard and was mortified by the headline 'CORRUPT SPORTS AGENT CONTROLS OUTCOME OF 1500 METRE FINAL'. The lead article reviewed briefly but accurately all he had planned in damaging the runners' chances in the race. The only thing the article failed to do was name him. The paper without doubt had chapter and verse on everything he had been doing, but surprisingly there was no specific mention of his name. He had been extremely careful in all his activities, choosing his contacts with care and only involving himself when there was a minimal chance of detection. Gressley took this as a lifeline. How the paper had obtained this information was beyond Gressley's comprehension, but the important thing was they didn't know it was him. For now he was in the clear. Or, thought Gressley, they were holding something back. Gressley felt the same tightness across the chest he had been feeling for months now. He stopped to take an antacid tablet, and turned to go through the revolving door of the squash club. Sweating slightly as he went into the changing room, he saw his long-term playing partner, Jeremy Theakson, already changed.

"I'll get on court and warm up the ball," said Jeremy cheerily, "I'm giving you five minutes, no more."

Jeremy had played squash almost every week with Nigel, but unlike Nigel, who did little else physical during the week, Jeremy also played league squash on two other days and ran every Sunday morning in a local 5k race. On the squash court they were a good match for each other, with Nigel's skill compensating for Jeremy's fitness. After exactly five minutes, Nigel arrived on court and after a short warm up the match started in its usual highly competitive manner. The game was close and Jeremy could see that after 25 minutes Nigel was visibly tiring, missing the odd shot that he would usually deal with easily and contemptuously. At the end of a long, hard rally, Nigel stopped rested his hands on his knees and took a while to control his erratic breathing.

"Had enough old man," enquired Jeremy, "you look all in."

"Sorry, Jeremy, I feel a bit out of sorts today. Shoulder's a bit painful."

"I'm happy to call it a day, Nigel. We've only time for one more game anyway."

"No, we'll play the decider, just give me a minute."

After a short break the game continued with both players putting everything into the cut and thrust of the play, and each trying to find a weakness in the other's moves. As Nigel ran to front court to try to deal with a wicked drop shot, he seemed to trip and fell heavily against the tin. Jeremy's initial amusement turned quickly to concern as he could see that Nigel was not moving with his face taking on a ghastly grey hue. Jeremy was uncertain whether to stay to help his friend or to call for outside assistance. It looked bad, so Jeremy ran to the changing room, grabbed his mobile phone from his locker and dialled

999. After Jeremy had given details of the club's location to the ambulance service, the operator then offered Jeremy some basic resuscitation procedures. Jeremy, phone in hand, headed back to the court and was alarmed to see that Nigel hadn't moved. Following the operator's instructions, Jeremy, having been unable to find a pulse, pumped hard on the rib cage above the heart with a steady rhythm. Jeremy had no notion of time, but it seemed only a matter of minutes before the paramedics arrived and took over. They went into a well-rehearsed routine and Jeremy was impressed with their inherent professionalism.

"Anything I can do?" said Jeremy, feeling rather inadequate.

"It's not looking good," was the reply, "why don't you get changed and come to the hospital? We'll be taking him to Tommy's. It's the nearest. I have your mobile number in case of any developments."

With that rather brusque dismissal, Jeremy watched from the outside of the squash court as Nigel was stretchered out into the waiting ambulance. He was concerned that Nigel didn't seem to respond to the treatment from the paramedics, but knew there was little he could do and that Nigel was now at least heading for the best possible treatment. Jeremy took a long shower and uncertain what his next move should be, he headed to the bar. After a refreshing drink, Jeremy felt better able to plan his evening. He had hoped to attend a lecture on the South Pole at the Royal Geographical Society but felt a degree of responsibility towards Nigel. He decided that perhaps a short visit to the hospital would still give him time to go to the lecture. With that resolve he grabbed his sports bag and headed for the car park. His phone rang as he was putting his bag in the boot of his car.

"This is Guy's and St Thomas' Hospital, Is that Mr Jeremy Theakston?" enquired a woman's voice on the line.

"It is."

"I understand that you were playing squash with Mr Nigel

Gressley when he took ill."

"That's correct."

"I'm afraid I have some bad news for you. I'm sorry to tell you that Mr Gressley was pronounced dead on arrival at the hospital. Would you be in a position to help us inform his next of kin?"

Jeremy now knew that he would not be hearing Ranulph Fiennes talk about his polar expedition.

Earlier in the day Christine Gressley had cleared out her spare freezer. She had come across her husband's carp bait. She was still revolted that Nigel should keep such things in her freezer but she couldn't help having a quick look at it before deciding whether it justified the space. She was surprised to find it kept in petri dishes. On closer examination, by prodding the amorphous substance, she wondered how the jelly-like substance could ever stick on a hook. Still, it was none of her business and she decided to return it to the freezer. She assumed that Nigel knew best.

Christine Gressley was on a life support machine in Guy's and St Thomas' hospital when Nigel Gressley died. The hospital staff were desperately trying to contact her next of kin.

CHAPTER 35

August 11th, 2012, 10:00 pm
Thamesview, London, UK

"Good evening. Here is the ten o'clock news for Saturday 11th August, 2012.

Josh Silverman, Olympic champion and world record holder in the 1500 metres has announced that in view of the circumstances surrounding his win, he will............."

"Rachel, turn it off will you?" said Josh, taking her by the hand, "We've heard it all before and it's time to move on."

The television was switched off and Rachel put on one of their favourite CDs. As the deep, sonorous voice of Barry White filled the room, they instinctively held each other tightly and danced slowly to the gentle rhythm of the ballad. The words of the song combined with the overpowering emotion of the last few days found them soon weeping in each other's arms. They let the tears flow as they continued to dance and tenderly they helped each other to undress.

A NOTE ON THE AUTHOR

David Brodie was most recently Professor of Cardiovascular Health at Bucks New University and previously held a personal chair at The University of Liverpool.

During his academic career, he published six academic texts and over 150 journal papers. He was awarded a DSc in 2011 in recognition of 'distinguished, original research work' over a twenty year period.

He took semi-retirement in 2011 and spent the next year writing this book, in between ongoing academic work, family responsibilities, dog walking, church, bridge, running, rowing, undertaking charity work in the UK and Nepal and the occasional foray to high places such as the Andes and the Himalaya.

This is his first novel.

He lives with his wife and their dog, in South Buckinghamshire.